Praise for Amanda Foody
and *Daughter of the Burning City*

"Wow! A dark and dangerous tale, a world like no other, and heroism of the weirdest kind!"

—#1 *New York Times* bestselling author Tamora Pierce

"Gomorrah makes for a fantastic, magical setting, a seedy mix of titillation and sin… Readers who enjoyed their whirl in Garber's *Caraval* will want to get in line for entry to Gomorrah."

—*The Bulletin of the Center for Children's Books*

"Amanda Foody's stunning debut is full of velvety language, intricate worldbuilding, and a story that treads the fine line of horror and fantasy. This is the kind of read that makes your spine shiver, and your heart beat faster."

—Roshani Chokshi, *New York Times* bestselling author of
The Star-Touched Queen

"The world…is astoundingly vivid and complex, the smells, sounds and sights of the smoldering city/traveling carnival near tangible. Amanda Foody's deliciously dark and magical whodunit has world-building so rich, the reader (like visitors to Gomorrah) is likely to leave with a hangover."

—*Shelf Awareness*

"Utterly original. Amanda Foody has a wicked imagination. If you enjoy your fantasy on the darker side, then you will love Gomorrah!"

—Stephanie Garber, *New York Times* bestselling author
of *Caraval*

"Foody's colorful setting is vast—filled with magic, political intrigue, and the potential to grow."

—*Publishers Weekly*

"I love the vivid, sumptuous world Amanda Foody has created: Sorina's magic, her illusionary family and the Gomorrah Festival make for a wildly inventive mystery I won't soon forget."

—Virginia Boecker, author of *The Witch Hunter* series

**Books by Amanda Foody
available from Harlequin TEEN**

Daughter of the Burning City

AMANDA FOODY

ACE OF SHADES

HARLEQUIN®TEEN

Recycling programs
for this product may
not exist in your area.

ISBN-13: 978-1-335-69229-0 (Hardcover)
ISBN-13: 978-1-335-92042-3 (Chain Exclusive edition)

Ace of Shades

This edition published by arrangement with Harlequin Books S.A.

For questions and comments about the quality of this book, please contact us
at CustomerService@Harlequin.com.

® and TM are trademarks of Harlequin Enterprises Limited or its corporate
affiliates. Trademarks indicated with ® are registered in the United States Patent and
Trademark Office, the Canadian Intellectual Property Office and in other countries.

Printed in U.S.A.

To Mom–Mom.

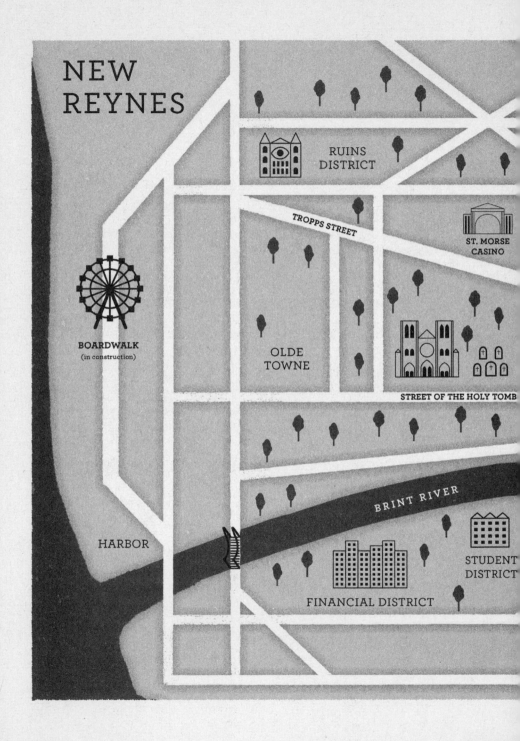

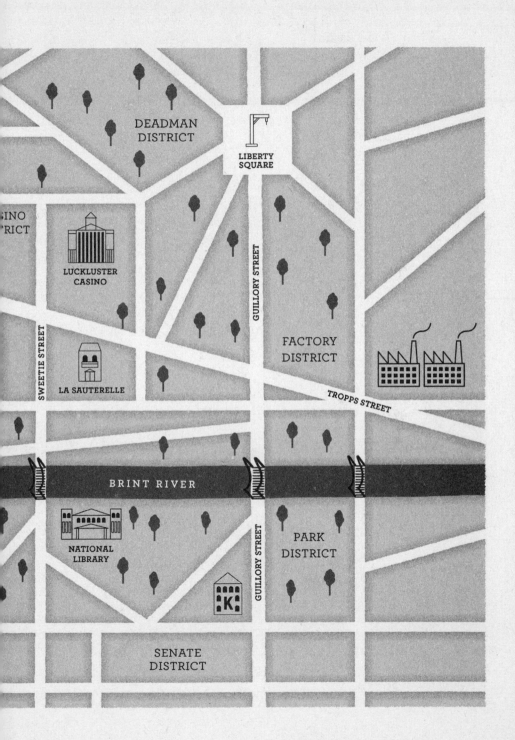

DAY ONE

"To be frank, reader, you'd be
better off not visiting the city at all."

—*The City of Sin, a Guidebook:
Where To Go and Where Not To*

ENNE

If I'm not home in two months, I'm dead.

Her mother's warning haunted her as Enne Salta lugged her leather trunk down the bridge leading off the ship, filling her with an inescapable sense of dread.

If I'm not home in two months, I'm dead.

It'd been four.

For the first time in fifteen days, Enne stepped onto dry land. Her balance veered from side to side as if she expected the gray cobblestones to tilt like the sea, and she white-knuckled the pier's railing to compose herself. If the ground weren't so littered with cigar butts and grime, she might've kissed it. Two weeks battling seasickness on a floating monstrosity could do that to a lady.

A woman shoved past her, not noticing Enne's petite frame. The force of it nearly knocked Enne over. She glared at the woman's ostentatiously feathered hat as it disappeared into the crowds.

Hmph, she thought. *A lady shouldn't rush.* Barely five seconds in the so-called City of Sin and already people were rude.

As more passengers disembarked from the ship, the crowds around the customs tables swelled with hundreds of people, hollering and waving passports and jostling each other in an effort to reach the front of the lines. Most were young men, probably visiting New Reynes to sample its famous casinos and nightlife—but the number of families present surprised her. This city was no place for children.

And, she reminded herself, staring up at the sinister, smog-stained sky, it was no place for her, either.

As Enne joined the queues, she dug through her belongings for her tourist documents. Her purse was stuffed: her passport, a handful of gingersnap cookies leftover from last night's dinner and a copy of *The City of Sin, a Guidebook: Where To Go and Where Not To.* As she fished out her papers, something fell and *clinked* when it hit the ground. Her token.

She scooped it up and clutched it to her chest. Her mother, Lourdes, had given her this token. It was two inches long and gilded, with an old Faith symbol of an eye etched on one side and a cameo of a past queen on the other. The Mizer kings had used these tokens as party invitations. It was probably illegal to own it—any remnants from before the Revolution twenty-five years ago had been destroyed, just like the Mizers themselves. But Enne couldn't bring herself to throw away something so rare and precious. She tucked it safely back into her pocket.

With nothing to do but wait, Enne pulled out her guidebook and compared its cover to the city in front of her. The photograph of Luckluster Casino matched the stories of New Reynes: red lights that flashed without flame, women of loose morals dancing on street corners in sparkling, skin-tight corsets, gambling den owners beckoning passersby with seedy smiles and the allure of fast fortune.

But neither the stories nor the cover bore any resemblance to the city before her. From what she could see, New Reynes was a wasteland of metal and white stone. The factories in the distance glinted as if coated in liquid steel, and the clouds were so black she swore the rain would fall dark as coal.

Panic seized her as she examined the skyline—white and jagged as teeth.

All you know are stories, Enne told herself. *And not all stories are true.*

"Next!" called the man at the customs table, and Enne hurried to his desk. He snatched the papers from her hands. "Erienne Abacus Salta."

She cringed at the sound of her full name. No one called her that but her teachers.

The man wore round spectacles rimmed in faux gold, making his eyes appear magnified as they traveled from her face and slithered down her body. "A Salta, eh? Then you're a dancer." By the way he said "dancer," drawing out the *s* sound and licking his lips, Enne knew he wasn't picturing her ballet at finishing school.

Her cheeks reddened. City of Sin, indeed. She was not *that* kind of dancer. She. Was. A. *Lady.*

He glanced back at her paperwork. "From Bellamy. Seventeen years old. You know, you hardly look seventeen."

She flushed deeper and counted backward from ten, lest she say something indecent and break one of Lourdes's sacred rules.

Ladies should never reveal their emotions. That was the first rule.

The man checked the birth date on her passport, shrugged and returned to her travel documents. "Blood talent is dancing, of course. What is the Abacus family talent?"

"Arithmetic," she answered. Every person possessed two talents, one inherited from each parent. The stronger one was known as the blood talent, and the weaker was called the split talent. Enne's Abacus split talent was so weak it might as well have been nonexistent, as if all her ability had gone to pliés and pirouettes rather than to simple math.

The man scribbled her talents and family names into a grease-stained booklet. "How long is your stay?"

"The summer," Enne said, trying to make her voice sound strong. School began again in September, and this was Enne's final year before graduation, before her debut into society. All her life she had perfected her fouettés, memorized her table settings and obsessed over every salon invitation…all to graduate and earn the title of lady. She wanted it more than she wanted anything. It was all she'd cared about…

Until Lourdes went missing.

No matter how scared or how alone she felt, Enne swore to remain in this disgusting city until she found her mother. For however long it took. But secretly, selfishly, she hoped she'd find Lourdes before September. Without her debut, she wasn't sure who she was supposed to become.

The man tapped his ballpoint pen at the bottom of the document. "Sign your name here. If you can't write, just put an X. And if you can read, go 'head and verify everything."

The document was a horror of fine print. At the top of the page was a check box for those with Talents of Mysteries. During the reigns of the Mizers, the various kingdoms had required every citizen to be classified into one of two categories based on their talents: Talents of Aptitude and Talents of Mysteries. Both Enne's blood and split talent were considered Talents of Aptitude; anyone could develop a skill in dancing or arithmetic, even if they would never compare to those born with a family talent.

Talents of Mysteries, however, couldn't be learned. Crudely put, they were magic—and even the Mizer kings, who'd had powerful Talents of Mysteries of their own, had considered them to be a threat. Before the Revolution, there had been harsh restrictions on where people could live and who they could marry based on their talents. It was one of the many reasons the Mizers were overthrown. And so Enne was shocked to find such a classification in an official document in New Reynes, the Republic's capital, the home of the Revolution. It was archaic. Distasteful.

She signed her name in her best calligraphic script, ready to move on.

With a dreadful thud, the man pounded her passport with a wooden stamp bearing the Republic's insignia, a circle with a bolt of lightning inside, meant to resemble an orb full of volts. The signature of Chancellor Malcolm Semper—the "Father of the Revolution," and still the Republic's leader twenty-five years later—was engraved over it.

Handing her the papers, the customs man said, "Enjoy New Reynes."

As if she could enjoy herself when her mother was lost in this rotten city.

Enne shoved her way out of the crowd and stared blankly at the vast New Reynes skyline. At the unfamiliar fashions of the people around her. At the bleakness of the city's polluted sky. She had no idea where to begin. As she crossed the street, the people waiting to be reunited with their families looked straight through her, as though she didn't exist.

On her tiptoes, Enne scanned the crowd for Lourdes, for her pale blond hair or signature crimson scarf. She was nowhere.

With the passing of each day beyond Lourdes's deadline, Enne had begun to crack. As weeks lapsed, then months, the cracks had deepened and spread. Now, as she held her breath and desperately searched the faces of the strangers around her, she felt that she was more broken than not. One exhale, one sob, and all her pieces would shatter.

Lourdes is alive, she assured herself, just as she had done every day for months. The repetition of the words steadied her more than the words themselves.

Lourdes was alive. She was in this city. And Enne would find her.

She repeated the mantra several times, like twisting the key in a porcelain doll, winding herself back together.

Never allow yourself to be lost, Enne recited in her head. That was Lourdes's second rule.

But she wasn't lost. She was terrified, and that was worse to admit.

She was terrified that—no matter how many times she recited Lourdes's rules, or how many times she wound herself back together—she'd made a dangerous mistake in thinking she could brave the City of Sin. If the stories were true, she was a schoolgirl who had just wandered into the city of the wolves.

She was terrified that Lourdes was dead, just as she had warned.

Lastly, she was terrified of finding her. For all of Enne's life, it had been only her and Lourdes and no one else. Lourdes was her home, but that home had many locked doors. Her mother had rooms full of secrets Enne had been forbidden to see, secrets Enne had pretended didn't exist.

Once she found Lourdes, it was past time Enne opened those doors.

Hands shaking, Enne pulled *Where To Go and Where Not To* from her pocket and turned the pages to the city map. The Brint River split New Reynes into two halves: the North and the South. She was currently in the harbor, the smallest district of the notorious North Side.

If a storm were to further delay my return or another unforeseen circumstance occurs, you can speak to Mr. Levi Glaisyer, a friend of mine who lives in New Reynes. He will be glad to help you.

That was from the mysterious letter Lourdes had sent Enne a month after she had left home. Enne had never heard of this Mr. Levi Glaisyer, nor had she the least idea how to find him. On the map, she scanned the various neighborhoods of the much more refined South Side: the Senate District, the Park District, the Student District…he could live anywhere.

Two police officers slumped against the wall of a warehouse, talking to a boy roughly Enne's age. The officers wore tarnished white boots and jackets buttoned from hips to throat, the threads frayed, the pits stained, the collars scuffed.

The boy speaking to them had a harsh face, like someone had carved his features with a razor so that they sharpened as he scowled. His shoulder bones, hip bones and wrist bones all jutted out uncomfortably, stretching his skin taut, and he wore an oversize collared shirt that only extenuated his gaunt frame. His brown hair was wildly disheveled.

While the officers' uncleanliness was off-putting, the authorities were probably a good place to start her search. Enne pocketed her guidebook and approached.

"Show us your hands," the first officer ordered the boy. He was tall with teeth like a shark—one of them gold.

The boy held up his palms. "Happy? No scars."

"How about rolling up your sleeves, then?" Shark asked slyly. The second officer nodded, a cigar dangling from his mouth. Enne fought the urge to cover her nose. The *stench* of it.

The boy reached for his sleeves, then stopped. Although Enne had little notion what they were discussing, she could sense the tension in their words. The boy seemed to be in some kind of trouble.

"What?" Shark said, an ugly smile playing at his lips. "Got tattoos you don't want us to see?"

Enne jumped forward at the boy's hesitation, both to save him from whatever unpleasant conversation was unfolding, and because she didn't have the time to wait. Who knew how long it would take her to find Lourdes?

"Excuse me," Enne interrupted. She flashed her best, practiced smile. All three of them ran their eyes over her plainly tailored suit and high-necked blouse. Amid the flashier haute couture of the women around her, she knew she stuck out as a tourist.

Enne cleared her throat nervously. "I'm looking for someone. I was hoping you'd be kind enough to assist me."

"Sure, missy," Shark said as he elbowed Cigar suggestively. "We'd be glad to help ya. But we have to deal with *him*, first."

"You can't arrest me," the boy growled. "I ain't done anything."

"Then show us your arms and prove you're not an Iron."

The boy didn't move, only glared at the officers.

"Please," Enne interrupted again. "I'm looking for a woman named Lourdes Alfero. She's been missing since February." Enne drew the letter from Lourdes out of her pocket and unfolded it. "She gave me the name of a Mr. Levi Glais—"

"Alfero?" Shark repeated. "Why you lookin' for her?" He shoved the boy aside and advanced on Enne. He was two heads taller than her, and twice as wide. Enne was swallowed beneath his shadow.

"Um…" Enne stammered, the words dying on her tongue.

The other man dropped his cigar and ground it into the dirt with his heel. "There's probably a mistake. Ain't that right, missy?" Enne glanced toward the boy, but he'd taken advantage of the distraction she'd provided and fled.

Her stomach knotted. Did they know something about Lourdes? Enne thought back to another line from Lourdes's letter: *I encountered a little trouble that has delayed my return…*

"Who's Lourdes Alfero to you?" Shark's fingers twitched as he reached for something at his side. A gun.

"No one," Enne said hurriedly, doing her best not to stutter. *Never let anyone see your fear.* Another one of Lourdes's rules— one Enne was certainly breaking. Her chest tightened as Cigar stepped closer, close enough to grab her. "My apologies. I believe there's been a mistake. Thank you very much for your time."

Enne dragged her trunk back into the crowd before they could stop her. Her mind raced as she attempted to conjure some sort of explanation for the officers' reactions. Surely, they must've confused her mother's name with someone else's.

An uneasiness settled into her stomach—maybe there'd been

no mistake. She was in the center of the harbor landing, but all around her were locked doors, locked doors.

Someone tapped Enne's shoulder. She shrieked and whipped around.

"Scare much?" The boy smirked.

"You know, it's rude to startle people, and—" And she needed to get out of here.

"Look over my shoulder." He leaned down like he was whispering in her ear, allowing her to see beyond him.

The two police officers pushed through the crowd in their direction. Enne's hands began to sweat inside her lace gloves.

"Who are you?" he asked. "First you're looking for Levi Glaisyer, and now you got the whiteboots tailing you."

"You know Mr. Glaisyer?" How could a boy like this know a gentleman? He smelled like he slept in a sewer, and there was something about his face that unnerved her—not so much his crooked frown as his crooked smile. He looked like a warning from her guidebook.

He rolled up his left sleeve to reveal a black tattoo of a club on the underside of his arm, like the card suit. It was small, halfway between his wrist and elbow. "I'm an Iron."

"I'm afraid I'm not familiar with…the terminology." Though, even as she said it, Enne realized it *did* sound familiar. Something she had read in the section about the North Side. Admittedly, she'd skipped most of those parts. The North Side's reputation was so dirty, even its chapters in her guidebook looked a little bit stained.

The boy leaned down a second time. The whiteboots watched them from the end of the block, and Shark kept one hand on his gun. "You're lost, missy. And walking straight into some muck. So take my advice: ditch your trunk, and scram. Playing nice is the same as losing in this city." Before she could adequately digest what he'd said, he whispered, "Three, two, one."

He took off.

Behind her, Shark and Cigar shoved their way toward her, cursing and knocking travelers aside. Enne whimpered, terrified, yet loath to abandon all her possessions.

But the decision took only a moment. She *was* lost, and the boy knew Mr. Glaisyer, Enne's only connection to finding Lourdes. Maybe Mr. Glaisyer could explain the misunderstanding between the whiteboots and her mother. Maybe he possessed the key to those locked doors. And besides, possessions could be replaced.

She dropped her trunk, yanked up the hem of her skirt, and sprinted after the boy.

He ran two blocks past the end of the harbor before turning down an alley. Wheezing, she forced her legs to move faster. Her heels clicked loudly with each step, and sweat dampened her forehead and undersleeves. Enne couldn't remember the last time she'd run. This behavior must've breached every one of Lourdes's rules.

The boy slipped down another alley up ahead, while Enne trailed fifty paces behind. What if she lost him? For every step she made, he'd already made three. He clearly had some sort of speed talent, which explained why his features were so angular— like he'd been made to be aerodynamic. She passed a pawnshop and an outdoor grocer, but no one looked twice at her, as if a girl fleeing from the authorities was a common morning occurrence in New Reynes. Maybe it was.

The next alley had no streetlights, and thanks to the black clouds and towering buildings, she could hardly see where her feet landed. Soon the noises of the main street—the motorcars, the shouting, the traffic whistles—disappeared, and it became eerily quiet. Only their footsteps remained. Enne's heart pounded so hard, she felt the beats in her back.

The buildings here looked different, too. In the harbor, the shipping houses were made of a weathered white stone—the kind her guidebook described as characteristic of the city. But the architecture around her now was gothic and black, full of spires and archways and wrought iron. Everything was sharp, a place designed to cut. To draw blood. It was the kind of dark where shadows didn't exist. Wherever she was...she shouldn't be here.

She turned a corner and found the boy waiting for her. He stood at the doorway of a house with boarded windows and shriveled ivy crawling up its gutters. He grabbed her by her blazer and jerked her inside. She crashed to the wooden floor.

They were in a dusty, unused kitchen. Two panels on the ceiling flickered with murky light.

The boy bent over her. "So, why are you looking for Pup?"

Enne scrambled to her feet and smoothed out her dress, hyperaware of how inappropriate their situation was. They were alone in goodness knows where. She didn't know his name. She didn't even know what he wanted.

What had she done?

No emotions, no fear, she thought. She smiled and adjusted her posture, but that couldn't have made much of an impression, panting and sweating as she was.

"Well, I'm actually looking for my mother, Lourdes Alfero," Enne explained. "She mentioned Mr. Glaisyer to me in a letter. She said he'd be glad to help."

"I never knew Pup to be glad to help anyone," he said darkly. "Sure you got the right man?"

Dread blossomed in her like black ink soaking through paper. Could there have been some other mistake? "I believe so," she replied meekly. "How are you acquainted with him?"

"Acquainted?" he echoed. With his thick New Reynes accent, he didn't pronounce the *t*. It reminded Enne that she was awfully far away from home.

"How do you know Mr. Glaisyer?" she asked.

"Everyone does," he answered. "He's the lord."

Footsteps thudded down a staircase, and two others entered the kitchen. The first was another boy, also about Enne's age. He had a soldier's look to him: broad shoulders, a shirt too tight for his muscular build and an expression like he was never much surprised about anything—that, or he didn't care. Black-and-white tattoos covered his arms, some disappearing into his sleeve, snaking up his neck. Among them were two small ones, the only ones with color: a red J on one arm, and a diamond on the next, in the same places as the first boy's. He wore his trousers cuffed and his blond hair slicked back underneath a newsboy cap.

Like a gangster, she thought. She took a step closer to the door.

The other person was a girl, maybe thirteen years old. She had golden skin and thick black hair, which was cut bobbed and jagged. She wore men's clothes that were several sizes too large and a pair of ruby earrings that Enne imagined she'd stolen. On the underside of her forearms, just like the boys, she had two tattoos: a black spade on the left, a five on the right.

The boys met each other's eyes sternly. "Where've you been, Chez?" the soldier one demanded. "And where—" his eyes wandered over to Enne "—did you find a missy like this?"

"Near Tropps Street. She was wandering around...an easy target, really—"

"You're a bad liar," the soldier one said. "You've been pick-pocketing near the harbor again. You *know* Levi has business with the whiteboot captain. Business worth a lot more than a few volts in some tourist's pocket."

Enne perked up at the mention of Levi. So they both knew him.

"Then where's my paycheck, Jac?" Chez growled. "Where's *her* paycheck?" He gestured toward the girl. When the soldier boy—Jac—didn't respond, Chez added, "I found this missy asking the *whiteboots* about Pup—I mean, about Levi. Levi and some other person. Then they started tailing her." Chez took a switchblade out of his pocket and flipped it between his knuckles—deftly, expertly. Enne's mouth dried, and she hugged her purse to her side. "She's kinda thick."

Jac tugged at his cap and nodded at Enne, who tried not to appear nervous. From his build, Enne guessed he had a strength talent. If he grabbed her, she wouldn't be able to escape. And if she ran, Chez would catch her.

They all knew Levi Glaisyer, but something was wrong. Without knowing why, she felt trapped. Fifty minutes in the city, and she'd already made a dangerous mistake.

Jac stepped closer to Enne and stared at her with such intensity that, if not for years of etiquette training, would've made her drop her gaze to the floor. Lost or not, strength and speed talents or not, she refused to let them know they intimidated her.

"What's your name?" he asked, arms crossed.

"Enne," she said, clearly, loudly, as if answering roll call rather than speaking to a potential delinquent.

Don't speak about yourself unless asked. Never show fear. Never allow yourself to be lost. No emotions. Don't trust anyone unless you must.

Lourdes had drilled dozens of rules into Enne in the hope that they would become second nature. Usually, they were. Sometimes Enne could *hear* her mother's voice in her head, whispering about etiquette and precautions. But right now, all she could focus on was Chez's knife twirling around his index finger and the seriousness in Jac's gray eyes. Even the girl looked threatening, and she was younger than Enne.

Enne held her breath, but even so, she felt herself cracking… shattering.

"Enne? That's a letter, ain't it?" Jac asked.

"Yes." She didn't hide her astonishment well, but the boy didn't seem to notice.

"You from around here?"

"I'm from Bellamy."

"Quite a journey." He smiled, and she relaxed a bit when she noticed his dimples and the way his ears stuck out. "When did you get here?"

"An hour ago." A wave of nausea crashed over her when she

remembered that she'd left her trunk with all her belongings near the harbor. Someone would've stolen them since then. Now her only means of paying for her stay in New Reynes and her ticket home were the thousand volts she was carrying, meant to last an entire summer. She hadn't anticipated buying new clothes or other necessities while in the city.

She was lost, surrounded by strangers, and all she had were the contents of her purse. And it was—mostly—her own fault.

When she caught Chez and the girl both staring hungrily at her bag, she hugged it closer.

Fear. Lost. Emotions. Trusting… Were there rules for when she was breaking every rule?

"I don't know why you wanna see Levi," Jac said, shaking her trembling hand, "but anyone who outruns two whiteboots on their first day here seems trustworthy in my book."

Even if he trusted her, Enne knew better than to trust him. She knew better than to trust anyone in New Reynes. Except, hopefully, this Levi Glaisyer.

"Levi will be here in an hour," he said, and those were the only words that held her together. "He's busy, and I can't make promises, but I'll make sure he talks to you." He took her arm and led her to the sitting room, his smile a little too wide, his grip a little too tight. "I'm Jac Mardlin. Allow me to be your official welcome to the City of Sin."

LEVI

Muck. Of all the gambling taverns in the city, why had the whiteboot captain chosen Grady's? Levi Glaisyer hadn't set foot in there since he'd handed Grady his resignation four years ago. He paced back and forth in the alley outside the tavern, dropping the copy of *The Crimes & the Times* he'd been carrying. On the front page, a photograph of Malcolm Semper, the oh-so-respected Chancellor of the Republic, soaked up the muddy rainwater.

After a few more moments of cursing, Levi gathered his nerve, straightened his felt homburg hat and strode to the door.

The inside of the tavern hadn't changed at all. It still reeked of tobacco and burnt food, and the patrons were loud, even now, early in the morning. A group of men seated at the main card table—what was once *Levi's* card table—were dressed in clothes with more patches than original fabric. A woman in fishnet stockings giggled and toppled into one of their laps.

The dealer at the table did a double take once he noticed Levi. Most gamblers considered Levi to be the best dealer in the city, and he didn't normally show his face in establishments as small-time as this one.

But he hadn't come to gamble. He'd come for business.

Levi searched the room for Jamison Hector, the captain of the city's whiteboots. The two of them were supposed to meet here at ten o'clock sharp, and Levi had been on edge about it for days. He wasn't usually the sort to rendezvous with authority—if only on principle—but lately, Levi had done a lot of things he'd never thought he would.

He locked eyes with the captain at a table in the back corner but made it only halfway to him before Grady slapped his shoulder, hard enough for him to wince.

"Levi, never thought I'd see you again," Grady said with a laugh. His enormous gut tremored. "How you doing?"

As if Grady didn't know how Levi was doing, what he'd become since his stint here as an amateur card dealer. Reputation aside, he was easily recognizable with his dark brown skin, his calculating gaze and his signature coarse curls—bronze at the roots, but black at the ends, like a burnt-out match. Levi had a look like he was trying to sell you something, and a smile that made you want to buy it.

"I've been busy," Levi answered. "How's business?"

"Just hired another new dealer and had some rotten luck. He barely makes ten percent profit. *Ten percent.*"

Levi whistled with feigned concern.

"It was better when you were dealing for me. No, don't bother apologizing. St. Morse must shell out three times what I paid you. At least."

Try ten times, Levi thought. *But that doesn't come without strings attached.*

"I could get you an Iron," Levi offered, always the businessman. He made a show of adjusting his sleeves to brandish his tattoos: the ace on one arm, the spade on the other. They marked him as the Iron Lord. "I found this new kid who deals pretty well—"

"I would, but I can't. The whiteboots keep paying me visits lately, and I don't want any trouble." Before Levi could point out that technically speaking, the Irons were the only gang that didn't break the law, Grady continued, "They think I'm smuggling."

"Aren't you?"

"Of course." He laughed again. "I'll get you a drink, on the house. Anything for my best dealer—and youngest, I might add. A Snake Eyes—that still your favorite?"

"Sure is," Levi said politely, though he'd never had a taste for the drink. It was also barely ten in the morning. "Thanks."

"You should stop by more often. Teach the new fellow how it's done."

"Maybe I will," Levi lied. He had no intention of revealing his tricks to anyone, especially a no-name dealer who wasn't an Iron.

When Grady walked away, Levi approached the whiteboot captain. The captain wasn't dressed in his usual uniform, but Levi never forgot a face—and the captain had an interesting one. His nose had been broken so many times that it was bent decidedly to the left, and an ugly scar traced across his jawline to the place where his right ear had once been.

"Not every day I have a drink with the Iron Lord," the captain said. He had a grandfatherly voice—all condescension, but with an added hint of malice. He looked Levi over more closely. "But you must be barely old enough to drink. Isn't that right?"

Levi tilted his head to the side and cracked his neck, a nervous habit of his. He hated the way people talked to him in this city—like he was nothing. No, like he was worse than nothing. Like he was a joke.

Levi reached into his pocket and pulled out a silk pouch filled with seven orbs. He set it on the table in front of the captain.

The man raised his eyebrows and opened it. He pulled out the first orb. It was a clear glass sphere, about the size of a billiard ball. White sparks, called volts, sizzled within the glass.

The captain held it up to the lamplight and examined it. "This is good quality."

"Only the best for my clients," Levi said smoothly.

"You make it?"

"No. I'm not in the orb-making business." *Not anymore.*

"Yes, we're all aware what kind of business *you're* in," the captain said drily. He pulled out a mechanical volt reader, flipped open the orb's metal cap and slipped the antenna inside. The meter read 180 volts. He did this with the other six orbs, even though it was widely known that Levi would never cheat a client. They were all there. Every volt he owed him.

Dealing in orbs was a very official way of doing business—it made Levi look more legitimate. As a currency, volts could be traded in two ways. Glass orbs, like the ones Levi had given the captain, were the traditional method. Alternatively, you could carry volts in your skin. This was the hardest to track, the most difficult to steal and the favorite method of the city's gangsters.

The captain slipped the last orb into the pouch. "It's a pity. The Glaisyer orb-making talent is the best of them all." He shook his head. "I don't want to know how you got these."

Levi's eyebrows furrowed. "The investment was a success. You're lucky you paid in when you did. The venture—"

"Was a scam, boy. Don't lie to me."

Levi's sense of alarm never crossed his expression—he had too skilled a poker face for that. But what exactly was the old man suggesting? He couldn't *know.* That wasn't possible.

"I've no idea what you're talking about," he answered coolly.

The captain leaned forward. "I've got it all worked out. You promise an investment with outrageous returns. One man invests, then another, then another. Then when their deadlines roll around, you pay them back with the volts from the newest investor and pocket a bit yourself. Not a bad scam. It just keeps going and going, all until you run out of investors and have no ways of paying people back."

No. No. No. Levi had covered every trace, tied up every loose end. After two years of running the scheme, he was nearly done with it. He had only two people left to pay back, and the captain was one of them. He was so close. He wasn't about to go down now.

He fingered the pistol at his side, even as he tried to think of a clever way out. He always did. Levi the card dealer. Levi the con man. There was no player he couldn't outplay. But he'd rarely been so easily backed into a corner.

Damn it, Vianca, he thought. *I could hang for this. And it would be your fault.*

As if his employer gave a muck about what happened to him.

"What do you want?" Levi growled.

"I don't want anything," the captain said. He was obviously lying. Everyone wanted something.

Grady set Levi's Snake Eyes on the table, bubbling in its champagne glass. "Anything else I can get you, Levi?"

"Nah, thanks, Grady," he muttered, forcing a smile. He still had one hand on his gun.

"What about you, um…sir?" Grady eyed the captain hesitantly. Grady was a good man, but he wasn't a respectable one. Whiteboots always made him tense. "What can I get for you?"

"Nothing for me."

Grady returned to the bar, where he yelled at an old man on a stool trying to order his fifth glass of absinthe.

"You know him?" the captain asked curiously, as if he still expected Levi to be capable of small talk at a time like this. Levi had a grim suspicion he was about to be blackmailed. Or worse.

"He's an old friend," Levi said curtly.

"That's why you're not like the others. The other lords don't *have* friends," the captain said matter-of-factly. "They have victims."

Levi was mucking tired of hearing how he wasn't like the other street lords. Tired of hearing each and every way they were better than him.

"How old are you?" the captain asked.

"Eighteen this October," Levi said stiffly, even though that was four months away. Better to seem older than be treated like a child.

"*If* you live to October. Have you ever considered that you might be in over your head?"

Levi clenched his fist beneath the table. He thought about it every night, during the hours when he should've been sleeping but couldn't. He didn't *choose* to start this scam. He didn't *choose* to involve the most dangerous people in the city. Ever since he started working for Vianca, he hadn't had many choices at all.

"Who else knows?" Levi murmured, the quietness of his voice betraying his fear.

The captain rubbed the scruff on his scarred chin. "I'm not the smartest man. So tell me, if I figured it out, who else might've, too?"

Levi caught his breath. He was referring to Sedric Torren, the twisted, perverted don of the Torren casino Family. The kind of man who could clear a room with the snap of a finger. The kind of man who could ensnare his prey with only a smile. The kind of man Levi didn't want as an enemy.

Sedric Torren was Levi's final investor. Once Levi paid Sedric back, he'd be done. Clean. *Safe*. But it'd taken Levi weeks to scrape up the nine hundred volts for the captain, and he owed Sedric ten thousand.

If Sedric *did* figure out the scam, would he wait for Levi to pay him back, or would he kill him to make a point? Conning a Torren was flirting with destruction.

The captain stood. "I'd prefer not to keep hearing your name." Then he nodded at Levi and left the tavern. No blackmail, no coercion. Just a warning.

Levi let out a breath of relief. He supposed he was lucky—he could've been arrested, or worse. But he didn't feel lucky. The whiteboot captain didn't bother arresting criminals he considered dead men walking.

I'm almost done. I'm almost safe, he reminded himself. *The only person I have left to pay is Sedric, then I can finally focus on the Irons.*

With all the time he'd been spending on Vianca's scam, his gang was slowly crumbling. Their income was tight, their clients were irritated and Levi hardly recognized some of his own kids. But Levi refused to fall with this scheme. He had a destiny to forge and an empire to build.

Levi stood to leave. As he made his way out the door, he tried not to notice Grady's face fall at the full drink he'd left behind on the table.

Levi headed to the newest abandoned house Chez and some of the other Irons had made their own. As he put more distance between himself and Grady's tavern, his shoulders relaxed, and the tightness in his chest loosened. Walking always cleared his head.

Around him, the white stone shopfronts and gambling dens gave way to the signature black scenery of Olde Town, the most historic neighborhood of New Reynes. With the buildings so tall and the alleys so narrow, there was little light here, which was why Levi had claimed it when he founded the Irons five years ago. It was nearly abandoned—nicknamed the "stain of the city," it was the sort of place you didn't want to find yourself, no matter the time of day. There was an art to navigating its maze of alleys, of slipping oneself into its endless shadows. Here, it was always night. And sleights of hand were easiest in the dark.

When he reached the Irons' hideout, Levi paused, running his hand across the wrought iron bars bolted over the windows. He knew every inch of Olde Town. *Because you own it,* he told himself, convinced himself. But did he really own it anymore?

Levi cracked his neck, mustered up some bravado and knocked on the door. Chez unlocked it.

"There's a missy here to see you," Chez said, crossing his

heart, as gangsters always did for their lord. As Chez *usually* did for him, though his sign of respect was often forgotten lately.

"What? Who?" Levi hadn't scheduled any meetings today.

"A real prissy one. From one of the territories."

Before Levi could ask if he was joking, Chez skulked off to the living room. Levi followed, ripping his arms out of his jacket. He didn't have time for this. He needed to figure out how to deliver ten thousand volts to Sedric Torren before Sedric Torren delivered him.

In the living room, Levi found Jac leaning against a quilted armchair, his aura drifting lightly in the stale air. Levi had inherited his split talent of sensing auras from the Canes, his mother's family. He couldn't sense everyone's auras—his split talent wasn't strong enough for that—but those of the people he knew well were often discernable to him.

His best friend's aura flowed toward him in waves and smelled like linen and the color gray.

Mansi perched at the end table, practicing a card trick Levi had taught her yesterday. She crossed her heart and beamed at him, just as she always did. Mansi was one of the best up-and-coming dealers in the Irons. Some called her Levi's protégée, though Levi hadn't made that decision yet. Still, her unwavering loyalty held appeal—there wasn't enough of that to go around, these days.

The missy in question sat on the couch, her back straight as a billiard rod, her legs resting to the side with one ankle tucked delicately behind the other. She was tiny, only about five feet tall, with fair skin and brown hair falling out of a tight ballerina bun. She was real pretty in a second-glance kind of way, though she looked like she was on the wrong side of the city—a strand of rose pearls caught on one of Olde Town's serrated spires.

She stood when Levi entered, like he was some dinner guest. "You must be Mr. Glaisyer." He cringed at the sound of his father's name. The others snickered.

"What's going on here, Jac?" he asked, keeping his gaze fixed on her. It wasn't every day such pretty or strange girls showed up asking for him.

"She said you could help her contact someone. And before you say no—" Levi snapped his mouth shut, and Jac continued "—she outran two whiteboots this morning after just arriving. Not bad, eh?"

Not bad? By the looks of her, Levi would say unbelievable. What could *she* have done to anger the whiteboots? Curtsy the wrong way?

"Who is she?" he asked.

"I'm right here," she said haughtily. "You might as well ask me."

"Exactly," Levi snapped. "But I didn't. Which means I didn't want to."

That shut her up.

"She's from Bellamy," Jac explained. Bellamy was one of the Republic's territories, a mostly self-regulated island that paid taxes to the wigheads. It had a reputation for being twenty years backward, which explained her conservative clothes. "Bit of a snob, really."

She cleared her throat with a sharp *ahem*.

The only person Levi knew from Bellamy was Lourdes Alfero, but he hadn't thought about her in years. She was one of those "anonymous" journalists who wrote for the monarchist papers. Though the Mizers were all dead, the monarchists kept lobbying for a reinstatement of the old kingdoms and the crowning of new families to rule them. The monarchists were the only ones in opposition to the First Party, the core political party of the Republic.

Levi owed Lourdes Alfero a big favor, but that was from four years ago. He'd always assumed she'd gotten herself killed—all the monarchists did eventually.

"Are you quite certain this is Mr. Glaisyer?" the missy asked Jac.

"Think carefully," Levi said, winking at him. "Better be sure."

Jac plopped on the couch, and the girl tried to subtly scoot away from him. He made a show of throwing his hands up in the air. "You meant the *other* Levi Glaisyer. Terribly sorry, missy. But dont'cha worry, the other Levi Glaisyer is a real nice fellow. Nothing like this guy."

Levi tossed his jacket and hat on the coffee table. "He's a bank teller. Three kids. Nice house on the South Side. Not even a *splotch* on his criminal record. Instead, you've got me. Best card dealer in the city. The Iron Lord." Chez rolled his eyes. "Though I like to call myself a businessman more than, well, a con man." He claimed the seat on her other side.

"There's no other Levi Glaisyer," she whispered, her lip quivering.

"Jac, you didn't tell me she was a smart one."

"Then...there must be some mistake," she stammered. To her credit, she managed to keep her chin snobbishly high. Maybe Levi wasn't the only one here with some bravado.

"Why else would such a fine Bellamy lady like yourself be looking for someone like me in the City of Sin, if not by mistake?" By her large purse, well-made clothing and leather pointed-toe heels, Levi bet she carried some decent voltage. "How about you give us your purse and we forget this ever happened? Maybe I'm not the other Levi Glaisyer, but I'm still a generous man."

"No," she said. Her voice cracked, and he couldn't tell if the word was a plea or a refusal.

"Might want to repeat that," Levi warned. "I don't think I heard you right." Chez walked up beside him, flipping his knife between his hands so fast the blade was a blur of silver.

She shrank away and choked a bit, like she was trying to keep from crying, holding her hand over her mouth and shaking all over. Muck. He hated when missies cried.

Unmoved, Chez ripped her purse from her hands and threw it to Mansi, who caught it as nimbly as in one of her card tricks. Half the contents fell out—a passport, a few loose buttons, several cookies and a folded piece of paper. Smirking at the mess, Levi picked up the last item. It was a letter with fancy, precise handwriting:

Dearest,

I hate to think of the worry I've caused you. I am well and missing you. Although I have encountered a little trouble that has delayed my return, I plan to leave in a few days. By the time this letter reaches you, I'll be eagerly sailing home.

If a storm were to further delay my return or another unforeseen circumstance occurs, you can speak to Mr. Levi Glaisyer, a friend of mine who lives in New Reynes. He will be glad to help you.

With much love,

Lourdes

Levi's stomach knotted. Lourdes. He knew that name.

Chez peered over Levi's shoulder blankly. "What's it say?"

Levi didn't respond. The girl watched him with wide, puffy brown eyes, hugging her arms to herself.

He pointed to the letter. "By 'Lourdes,' I'm guessing this is…"

She shook her head indignantly and reached to snatch the letter from him. He moved it away from her reach.

"Relax, missy. It's just a question. Do you know Lourdes Alfero or not?"

She took a deep breath to compose herself and wiped away the tearstains on her cheek. "I do. That's why I'm here."

Jac stiffened with recognition and met Levi's eyes. His expression seemed to prod, *This changes things, right?*

Levi looked away. Of course it changed things. His best friend had a low opinion of Levi's conscience. Levi owed a debt to Lourdes—at the very least, he'd hear the missy out.

"Would you three leave me and Miss…" He paused and looked at her.

"Miss Salta. But you may call me Enne." Despite still tearing up, her voice remained controlled and steady. She spoke more formally than the managers at St. Morse did when addressing their rich patrons, but her jaw was locked, her fists clenched. She wouldn't forgive him so easily for trying to cheat her—not that Levi cared what she thought of him. He wasn't trying to be a gentleman; he was trying to pay his debts.

"Could you leave me and Enne alone for a few minutes? Leave her purse."

Chez's jaw dropped, but Jac put his hand on his shoulder and steered him away. Mansi tossed the purse on the table before they all left through the back door.

When Levi was certain they were alone, he asked, "How do you know Alfero?"

"*Lourdes* is my mother. I traveled here because I need you to find her."

I take it, after writing this letter, Levi thought, *Alfero never did make it home.* He was liking this day less and less, and it was barely eleven in the morning. "You came a long way, and this place isn't much like Bellamy."

"No, it's not," she said flatly. "But the reputation of New Reynes is the least of my worries."

That was her first mistake.

If she'd known anything about her mother, she wouldn't have gone within a hundred feet of whiteboots, much less actually approach them.

Which meant Levi had the unfortunate job of telling her that her mother was almost certainly dead.

He studied her. If she didn't share Alfero's blood name, she must've been her split daughter, with a blood talent inherited from her father. Enne Alfero Salta. From what he remembered of Alfero—a devoted journalist, a staunch progressive and a profound political mind—Levi couldn't picture her walking out with someone with a dancing talent. She'd seemed too serious for that. Nor did he recall her being particularly interested in men. It'd been four years ago, but Levi still remembered the determined fury in her eyes. The Republic had wronged her in a way she could never forgive.

Whatever her cause had been, Levi wondered, was it worth dying for? Worth leaving behind a daughter for?

He doubted it. Nothing was worth that price.

She cleared her throat. "Tell me, Mr. Glaisyer—"

"Call me Levi."

"Tell me, *Levi*, why would the whiteboots be so interested in my mother?" She slipped her hand into her pocket and pulled out a bronze coin, which she squeezed the way gamblers squeezed dice before they tossed them. Like a prayer.

Levi hesitated, not wanting to deliver the bad news so fast. She'd only just she stopped crying. Instead, he said, "You don't look much like her." The Lourdes Alfero he remembered was tall, nearly as tall as him, and with blond hair much lighter than Enne's brown. She'd dressed fluidly—some days as a woman, sometimes as neither male nor female—and her angled features lent themselves easily to her identity. She preferred to be addressed as "she" and "her."

He didn't see any of Lourdes's face in Enne's.

"Lourdes is my adopted mother," Enne explained. "But I can tell you're stalling. Why were the whiteboots so interested in her?"

Levi sighed. She might not know much about New Reynes, but she wasn't thick. "She's a Mizer sympathizer. A famous one, at that."

"What?" Her voice came out in a screech. Maybe she wasn't as controlled as Levi had first thought.

He supposed he couldn't blame her slip. Even if the way Chancellor Malcolm Semper governed the Republic was wildly unpopular, the Mizers had been tyrants. In New Reynes, where the Revolution began, men, women and children had cheered in

Liberty Square as the royal family was beheaded. Most viewed the monarchists as radicals.

"Ever since the Revolution—especially during the Great Street War, which occurred seven or so years after—there's been a group of journalists writing for monarchist newspapers. They use code names to expose stories the wigheads try to keep quiet, and they work in secret. They call themselves the Pseudonyms. Lourdes is one of them." *The most famous of them all, even.* "The whiteboots have been searching for her for a long time." *And, sometime in the past four months, they'd probably found her.*

Levi paused, gauging Enne's reaction. "Did you really have no idea?"

She bit her lip. "I knew Lourdes had her secrets, but no, I never would've guessed this."

Levi held his breath as he watched the gravity of her mother's situation dawn on her. He didn't need to tell her that Alfero was dead. She could probably guess it herself now.

"Do you know where Lourdes might be?" Enne asked, still using present tense. Levi sighed inwardly.

"I haven't spoken to her in years," he told her.

"What?" She frowned. "Then why would she recommend you?"

"I've got no idea. About four years ago, I got myself into a lot of trouble with a con gone wrong." *And apparently,* he thought, *I haven't learned my lesson.* "Lourdes paid my way out of it and got me a steady job at St. Morse."

"St. Morse?"

"The casino. You must've heard of it. It's one of the two largest in the city."

She pulled a book out of her pocket, and Levi snorted. A tourist guide. "I think I've heard of it," she said, skimming through the pages until she found the passage she was looking for. "Oh. It says not to go there."

He glanced at the title. *The City of Sin, a Guidebook: Where To Go and Where Not To.* If she'd paid more attention to her guidebook, then she'd never have followed Chez into Olde Town, the heart of Iron territory. She would've left the harbor and gone straight to the South Side, where she clearly belonged.

Levi stood up and reached for his hat on the table.

"Where are you going?" Enne asked.

"Out. There are volts to make and people to cheat." He flashed her a smile. She was lucky he hadn't cheated *her*. He was feeling sentimental today.

"But you didn't finish your story," she blurted.

"That *is* the story. Lourdes helped me out, she got me a job and then she disappeared. I haven't spoken to her since."

Enne stood up, her shoulders square and her expression a challenge. He wondered if she really felt that brave, or if she was a breath away from tears again. "But you *must* help me. I have to find her."

"I *must* help you?" he said, taking a step closer. She wasn't very intimidating, small as she was. Not many spoke to him the way she did. "Why should I? I don't know you. I barely know your mother."

"Because..." Her voice wavered. "Because I'll pay you."

"You lost your luggage. How many volts could you possibly have on you right now?" His eyes traveled from her purse to her pockets. He doubted she had more than a few hundred.

But...that was a few hundred closer to his ten thousand. Maybe he was feeling a bit altruistic after all.

"Lourdes has a bank account," Enne said, with the kind of seriousness that made Levi think she wasn't lying. He searched her face for a tell—everyone always had a tell, a break in their poker face. But he found none.

"It has more volts than you could want," she continued. "If you help me find her, I'll pay you."

"How much?" he asked.

"Five thousand volts," she said unflinchingly.

He stilled. Did she really have that kind of voltage? She *did* look like she came from money, as Lourdes always had, too.

Maybe she had five thousand volts. Maybe she had more.

"Sorry," he said, faking disinterest. "I don't have time for this. I'm not the sort of guy who helps damsels in distress."

"*Ten* thousand volts," she declared.

Gotcha.

He narrowed his eyes, as if considering. He let a few moments pass, and as he waited, the boldness in her dark eyes never faded. A few minutes ago, she'd been in tears, but she wasn't broken.

But would she be, once she realized her mother was probably dead?

Maybe Alfero is still alive, Levi thought. After all, she'd survived this long. That alone was impressive.

But unlikely. And a good player knew better than to bet against those kind of odds.

"I'm listening," he said. "But I'm going to need some incentive up front. Who knows how long it could take to find her?"

"I'll give you one thousand volts," she offered, "but not until the end of the day. You said yourself that you barely know Lourdes. I want to make sure you can help me at all."

If he pressed her for more, she'd probably relent. After all, she could play at being brave all she wanted, but Levi knew better. She'd left her belongings behind to follow Chez straight into the heart of the North Side—she was desperate.

But he didn't haggle. He didn't want to scare her away and lose the possibility—even if it was slim—for ten thousand volts, for a chance to save himself. After all, he was desperate, too.

If the day ended without a lead, then Levi would take his one thousand volts tonight and leave her in the dust. Even if ten thousand would cover his entire debt to Sedric, he still doubted that Lourdes Alfero was even alive. He couldn't afford to waste time on a pointless search.

"We'll start with a friend of mine," Levi said. "He can answer our questions."

Enne's shoulders relaxed, and she let out the breath she'd been holding.

"Is your friend an…Iron?" she asked.

He smirked. "What? Don't like my friends much?" Jac might look threatening, but he had all the aggression of a baby rabbit. Mansi was practically Levi's younger sister. And Chez… Well, Chez and Levi weren't on the best of terms as of late, but when Chez wanted to, he could be tolerable. Sometimes, when the stars aligned, even pleasant.

"No, my friend's not an Iron," he said. But Levi got the feeling Enne would be missing Olde Town's charm within the hour.

"Good," she huffed.

He opened the door for her. "After you, missy."

"But what about the whiteboots?" she asked. "They could still be searching for me."

"You think I'd go someplace with whiteboots? Please, I know better than that. You should learn to trust me." His smile was filthy with insincerity.

"I'll work with you because I have to, but I'm not going to trust you until I find Lourdes."

She lifted her head and marched outside.

"One thousand volts," Levi grumbled to himself. If he could tolerate her for a single day, then he would wake one thousand volts richer tomorrow.

Besides, Enne Salta wouldn't last more than a night in the City of Sin.

LEVI

Levi and Enne emerged from the edge of Olde Town, squinting into the light. Not the sunlight—the New Reynes sky was overcast, the smog leaving foul smudges against the clouds. No, they were squinting at the flashing lights of Tropps Street, the center of the Casino District, and—as far as anyone on the North Side was concerned—the center of the city. Everything shone on Tropps Street: the glint of costume jewelry, the golden teeth of the bouncers' smiles, the waxy sheen of faux leather and, of course, the neon reflections in the puddles of rainwater, piss and emptied liquor cups along the sidewalks.

There was nothing like the Casino District. From the moment Levi had arrived in New Reynes, he'd made it his home. Then he'd made it his territory. One day, he would make it his kingdom.

To the right, a man played an accordion along the curb. He sang about the woes of unrequited love, but it wasn't clear if he was referring to a sweetheart or the bottle of absinthe at his feet. Enne cringed each time the singer cursed.

"You seem nervous," Levi said.

She hugged her arms to her chest and darted an anxious glance over her shoulder. "This street is so crowded, but it's not even noon. Don't these people work?"

He snorted. "Crowded? You should see this street at night."

Half a block ahead, a man in a trench coat stared at them from beneath a dull and flickering yellow sign. Rusted chains dangled from it like metal streamers. The man's face was sallow and sunken, and he reached a shaking hand forward like a prisoner trapped behind bars, begging for food or volts.

Enne stiffened and knocked into Levi's shoulder, piquing his annoyance. "Why is he watching us?" Enne whispered.

"He's a street slave. Don't worry—he can't follow us."

"What does that mean? What's stopping him?" She ducked to his other side so that Levi was between her and the man.

"He's trapped on that street," Levi explained. "The families there have a talent that binds people in debt to them within a certain area. That street is like a jail cell."

She shivered. "What are they in debt for?"

"Drugs. Mostly Rapture, Mistress and Lullaby—all from Torren and Augustine suppliers. Try to avoid Chain Street."

She nodded fearfully and fiddled with something in her pocket. If Levi didn't know better, he'd guess she was an antsy runner carrying an expensive package. The farther west they walked down Tropps Street, the closer they came to Scarhand territory. Even if it wasn't peak hours, there were probably still a few gangsters roaming the alleys, hunting for orb pouches or—for the particularly skilled—grazing trace volts off unlucky passersby's skin. Enne was marking herself as a target.

Then, to Levi's ever-increasing aggravation, Enne removed her coin from her pocket and began fiddling with it as she walked. He glanced at the cameo of the queen on the front. If it was from before the Revolution, it was probably worth more than sentimental value. All the more reason to avoid wandering eyes.

"Put the coin back," he snapped. "That looks like gold from far away." This missy was bound to be more trouble than she was worth. He didn't have the time or patience to teach her the rules of New Reynes.

Enne bit her lip and slipped it back into her pocket. At least she listened to what he said.

"What's the coin from, anyway?" he asked.

"It's an old token. Lourdes gave it to me."

She's alone and agitated, Levi reminded himself. Of course she was acting jumpy. What she needed was a distraction.

"So just how different is New Reynes from Bellamy?" he asked, even though he already knew the answer: completely.

"Well, to start with, it's a lot dirtier," she said, her nose crinkled. Levi was beginning to think that was her signature look. "And it smells foul."

"What? This city?" He inhaled deeply through his nose. "That's the smell of opportunity. And maybe a little piss."

"Yes, well, I suppose you might be fonder of it if you were born here."

"You can't tell from looking at me, but I wasn't born a Sinner," he said. "But yes, I *am* rather fond of the eau de New Reynes. Maybe you will be, too, after a while."

She crinkled her nose again. Pretty or not, Levi wondered if he had ever met such a delicate, unpleasant creature. "Where are you from, then?" she asked.

"My family lives in Elta." The word felt like a shard of ice on his tongue. It was a city a few hours east, on the opposite coast. "Before that, my parents came from Caroko."

Caroko was once a great capital of one of the seven Mizer kingdoms. During the Revolution, like many orb-maker families who'd been loyal to the Mizers, the Glaisyers were forced to relocate near the ever-suspicious eyes of New Reynes, the capital of the Republic. His mother, who'd been a bit of a world traveler in her youth, hadn't resented the move. His father, however, had mourned the loss of his home and the king he'd once served. Rather than teach Levi about Caroko, his father had refused to discuss it, as if the city itself was gone, left in an unspeakable state of grief. He considered himself a martyr.

"How long have you lived in New Reynes?" Enne asked, bringing Levi's focus back to the present.

"Since I was twelve." Levi had fled the brutality of his home seeking the brutality of somewhere else—a place where, this time, he could fight back.

Frowning, he shook away the unpleasant memories. In less than a minute, she'd managed to steer the conversation entirely away from herself. He didn't like it when people didn't talk about themselves. In his experience, that usually meant they had something to hide.

"You're full of questions, aren't you?" he commented.

"You're a stranger leading me through an unsightly area in an unseemly city. Of course I'm full of questions." He supposed that was a reasonable response, though he'd hardly call his own territory "unsightly."

Someone cooed to their right.

"Welcome to Sweetie Street," he said, not bothering to hide his grin. He could think of no place better to watch Enne squirm.

Swarms of people stumbled down the alley, all flushed and in some degree of hungover stupor. The women dressed in dark skirts with lacy tulles, lipstick every shade of red, faces white or pink with powder. The men wore black-and-white-striped suits, with jewel-studded pipes resting suggestively between their lips. At night, the dancing silhouettes in the windows beckoned customers from all across the city with promises of warm beds and warmer embraces.

"Whatever you do," he whispered in Enne's ear, "don't look anyone in the eyes."

"Why not?" she asked, jerking her gaze from the window displays to the ground, which was covered with broken glass and sparkly confetti.

"Their talent is seduction." He swore he saw goose bumps prickle against her skin, and he fought to contain his laughter. "You can't let them get too close, either. One touch—" he squeezed her shoulder "—and even you would be discarding your skirts and stockings. One kiss, and you'd be overcome by an almost primal sort of lust."

Enne narrowed her eyes like she'd realized he was mucking with her, but then a woman giggled to their right, and Enne jolted as if she'd heard a gunshot. The woman swayed back and forth, wearing only a ruby corset covered in black lace, her glitter-covered chest spilling out the front. The number ten was written across her cleavage in violet lipstick.

"Oh goodness," Enne gasped, her gaze darting wildly between the cobblestones and the woman's breasts. "What does the number mean?"

"Price."

The whimper that escaped her lips was enough to send Levi into hysterics. He laughed so hard he needed to clutch his abdomen to steady himself.

"Oh, I'm glad you find my decency *so* amusing," she snapped. "So is Sweetie Street frequented by everyone in the City of Sin? Is this where *you* come every night after…whatever illegal things you do?"

"Me? I don't need to come here," he said, only somewhat in earnest, but mostly because he couldn't help himself. His cockiness earned him a disgusted but embarrassed look from Enne. "Think of it this way," he said. "When you go back to Bellamy, you'll be able to scandalize all your uppity friends."

Enne laughed hollowly. "As if I need them thinking any less of me."

"Less of you? Are you not snobbish enough for their preferences?"

She rolled her eyes. "I'm a Salta. There are much better, richer families at my finishing school with more impressive dancing talents. No one notices me. Most of the time, they hardly acknowledge I'm there."

Must've hit a nerve, Levi thought. That was the most she'd said about herself yet. It also struck him as rather unbelievable. Her doll-like features, her determined dark eyes—how could anyone not notice her?

"Then why go back there?" he asked.

"Because I have only a year left of school before my debut. It's why...I'd really love to be able to return before the start of term." If Levi didn't find the thought of a "debut" so ridiculous, he might've felt sorry for the longing in her voice. She was sacrificing a lot to find Alfero, assuming Alfero could even be found.

"And if you don't find Lourdes before the summer ends?" Levi asked Enne quietly. "You're willing to risk that?"

"Of course I am. She's my mother."

Levi's stomach tightened, and—to his own surprise—he was about to say something consoling, but then she bit her lip. Maybe dealing cards made him hyperaware of bluffing, but that was a straight-from-the-book tell. He wondered if she *was* hiding something after all, but he didn't press her on it.

For now.

"We're here," he announced as they crossed the border from Iron territory into Scar Land.

Tents, stands and carts lined the sidewalks, and people crowded around them, waving merchandise in the air to tempt customers or yelling at the kids trying to steal food and trinkets. Several paperboys approached him and Enne, advertising this week's copy of the South Side's *Guillory Street Gossip* or the North Side's version, *The Kiss and Tell*. Levi grabbed Enne's shoulders and pushed her ahead. If she spent too long gawking at everything, a pickpocket would nab her in a blink.

"This is Scrap Market," he said. "It changes location every day, and it's in only one place for a few hours at a time before it disappears."

She broke away from his grasp and glared at him with annoyance. "Are all your markets like this? How disorienting."

"No, just this one. People here don't pay in volts—they don't really have them. Instead, they trade. It changes time and place to make it harder for the whiteboots to find them. The goods here aren't all legal, and it's all under the table."

They passed a food stand, and Levi's stomach rumbled at the smell of sausages and sizzling bacon. He'd forgotten to eat breakfast. Enne must've been hungry as well, judging by the longing look she cast at the doughnut cart.

"Illegal? Then why are we here?" she asked nervously.

"The Scarhands live under Scrap Market."

"The Scarhands?"

"One of the gangs."

She halted in the middle of the street. "You said your friend wasn't in a gang."

Levi hauled her along, this time not letting her shrug him off. She was going to lose her purse.

"No, I said he wasn't an Iron," he grunted. Besides, Reymond Kitamura was a good place for them to start. Not only had Reymond introduced Levi to Lourdes, but he was the Scar Lord, and all secrets of New Reynes flushed down to him eventually.

"Let *go* of me. It's terribly impolite—not to mention improper—"

"I'm trying to keep you from getting your purse stolen. You've already lost your luggage. Wanna lose your volts, too?" Levi refused to suffer through this entire morning only for Enne to lose his reward.

She stopped struggling, and he led her into a ramshackle

building with a sign reading Cheep Orbs and Metalwork. They slid between a couple examining a box of empty glass orbs.

"Those are real shoddy quality," Levi muttered. "Probably can't hold over twenty volts without shattering." He could make better blindfolded…not that he'd made orbs in years. His blood and split talents didn't mix together well, so he'd decided a long time ago to avoid orb-making altogether.

Enne stared at a crate full of knives, each with a little rust on the handle or cracks in the blade. "How many street gangs are there?"

Levi cleared his throat. Really, there was no person better suited for introducing Enne to New Reynes than himself. "There are three: the Irons, the Scarhands and the Doves. They all live on the North Side." There were also the two casino Families, the Augustines and the Torrens, but Levi didn't want to overwhelm her. Besides, he'd rather not think about the Families right now. It was a mistake involving himself with either of them.

"Why do you call yourselves the Irons?" Enne asked.

"It's a nickname. We didn't have a name at first—the dens just called us 'mechanics.' People who fix games." He shook his head. "Of course, our clients didn't actually like to call us that—bad for business. Somehow the name Irons caught on."

"So you cheat," she said, the contempt obvious in her voice.

"We make a business out of winning."

Levi took her to a door in the back of the shop. A rusted lock dangled from the knob.

Although Levi never used his blood talent anymore for its actual purpose—making orbs—he often relied on his skill for fire. Levi could do a few tricks: light a match with the snap of his fingers, walk through open flame without being burned, craft a glass ornament with only his bare hands. Nothing powerful, but his talent was often useful.

Levi grabbed the lock and concentrated on heat. After a few moments, it glowed red and hissed with steam.

"How are you doing that?" she asked.

"It's my blood talent." He tugged it, and it snapped. He would've thought that obvious, given the orb-maker colors in his hair.

"Which is—"

"Someone will hear you." He didn't need the Scar Lord blaming him for giving away today's location to all of Scrap Market. Reymond liked to lie low.

Levi slipped inside the crack of the door into a dark, narrow staircase. When Enne closed it behind them, everything went black.

"You'd better leave. We're not seeing anyone today," someone growled. Enne made a sound somewhere between clearing her throat and a squeak.

"It's me," Levi said.

"Pup?"

He *hated* that nickname. People assumed that Canes smelled auras like bloodhounds, even though they read them with all their senses. The nickname was, in Levi's opinion, the embodiment of everything he needed to change about his reputation. Once upon a time, the Irons had been the richest gang in the city. Even if he was young, Levi deserved to be taken seriously.

"Nice to see you again, Jonas," Levi lied.

Jonas Maccabees, the Scarhands' second-in-command, sneered, "You should stick to Olde Town where you belong."

"That's a shame, because I came here to see you. It's hard to resist that smile of yours."

Jonas turned on a light, and Levi squinted as his eyes adjusted. The room had concrete walls and a mess of exposed, leaking pipes. It smelled faintly of cigarettes.

"Reymond isn't seeing anyone today," Jonas grunted. A scar ran from his left eye down his cheek, disappearing beneath his shoulder-length black hair. More scars crisscrossed his palms, and his skin had a gray tint to it. Like a corpse. Beside Levi, Enne stiffened.

"But he'll see me," Levi challenged.

Jonas glared because he knew Levi was right, then mumbled something under his breath and turned to a door at the other end of the room. The undeniable stench of rotting bodies trailed after him.

"Is Reymond their boss?" Enne whispered.

"He's the Scar Lord."

"You failed to mention that."

"Does it matter? I'm the Iron Lord, aren't I?" Apparently *his* lordly title didn't warrant the same concern.

"Maybe this was a bad—"

"Do you want to find Alfero or not?"

She quieted.

Jonas opened the door and ushered them into an office. Reymond perched on the desk. He was short and slender to the point of looking starved, with black hair and brown, hooded eyes. He wore a shiny gold vest and a crimson jacket, a belt of reptile scales and huge rings on every finger, which made eight rings in total—both his middle fingers were stumps.

"He brought a missy," Jonas said.

"Yes," Reymond answered, scanning Enne up and down with interest. Levi didn't usually introduce missies to his friends. "I can see that."

Levi pulled up a seat at the desk and nodded for Enne to do so, as well. As he sat, he got a whiff of Reymond's cheap cologne and nearly gagged.

"We won't take long," Reymond said, dismissing Jonas, who closed the door as he left. Then he held out his hand to Enne. "I'm Reymond Kitamura," he said.

She shook it and gave a winning smile to rival Levi's own. All of her apprehension from before was concealed. "It's a pleasure. My name is Enne Salta."

"You don't dress like any Salta I've ever met," he remarked, which made Enne lift her chin indignantly. Levi snorted, picturing Enne in a burlesque costume. Well...it wasn't so terrible a picture, if he was being honest with himself. "Or any of Levi's boys or missies, for that matter," Reymond added, smirking at Levi.

He shrugged in response. Levi had a long romantic history of scattered affairs—a few girls and many boys—that had become the subject of teasing from his friends. They claimed he had a hopeless habit of kissing and telling.

"I'm not his missy," Enne said hurriedly.

"Good. Glad to hear you got taste," Reymond joked.

Aside from the dons of the casino Families, Reymond Kitamura was arguably the most powerful person in the North Side, a reputation he enjoyed flaunting in Levi's face at every opportunity. When Levi had first arrived in New Reynes—twelve years old, scrappy and eager—Reymond had taken him in. The two were like brothers, though, as Jac had pointed out on more than one occasion, they fought more often than they got along.

Two Octobers ago, when Vianca Augustine had dumped the investment scheme on him, Levi had turned to Reymond as a business partner. Since then, Levi had tried to keep their working relationship under wraps, but Chez had discovered it several months ago. His third considered it a betrayal. Officially, the Irons and the Scarhands were far from friends, and the gangs took their rivalries seriously. So Levi visited Reymond only when it was absolutely necessary these days, even if he sometimes missed their squabbles.

Reymond pulled a cigar out of his pocket. He pointed it at Levi, almost like he was offering it to him, except he wasn't. Levi snapped his fingers, igniting a small flame at his fingertips and lit the end. Reymond cupped it and took a deep inhale. The smoke billowed out his nostrils, and Enne crinkled her nose.

"We're still late on the Torren payment," Reymond reminded him, as if Levi needed reminding. "Two weeks or so."

"Let's talk about this another time," Levi muttered. Enne already knew he ran a gang; he didn't want her knowing about the scam, too. He couldn't have her running off on him...at least not until she paid him tonight. And if Reymond *did* have any leads on Alfero, then it was in Levi's best interests to stick with Enne. He couldn't lose the potential for a ten-thousand-volt reward for finding her mother, even if the chances were slim.

"*Now* seems fine to me." Reymond blew out a cloud of smoke, and Levi seriously considered the repercussions of wringing his skinny neck. Clearly, he'd caught his friend in a bad mood. "And the whiteboot captain?"

Levi debated with himself for a moment, then decided that, after being chased just this morning, Enne was unlikely to talk to anyone about this conversation. She didn't know anyone in this city except for him. Still, they needed to be discreet.

"I paid the captain this morning," Levi answered begrudgingly. "But he knew. He knew about the scam."

Reymond's eyes widened. "Did he tell anyone?"

"I don't think so, but he said some things about Sedric Torren that have me concerned."

Reymond anxiously tapped the soot off his cigar. "You talk to Vianca yet?" Powerful as Reymond was, the only person who could truly protect Levi from Sedric was Vianca, the donna of the Augustine family, the owner of St. Morse Casino, and—as far as Levi was concerned—the foulest woman in New Reynes.

"Not yet. I'm not sure what she'll do to help." St. Morse was a sinking ship. Vianca's radical political beliefs made her unpopular on the South Side, where many of her patrons lived. Meanwhile, the Torren Family had the wigheads in their pockets.

"You're Vianca's favorite. She'd do anything for you," Reymond said, blowing out another exhale of smoke. "You're her bitch."

Levi's fury simmered as Reymond smirked. "We're not here to talk about this," Levi snapped.

He wanted to add that Enne and Alfero's volts might've been the solution to their problem, but he couldn't think of a way to say that without Enne picking up on it. He'd have to discuss that with Reymond another time.

But he already knew what Reymond would say. *Alfero is dead, Levi. Of course she's dead. You're too easily persuaded by a pretty missy.*

"But *I* wanna talk about business," Reymond insisted. "Ever since Vianca lost our thousands of safety volts, this is starting to sound a lot more dangerous. I have skin in this game, too."

"If you wanna pitch in more, partner—"

"No can do. Fifteen percent was the deal." Reymond flicked his ashes in a porcelain bowl that was broken on one side. "No can do."

"Are you both quite done?" Enne snapped. "It's very inconsiderate to talk business in front of a stranger."

Reymond snorted and picked at his well-manicured cuticles. He took precise care of the fingers he had left and never liked to get his hands dirty. "She's a real charmer, Pup."

"I'm afraid I didn't come here to charm you," she snapped. "I came here in search of information on Lourdes Alfero."

Reymond paused. "Did you, now?"

Despite Enne's numerous flaws—namely that she was mucking annoying—she knew how to weasel in and out of a conversation. Levi respected that.

"Have you heard anything about Alfero lately?" Levi asked Reymond, more than eager to steer the discussion away from their failing con.

"She comes and goes," he answered. "The usual spots. But I haven't heard anything noteworthy recently. What do you need to know?"

Enne's face lit brighter than a neon sign outside of Luckluster Casino. "I need to find her. She's missing."

"How do you know her? You don't look like the type to read monarchist papers."

"You can tell this just from looking at me?"

The Scarhands worked in the business of counterfeiting, arms dealing and information, and Reymond had sacrificed ten years, dozens of men and two fingers to carve out his gang's place in the North Side. Reymond credited his power to his blood talent: he could see through any lie. But he probably didn't need it to guess that the dare in Enne's words was empty.

"Most of the Pseudonyms are dead," Reymond said flatly. "Lourdes Alfero is smart. She survived this long. If she's missing, though…"

"Please, where was she last seen?" Enne's voice quivered.

"She frequented the Sauterelle. It's a cabaret a few blocks off Sweetie Street. There, they'd probably know her as Séance, her pen name."

Enne paled at the mention of Sweetie Street. "Are you sure—"

"Levi and I both have friends there. We can get you in."

Levi nodded. Mansi worked at the Sauterelle. "My shift is this evening. But tomorrow we'll pay a visit," he said. This was perfect. With the promise of a lead tomorrow, Enne would need to stay with Levi and pay him tonight. He doubted she would attempt to brave Sweetie Street by herself. And if he could promise her this night, then the next, then the next, maybe they really could find Lourdes. Maybe she was the answer to all of his problems.

He just needed Lourdes to be alive. And he needed Enne to stay.

"What's wrong?" Reymond smirked, seeing Enne crinkle her nose. "Got a problem with variety shows, doll face?"

Enne shook her head.

"No…" Reymond tilted his head to the side. "That's not it. It's that you're afraid Lourdes is probably dead." Reymond had many good qualities, but no one would call him considerate. He didn't hold back any blows. "You know, you still never mentioned how you knew Alfero." Reymond was already using past tense.

Enne's face was pale as she rose from her seat in a rush. "Thank you, but I need some air." She nearly tripped on her dash to the door. Levi stood hurriedly and followed her. He didn't like Enne much, but even he admitted that Reymond's words were harsh, considering the morning she'd already had.

Enne pushed through the back room and up the stairwell. By the time they exited the orb shop, tears glinted in her brown eyes.

Outside, the wind had picked up, and the clouds—black from factory smoke and an oncoming storm—cast a shadow over the city. The tents were gone. Carts, gone. Stands, gone. Scrap Market had picked up and left, and Enne and Levi were the only ones standing on the empty street.

"Is she really dead?" Enne asked, her voice high and broken in a way that stirred his own memories.

For a moment, Levi was eleven years old again, kneeling at his mother's sickbed. He swallowed.

"Don't," he warned.

She didn't listen. She let out a gasp, then a sob.

Levi stepped back from her, unsure what to do or how to comfort. Tears pooled down her cheeks, and she blotted them away with the back of her hand.

"I don't know if she's alive," he said truthfully but gently.

"But I'd feel it. I'd know if she was dead."

If Jac were here, he would've agreed with Enne. Jac was sentimental like that. Levi was usually too cynical to indulge such hopes, but, this one time, he needed to believe. He needed Enne's reward.

I need her to stay.

But it was also something more than that. He recognized his own ghosts in Enne's eyes.

He put a hand on Enne's shoulder and bent down to her level. "Look at me. We can't talk here, in the middle of the street for the whole world to hear. You know that, and you know why, don't you?"

Enne nodded, her hand fiddling in her coat pocket. Even with her limited knowledge of New Reynes, she understood why the monarchists were a dangerous subject.

"I have a shift tonight at St. Morse Casino, so I'm going to take you there now." Levi swallowed hard, hoping he wouldn't regret his next words. "But I promise, I'll help you find your mother, no matter what."

ENNE

Levi and Enne passed through the revolving doors of St. Morse Casino. Enne had never set foot in a casino before, but she'd glimpsed some of the smaller establishments on Tropps Street, and none of them came close to resembling St. Morse's old-world glamour. A crystal chandelier stretched across the entire ceiling. Emerald green carpeting trailed up the stairs, matching the velvet curtains draped over the windows and the uniforms of the concierges. Metallic silver archways led into rooms labeled Tropps Room, Theatre and Ballroom with sapphire-blue calligraphy. Everything smelled of fine leather and whiskey, and each patron donned the Republic's most famous designers: Gershton, Ulani Maxirello, Regallière.

It was, without a doubt, the gaudiest place to ever affront Enne's senses.

At least fifty guests mingled in the lobby, champagne glasses in hand. They wore elegant tea gowns with pleated skirts, feathered hats and long strands of black pearls. In her tailored suit and scuffed heels, Enne felt exposed in more ways than one.

She'd lied to Levi about the volts.

At first, she hadn't felt guilty in the least. Levi was a criminal after all. He probably cheated tourists like her every day. But that didn't make it right. And after what he'd said to her earlier, like he had more at stake in this than his wallet, it didn't make her feel good, either.

It hadn't been a total lie. The volts *did* exist. Last summer, when Enne had sneaked into Lourdes's private office for the first and only time, she'd seen the bank slips. She and her mother certainly didn't live like they had millions of volts, but Enne had read the documents herself. It was...wealth beyond imagination. And Lourdes had kept it from her.

So the volts *did* exist, and paying Levi would hardly put a dent in their fortune. But Enne had no idea where the bank account was. Or where the volts came from.

It didn't matter. Once she found Lourdes, she'd have her answers. Once she found Lourdes, Levi would have his volts. It wasn't a lie. It just wasn't the truth.

She and Levi walked into a hallway lined with portraits of men, women and occasionally whole families, each with blazing purple eyes. *Mizers*, Enne thought with a chill. She wondered whether or not it was dangerous for the casino to have portraits of the royal families on display, as if they were people to be revered. Most people alive today had witnessed the Revolution, and, however corrupt the Republic might've been, it was nothing compared to the tyranny of the Mizers.

The deeper they ventured into St. Morse, the more Enne felt like she was walking into a castle out of a history book. The mahogany woodwork. The blue and green, everywhere. The white stone walls. *A hotel casino*, Levi had called it. Really, it was more of a fortress. In the nighttime, it might even resemble a mausoleum.

They stopped in front of an elevator, where Levi pulled a lever that illuminated an up arrow above the doors.

"How many volts did you bring?" Levi asked. "Enough to last until you leave?"

"No, not with all of my belongings gone." A jolt of panic shot through her. She had no clothes. No toiletries. And not enough volts to replace them and still purchase her ticket home, after paying Levi tonight.

"That's what I thought," he said. The elevator doors opened, and they stepped onto a shaky metal platform. The black iron gates creaked closed as the operator turned a crank. "How are you with heights? This is the tallest building on the North Side."

"I'm all right," she lied. The floor shifted beneath her feet, almost like the deck of the ship she'd traveled on to New Reynes—but then, she hadn't been terrified of falling to her death. Enne held her breath and squeezed the railing.

Levi watched her with amusement, much as he had all morning. At first, when Levi had tried to steal from her, Enne had considered him a crook. But after they left Scrap Market, there had been an unmistakable sincerity in his voice. It had improved her opinion of him, if only slightly. Still, he was terribly rude. She reminded herself that she needed to tolerate him only until they found her mother.

"Never ridden in an elevator before?" he asked.

"Not one quite so in need of maintenance."

The operator grunted.

The doors opened to a hallway with emerald wallpaper and silver trim. It looked opulent and grand, but beneath, Enne could see that it was royal only in the cheapest, most obscene manner possible. Every metallic finish was paint; every bit of crystal was actually glass.

"The top floor is only for Vianca Augustine's favorites," Levi said, except with more disgust than pride. "This includes the highest-paying guests, close friends of the Augustines, Vianca herself and, of course, me."

"You mentioned Vianca earlier. Who is she?" Enne asked.

He scowled like he had a bad taste in his mouth. "You should pay better attention to that guidebook. Vianca is the donna of the Augustine crime Family, and she owns St. Morse Casino."

As Enne digested his words, Levi led her to a room labeled 2018 and unlocked the door. He held it open for her, but she couldn't tell whether his politeness was meant to mock. It was impossible to differentiate between his smirk and his smile.

The apartment was unnaturally clean. Levi took a seat on the stiff armchair in the living room while Enne examined the shine of his counters and the strange black oven that looked out of place in his cramped kitchen. Bookshelves covered every wall, filled with volumes and papers arranged by height, and a glass conch shell glittered on the coffee table.

Enne took a seat on the couch.

"What?" Levi asked, studying her face. "Missies always expect that I live in a gutter," he muttered. Then, as though he were actually going to play host, he offered her a green candy from the bowl on his table. "Tiggy's Saltwater Taffy. Absinthe-flavored. It's the signature New Reynes treat."

Enne shook her head, certain anything signature to this city would prove repulsive. "Why are we here?" She'd never been alone in a young man's home before, and she hoped he couldn't see her cheeks redden, couldn't tell what she was thinking. Surely there must've been other places in St. Morse to talk in private besides his apartment. The whole ordeal of Sweetie Street and the unfamiliarity with New Reynes didn't ease Enne's mind, nor did the pleasing slopes and angles of Levi's jawline.

"I'm gonna get you a job," he declared.

She startled. "A job? *Here?*"

"What? Too below you to earn an income?"

She doubted her teachers at finishing school would have approved of a lady working at a casino. Or a lady working at all, for that matter. "What kind of job do you have in mind?" she asked coolly, refusing to rise to his provocation.

"You're a dancer. We've got several groups of performers—"

"I'm not *that* type of dancer."

"And St. Morse isn't *that* type of establishment." He stood and turned into a narrow hallway, motioning for her to follow. By the time she got up, he'd disappeared into the room at the end, and she realized with no small amount of horror that it must have been his bedroom.

"What are you doing?" Enne called from the doorway, unable to even peek inside.

"Finding you something to wear. Your clothes belong in an antique shop."

Enne sniffed in indignation. Her outfit was considered fashionable in Bellamy, where women had a sense of modesty.

"What do you expect me to wear?" she asked. "Trousers?" Or worse, one of those fishnet numbers she'd seen all over Tropps Street?

He emerged with a dress and an easy smile. "What? Don't you trust me?"

"Hardly." And certainly not with that gleam in his eyes. Or with the not-entirely-unpleasant smell of his citrus cologne.

She allowed herself to admit that Levi Glaisyer was very good-looking—at least, in an up-to-no-good way that she supposed *some* people found attractive. He was of fairly average height, but his build was slender and trim. Of all his noteworthy features—his smooth brown skin, the sharp slopes of his cheekbones—the most identifiable was his hair. It started bronze at the roots, but the tight curls gradually turned to black at the ends, as if singed.

Sometimes talents, especially Talents of Mysteries, carried a particular physical characteristic with them—like the purple eyes of the Mizers. She remembered Levi melting the lock earlier and lighting Reymond's cigar. He might have had a fire-making talent, but the fire-makers she'd met in the past were different—they smelled of smoke and depleted the oxygen from the air around them, suffocating anyone in close contact. He didn't *smell* like...

Levi smirked, and Enne realized with a start that she'd been staring.

To avoid his gaze, she spent several moments examining the dress. It was floor-length, with a gold ribbon trim lining the silky, sage-colored fabric. It was actually rather nice. "Where did you get this?" she asked as she daringly entered his room and took it from his hands.

"I've got a collection of lost things."

Lost things? Oh. He meant left behind. She lifted the dress up to hide her mortified expression.

"You get dressed," he said. "I'll be out here."

"Levi," she protested as he walked away. "This is ridiculous and unnecessary. My clothes are *perfectly* fine." Although, as she looked down, she noticed that her hemline was rather filthy.

"Look, missy," Levi said flatly. "You can call as much attention to yourself as you want, but I prefer to keep my head down. Time to fit into *our* society." He closed the door but kept talking, his voice diminishing. "Now get changed. I've things to do and only time for half of them."

Hmph. Though her attire did stand out in this city, it was for the right reasons. But the dress he'd chosen didn't appear too outrageous, and the color would suit her nicely.

As she changed, she realized how low the neckline was cut. *Goodness,* she thought, *it would be almost like strutting around topless.* She turned to his wardrobe and rooted around for a new outfit. Nudged between another blouse and several pairs of men's undershirts in various sizes—this was *quite* the collection—she selected a red dress with a more conservative front.

When Enne returned to the sitting room, she found Levi in the armchair turning the glass conch shell over like an archaeologist examining a fossil. He raised his eyebrows upon seeing her in a different dress.

"Where did you buy it?" she asked, referring to the conch. "It's beautiful."

"I made it. There was a shell like this in my house when I was young, so I tried to replicate it."

"You have a glassmaking talent?"

"No, an orb-making talent. But I don't use it much." He talked with a kind of bitterness, as if admitting to something shameful. The orb-making talent certainly explained his hair and his affinity for fire; she'd never met an orb-maker, but she should've guessed it before. They had nearly as much lore surrounding them as the Mizers did. Most of them were even executed alongside the Mizers, so there weren't many families left.

"Then why be a card dealer and a…" She didn't say *criminal*, in case she might offend him, though Levi seemed to take pride in his particular line of work. "Orb-makers could make a very fair living."

"You mean, why be poor when I could be rich?" He laughed hollowly. "For plenty of reasons. For one, most people assume orb-makers are Mizer sympathizers, and I'd rather not associate myself with that muck. The only reason my family survived was because we haven't called attention to ourselves."

Enne flinched at *Mizer sympathizers* and *survived*. She didn't like how, in only one morning, New Reynes had drawn a heavy, black line connecting those two phrases to her mother, followed by a bloodred question mark.

For the second time that day, Enne wondered how she would face it if she never learned the truth about Lourdes's other life. The newspapers…the monarchists…the Mizer sympathizers… it was so far from what she knew about Lourdes.

But what *did* she know about her mother?

Lourdes had taught her how to analyze people meticulously. She had a method to this, and a set of rules that she observed with an almost religious reverence. Enne could replicate her skills in a heartbeat.

But they never worked on Lourdes.

It began with a person's air. Lourdes was tall with features full of right angles and fair colors. She dressed fluidly—a practice uncommon but not unheard of in Bellamy, where reputation depended on social circles and income and nothing else. Her Protector talents—her blood and split talents were the same, making her exceptionally powerful—made her every word sound consoling, soothing, no matter how sharp her tone. She followed each code of societal etiquette, but did so with such precision that it always seemed as if she were poking fun.

Next was what you could've gathered from pleasant small talk. Lourdes claimed she was thirty-seven years old, but she looked no more than thirty. Her family—now all dead, as far as Enne knew—had vacationed in Bellamy when she was young, but she hadn't moved there until she'd adopted Enne, and no one in Bellamy knew her from her childhood.

Last were the more intimate details. Within the privacy of their home, Lourdes cursed. She read New Reynes newspapers. She sang loudly and terribly. Enne had seen strange scars shaped like perfect circles on the inside of her elbows. She'd heard her laugh too hard or yell in a way that made the beads on their chandelier quiver, but she'd never seen Lourdes shed a tear. She'd seen Lourdes walk into her office each morning with a cup of coffee and lock the door behind her, and Enne, for years, had been too nervous to follow her inside.

Enne loved her, but she didn't understand her. No one in Bellamy did. It was why their names rarely graced the guest lists of balls and salons, why no one ever paid attention to Enne.

Now Enne wanted to understand, and she regretted, more than anything, avoiding these questions before.

"I want to hear everything," Enne told Levi seriously. "Everything you know about the monarchists, the Mizer sympathizers, this *world*. Lourdes never shared any of this with me, and I need to—"

"Have you ever considered that your mother purposely kept you in the dark?" he asked—not unkindly, but not gently, either.

Yes, she thought.

Instead she answered, "Why would she do that?"

"No idea, but before we chat with Vianca Augustine about hiring you, it's very important that we're on the same page. If you haven't noticed by the decor of this casino, Vianca has a fetish for all things Mizer. She certainly knows who Lourdes is, *but*—" he said loudly as Enne began to interrupt "—under no circumstances should you *ask* Vianca about Lourdes. Under no circumstances should you ask Vianca *anything*."

The way Levi spat out Vianca's name, Enne wondered what exactly *he'd* asked of Vianca. Or what she'd asked of him.

"Mizers created volts, that was their talent," he began.

"I know that—"

He shushed her. "Being an orb-maker, I was taught a lot about Mizers—I'm sure I know more than you. We're different from the metalsmiths or glassmaker families. As you might know, Mizers don't technically make volts—they make energy. Orb-makers filter that energy into volts, sort of like a by-product. Without orb-makers, no one would've ever started using volts as money. Without orb-makers, holding that energy in your skin would be unbearably painful."

Enne was tempted to interrupt and remind him that very few people stored volts in their skin. In Bellamy, it was considered too lowbrow not to use orbs—they weren't *that* expensive. And in New Reynes, she imagined such a method could prove risky. With enough practice, someone could steal your volts with only a graze of your skin. Forgoing orbs was impractical.

"The Mizers were all systematically murdered during the Revolution. Adults and children alike," Levi said gravely. "There were protests, of course, but the Phoenix Club didn't much care. Twenty-five years ago sounds like a long time, but not for the North Side. Mizers are still a political topic, but we don't need them anymore, now that volts can be manufactured artificially. Still, the monarchists have been slowly gaining momentum to fight against corruption."

"Do you agree with the monarchists?" Enne asked quietly. Levi almost made it sound like the monarchists were in the right, when all Enne had ever associated them with was extremism and violence.

He smiled in a way that wasn't much of a smile at all. "I don't involve myself in politics."

Seeking reassurance, Enne took her token out of her pocket. It'd always seemed like a unique trinket, something pretty Lourdes had thought Enne might like. Now Enne saw the woman in the cameo as a Mizer queen. She saw the Revolution. The queen's execution. The murder of every Mizer and their sympathizers. She couldn't decide which was more horrific: that Lourdes had gifted her an object with such a blood-soaked history, or that Enne had treated it as a trinket.

"I still..." She squeezed the token, and it felt warm and steady in her palm. It was her only comfort away from home, alone in this city. "I still can't picture Lourdes being involved with monarchists."

"She was *more* than involved. She was Séance, practically the face of the Mizer sympathizers' crusade." He gazed at Enne fiercely, the judgment clear in his dark eyes. What exactly did Levi Glaisyer think of her—that she was desperate? Foolish? Childish? She wondered why she cared. "Why did you think she came to New Reynes so often?"

"She said she was visiting friends," Enne answered.

"She never thought to bring you to meet those friends?"

"It was more important I stay in school."

"You never questioned that?"

She squeezed the token in her fist. Was this some kind of interrogation?

"She's my mother. Why should I have questioned her?" Although Enne had certainly had her suspicions, she'd ignored them. Admittedly, there had once been a time when Enne resented Lourdes for her secrets, for her strange behavior, for the way she alienated Enne from any chance of society's approval.

But now, with Lourdes's whereabouts and even survival unknown, she hated herself for those thoughts.

"It's easy for Protectors to keep secrets," Levi prodded. "They never *seem* as if they're lying. It never occurred to you—"

"No. It didn't." Enne's voice rose, marking the dozenth time she'd broken the *show no emotion* rule. She didn't appreciate what Levi was suggesting, that Lourdes would use her talents to purposefully keep Enne in the dark. If a Protector officially swore their powers to someone, they were forever bound to act in that person's best interest, no matter the implications for themselves. Lourdes had never sworn to anyone, thank goodness. The practice was barbaric and unused since the Revolution. Levi was suggesting Lourdes *was* protecting someone—probably someone in New Reynes—and, by extension, that Enne hadn't even noticed that her mother's life was barely her own.

"I trust her," Enne snapped. What did he want her to say? That yes, it had occurred to her that Lourdes had purposefully kept information from her? Of course it had. Enne knew Lourdes kept secrets, but he made it sound as if their entire relationship was a lie, and Enne would never believe that. "I trust her. Maybe trust is a foreign concept to you."

She realized, once she said it, that the words had come out rather harsh. This whole time, Levi had kept a remarkably cool expression. She was the one working herself up. For a moment, she considered apologizing. Then…

"Maybe naïveté is a foreign concept to you," he said drily.

That thought vanished.

"How *dare*—"

"If you're so jumpy answering *my* questions, how are you going to last one night on the North Side? How are you going to face Vianca Augustine?" He shook his head, and Enne couldn't decide if she felt ashamed or aggravated. He wasn't being fair. "I'm just trying to keep you from getting yourself killed."

"What do you mean?" she asked. It wasn't as though *she* was in any real danger. At least, as long as she didn't speak to any whiteboots again.

He leaned forward and steepled his fingers, his expression grim. "Have you ever heard of the Phoenix Club?"

"Only now, when you just mentioned it," she answered.

"They're the most powerful and dangerous people in the Republic. Businessmen, wigheads, scholars…all with a talent for immortality. They're the ones who orchestrated the Mizer executions. The whole Revolution, even."

She searched his expression for one of his telltale smirks, but found none.

"There's no talent for immortality," she said. "That's impossible."

He sighed, cracked his neck and checked his watch. Enne's nostrils flared. If anyone had a right to feel impatient, it was she. "Chancellor Semper himself is part of the Phoenix Club. He's their leader."

She barked out a laugh. "You expect me to believe that?"

Levi stood. "Fine, missy. I was trying to prepare you. But if you're so sure of yourself, you're obviously ready for Vianca."

He walked to his front door and motioned for her to follow. Enne hesitated, wanting to challenge him. But if she kept arguing, she might start crying again. The urge to do so throbbed in her chest, and if she even used enough breath to say *fine*, it would explode. She'd already cried twice this morning. She didn't know how she had enough tears left for a third.

They were silent until the elevator reached the bottom floor, where she followed Levi through another hallway lined with portraits of Mizer monarchs with amethyst eyes.

"You should address Vianca as Madame," he said, more like a warning than a suggestion. "She likes that."

"I'm more than comfortable addressing superiors." Her voice sounded steady and precise. The streets might've been Levi's arena, but etiquette was hers. After everything she'd faced so far this day, an interview with Vianca Augustine hardly intimidated her.

Enne held her head up high, smoothed down her hair and focused. She repeated Lourdes's rules in the back of her mind.

His eyes trailed over her—almost enough to ruin that focus. "I take it you didn't like my choice of dress for you."

"It was inappropriate. Particularly for an interview."

"Maybe that's why I liked it."

He smiled, and no, *no*, she wouldn't let that smile break her resolve to be aggravated with him. She stared in the direction of her pointed-toe heels, hidden underneath the hem of the dress, and hoped with every fiber of her being she wasn't giving him the satisfaction of blushing like a Bellamy schoolgirl.

"Though I will admit, this dress is a bit long," she commented, trying to remain aloof.

"Yeah, you should grow some."

She couldn't think of a snappy enough retort, so, left with no other options, she let out a *hmph*.

He snorted, but then his smirk receded. "I'm sorry, Enne. I haven't been trying to upset you. But this city...it's rotten, down to its very core. And you need to be prepared for what you might face. Or learn." He looked away and stared at his oxfords. "I'm trying to help you."

He was attempting to soothe her, but his honesty made Enne only feel worse. Maybe she was no match for this city. Maybe the North Side would take everything she had and spit her out into the harbor. Maybe the streets where Lourdes walked freely would spell ruin for her daughter.

They walked into a waiting room with several marble busts

lining the walls. A pale, fragile-looking woman hunched over a desk in the corner. She startled at the sight of them.

"Levi," she exclaimed, standing as he approached and even giving a slight bow of her head. She had a pinched nose and a collar so tiny it was a wonder she could breathe. She drank in the sight of him, never once glancing at Enne. "I wasn't aware you had an appointment."

"I don't. Is Vianca available right now?"

"Yes." She hesitated before adding, "I can announce you if you wish—"

"We'll announce ourselves." He grabbed Enne's wrist and tugged her to the door on the far side of the room. "Here we go."

He knocked.

"Come in," a woman's voice invited.

Before opening the door, Levi bent down, his lips inches from her ear. "Whatever you do, don't let her see you squirm."

ENNE

Enne and Levi stepped inside a dark office with emerald velvet curtains and matching chairs. Behind Vianca's desk hung a mural of another Mizer family: two parents, two daughters and an infant on the mother's lap—the last royal family of Reynes, executed twenty-five years ago during the Revolution. Mahogany bookcases lined the side walls, filled with more vases, marble busts and antiques than books.

Amid the darkness of the room, Vianca Augustine was fair. Her white hair and ivory, sallow skin made her appear ghostlike, and there was certainly something haunting about the emptiness of her gaze. Soulless. She looked to be in her sixties, and her age was exaggerated by the powdery makeup caked within the creases of her face. Despite her ornate dress and overwhelming amount of jewelry, nothing about her was elegant. She had clearly never been beautiful, and—judging from the severe frown lines and pruned wrinkles around her pursed lips—she had never been kind, either.

"Levi," Vianca said. She spoke his name slowly, as if savoring its taste. "I wasn't expecting you."

"I owe this girl a favor. She needs work, and with all I need to juggle at the moment—" He smiled, a bit too widely. "It would put my mind at ease knowing she gets settled."

Vianca raised her pencil-drawn eyebrows and shifted her gaze to Enne. "What's your name, girl?"

Grace, Enne told herself. *I am grace and ease.*

"Erienne Abacus Salta, Madame."

"A dancer? I already have more dancers than I need. And usually my dancers come with a vocal or instrumental split talent. What use do I have for a dancer who can count?"

Enne wasn't sure how to respond, especially as, truth be told, she wasn't much of a counter at all.

"She's a gymnast, as well," Levi added quickly. "I heard there's a spot open for a new acrobat."

Enne struggled to contain her alarm. She hadn't bargained for that. She didn't know the first thing about gymnastics.

"Is she, now?" Vianca asked, not looking *at* Enne so much as through her. "You may go, Levi. I'll speak to Miss Salta in private."

He blinked in surprise, then nodded. After giving Enne a final weary look, he slipped out the door. Enne tried not to let his apparent nervousness bother her. She had faced worse interviews for admission to her finishing school.

Vianca beckoned her forward, and Enne moved to stand in front of one of the chairs before the donna's desk.

"Do you plan on taking a seat, Miss Salta?" she asked.

"Not unless you ask me, Madame."

Vianca's green, lizard-like eyes inspected every foot, inch and hair of Enne's body. Her lips curled, and Enne couldn't help but notice her uneven red lipstick. "Sit." Once Enne had taken a seat, Vianca asked, "Where are you from?"

"Bellamy, Madame."

"That's quite a journey. How long have you lived here?"

"About half a day, Madame."

That made Vianca smile. For a moment. Enne hadn't been trying to be humorous.

"Is Levi trying to court you? He serves a number of roles for me, and I require him to have a clear head. If his belle is living within St. Morse, it will distract him."

Enne would never walk out with a card dealer, not if she planned on keeping the last shreds of her reputation intact. And if the card dealer in question was Levi, she'd also need to salvage what remained of her dignity. Even if he *was* attractive, she had no patience for his jokes and smirking. "No, Madame. Nothing like that."

"Then why is he so interested in your well-being?"

Enne uttered the first lie she could think of: "He owes a favor to my father."

"I should've guessed Levi would be in debt to a counter. How good are your counting abilities?"

Enne could barely add or subtract without the use of her fingers. "Quite good, Madame."

"Are you literate?" With each new question, Vianca leaned closer to Enne over her desk, almost close enough to grab her.

"Yes, Madame."

"How well you can read?"

"I read very well, Madame," she answered, barely able to hide the bite in her voice.

"Who taught you?"

"I went to finishing school. The Bellamy Finishing School of Fine Arts."

"Did you really? They don't accept just anyone. You must be the only Salta in your class."

Enne kept her hands folded calmly in her lap, despite the fury shooting through her like an electric current. The Saltas might've been the lowest and most common dancing family, but she wasn't ashamed of her name. It didn't matter that her talents didn't compare to her classmates. She'd *worked* for her place at that school, for her future.

"I was, Madame."

Vianca was now bent so close to Enne that Enne could smell her musky perfume. "And you must be quite intelligent to have passed the entrance exams."

It wasn't a question, so Enne stayed quiet.

"Is there anything else I should know about you, Miss Salta? Anything else that could be useful to me?"

"No, Madame."

"Pity." At last, Vianca leaned back in her seat and drummed her fingers against a stack of papers. Each of her rings—there were almost a dozen—shimmered. Unlike Reymond's, these appeared to contain real jewels. "How old are you, Miss Salta? You must be at least fourteen to work here, and I don't make exceptions."

Enne cringed inwardly. This interview had already been the best test of her etiquette skills she'd ever experienced, and it had been only a few minutes.

"I turned seventeen in February, Madame," she said.

"You look quite young. Oh, he *would* like you," she murmured, more to herself than to Enne. Enne didn't ask what or whom she meant. "I'm glad to hear you have a background in gymnastics. Levi was quite right; we *are* looking for some acrobats."

If Levi's smile looked like a smirk, then Vianca's looked like a sneer.

"But I think I've found an additional use for you," Vianca purred.

Enne nodded and pretended like she was following along, though the unsettling satisfaction on Vianca's face sent an uneasy feeling through her stomach. This interview was highly unlike any that she had experience before.

"This casino has been in my family for generations," Vianca told her. "But New Reynes isn't the city it was when St. Morse was first built. Have you ever heard of my family, Miss Salta?"

"No, Madame."

"So you don't know what kind of business we run?"

"A…casino, Madame?"

Vianca stood and turned her back to Enne, facing the Mizer family portrait. "There are people in these halls who can unhinge your mind with a kiss. Who can distill poisons and narcotics from a single flower fallen from a bouquet. Who deal in tricks, deceit and even death. And they are all under my employ."

Sweat broke out along Enne's neck. *Donna of the Augustine crime Family,* Levi had told her. This must've been what he'd meant.

But what would that have to do with Enne? She was a simple performer. If Vianca truly had those kind of people within St. Morse, then what use could she have for her?

Vianca turned to face her. Her green eyes looked nearly black. "Among my friends, I keep a few *favorites* who perform a little extra for me. There are enemies everywhere in this city—even within this casino—who seek to destroy me. I need to know their plans. I need listeners. And I can no longer afford to be short on ears."

Before Enne could process Vianca's words, the donna ushered Enne out of her seat and to the center of the room. She made a twirling gesture, and Enne, confused, obliged. Enne kept her shoulders back to make them appear larger, stronger—the right build for an acrobat. Whatever this was, it felt like a test.

"You're young. No one ever notices the young," Vianca commented wistfully. She grabbed Enne's cheeks and brought her face closer, then absentmindedly ran a bony finger down Enne's Cupid's bow to her chin. Her fingers tasted foul, like rancid perfume.

Enne resisted the urge to free herself from Vianca's grasp and ignored the sickening feeling in her stomach. She needed a job. She needed to survive in this city long enough to find Lourdes.

"But you're a performer," Vianca continued, unaware of or unbothered by Enne's unease. "You can be noticed if you want. You're smart and can move in higher society, but you also know Levi—and I'm sure, if you ask nicely, he'd be willing to show you a thing or two about the streets. You've only just arrived— this city hasn't corrupted you. Yet." She relaxed her grip on Enne's face, and Enne backed away, her cheeks sore. "And I could use a *girl*."

Whatever Levi had told her about Vianca Augustine, she hadn't been prepared for this. The way Vianca looked at her, touched her…like she was a possession. This meeting felt more like an appraisal than an interview. Under different circum- stances, Enne would have fled the room and the donna's fright- ful presence.

"I'm going to do you a favor, Miss Salta. I'm going to give you this job."

"Thank you, Ma—"

"But I need a favor in return. I need you to do another job for me."

I will find Lourdes, Enne recited, winding herself back up. *I will find her and bring her home. No matter what it takes.*

"Of course, Madame," she responded swifly, despite her ner- vousness.

"I need you to deliver messages to my enemies. Can I trust you to do this for me?"

Enne swallowed, staring into the woman's predatory gaze and vicious smile, and wondered who would be reckless—or dangerous—enough to make an enemy of someone like her.

No matter what it takes.

"Yes, Madame."

"Hold out your hand," Vianca instructed. When Enne obeyed, she clasped both of her wrinkled hands around Enne's.

She whispered something that Enne couldn't hear, and a cold tingling shot up Enne's arm. Enne gasped, but when she tried to yank her arm back, Vianca held it in place. The tingling accumulated in Enne's chest, and her lungs shook and hardened as if surrounded by a shell. No air would release. She couldn't breathe. Her balance swayed, but Vianca just gripped her hand tighter, her face unconcerned.

Her nails dug deep into Enne's skin, and Enne choked for breath. Nothing. Nothing. There was no panic like the panic of suffocating, and she stared wildly at Vianca's apathetic green eyes, pleading for aid.

Help, she mouthed, but no air came out.

Just as her vision began to darken, the feeling released. Air rushed down her throat, and Enne coughed as her lungs stretched like cramped muscles. She collapsed on the floor, tears welled in her eyes.

"*That* was my omerta," Vianca said, looming above her. "It's not an oath I bestow often. But now you are mine."

Enne grasped for Lourdes's rules, for something to tell her how she should react, how she should behave, when confronted with the worst. Words to recite. Words to wind herself back up.

Don't let her see you squirm, Levi had said.

Never show them your fear, Lourdes had warned.

But the loudest word, the only word, was Vianca's.

Mine.

Mine.

Mine.

Enne stared at Vianca in horror. The woman had strangled her without touching her. Though Enne's lungs had returned to normal, a phantom soreness lingered, and panic still clawed up her throat. For several moments, she'd thought she would really die, that Vianca would kill her in this dreadful office, while her secretary and Levi waited outside. She could've died. And no one had heard a thing.

Enne felt small. She felt ill. What had Vianca done?

"You may sit now," Vianca told her, a smile playing on her lips.

Enne sat down slowly, carefully, and she watched the old woman with growing alarm. She needed to run. To be alone. To bathe. She needed comfort, and there was none to be found in Vianca's domineering expression, in the stiffness of the desk chair or the uncomfortable heat of the office.

Vianca called it an omerta, but Enne had never heard of such a thing. What had she done to her? And Levi...had he known she could do this? Why hadn't he warned her?

"Sedric Torren will be paying St. Morse a visit tonight," Vianca said, already returning to business. "Your first assignment will be to bring a message to him in the Tropps Room at ten o'clock."

The name sounded familiar for some reason, but Enne was too traumatized to place it, picking at a scab along her thumb to focus on anything other than the woman before her. By the way Vianca spoke the name, it sounded as if everyone should know him.

Her scab popped off, and blood trickled down her palm.

"Look at me while I'm talking to you," Vianca snapped, and Enne's head jolted toward Vianca of its own accord. Enne's heart thundered. This woman could control her like a puppet, force her own body to betray her. She was trapped within her own skin.

"What is the message, Madame?" She wasn't sure if she had spoken those words on her own, or if Vianca had made her.

Vianca pulled a vial of clear liquid out of her drawer and handed it to her. "This is your message. See that he receives it. I'm tired of young Mr. Torren playing with my *things*." Once again, Vianca leaned closer, and this time, Enne winced and put as much distance between the two of them as possible. She knew her terror must have been plain on her face. "This won't kill him, but it will incapacitate him for several days. That should send him a message, don't you agree?"

"Y-yes, Madame."

Enne's conscience twisted when she realized what she'd agreed to do, even if Sedric Torren was a stranger. Surely, he didn't deserve to be poisoned, and she couldn't possibly be the one to do it. She was a schoolgirl, for goodness' sake, not some kind of assassin.

But Vianca's menacing glare rooted Enne to her seat.

This was her chance to refuse. To run. But the more she considered it, the more air was sucked out of her. Her breath thinned until she was gasping again. Each inhale was weaker than the next. While Vianca thoughfully twisted an emerald ring around her finger, Enne gripped the edges of her seat, her lungs aching as they demanded oxygen.

Then Vianca's lips coiled into a smile, and Enne's chest expanded in relief. She took large, gulping breaths and blinked the tears away from her eyes.

Somehow, the omerta knew what Enne was thinking. It knew Enne didn't want to do this. And it was playing with her, punishing her.

This woman could murder her at any moment she wished.

Enne bit her lip to hold back the helplessness squirming in her throat. *Breathe.* Sedric was a stranger. Someone who meant nothing to her. *Breathe.* This wasn't permanent. She was leaving this monstrous city the moment she found Lourdes.

"We've come to an agreement, then," Vianca said. Clearly, Enne's silence was what she'd wanted to hear. "The acrobats are in the middle of a show. Tonight is their last performance, so you can begin rehearsing a new act with them tomorrow. I'll be sure to send you something special to wear tonight for your date with Mr. Torren. Time to abandon your Bellamy values."

Enne didn't need to worry about the city corrupting her.

Vianca Augustine seemed confident in achieving that all on her own.

Vianca retrieved a bronze key out from a filing cabinet. "As part of your newfound employment, you will live here in St. Morse. Your apartment, room 1812." She handed the key to her, and Enne mumbled a thank you, sliding it into her pocket beside the vial and her token. "Welcome to the greatest casino in New Reynes, Miss Salta."

Enne stood so fast her knees cracked. She needed to get out of here. Away from *her*. She needed to get out of this city.

This had all been a terrible mistake.

"I'll contact you again when I have a new task for you," Vianca promised, her eyes flinty. "Or if you disappoint." The threat in her words was clear.

As Enne stumbled on her near-run to the door, Vianca didn't even look at her. She returned to her papers. No smile. No nod. Not even enough acknowledgment to call it indifference. And that was what terrified Enne most of all.

Levi stood in the waiting room, repeatedly checking his watch. He looked up as Enne closed the door. "Well?" he asked impatiently.

Enne hesitated a few moments, waiting for Levi to add something else. *Anything* else. Had he known this would happen? Surely he wouldn't have brought her here if he knew about the omerta. He would've warned her. He wouldn't have let her anywhere near St. Morse Casino. She'd only just met Levi, but criminal or not, she had heard true sincerity in his voice when he promised to help her. Unless everything in this city was a lie.

She opened her mouth to tell him the truth, but her chest constricted. It was a simple word, *omerta*, but when she tried to form it, no sound would come out. Enne realized that, whatever Vianca had done to her, Enne couldn't talk about it. So she smiled to hide her panic, as she had always been taught to do.

Wasn't that one of Lourdes's sayings about being a lady? *Smile widest when you are about to cry.* Enne had already broken rule after rule, and she needed this one. She needed to do something right. She needed to feel in control.

More than anything, she needed to be alone.

"I got the job," Enne managed, though she didn't sound excited. Everything felt numb. Tonight she was going to…going to…

"You got the job?" Levi echoed, and Enne hated that he looked impressed. Hated that she'd wanted that minutes ago, when now she felt so shaken.

"I'll walk you to your new room, then." He opened the door to the hallway, and Enne avoided staring at the Mizer portraits, suddenly all too aware that these faces belonged to the dead. When she stared into their purple eyes, she felt Vianca's green ones gazing back.

"How kind of you," she muttered, wishing he would instead leave her to herself. As intent as she was on finding her mother, she didn't know if she could do anything else today, with all the questions and stress of this morning and tonight's assignment weighing on her shoulders.

"Ever the gentleman," he said cheerily as they stepped inside the elevator.

The pulleys above them spun, and the platform jerked as they ascended. Enne held the railing in a steel grip.

"What did you say that impressed Vianca so much?" Levi asked. Everything about his tone was pleasant and friendly. It made her want to scream.

"*She* appreciated my etiquette skills," Enne snapped. That was another broken rule—she couldn't pinpoint which one. Not in this death trap. Not with the curse Vianca had cast on her. Not when she kept picturing Lourdes in a similar metal cage, only one that was descending and descending, never to reach a bottom.

She was still smiling, though. Her teachers would've been proud.

"Ah, there's that attitude again," Levi said.

"Are you quite finished?"

For some reason, that made him smile. He didn't hear the panic in her voice. Didn't realize he'd just introduced her to a monster.

"Why do I have the feeling I need to watch out for you?" he asked.

Goodness, he's exhausting. "I'm not helpless, you know."

"That's not what I meant. I meant that maybe I should watch out for you, because you *seem* like the kind of person someone might underestimate."

Enne blinked in surprise. "What gave you such an idea?"

"I don't spend my mornings helping out just *any* pretty missy, you know."

Was Levi Glaisyer *flirting* with her? The boys in Bellamy never flirted with her unless they hoped she'd introduce them to her richer classmates. Few people paid attention to someone as common as a Salta.

He must've been making fun of her again. She was emotionally wrung dry, and she didn't have the patience to watch Levi fling one smirk after another. He'd sat unaware while, in the next room, Vianca had assaulted Enne in the most terrifying way. He'd mocked her at every opportunity. He might've been helping her find Lourdes, but only because Enne would pay him that night.

"I'm flattered," she sneered, her voice vicious. "Truly."

He stiffened, wilted. "Excellent," he said drily. "Wouldn't want to get off on the wrong foot with a new coworker."

The word *coworker* sounded stranger the more Enne let it sink in. Her teachers—and probably Lourdes, for that matter—never would have let her within fifty feet of a casino, and probably not within one hundred feet of Levi and the collection of *lost things* in his closet.

But the Lourdes Enne knew and the Lourdes Levi remembered seemed to be completely different people. To think that Lourdes spent so much time in this wretched city boggled Enne—disturbed her, even. Maybe Lourdes knew how to survive in New Reynes. Maybe the reason Lourdes never told her the truth was in case Enne might have been foolish enough to believe that she could survive here, too.

Her mother had been right to keep her daughter in the dark, because each hour spent in New Reynes formed a new crack, and there was no way Enne was going to emerge from this city unbroken.

LEVI

Levi's poker face didn't waver as he studied his hand: a four-card straight and the kings of clubs and spades. Clearly luck was on his side. The player to his left eyed him warily and threw in five green chips. Two hundred and fifty volts.

From beside him, Sedric Torren also slapped five green ones in the pot.

Levi equaled their wagers on behalf of the house. Normally with the betting so high, he'd fold. But tonight was different. He hadn't expected Sedric Torren himself to visit St. Morse. He could've been there for only one reason, and that was Levi.

Which meant that Levi couldn't afford to look weak—not even for a moment.

When the hand ended, Levi had managed to earn a 27 percent profit. At this rate, he'd have thirty in the next hour, which was the highest he'd ever made in one shift. Unlike poker or blackjack, where the dealer was little more than a moderator in the game, Tropps treated the dealer like a player who represented the house. The game placed a heavy emphasis on strategy and bluffing, and it was so well-known across the city that the main street of the Casino District was named after it. Dealers like Levi were famous for their skill, and Levi was one of the best of them all.

The other players grumbled and stomped their way to the next table, their pockets significantly lighter. Levi took a break to collect the cards, as well as his bearings.

The only player who didn't leave was Sedric Torren.

"'Lo, Pup," he murmured. His brown hair was slicked to the side and shiny with grease, and his smile was wolf-like. He switched to the seat beside Levi.

"Sedric," Levi gritted, concealing the ugly feeling of dread in his stomach. The Tropps Room around them was loud with jazz and the chatter of guests, all gussied up in designer gowns and carrying cigarettes in long jewel-encrusted holders. Surely Sedric wouldn't try anything in public. Even the don of the Torren Family wouldn't do something that reckless. "What can I do for you?"

Sedric turned to one of the waiters carrying a tray of champagne. "Two glasses." He set one in front of Levi, who didn't bother to reach for it. Drinking with a Torren—least of all the don—sounded like asking for trouble, and Levi needed all his concentration to survive this encounter unscathed. "Should we make a toast?" Sedric suggested.

"To what?" Levi asked, keeping his voice steady as he shuffled the Tropps decks. Sedric Torren had a reputation for playing with his prey before he killed it, and Levi needed to make it clear to Sedric that he wasn't afraid. As far as Sedric should have been concerned, Levi had no reason to fear his family. If anything, this should be an exchange between two businessmen, a celebration of an advantageous trade.

Sedric raised his glass. "We toast to your continued good health. You've managed to push back the date for our investment return not just once or twice, but three times."

Levi's skin went clammy. This was no celebration—this was a threat.

"Cheers, Pup." Sedric clinked Levi's glass before taking a swig. "So where are my promised returns?"

Levi swallowed. "They're coming."

Sedric leaned closer. He had a sickly sweet smell to him, like toffee. "I'm not a thickhead, you know," Sedric said. "Just tell me what you've *really* been doing this whole time."

He suspects, Levi thought with panic. *Or he knows. And he's forcing me to lie.*

The truth meant death.

"You'll get the volts soon," Levi rasped, shifting away from him.

Sedric laughed, then adjusted his suit jacket. A silver knife gleamed from an inside pocket, a ruby winking at Levi from its hilt. Only a Torren would carry a weapon that flashy.

Levi reminded himself that he couldn't look vulnerable. He searched around the Tropps Room for some of Sedric's cronies, and sure enough, he spotted several men lurking near the door in crisp suits with black-and-red-striped ties—Luckluster colors. He fought to maintain his poker face. He was surrounded.

"You gonna kill me in St. Morse?" Levi dared, mustering up the appearance of confidence. "Doesn't seem you'd get your volts back, then. And Vianca would never forgive you."

"I'm not here to kill you. I'm here to warn you." But despite his words, Sedric removed the knife from his jacket. With only an arm's length of space between them, it would take Sedric only a heartbeat to stab the knife through Levi's neck.

Any rational man would run, but Levi was frozen. Maybe that was a good thing. It made him appear bold, even when he was terrified.

Sedric ran his finger along the blade, then inspected the red droplet on his fingertip, as if assuring Levi the knife was sharp. He licked away the blood. The sight of it made Levi shudder.

"Whatever scheme you've been running," Sedric murmured, "it's over. Maybe you will be, too."

Sedric flipped over the top card on the deck.

"Ten of hearts. You got lucky, Pup. We'll give you ten days. With reminders." He stood, slid his knife back into its sheath and drained the rest of his glass. "A present from my family." He tossed a silver card face down in front of Levi. Sedric whistled and walked to a different table.

Levi's heart hammered, both from Sedric's threat and the gift he left behind. He recognized the card instantly—its metallic back was signature to the Shadow Game, the rumored execution game of the Phoenix Club. It was a North Side legend, as notorious as the Great Street War or the original lords. To Levi, it was an object plucked out from a story, from a nightmare.

It can't be real, Levi thought, hoped. But even his cynicism couldn't rationalize away the card's plain existence right in front of him.

The tales claimed the cards had magical properties once you touched them. Even though Levi didn't believe in those shatz superstitions like Jac did, he flipped it over with a morbid curiosity, seeking some assurance that the legends weren't true.

The moment he touched it, the lights of the Tropps Room faded, and silence pierced through the music.

Levi stared down a long hallway that stretched endlessly in both directions. The impressively tall doors alternated black and white, each parallel to the other. The walls and ceiling were marble, clean enough to glint off the hallway's collection of mirrors and crystal. The floor was tiled in black and white, as well. Like a chessboard.

Vaguely, he got the sense he was dreaming. But if he was, he couldn't seem to wake up.

He reached for a black door, but it was locked. He tried the white one next to it, and it clicked open. The air that rushed past felt like a sigh against his skin.

Once he crossed the threshold, he found himself dressed in a smart suit, far nicer than his St. Morse uniform. The mud squished beneath his oxfords, and it smelled of earth. He was in a graveyard. The sky was gray, as the sky in New Reynes tended to be. The City of Sin followed him wherever he went, even in his dreams.

Levi moved to return to the hallway—graveyards unnerved him, as cliché as that was—and tripped over one of the headstones. It was painted metallic silver.

Levi Canes Glaisyer, it read.

Levi scampered to his feet and backed around it. On its other side was a face: the Fool, one of the Shadow Cards, the invitation to the Shadow Game. The bells on the Fool's hat chimed, high-pitched and eerie in the silent graveyard. The diamonds and triangles painted on his face spun like pinwheels, and he strutted toward the cliff in front of him. Levi reflexively took a step back, as though he could also fall.

The Fool laughed. And laughed and laughed and laughed.

It's not real, Levi assured himself. *It's only a nightmare.*

But it didn't feel like one. The earth sticky under his shoes, the cold sweat dripping down his neck, the Fool winking from his headstone—how could this all be in his head?

He whipped around and faced a new row of fresh, unfilled graves. He peered into the first hole, above which the headstone said *Jac Dorner Mardlin*. Jac's coffin was lidless. Soot coated his blond hair and cap, and his eyes were wide-open, his mouth twisted into an unnatural scream.

Levi jolted back with horror and nearly stumbled into the next grave. It was Chez's, and beside him, Mansi's, and dozens of other Irons from around the city. Levi bit back a wave of nausea looking at Mansi's gray-toned skin and lifeless eyes, matching the bodies of the other kids around her. Even if the investment scheme had gotten in the way of most of Levi's responsibilities as lord, he still cared. They were his kids. His to protect.

This was all Levi's fault.

He ran back to the hallway. The moment he crossed the threshold, his shoulders relaxed, his guilt and fear fading along with the nightmare.

There were hundreds of doors, but none of them was the right one.

Suddenly, a white door blasted open. Fire spewed out, reaching into the hallway, reaching for him. Levi raced out of its path. His back pressed against one of the black doors, the heat licking his cheek. Ghost-like faces flickered within the flames, their eyes an eerie, glowing purple, watching him.

All at once, they screamed.

Levi gasped and woke in the Tropps Room at St. Morse. His suit and vest were wet from his spilled glass of champagne. A few people at neighboring tables pointed at him as he dried off his pants with a handkerchief, his fingers trembling.

A dream, he told himself, shaking his head to clear it. *A nightmare*. But he could still hear the Fool's laugh. He could still picture Jac's contorted scream.

On the face of the Shadow Card, a metal tower stretched toward the night sky, disappearing amid clouds and stars. Several men climbed its spiral staircase, and one fell from it to the ice below.

The Tower. In the Shadow Game, it represented chaos and ruin.

He shoved it in his pocket as nausea stormed in his stomach. The Phoenix Club's private execution game was a myth, and Levi had always taken the North Side's legends with a grain of salt. There was no house of horrors hidden within the city. There was no wandering devil bargaining for your soul. And there was no game you couldn't win.

But there could be no mistake—the Game did exist. The card and the visions proved it.

Have you ever considered that you might be in over your head? the whiteboot captain had asked him this morning, and the words made Levi sick. He'd always known Vianca's scam was dangerous, but he was the Iron Lord. He was cunning. He was clever.

If he didn't collect Sedric's volts in time, he was dead.

Levi's break ended, and a new group of players sat down. Every card he drew was lousy: a single queen and the lowest of every other suit. The house's pile of chips shrank, and his profits slumped to 20 percent.

A man in a bowler hat took his eighth pot. Levi tried to focus on his game to see if he was counting cards, but he was panicked. He was sloppy. And his mind kept straying back to Sedric Torren.

If the Torren Family wanted him dead, why would they use the Shadow Game instead of one of their own men? Sedric's cousins—the brutal, notorious siblings, Charles and Delia— never turned down an opportunity to kill. Levi had heard rumors that Charles was experimenting to see how many times he could shoot someone before they bled out, and that Delia had a knife collection made from the bones of each of her victims.

If Sedric wanted Levi dead, he didn't need the Shadow Game to do it.

Which meant Sedric was showing off his friendship with the Phoenix Club. Sedric had inherited his position as don less than a year ago, after his father's death. Since then, in an effort to squash his rival, Vianca Augustine, he'd befriended the wigheads, begun a campaign for office and declared himself an honorary South Sider.

He would make a spectacle of Levi, just to show he could.

After another round, the players headed to the poker and roulette tables. Levi's profits plummeted to a meager 18 percent, a good percentage for a mediocre player. Not for him.

Even if he played his best at St. Morse, ten days wasn't enough time to come up with ten thousand volts.

He traced his finger along the edge of the Shadow Card in his pocket. In the stories, receiving one meant only one thing: a warning. Make the Phoenix Club happy, or go buy a cemetery plot.

Lourdes Alfero has to be alive, he thought. *Because if she's not...*

Ten days.

Ten days to figure out how to beat his enemies at their own game.

ENNE

Enne found a mention of Sedric Torren in her guidebook, buried within a chapter called "A History of Organized Crime on the North Side."

He was the don of the Torren Family.

He owned a narcotics and gambling empire.

He was one of the most powerful men in New Reynes.

And Enne was going to poison him.

A knock at her door summoned her from her bed. She'd fallen asleep, but she hadn't truly rested. In her dreams, she was running through the city's streets, reaching for her mother's slender shadow as it disappeared down alley after alley. She'd been paying too much attention to the diminishing sound of Lourdes's footsteps to notice the second shadow lurking behind her. It tore the jacket from Enne's arms and ripped the purse out of her hands. She'd woken just before it had plunged a knife into her back.

Enne opened the door.

A woman stood in the hallway with a grim expression, holding a dress. "From Madame Augustine," she said.

Enne's hands shook as she took it and held it up to her small frame. It was pink as peonies, with a crescent moon collar and a ribbon tied around the waist, its skirt a mess of tulle and bows. It was a dress meant for a doll.

"What is this for?" Enne asked.

"For tonight," the woman answered, already turning to leave.

"She can't be serious."

"It's nonnegotiable."

Enne had always enjoyed dressing up, especially for a performance. In a way, the outfit reminded her of a ballet costume, so as she slipped it on, she tried to convince herself she was preparing for an elaborate show rather than her potential demise. Her makeup calmed her, even if her hands were shaking. Some powder around her nose. Some rouge on her cheeks. Some tint on her lips. Whatever it took to persuade herself that she was another person, that this was not her life, this was not her end.

She repeated Lourdes's rules to herself in the mirror.

Do not reveal your emotions, especially your fear.

Never allow yourself to be lost.

Trust is a last resort.

The words didn't mean much now—after all, those rules couldn't save her. She tucked the clear vial into her pocket and, on her way out the door, left one thousand volts in an orb for Levi on her table—nearly everything she had—in case he came looking when she didn't return.

She'd never felt so alone.

If St. Morse were a palace, then the Tropps Room was the throne room, and greed was king. The stained glass windows, the iron candelabras, the glimmering marble floors and white tables—the room was decorated as though for royalty. The throne itself was in the center of the room, raised above the rest of the floor. There Levi sat, collecting and shuffling a deck of midnight blue cards. He was speaking to a man with slicked brown hair, fair skin and an expensive suit.

Of course Levi was at the throne. Reymond had said he was Vianca's favorite.

Levi wore a three-piece blue suit and a green tie that matched St. Morse's signature colors. For a brief moment, Enne allowed herself to see what the other girls and boys had seen—the girls and boys whose clothing now filled half of Levi's wardrobe. He cleaned up nicely, and Enne had a soft spot for men in suits. She appreciated the way the jacket made him look broader, and the way his dark suit and features contrasted with the copper roots in his hair...

She stopped herself. She needed to focus.

Levi watched the man next to him while shuffling a deck of cards. He half smiled, then he adjusted his tie, the muscles in his jaw clenching as he—

Focus. What would her teachers have said? Levi was...hardly someone to admire. And even if his *appearance* was nice, his character left quite a lot to be desired. She didn't feel like herself, not in this dress, not with the vial in her pocket, not so far from home.

More problematic than Levi's dashing appearance was the fact that he was so prominently seated above everyone else in the room. She would be easy to spot, looking like a walking piece of cotton candy. But Vianca had claimed Sedric would be here, in the Tropps Room. Thankfully, Levi wasn't directly facing her. Maybe he wouldn't see her at all. He *did* look rather preoccupied with the man beside him.

If only she was wearing something less conspicuous. She was small enough that, with some luck, she could have slipped the poison into Sedric's glass from behind him and he'd have been none the wiser. But the dress made this impossible. Enne had spent her entire life being overlooked, but tonight, Vianca had dressed her to be noticed.

A man in a green St. Morse uniform stood by the door, the pallor of his face nearly matching the white busts lining Vianca's hallways.

"Excuse me?" Enne asked.

"What can I do for you, miss?"

"I'm looking for Sedric Torren. He promised to meet me here." The gravity of the evening felt much more real now that she'd spoken his name out loud.

"He's there." The employee pointed to Levi's table. Just as he did, the man with the slicked hair drained his glass and strode away with a swagger to his step. Enne paled. What was Sedric doing talking to Levi? "He just left."

"Thank you—"

"Miss?" the employee called, his voice heavy and weary.

Enne turned around. "Yes?"

"Are you, um, here alone?"

This dress, Enne grumbled internally. *As if I don't look young enough already.*

Seeing her annoyed expression, the man looked down at the floor, flustered. "Never mind. Please, forget I said anything."

Enne took a deep breath and repeated Lourdes's rules to herself. She followed Sedric to another card table and, before she could talk herself out of it, slid into the chair beside him. It was conveniently behind Levi, so he wouldn't spot her unless he turned around. She almost wished he would—maybe he could help her; maybe he could save her. But the omerta was a secret. She hadn't been able to tell Levi before, and even if she found a loophole, the memory of suffocating made her stomach turn. She couldn't risk that again, even if it meant acting alone.

She didn't look at Sedric for several moments. Her heart pounded. He was the don of a casino Family, just like Vianca, and if he was anything like her, then Enne was right to be afraid. She should be petrified. She should run.

But that wasn't an option. She might need to poison him for Vianca, but she would survive this night for Lourdes.

At last, she turned to him.

He was already smiling at her.

He was attractive. Not in a beautiful or even a handsome way, but in how he carried himself. As if he had power over everyone, and he knew how to use it. But the more Enne stared at him, the more she noticed the heavy grease in his hair and the outrageous, gaudy details of his suit—as if anyone really needed a diamond-studded necktie.

Yet as attractive as he was, it wasn't a good-looking smile. It was threatening, like a wolf who had just spotted his prey.

"I don't believe we've met," he said smoothly. His age was difficult to discern—his receding hairline didn't match the few lines on his face. She guessed about thirty years old. "Are your parents here?"

"What? No, no," she said, her voice distressed. She was breaking the first rule. He could see her fear. She needed to do better than that if she was going to live through the night.

A knife winked at her from his pocket. She almost whimpered.

"And are you a fan of Tropps, miss?" Sedric asked.

She didn't have any chips. She didn't know how to play. Her lie was unraveling before she could even spin it.

Forget you noticed me, she pleaded. She wanted to go home. She wanted to be invisible again, so long as she was safe.

But she was trapped under Sedric's snare of a smile and the other players' bewildered looks. She was in the spotlight. For once, she had people's attention.

So she did the only thing she knew. She smiled innocently and lied. "Yes. I play all the time."

She could tell from his expression that he didn't believe her.

But there was no suspicion in his eyes—only amusement. She was simply a silly girl to him.

She relaxed—barely. Young, innocent…she could keep up that charade. She was a Bellamy schoolgirl lost in the City of Sin. She knew this role well.

Sedric slid her a stack of ten green chips. "Compliments to a pretty young lady."

"Thank you." She placed one of the chips in the center, and the dealer handed her three cards. She mimicked how the other players held them and moved some cards around here and there for good measure.

Each round, the players placed their bets, and the dealer passed them a new card. This continued for a few turns, until each of them was asked to reveal three cards from their hand. Enne flipped over the ace of spades, then the queen and ten of hearts. The others watched with raised eyebrows. Perhaps she'd made the wrong move.

One of the players folded, and so did she. With four chips left, she waited for the game to finish, the hairs on her neck rose on end. She felt the heated gazes of the whole table. She looked obviously lost. If this continued, Sedric might grow suspicious.

When the game finally ended and the dealer collected the pot of chips, Sedric turned to her. "I take it you're not a regular. Are you sure you've played before?"

"Was I that obvious?" she asked, trying to appear sheepish. She wiped her sweaty hands on her tulle skirt.

He smirked at her as if, yes, she was. "Waiting on someone? You can't be here by yourself."

"I'm here alone," she replied cautiously. "I thought I'd watch the dancers."

"Then you're a little lost. The theater is across the hall." He scanned at her up and down, and she resisted the urge to look away from his dark eyes. She was supposedly playing the role of the assailant, yet *his* gaze was the one growing more and more predatory. Her skin prickled with unease. "Would you like me to accompany you? I wouldn't want you to get lost again."

"That would be lovely…"

"Sedric."

"Sedric," she echoed nervously.

"And your name, miss?" He took her arm and led her around the tables. She peeked at Levi, who was—thankfully—still too focused on his game to notice her.

"En… Emma. It's Emma."

"A pleasure, Emma."

In the lobby, the air reeked of floral perfumes, cigarette smoke and the perpetual stink of Tropps Street. Groups in ruffled gowns and tuxedos shuffled between the restaurant and the casino rooms, but they all parted for Sedric as he approached. Enne couldn't tell if it was out of respect or fear—in New Reynes, they both seemed like the same thing. She tried to avoid their wary gazes in her direction to keep herself from trembling.

"The performance doesn't start for a half hour," Sedric said. "Do you like dancing as much as you like watching it?"

In order to poison him, she'd need to stay with him until he bought himself a drink. But the way he held her, his arm linked so tightly with her own, her side pressed against him, she felt the urge to flee. It was nothing he had said, but the way he looked at her. It made her feel…wrong.

"I love dancing, but only if I have a good partner," she said, swallowing down her longing for escape. She had lasted this long. She could do this.

She had to.

He smiled. His teeth were alabaster white. "I promise you will find me more than acceptable."

He steered her to the dance floor of a grand ballroom of twinkling lights and waxy floors. The other couples danced chest-to-chest, and Sedric pulled her close. His breath warmed her forehead, and she wished she was tall enough to look him in the eyes, or at least anywhere above his neck.

She did her best to follow his steps—they didn't have this dance in Bellamy. Left. Right. Right. Turn. A left kick. Repeat. She caught on quickly, and he smiled as she accidentally turned tighter than intended and pressed her back into his chest. His cologne smelled sweet, like toffee.

He raised his eyebrows. "You didn't tell me you have a dancing talent."

"You never asked."

"Are you a Tanzer? A Glisset?" Those were the names of wealthy dancing families at her school. Enne had attempted to compete with them her whole life, even when her toes blistered and her muscles ached. She knew his words were flattery—Saltas and Tanzers were simply incomparable, no matter how hard she practiced—but the compliment still sent a thrill through her chest.

"A Salta," she corrected him.

"There's no need to keep secrets from me." Left. Right. Right. Turn. "You're too graceful for a Salta. You're a rarer form of dancer. Or your parents must spoil you with lessons."

Her annoyance piqued. "My name *is* Salta."

"I'm sorry," he amended quickly, but he looked more amused than apologetic. "I meant no offense."

The song ended on a low minor chord, saving Enne from responding. He took her arm and led her to a near-empty side of the room, to a lone velvet love seat in a shadowy alcove. It felt awfully private here, so far from the other dancers. Enne felt a prickle of unease. What exactly was he considering?

"Why here?" she asked.

"Away from prying eyes. I'm determined to learn more about you, Emma Salta. I don't usually meet girls your age quite so…"

"Quite so what?"

"Confident." He gave her that snare of a smile. "You must give your teachers a lot of trouble."

He truly thought her to be young, treating her as though she weren't old enough to be a teenager. As he leaned forward, the way his gaze roamed over her delicate hands and her small chest, she realized with horror why the dress was nonnegotiable. And she felt ill. She couldn't decide who was more of a monster: Sedric...or Vianca?

Oh...he would *like you*, she'd said. This was the part Vianca had designed for her to play. She wanted to leave him in disgust, but then she felt the omerta squeezing her lungs, coercing her forward, trapping her. She had no choice but to continue the act.

"My teachers love me," she played along, feeling vile inside and out.

"Of course they do." Sedric snapped his fingers at a footman. "Two glasses of your house's finest wine." Her heart lifted for a moment. A drink meant the opportunity to poison him and be done with this despicable man—something she was feeling less guilty about by the minute. "Once he returns, we can make our way to the theater."

"I didn't realize you were so interested in dancing," Enne replied with an attempt at a girlish smile.

"I don't mind dancing, but I'm more interested in sitting beside you. A person's first show at St. Morse is always a treat. But..." He smiled, a hint of arrogance in his expression. "I'd love to show you Luckluster. Our shows are spectacular."

"What do you mean 'our shows'?" she asked, as though she didn't know he also owned a casino. "Do you run them?"

"Not exactly," he answered. "Your parents wouldn't mind me showing you, would they?"

"No, they wouldn't." She attempted to feign excitement to hide her revulsion. No, perhaps it wouldn't be so terrible to poison him.

The footman returned with two glasses of red wine. She'd never had it—alcohol was illegal in Bellamy—but she recognized it from the bottles other girls had smuggled into their dormitory. She sipped it and tried not to wrinkle her nose; it was horribly bitter.

"Have you ever had wine before?" Sedric asked conspiratorially. "I was twelve when I tried it for the first time. Didn't have a taste for it then, either."

"No, I haven't. It's..." She didn't want to sound rude and risk ruining her charade. "It's nice."

"I wouldn't tell your parents, if I were you."

"Why not?"

He scooted closer to her until their legs touched. "That's how parents are. They won't like how fast you're growing up."

Enne had always been a good liar. She'd lied to Levi about the volts. She'd lied to her mother's house staff about how she was spending her summer. She'd lied over and over to her classmates about where Lourdes always traveled. But there was no lie as disgusting as this one. Because the truth of it wasn't that she'd been selfish, or that she'd run away to the City of Sin, but that, probably many times before, there'd been a real girl who sat where she sat, who smiled as she smiled. This game was a familiar one to Sedric.

She was suddenly grateful for the vial in her pocket. Before, she was going to poison Sedric Torren because she had no choice. Now, she was poisoning him for the girls who hadn't known better. For all the girls fed to the wolves.

She was still scared—she was still *terrified*. Sedric wasn't simply a predator; he was one of the most powerful people in the North Side. He was a beast wearing a man's skin.

But she was also decided. There was no shame in poisoning him.

"Shall we go?" he asked, offering his arm.

She took it, her wine in her other hand. "We shall."

In the lobby, three lines waited outside the theater. According to the posters on the wall, the dancing show was only one of the many varieties that St. Morse offered.

"Where do you take your dance lessons?" Sedric asked as they took a place in the back.

"I'm looking for a troupe, actually."

"That's awfully ambitious of you. Looking to dance here, maybe?" He took another sip of his wine. She'd better hurry, or soon his glass would be empty, and she would miss her chance. She didn't know what the omerta would do to her if she failed, but she refused to die in this city.

"Yes, I'd love to dance here," she responded, "but I don't think Ms. Augustine wants to give me the job."

"Why not? You're an excellent dancer. Though I suppose she might want someone older—"

"My split talent has nothing to offer her, and Saltas are a volt a dozen in the casinos." She spoke matter-of-factly, as if she'd been in this city for more than a day.

She must've sounded convincing, because he squeezed her hand comfortingly, and Enne felt weary with nausea. "She doesn't know the talent she's missing. But you wouldn't want to work here, anyway."

"Why not?"

"Because the Augustines are the cruelest family in the North Side," he said, dropping his voice to a whisper. They were, after all, surrounded by Vianca's patrons. "Their blood talent is omertas, an unbreakable oath. Like a swear of fealty and silence. Vianca is no better than a glorified street lord."

Unbreakable? The word echoed in her mind, unraveling her, shattering her.

It couldn't be true.

Before his words could fully sink in, she pushed them away. She had a job to finish.

She and Sedric reached the ticket booth. "Do you mind holding this for a moment, Emma?" Sedric handed her his drink and rummaged through his coat pockets, then turned to talk to the ticket salesman.

Enne hardly believed her luck. This was her chance. She turned around and quickly slipped the vial from her pocket.

She didn't hesitate. She dumped the poison into Sedric's glass. It was so easy. She'd done it, just like that.

Returning the vial to where it was before, she waited for Sedric to finish purchasing the tickets. Her heart beat faster with a mixture of fear and exhilaration.

When he finished, brandishing two blue Admit Ones, Sedric plucked his wineglass out of Enne's hand. "To the show," he said, leading her in with his arm around her waist.

The theater was dark. A blue curtain draped over the stage, and a single spotlight shone at its center. There must have been over five hundred audience members already present, not counting the few in balconies along the walls. They took their seats in one of the side rows by the front—the tickets, she realized, must have been quite expensive. The piano tapped out a light, staccato tune, and the audience quieted in anticipation. Gradually, the spotlight faded.

Sedric took a sip. When he didn't gag or convulse or immediately vomit, Enne realized the poison might not take effect for a while. She also realized that she didn't feel even a twinge of guilt. She didn't care—he was a contemptible man.

The curtains rose.

Sedric Torren placed his hand on her knee and smiled triumphantly, but Enne had already won.

ENNE

When Enne returned to her apartment two hours after pouring the poison into Sedric's glass, the first thing she did was take a shower. She smelled of Sedric's vomit. However, more nauseating than that, she felt filthy with this city, with what she'd done and how little she cared.

Unbreakable, Sedric had called the omerta, but she refused to believe it. She couldn't be trapped within Vianca's grasp forever.

Enne turned the water temperature up to steaming, but she didn't feel clean. She could still feel the heat of Sedric's gaze and the touch of his hand against her thigh.

She had no other clothes to change into after bathing, so she put her slip back on, and over it, the robe she found in the bathroom closet, embroidered with St. Morse's logo. Then she returned to the page she'd bookmarked in her guidebook.

What if Vianca died? Would the omerta break then? Enne intended to survive here, so she needed to learn more about Vianca, about New Reynes.

She continued reading the guidebook's chapter about the

city's organized crime. The topic shifted from the Augustine and Torren casino Families to the street gangs. Although the Families had control of the narcotics trade, the street gangs managed everything else. They'd divided the North Side into territories and turned crimes into monopolies. She followed along, occasionally referring to her guidebook's map.

Once upon a time, there had been dozens of gangs. But now there were three.

The Scarhands. They were the largest gang, run by the slimy Eight Fingers, Reymond Kitamura, who Enne—despite all of her guidebook's warnings—had managed to meet during her first morning in the City of Sin. Not only did the Scarhands provide counterfeits and forgery services to the city, but they also operated the weapons trade. Their territory spanned throughout the Factory District. You could spot a member by the scars that crisscrossed their palms and wrists.

The Doves were the assassins, their territory known as the Deadman District. They dyed their hair white to match their lord, Ivory, who was credited with over sixty-three murders. No one had seen her face and lived. Perhaps she was so good that no one had ever seen her face at all.

Last were the Irons. The gang of gamblers and cheats who called themselves consultants, and who occupied Olde Town and the Casino District like an infestation. They dealt in cards, ambition and opportunity. Anything you could do, they could do better. They were the smallest gang, with the smallest paragraph in the guidebook. Levi wasn't even mentioned at all.

Someone knocked on her door.

Enne's stomach dropped, half expecting Vianca's woman again. She walked to the door and cracked it open, only to find it was Levi.

"'Lo," he said. He looked pale.

After all the night's stress, she'd utterly forgotten he would come for his volts. "I'm not dressed properly."

He held up a bag. "It's fine. I brought you clothes. Figured you might need them."

She sighed and opened the door fully, even though she'd rather be alone and not deal with Levi's condescending smirks. He handed her the bag, and she rummaged through it. The fabrics were colorful and flashy—very unlike her typical style. "Are these from that collection of yours?" she asked suspiciously.

"Not this time. Jac swiped them from some clotheslines."

She grimaced as she wrapped an oversize sweater around herself. They'd have to do for now. She could buy her own clothes once she got paid.

Beneath the clothes were food items, flour and eggs and other necessities. Her mood improved almost instantly—she was starving. She eagerly unloaded them onto the kitchen counter. To her delight, she now had all the right ingredients to make cookies. Dessert was such a simple comfort, but she nearly wanted to cry in appreciation. When she turned around to thank him, she realized he was no longer standing beside her.

She heard him rummaging around in the living room. "What are you doing?" she called.

"Where did you find this trash? I'm not even mentioned!" He appeared in the kitchen, waving her guidebook. "Look at all the places the author says not to visit. Hundreds! We'll have to go on a tour, you and I. We only managed to hit up a few of them this morning." He paused as she broke some eggs into a mixing bowl. "What are you making?"

"Cookies. Our cook used to make them with me." Enne had spent a lot of her childhood keeping company with the staff, when Lourdes was traveling and she was lonely.

"It's almost midnight."

"I'm hungry."

He shrugged and took a seat on the counter beside her. "You look flushed, missy. You go out on the town while I was working?"

"I stayed in," she lied. As she mixed in the flour, she gathered up her nerve to tell him what happened. Levi was Vianca's favorite, so he had to know about the omerta. She wasn't allowed to speak its name or reveal the truth, but somehow, she'd need to find a way around that. She needed to tell someone and, tolerable or not, Levi was the only person she had in New Reynes. "I read about Vianca in the guidebook. It...it mentioned the family blood talent." When she tried to form the word, no breath would come out. She couldn't say it. Still, she persisted. "I forget what it's called."

Levi's face darkened. "I'm surprised they printed that in a guidebook."

"Oh, um..." Her chest tightened. The omerta knew she was feeling for its cracks, searching for loopholes. But she needed to find a way to tell Levi. He was the only one in this city helping her. Maybe he could even convince Vianca to let her go.

"Now that you're hired, keep as far away from Vianca as you can," he warned. "Believe it or not, she's a woman you would rather have hate you than like you."

And you're her favorite, Enne thought, wondering what exactly that meant.

She returned to the cookies, while Levi, now in a foul mood, stormed off into the living room. Every now and then she heard him groan something, like "They mentioned *Jonas mucking Maccabees* but not me" or "*Veil* founded the first street gang. Not Havoc. Who wrote this shatz book, anyway?"

Then a few minutes passed in silence. Enne laid the cooling sugar cookies on the counter and walked into the living room, expecting to find him asleep.

Instead, he was sitting up on the couch, turning over the empty vial of poison in his hands. Enne froze.

"Black Maiden," he said grimly. "It's Vianca's poison of choice."

"Where d–did you find that?" she stuttered.

"I went looking. They don't mention Vianca's blood talent in the guidebook." He nodded to it open on the table. "Enne, *why do you have this poison?*" There was an acute desperation in his voice, in his expression. He stepped close enough that she could smell his cologne, too close to avoid his gaze.

Enne tensed beneath that look. She took a deep breath and tried to form the words, testing the limits of the omerta, what she could say and what she could not.

"Vianca Augustine is a monster," she managed carefully. "And you knew that. So why did you bring me to her?" Her voice was full of accusation. She didn't mean that. Or maybe she did.

He blanched as the realization settled in. "What kind of job did she give you?"

"Why would you *bring me to her*?" Enne hadn't realized how angry she was until she shouted the words. "You were supposed to help me!" She laid her hands on his chest and shoved him back. "You told me to trust you!"

He looked as though she'd punched him. "I didn't know. How could I? Vianca can give only three…" He shuddered and didn't speak the word. "At any time. They're precious to her. I never would've guessed she'd give one to you. You have to believe me." He sounded genuinely wounded, genuinely desperate. For her? No—it had to be something more.

Then it dawned on her.

Levi continued, his voice strained, "If I had suspected, I'd *never*—"

"You have one, too," Enne whispered. "That's why Reymond said you're her favorite."

His nostrils flared. "Of course I have one." He turned away from her and paced around the living room. "As if I *chose* to start a scheme that was born to fail. I've been scrambling around for months trying to clean it up. Meanwhile, the Irons are as good as broke. They can barely look at me anymore. I can barely look at myself anymore." He stopped pacing, but he still never faced her. "I was supposed to be something. Instead, I'm *hers*."

His voice grew hoarse at the last word, as if he might also break down. He fiddled with something silver in his pocket.

"Is it truly unbreakable?" Enne asked quietly. She couldn't tell who was supposed to be comforting whom. She didn't know what scheme he was talking about.

He turned to look at her. "Yes," he whispered hoarsely. "Unless she dies."

She gave him a questioning look.

"I'm not a killer, no," he murmured. "But, oh, I would. But I can't. We can only pray someone else does."

Any lingering anger she had left disappeared. She'd never seen someone else's expression so perfectly reflecting her own. They were both trapped. And he hated Vianca. She could hear it in his every word.

Leaving him to cool down for a moment, she brought in a plate of cookies from the kitchen. Six for her, two for him. She sat on the couch, her knees against her chest, making herself small. She ripped a cookie in half and nibbled it from center to crust. Eating felt normal. She'd barely eaten all day.

Levi sat opposite her in an armchair. "I'm sorry." He said it like he meant it. "I'm so, so sorry."

"I know." And she really did.

"What did she make you do?"

"She didn't *make* me do anything." Enne moved on to her second cookie, her voice low and cold and unrecognizable. "Initially, she did. But by the end, I wanted to, and I don't feel guilty in the least bit. I'd do it again." She paused to examine his reflection for any judgment, but his face was unreadable. "Does that make me a bad person?"

"I suppose it depends on what it is you did," he said uneasily.

She braced herself for the omerta's constrictions, but felt none. "In Luckluster Casino, Sedric Torren is likely overturning his dinner, and he deserves it." Apparently, once the secrecy of the omerta was broken, Enne could speak the truth freely. She sighed with relief.

Levi froze while reaching for a cookie. "You poisoned *Sedric Torren?*"

"He's not dead—just sick." Enne shuddered. "There was a childish pink dress. Vianca made me wear it. And it worked. Vianca dressed me up to send me to the slaughter."

A long moment passed before he whispered, "Are you hurt?"

"I'm fine."

"You're not crying."

"I said I'm not hurt."

"But you cried all morning."

"I'm *tired*," she seethed. And if he kept prodding her, she would cry. It wouldn't take much. She wasn't trying to be strong. She just didn't have it in her to be anything right now.

She stood and grabbed the orb she'd left on the table earlier for Levi, thrusting it at him.

"I'm not taking that," he said defiantly. "It's my fault that she found you."

"You said the Irons were broke."

"And that's my fault, too."

"So fix it." She shoved the orb into his chest.

"Does she know that you're Alfero's daughter?" he asked, and she shook her head. "Good. She can't know. *Ever.*" He laid the orb back on her table. "I'm not taking it."

"But—"

"Don't you get it?" he yelled. "She *owns* you. For as long as she's breathing, you're trapped in New Reynes. There's no way out. All those things you said earlier about wanting to return home in the fall? Wanting to finish school? You'll be lucky if you ever see Bellamy again. You'll be lucky if you make it out of this city alive."

The walls of the room suddenly felt smaller, closer. And, at last, Enne began to cry.

"I…" He blinked at her as if seeing her for the first time. "I'm sorry. I didn't mean to yell." Slowly, hesitantly, he moved closer to her as her shoulders heaved and took her in his arms.

His touch was warm. Enne almost slid away, but truthfully, she welcomed the comfort—even from him. She had no one else.

"I've never met one of her others," he murmured. "I've always been alone."

"I want to go home."

"I know."

"I want to find Lourdes." She'd never needed her mother as much as she did in this moment. Missing her felt like missing something vital in her chest. It ached as she steadied her sobs.

"I promise we will," he said. She clung to his words like a life raft.

"But what if Vianca gives me another assignment?" she asked.

"Then you do it. That's all you can do." He let her go, and she pulled away from him and wiped her nose. "Tomorrow night, we'll go to the Sauterelle. We'll learn what we can about Lourdes."

She nodded. It was a start. She picked up the orb and handed it to him one more time. "I *want* you to have it."

He took it, though she could tell it hurt him to do so. "I promise, Enne." Her name sounded strange on his lips. He'd always called her "missy."

"I'm going to help you. We're in this together, you and I."

She smiled weakly. They were, in more ways than one.

As he opened the door to leave, she asked, "What were you talking to Sedric about? I saw you speaking earlier, in the Tropps Room."

He paused and looked back at her for a moment, his expression perfectly blank.

"Nothing," he said. "We were only talking about a card game."

Before Enne could ask another question, Levi was already closing the door behind him.

DAY TWO

"If you must visit, reader, then I implore you: remain only on the South Side. Do not cross the Brint. Do not believe their smiles. Do not stray into their lairs. Or you may never come out."

—*The City of Sin, a Guidebook: Where To Go and Where Not To*

LEVI

In an abandoned park in Old Towne, Jac Mardlin leaned against a wrought iron fence, his newsboy cap tilted down over his face. A briny morning mist hung in the air from last night's rain. Everything was dark; it was perpetually dark in Olde Town. The buildings were made of glossy black stone, their spires and archways casting barbed shadows into the alleys. It all looked and smelled like a grotto.

Jac was a mere silhouette in the mist, still and quiet.

Levi might not have recognized him if not for the signature gray aura encircling his friend's body. It was light and smelled of linen, and Levi felt himself relax from its familiarity, like returning home after a long day.

Levi tapped him on the shoulder, and Jac opened one eye. It was gray. Everything about Jac seemed gray and colorless, except for the red card tattoos on his arms and the faded scars beside them.

"'Lo, Levi." He yawned and crossed his heart.

"Long night?"

"I had a shift." Jac worked as a bouncer at a gambling den

called the Hound's Tooth a few blocks from St. Morse. The den's owner was one of the Irons' oldest clients.

Unlike the other gangs, which operated on crime and on New Reynes's constant appetite for sin of all sorts, the Irons appealed to only a single vice: greed. They worked as contractors. Every few months, Levi selected a new gambling establishment and promised the owner that, if they hired his kids, he could raise their profits by 20 percent in three months. First, Levi brought in the card dealers, his expert cheats. Then he brought in the bouncers, the actors, the bartenders. He could sweeten every pot and rig every game—he had his consulting down to an art—and all he asked for in return was 15 percent of any growth. It was a deal very few could refuse.

"You look like you had a long night, too," Jac said.

Levi rubbed his eyes wearily. He'd lain awake for hours last night, replaying his vision from the black-and-white hallway, revisiting the moment he'd held Enne and promised her he'd do the impossible. Then, around five in the morning, he'd pounded on Vianca's door to let her know exactly what he thought about Enne's new permanent position in her empire, only to learn that Vianca was gone for the day. Out of town at some monarchist rally, preparing for a hopeless campaign for the November senate election. Typical.

"Sedric Torren brought me a gift last night," Levi explained. He probably shouldn't have said it—worries had a way of undoing his friend—but he needed to tell someone. He hadn't told Enne last night. Hadn't had a chance to tell Vianca this morning. And he needed some of the burden lifted off his shoulders.

"I wouldn't accept a gift from the Torrens if it was a kilovolt tied with a ribbon," Jac said seriously. "What did Sedric give you?"

Levi pulled the Shadow Card out of his pocket. Jac paled, then snatched it from Levi's hands and turned it over, running his thumb across the metallic silver back. "This is some serious muck. He didn't…he didn't *invite* you, did—"

"No. It's a warning." The invitation card was the Fool, not the Tower. And *invitation* was a misnomer: the Fool card warned you of your upcoming execution. Upcoming as in immediately.

"A warning about what?"

"The investments. He said I have ten days." *Nine days now.*

"Ten days?" Jac croaked. "You… You'll think of something. You always do."

Jac had always had too much faith in Levi, starting from the first day they'd met. Levi had been twelve, crouched in an alley off Tropps Street. He'd worn all black and kept his face covered—as was the signature look of Veil, a legend of the North Side and Levi's hero—and he'd dealt out a deck of cards, goading passersby with a game of fifty-fifty chances. But no one had stopped. They'd all recognized him and his cons by then.

"How would you like to make a hundred volts today?" Levi had asked Jac as he walked by. Even then, Jac was big. Not tall—he'd never been tall—but in his shoulders, in his build. The sort of strong that could've been concealed. He looked like a card Levi might want up his sleeve.

Jac tapped Levi's near-empty orb jar with his boot. "That's big talk."

"I aimed low."

They'd earned two hundred volts, and they'd spent them all in one night, feasting and drinking at a lousy cabaret. So they met up again the next day. Soon it was every day, a new place, new con, new spoils. It lasted for one year, until Levi met Vianca, and Jac met a drug called Lullaby.

"Did you get a…vision or something?" Jac whispered. "Ain't the Shadow Cards supposed to be jinxed?"

"Nah, nothing like that," Levi lied, because Jac was already pulling out his Creed, the necklace he wore that was a symbol of the old Faith. Not many believed anymore; the Mizers had perpetuated its stories for their own gain, and, after the Revolution, the wigheads had declared the Faith illegal. If Levi told Jac about the hallway and the graveyard, Jac wouldn't sleep for a week, and he'd spend the next few days quoting Levi verses from some text Jac couldn't even read himself.

Jac rubbed the Creed—which looked like an intricate knot in the shape of a diamond—between his fingers.

"Speaking of warnings, do we have anything to give to Chez?" Jac asked. "More than, you know, the usual?" Lately, the usual hadn't been much. Levi could manage to give him and the other Irons only the minimum at the last few weekly meetings.

"We don't collect from the dens for a few more days," Levi reminded Jac. It was the only excuse he could offer.

Ever since the investment scam began to crumble, Levi hadn't been able to run the Irons like he used to, and they were falling apart. The minimum wasn't going to cut it much longer. It wasn't enough. And it killed him.

Membership in a gang was more than a simple contract: it was an oath. Once you swore to a lord, they had power over you. Nothing unbreakable, like an omerta, but a power that carried orders down a chain of command and prevented the gang's circle of trust from being violated. There was magic to an oath, and even if Levi didn't understand it, he respected it. Everyone on the streets did.

They'd sworn Levi their loyalty, and he'd promised them more. If not greatness, if not wealth, then at least roofs over their heads and dinner in their stomachs.

Enne had given him one thousand volts last night, volts she thought were going to help the Irons. And Levi wished they were, but he needed them. They brought him one thousand volts closer to paying Sedric. He'd be no good to the Irons if he was dead.

Nine more days. All he needed was to survive the next nine days. Then the Irons would go back to being the richest gang in the city. Then Levi could finally give his kids what they deserved.

Levi checked his watch. "We need to get going."

Jac walked beside him, his shoulders slumped with weariness. "You haven't said anything about that missy you were with yesterday. *N*-something."

Levi would rather not involve Jac in all that muck, not if he could help it. The monarchists were a dangerous lot. "I got her a job at St. Morse."

Guilt simmered in his stomach as he remembered where exactly that job had led Enne. He had admittedly thought her a bit snobbish when they first met, but he wouldn't wish Vianca's omerta on anyone. Had he even suspected Vianca would take interest in Enne that way, he would never have brought her near St. Morse.

You were supposed to help me! she'd yelled at him. *You told me to trust you!*

Levi had failed her in the worst way. At the start, finding Alfero for her had been a way to save himself, and since Sedric had given him a Shadow Card, it meant salvation now more than ever. But since last night, it was also more than that—it was about Enne's forgiveness. It was about making things right.

He'd originally thought Enne wouldn't last more than a night in New Reynes, but he'd been wrong about her. Sedric had terrified Levi down to his very core, and Enne—*Enne*—had poisoned him, the wolf of the North Side, and she felt remorseless. No, she wasn't what he'd expected at all.

Jac snorted. "A job doing what?"

"I told Vianca she was an acrobat."

"Think you could get me a free ticket to their next show? I need a good laugh." Jac kicked an empty beer bottle across the street. It clunked loudly—too loudly. This section of Olde Town was lifeless except for them.

Then footsteps thumped through the silence. Chez strutted

out from the alley next to the old church, Mansi following close behind. Chez was scowling, which had lately become as permanent a feature of his face as his protruding brow bone and sharp sliver of a nose. He saluted Levi, quickly and haphazardly.

Mansi, however, brightened the moment she saw him and didn't hesitate to cross herself. Like most kids in the North Side, Mansi took the laws of the streets seriously. Every rule. Every myth.

She looks skinny, Levi thought. Skinnier than usual.

He sighed. He was so tired, in his body as much as his soul. It exhausted him, carrying all this guilt. If all his failures were a sea, then he was drowning, and the omerta was the ball and chain dragging him down to rock bottom.

"'Lo," Levi greeted them.

"Where were you last night?" Chez demanded. "Either of you?"

"Working, same as we both have every Saturday for the past year," Levi grunted. Chez already knew this. "Why? What did we miss?" That was a question that, as the Iron Lord, he should never have had to ask.

"A run-in with the Scarhands," Mansi blurted. Her gaze shifted wildly from Levi to Chez.

"What?" Levi growled. He would've never sanctioned such a brawl. Nor would Reymond. But street law had more power than the lords, in the end. Besides, Levi's history with Reymond wasn't common knowledge outside of this circle. The other Irons would view it as a breach of loyalty—Chez certainly did.

"Where was this?" Jac asked sharply.

"Near Revolution Bridge." Not far from the border between Iron and Scar Lands.

"Was anyone hurt?" Levi asked, searching Mansi for scratches and bruises but, thankfully, found none.

"One of our rats pulled a knife but didn't get a chance to

use it," Chez answered, his chest puffed out. "Scavenger had it coming."

"Someone pulled a knife on *Jonas*?" Levi couldn't imagine which of his kids was that thick. Jonas was the deadliest agent in the Scarhands. He'd even killed a Dove once.

"Will Reymond be upset? Didn't mean to anger your missy, Pup," Chez said, then instantly froze.

Both Jac's and Mansi's mouths fell open. It took everything Levi had not to cringe, to remind himself that he didn't deserve this.

He was meant for more than this.

Levi slowly slid his knife out of his jacket. Not the smart one Vianca paid for, but the one with the rusted handle he'd used in the old days.

Chez eyed the knife but didn't move. Levi flipped it a few times in the air as he walked toward him, and the blade's edge twirled around Levi's fingers with deadly finesse. Chez wasn't the only one who could show off.

"It was a joke. You gonna gut me?" Chez said it more like a dare than a question, but they both knew that this was more than that. Six months ago, these comments were a joke.

Now they were a threat. To Levi's power. To his pride.

Levi didn't know how far he would go, but, oh, that knife felt good in his hand. Reymond or Ivory would've never allowed their third to talk to them like that. But Levi had sworn long ago he wouldn't be like Reymond or Ivory. He wanted glory, not fear.

Besides, it wasn't as if Levi *could* gut Chez, or simply kick him out. He'd need to replace him with someone else who could relay Levi's orders to the other Irons—Jac couldn't do all that himself. Mansi would run to the edge of the world and back for Levi, but she was only thirteen—how would it look if the third of the Irons was just a kid? The other gangs thought *Levi* was just a kid. If he made Mansi his third, they'd think he was a punch line.

He hated to admit it, but he needed Chez—at least until he got Sedric his payment and could focus on the Irons again. Or maybe Chez would grow more tolerable after that. He used to be better, before he'd decided the Irons' problems were his responsibility, not Levi's.

They'd been friends, once.

It all came back to respect, in the end. Levi would rather earn his respect at the card table than demand it at gunpoint. But it was Reymond who had once told him that respect and fear were two sides of the same card. Since it had come this far, Levi needed to play his hand.

He placed the edge of the blade against Chez's throat. Chez went rigid. He didn't dare to breathe. But he didn't fight back, either. He didn't think Levi would truly hurt him.

Levi barely recognized his own voice as he growled, "I *could* gut you." Beside him, Mansi's eyes widened with uncertainty. It was a look Levi wouldn't soon forget.

"Oh, is that how you're playing now?" Chez rasped.

"The question is how *you're* playing," Levi hissed. "What makes a lord isn't the bravest, the smartest or the first person to whip out a knife. It's the one who earns the volts and keeps everyone alive. No one else can lead like me."

Levi felt the wisps of Jac's aura grazing his shoulder, as if trying to calm him. Jac probably didn't even realize his aura was doing it. Levi knew he wasn't acting like himself; the Iron Lord didn't have a reputation for pressing knives to his subordinates' throats. But this was the hand he'd been dealt. He didn't know how else to play it.

"The Irons have more volt flow than any other gang in New Reynes, thanks to me," Levi continued.

"Maybe once," Chez challenged. "Not anymore."

"This is temporary. Give me nine days, and I'm going to solve all our problems."

Chez's eyebrows furrowed. "What comes after nine days?"

My freedom, Levi thought, although that wasn't entirely true. In nine days, if he did manage to pay back Sedric, he'd be free of the investment scheme. But he'd never be free of Vianca. When all this was over, she'd just give him a new assignment, a new way to get himself killed and put volts in her pocket.

But maybe not. This was by far the worst job he'd ever done for her. She wouldn't demand such risk from him next time. He hated how much he was under her power, how he had to cling to the hope that next time, she'd take pity on him. That next time, she'd show compassion.

You're her bitch, Reymond had said yesterday. He'd been joking—Reymond was always joking—but it'd stung.

Levi was and always had been the Iron Lord, and it was time that meant something again.

"Our paycheck comes after nine days," Levi answered. This wasn't a lie; once the scheme was over, Levi could pay the Irons what the Irons were actually earning again. They were *still* the richest gang in the city, even if no one but him and Jac knew it.

"From now on," Levi commanded, dropping his knife and stepping back from Chez, "if you're thinking about pulling a knife on another gang, you clear it with me."

Chez's eyes narrowed. Levi could tell he was debating whether to challenge that order. Chez was coming awfully close to learning the truth of it: that Levi was stealing from his own gang. But it wasn't that simple, and Levi wouldn't do it if he didn't need to. He loved the Irons, but he wasn't sure he loved anything enough to die for it. Not when the problem was so close to vanishing.

Much to Levi's relief, Chez nodded. Mansi nodded even more fervently, beaming with the kind of loyalty that made Levi's stomach hurt. He didn't deserve it.

Only Jac failed to react. He was exceptionally gray and still and quiet, even for him. It made Levi uneasy.

"Any other news to share?" Levi demanded. "Any questions?"

Chez shook his head.

"Then maybe we can get on with our meeting."

Levi pulled out the bag of orbs in his pocket and handed them out. As the third, Chez was responsible for distributing the shares to the other Irons.

Chez didn't waste any time. He pulled his meter out of his pocket and counted the volts, as if Levi would sting his own crew to their faces. "We need more," Chez said, "for the dealers taking more shifts. They're pulling extra weight, and they could use the volts."

"We don't collect from the dens for a few more days," Levi said, echoing the excuse he'd given Jac earlier. "I would if I could." He was tired of those words. Even if they were the truth, they felt like a lie. He could always do something more, give something else. Except, this time, he was truly out of options.

Chez's eyes narrowed. "There should be more. Where are the other volts going? Where are the extra shares from last week?"

The extra shares were now in the whiteboot captain's pocket.

"There weren't any," Levi said, swallowing his guilt.

It's not supposed to be this way, he thought.

"But things are going to change," Levi swore. "Real soon. In fact, an opportunity has come up, and I have a favor to ask both of you because of it." Mansi nodded enthusiastically, but Chez didn't respond. As always, he looked skeptical. Levi supposed Chez had little reason to believe him anymore. His word didn't hold much value these days, and Chez needed more than promises from him—he needed action. "I'm looking for information about someone called Lourdes Alfero."

"The one the missy yesterday was talking about?" Mansi asked.

"Yeah, but you need to be on the low about it. People will be after Alfero, I think, if they haven't already found her."

It was a dangerous favor to ask, which was why he didn't add that Lourdes was a monarchist. He didn't intend for Chez or Mansi to go digging and leave an incriminating trail. Lourdes was well-known, but only in a few circles—nothing that would've touched the Irons. The less they knew, the better.

He turned to Mansi. "I also need your help tonight."

"For what?" she asked eagerly.

"I need you to help me sneak four people into the Sauterelle." Mansi worked there as kitchen staff, as well as an amateur card dealer.

"Celebrating something?" Chez asked, a slight sneer in his voice.

"A business meeting of sorts," Levi said.

Mansi nodded. "I can do that. No problem. Who's going?"

"Me, Jac, that girl you met yesterday and a friend." *Reymond.* He couldn't say that in front of Chez. Tonight, he'd make Mansi swear to keep it a secret. It wasn't fair to her, but Levi didn't have the luxury of playing fair. "I'll even bet a hand or two at their tables. You should play, too."

She beamed. "I've been practicing. The boss says I could be as good as you someday."

"You could even be better."

Behind her, Chez glared. It was an empty glare, Levi thought. He *suspected* the truth, but he didn't know. Like Mansi, the Irons were loyal to him. And no matter what Chez told them, no matter how bad it got, they all needed to believe in him for nine more days. He needed to believe it, too.

Nine more days, and he would fix this.

ENNE

Enne stared down an impossibly long hallway. The tiled floor, the alternating doors, and the stone columns all repeated the same pattern of black and white.

She knew she was dreaming, but she couldn't wake up. Not until she found the right door.

She turned the knob on a white door to her left. Locked. She tried the black one beside it, and it clicked and swung open. Once she stepped across the threshold, she slipped back into her own mind from four months past...and entered a memory.

She was in a wool coat. February—she didn't detest anything quite so much as she did February, even if it was her birthday month. She stomped through the snow. Look at her. Stomping. Ladies were supposed to *glide*. A girl from her class passed by in a motorcar whose two flags bore her family's crest. Enne froze and tried to make herself appear smaller. This really was a hideous wool coat. Perhaps if she didn't move, the girl wouldn't see her.

The girl didn't. But to Enne, that was almost worse.

The motorcar drove away, and Lourdes was behind it, standing beneath a streetlamp with a newspaper tucked under her arm, wearing her favorite crimson scarf. She smirked; she must've seen Enne stomping. *Hmph.* Well, Lourdes might think it was amusing, but *she* didn't have her society entrance in a year. Besides, Lourdes didn't glide, either. Her mother *strode*, the heels of her boots clicking rhythmically, deliberately. Not that Lourdes was a lady every day, like she had dressed this morning.

Lourdes hugged her when Enne crossed the street, and despite Enne's worries a few moments ago, she instantly felt safer. Lourdes smelled like fresh ink, which meant she'd spent all morning writing letters to her friends in New Reynes. Honestly, Enne didn't understand why Lourdes associated with them. Everyone knew *they* defined reputation by the amount of voltage one gambled away or the number of mistresses one kept.

They entered a nearby café and were instantly enveloped in the aroma of fresh bread. Lourdes and Enne shared a cheese pastry to start, as they always did when Lourdes visited on Thursdays. Lourdes ate delicately, her slender fingers easing the crust from the filling. Enne refrained from tearing at it and tried to mimic Lourdes's easy grace.

"How are your classes?" Lourdes asked, sipping her tea. It was in that moment that Enne admired—as she had many times before—how striking her mother was. Her blond hair was as pale and thin as the threads spun from a silkworm, her features serious yet elegant, from her aquiline nose to her deep-set eyes. Enne considered her best quality to be her skin, free of freckles or blemishes of any kind, and surprisingly youthful despite her age. Lourdes had an effortless grace that Enne was convinced she'd never possess. No matter how many etiquette lessons she took, how many classes she spent walking with books upon her head—nothing in Enne's life had ever felt effortless.

"They're horridly dull. Algebra is illogical. My history teacher's voice puts everyone to sleep. Madame Tensington threatens to strap a ruler to my back to keep my posture straight—"

"Breathe, Enne. You'll impair your digestion." Lourdes laughed. "You know, I bet algebra isn't all that illogical."

"It is to me. Some days, if it were not for my ten fingers, I don't know how I'd survive."

"Surviving with fewer than ten fingers would be taxing, indeed," she said solemnly. Somehow, Enne still suspected she was joking.

They picked at the last pieces of the pastry, or rather, Enne did. Lourdes seemed to have lost her appetite.

"I'm leaving for New Reynes tomorrow," she said. "I have some business there."

What business? Enne wanted to ask, but she never did. She'd decided long ago that she didn't want to know.

"I'll be back before school finishes, of course."

Enne sighed. She didn't have many friends, so Lourdes's business trips typically meant months of loneliness. Enne would go home every weekend to an empty house.

"Be careful while I'm gone," Lourdes said seriously, though maybe Lourdes was the one who should have been careful. Enne had heard some appalling stories about the City of Sin. "If I'm not back in two months, I'm dead."

Enne stiffened, even though Lourdes had given that warning before. "Don't be so dreadful."

Then the memory deviated from what had actually happened, and the dream took over.

"I don't want you to go," Enne whispered. In that moment, she was no longer the same person from last February. She was present Enne, the one who'd spent a day in New Reynes, who knew what the future held. "Please don't go." Her voice was stronger this time.

Lourdes shushed her. "I have to go."

"Why?" Enne demanded. "What could be so important? You're the only person who matters in my life. What else is out there that matters to you? That is so dangerous?" She grasped for Lourdes's hands, but Lourdes leaned back in shock. "Why do you keep secrets from me?" Hot tears sprang from her eyes. "Why didn't you tell me the truth about what you do—"

The black door opened to the hallway, suddenly, forcefully, and evicted Enne from her memory. She landed painfully on the black-and-white floor tiles, and the door slammed in her face. She cried out for Lourdes, but woke up before she heard a response.

Her sheets were damp with sweat. She rolled over and gazed out her bedroom window, where the sunrise illuminated the stunning view of the trash collectors in the alleys behind St. Morse. Enne waited for the details of her dream to fade, but even as she rose and readied herself for another day in the City of Sin, they never did.

The St. Morse acrobatics troupe huddled in a back hallway, bags slung over their shoulders, coffee in their hands, waiting for Enne. She was over ten minutes late. In her defense, the parcel Vianca's staff left at Enne's door had come only with a leotard, not directions, and every opulent hallway in St. Morse looked the same.

The troupe stared at her as she approached. Enne might've *looked* like an acrobat, with her small build and wide shoulders, but she wouldn't fool them for long.

So she'd decided to be honest. She couldn't have been the *only* one without any experience, and acrobatics talents weren't common. Vianca had already hired her. Certainly they'd be willing to teach her.

"You must be Enne Salta." A young man shook her hand, his grip firm to the point of hurting. "The *dancer*," he sneered.

She withered. "'Lo," she said, mimicking the way people spoke here.

He ignored her. "Everyone, this is Enne, the replacement."

"Replacement?" she echoed.

"Last week, a girl broke her leg and quit." He looked her over. "Clearly Vianca had to make due on short notice. Do you have any experience?"

"No," she answered weakly.

"Neither did the last girl." He shook his head. "We have a week until our next performance. Try not to break anything."

An acrobat, Enne seethed. *What was Levi thinking?*

Now that the troupe was complete at twenty people, they walked out the back doors into an alley behind the casino. Enne crept quietly to the back of the line. The cool morning breeze teased pieces of her hair out of her neatly coiffed bun, and she shivered. New Reynes didn't seem to understand the concept of summer.

Past several garbage bins—reeking and still awaiting the morning collectors—they reached the doors to a warehouse. It was no warmer inside, and it smelled of feet.

The troupe dumped their belongings in the corner of a massive square mat. There was equipment sprawled all around the warehouse: sets of bars, trampolines and even a full flying trapeze. She craned her neck back and stared at it, her palms growing sweaty. She hated heights.

They spent over a half hour stretching, and no one said a word to her. She didn't mind—she was accustomed to that treatment from school. The warm-up and the leotard felt familiar, normal, and she missed her dancing classes back home. She'd never been the best dancer in the room, but at least she'd been confident in her abilities. Today she'd consider it a victory if she left with all her bones intact.

After a while, the troupe split into groups. Enne lingered on the mat, awkward and alone, until a girl approached her. She was several years older than Enne, with blond hair and freckles covering her face and arms.

"I'm Alice. I write the routines." Enne shook her hand. "I get to spend the week rushing you through the choreography."

If she didn't want to make a total fool of herself and the troupe, Alice explained, Enne would need to manage a single back handspring and brave the flying trapeze. Alice had cut Enne's part down to the most basic material, and unless Enne also fractured a limb, she would be performing the number next Saturday with the rest of them.

Enne nodded along, feigning determination instead of fear. All she needed was to survive today's rehearsal so she could go to the Sauterelle tonight, to find information on Lourdes. One day at a time.

While Alice explained the different roles of each of the troupe members, Enne found herself imagining what it would be like to encounter her mother tonight. To spot her sitting at a table in the corner, smoking one of her foul cigarettes, a newspaper and a glass of bourbon in front of her. What would Lourdes say about finding Enne at the same cabaret?

I'm sorry. I was running late, that's all, Lourdes would apologize, her voice as soothing as the sound of rain on rooftops. *There wasn't any need to worry.*

And what would Lourdes say when she realized how quickly the city had corrupted her daughter? Enne had poisoned Sedric Torren. She was a prisoner to the unbreakable chains of a cruel mafia donna. Her only ally was a street lord.

Enne couldn't come up with any answers. She had no idea what Lourdes would say. As it turned out, she didn't know much about Lourdes at all.

"We'll start with the worst of it," Alice declared, her speech finished. "Once that group is done."

Enne realized with horror that she meant they'd begin with the flying trapeze. Enne studied the group of four rehearsing there. They soared effortlessly, fearlessly, even though they were at least fifty feet off the ground. Of course, there was a net between them and a broken back, but it looked thick and stiff.

Falling into it couldn't be much more comfortable than hitting the floor.

Enne swallowed as she followed Alice up the ladder, her legs wobbling worse with each rung.

"We don't always have the flying trapeze in the show," Alice said, while Enne crawled unsteadily on to the platform. "But guests like it. It looks impressive." As she spoke, she reached for the rope, then reeled in the closest trapeze. She handed Enne the bar, and Enne's stomach leaped as she reached out for it. "You won't have to worry about catches today, thankfully. There's nothing like that in *your* routine. But you need to be comfortable with the bar." She raised her eyebrows as she examined Enne's face. "I can already tell it's going to take you a while to be comfortable."

Enne reddened. "Dancing is generally done on the floor."

Alice didn't look amused. "Six days, missy. It would be awfully embarrassing for the troupe if you broke your legs in front of an audience."

Enne managed not to say anything unladylike…but she was certainly thinking about it.

Alice continued her lesson plan, but Enne was barely listening. She felt ill, even as she fixed her gaze securely above the floor, locked only on the space in front of her. She rehearsed the very angry words she intended to give Levi when all of this was over.

"*Go,*" Alice commanded.

Enne took a deep breath, held the bar and leaped. She lurched forward, and the world seemed to give out beneath her as she soared.

As she went backward, she reached her toes out behind her for the platform, coming a few inches short. Her breath tightened in panic.

"That's not how gravity works, missy," Alice said. Enne couldn't tell if it was amusement or annoyance in her voice. "You'll need to give it some push if you intend to come back."

That would've been nice to know ahead of time, instead of when she dangled limply fifty feet above the ground. She desperately tried to avoid looking down.

On her second return backward, Alice instructed again, more emphatically, *"Push."*

So Enne pushed. She kicked her legs behind her as she reached the peak, then brought them in front of her as she sped forward. Her body, much like the movement of the trapeze, was an arc. Her core ached from keeping her legs so straight, but it wasn't terribly difficult. She'd always been strong.

After two swings, Enne had generated enough force to make it back on the platform. She exhaled shakily and tucked a loose strand of hair behind her ear.

Alice pursed her lips. "Your technique is very precise." But her sour expression and complimentary words didn't seem to match. "Much better than the last girl. Did it feel good?"

Enne nodded. She wouldn't mind doing it again, now that she wasn't so nervous.

Alice relayed some more instructions. "If you can lock your knees around it, or even sit up, I'll be really impressed."

Enne had always considered herself someone who rose to the occasion. After all, being from one of the lowest-tier dancing families at her school, every challenge was an opportunity to prove herself. This might not have been ballet, and this certainly was not her finishing school, but her familiar competitive drive began to take over.

She leaped, this time more comfortable with her center of balance and with the trapeze. When she reached the highest point of the arc, she kicked her legs up, tucked them beneath her arms and latched them onto the bar. As she let her hands go, a few memories from her childhood returned to her, of similar games played at parks, of cartwheels and swings, of tumbles and scraped knees, none of which she'd thought about in years. Lourdes had never approved, she recalled.

As she glided, she almost had the urge to laugh. She didn't remember the last time she'd enjoyed herself like this.

When Enne returned to the platform, she did so only to catch her breath.

Alice handed her a cup of water, which Enne gratefully accepted. "None of it's difficult, what you're doing, you know." There was a strange edge to her voice. "I'm not surprised you can *do* it, but it's your form that's more interesting. You sure you've never done this before?"

"No."

"You're quite the natural." Enne had never been called natural at anything. Everything she was good at, she'd worked for. Everything she'd earned had been an uphill battle.

Then Enne placed the edge in Alice's tone—she felt threatened.

"What's your split talent, missy?" Alice asked.

"Counting."

"You any good at it?"

She hesitated, knowing what Alice was getting at. "No."

"Well, maybe mommy didn't really know the daddy after all," she said pointedly.

Enne glared at her as she took a sip of her water. There'd been times when Enne had wondered if her Abacus split talent was wrong—she'd never prided herself on her analytical or problem-solving skills—but it didn't make sense. It wasn't Enne's *father* who'd been the Abacus, but her mother. And Lourdes had known Enne's mother, the woman who'd entrusted Enne to Lourdes's care before she'd died. So if there was a case of mistaken paternity, she'd have to question her Salta blood talent, not her split talent. But she was a decent dancer. Decent enough for a Salta.

She'd always known she was a bastard. She wasn't ashamed about it, but that didn't mean she appreciated what Alice was implying. Lourdes rarely spoke of Enne's birth mother, so Enne knew too little about her to have any attachment. But still, the comment felt crass and unkind, even for New Reynes.

And Enne wouldn't take anyone's taunts any longer.

"I'd ask," Enne snapped, "but mommy's dead." It was a very unladylike thing to say, even if it felt oh-so-good to do so.

"Oh, so the doll has some bite," Alice sneered. "Fine, lie or play whatever game you want, but I want you to know how it works here. There are no favorites. There are no cheats. You get your roles on merit alone, but that doesn't mean anyone will take kindly to you if you're trying to play us for fools." Alice made a show of looking down at the floor. "You know, missing that net wouldn't be hard, with the right push."

Two days ago, Enne might've withered in the face of such a threat. But yesterday she'd poisoned Sedric Torren, one of the most dangerous men in the city, and today she wasn't in the mood to hear anyone else call her a doll. She wasn't so breakable.

She finished her water and handed Alice back the cup. "Then push me," she growled, her fury growing. But her anger had far less to do with Alice's words and everything to do with the doubt that was burying itself in her mind.

Lourdes had lied about a lot of things. Enne had braced herself for the truth when she'd decided to come to New Reynes, but this was different. These lies involved Enne. Lourdes had hidden her politics from her daughter, but Enne hated to imagine that she might've concealed Enne's very identity from her, as well.

Alice shrugged, but gave a menacing smile. "'Lo, Tommy! We need a catcher. Doll face here is getting cocky."

Tommy, one of the other acrobats, left his group at the bars and ran to join them. To Enne's surprise, she realized the rest of the troupe had stopped practicing. They'd been watching her.

No one had ever watched her before.

"We're going to practice some tricks," Alice told Tommy as he smiled, unaware and well-intentioned. "I think the new girl could use more of a challenge. I want to make sure she knows how it works around here."

Enne gritted her teeth. She hadn't asked for this. She wasn't looking to impress anyone or win anything.

But she'd spent her entire life fighting for next to last. So if she had to play, she would not lose. She would not break.

She had other business in this city.

LEVI

Enne was wearing some of the clothes Levi had given her, and whoever the original owners of that fur coat and blue dress might've been, he decided she wore them better.

"New Reynes looks good on you," he said.

She didn't grace him with a smile. She pulled the coat tighter around herself and shivered.

"She's in a mood," Jac warned. He leaned against the alley wall behind them, his presence quiet even though he took up so much space. He'd also worn his best—a gray vest and pin-striped shirt. His jacket was draped over his arm, and he smoked a cheap cigar. It smelled foul—Levi hated them—but it was preferable to the other substances these streets had to offer.

"We've been waiting for ten minutes," she groaned. "Are you sure Mansi is coming?"

"Of course she is." Levi flashed a smile, though the doubt had occurred to him, as well. But Mansi was more dependable than the sunrise—she'd be here. "It's a favor for her lord."

Jac grunted.

"Oh, is he in a mood, too?" Reymond asked. He stood on Levi's opposite side, grinding a pebble into the cobblestones with his blue-and-black-striped cane. It looked like something out of a candy shop.

The Sauterelle wasn't much to look at, even from the front, and, unfortunately, they were in the back. The alley was an offshoot of an offshoot off Tropps Street, a collection of discarded liquor bottles, random articles of clothing and food wrappers. Faintly, the ragtime from within the cabaret murmured in the darkness. Levi felt an itch in his fingers picturing the Sauterelle's numerous card tables. He was in the mood to win tonight.

"You went too far today," Jac said low enough that only Levi could hear.

Levi tensed, his winning mood already diminishing. "You tell me this now?"

"It wasn't you, Levi. It was an act, and Chez saw through it," Jac said. "He doesn't want a show. He wants volts."

"What else was I supposed to do?" They were already sneaking into the Sauterelle just so they wouldn't have to pay for tickets.

Jac shook his head. "I just have a bad feeling."

Reymond plucked the cigar from Jac's mouth and took a hit. "You always have a bad feeling. You're more jitter than person." He handed Jac back the cigar, who looked less than eager to have it returned. "What's the problem?"

"Nothing," Levi said hurriedly, because he already knew Reymond's advice: if there was a threat, squash it. Break the rules before they broke you.

Jac inspected the cigar, clearly decided he no longer wanted it, and offered it to Enne.

"What do I look like?" she asked.

Jac grinned. "Like a Sinner."

She *hmph*ed.

The back door to the cabaret opened at last, and Mansi poked her head out. Her eyes widened as she took in the sight of Reymond. "Oh, um, Eight Fingers," she said weakly.

"I'm a friend, little missy," Reymond said, his voice welcoming, though Levi knew each of his eight rings contained a different type of poison, memorabilia from his days as a Dove. "We've come to enjoy a good show."

Mansi looked hesitantly to Levi, who nodded, then opened the door. The four of them slipped in. He patted Mansi on the back. "This is our secret, isn't it, kid?" he asked.

"People will stare," she whispered. "People will recognize him."

Mansi was right—neither Reymond Kitamura's slimy face nor gaudy style was easy to forget. Levi preferred a more inconspicuous approach himself. In fact, he preferred almost any approach Reymond didn't. He figured this was why Reymond had taken such a liking to him.

"He'll behave," Levi promised, as if he had any control over the Scar Lord.

Mansi nodded uncertainly and scampered off, back to her post in the kitchens.

Enne lingered in the hallway, clearly waiting for Levi. The music from the show grew louder, the cigarette smoke stronger, the lights brighter. But they paused briefly in the hallway's darkness.

"What if she's in there?" Enne asked breathlessly. It was obvious who she was talking about.

Levi had considered this, but it seemed unlikely. Lourdes wouldn't let her daughter worry while she passed her nights at a variety show.

"She probably won't be," he said gently. "But this is the arts neighborhood. A lot of her associates come here."

Enne nodded, but Levi could tell she didn't feel much better by the way she reached out and grasped his arm. She might've been collecting herself, but the touch was enough to make Levi unravel. Her eyes were wide as she stared at the lights ahead, her breath hitched. Just the look of her like that made his chest knot.

She was dangerous, this missy. Barely two days of knowing her, and Levi was so fixedly intertwined with her troubles. He'd been Vianca's prisoner for four years, and never had anyone else shared his cell. Never had anyone else understood.

He let her compose herself, even though his own heart was pounding. It was nice to feel needed, nice to provide. For the past several months, he had only taken, never given, and he couldn't give her much, except some measure of comfort.

"We're going to find her," he promised. She nodded again. He wasn't sure she was even listening, so he squeezed her shoulder. She shied away, wincing.

"Did I do something wrong?" Levi asked.

"Sorry. I'm just terribly sore," she said, rubbing her arm.

Levi grinned. "Already had your first rehearsal? Well, you seem to be in one piece. Are you that terrible?"

She hesitated, then gave him a weak smile. "I soothed myself by imagining telling you off later."

"Is that so?" he asked, stepping even closer to goad her. He probably deserved to be told off. He'd definitely pulled the acrobatics idea out of his ass. "Well, I'm ready. Let me have it."

Then the music stopped, and they heard the audience clapping. Enne's attention turned back to the show, and Levi found himself a bit disappointed. "Let's go find the others."

They emerged on a second-floor balcony, the show itself below them. Jac and Reymond perched at a high-top near the railing, drinks already in their hands. They hollered at Enne as she approached, real rowdy, though Levi couldn't figure out why until he saw the stage, where a woman posed in nothing but a slinky garter set and silver tassels dangling from her nipples.

Enne went red as a cherry, and her lips formed a small O.

"I see why your mother likes it here," Levi said.

Levi could tell from Enne's expression that she was attempting to remain nonchalant about it all. But he still recalled their delightful experience yesterday passing Sweetie Street. She hadn't given up her sensitivities that quickly.

"Yes, well," Enne breathed, examining the mostly nude woman. "I imagine Lourdes probably does."

Levi drummed his fingers against the countertop, then searched the floor below for a card table to make his own. He nudged Jac and pointed to the far corner. "That one," he declared.

"Why that one?" Jac asked.

"Just a feeling." Truthfully, the card dealer at the table—who wasn't an Iron, wasn't anyone Levi recognized—was devastatingly attractive. They were here to find Lourdes, and this was an opportunity for Levi to win some of the voltage he needed to pay back Sedric, but there was no harm in a little fun.

"Are we splitting up, then?" Enne asked, scanning the crowd below. Lourdes and her head of blond hair were nowhere to be found.

"Of course not," Reymond said. "*They* are, but you can't be wandering around a place like this all alone." He put his arm around Enne's shoulders, but—just as she'd done to Levi earlier—she groaned and batted him off, muttering about trapezes and bruises and handsprings.

Levi shot Reymond a questioning glance. Levi didn't have the right to feel possessive—in fact, he would much prefer that he didn't feel this way, would much prefer the idea of the handsome card dealer whose problems were so distant from his own—but he couldn't imagine what interest Reymond might possibly take in Enne. While Levi leaned either way, Enne was most assuredly not Reymond's type.

"You need a local with you, missy," Reymond told her. "Levi will be asking around at the card tables, Jac will be keeping an eye on the floor and you and I can chat with the staff, who I'm sure see more here than anyone."

Levi couldn't argue with his logic, though it irked him how easily Reymond had taken the lead...even if Reymond *was* the one who'd suggested they survey the Sauterelle in the first place. Whereas Levi had always needed to work for his authority as a leader, being a lord came naturally to Reymond.

"Fine," Enne said.

It also irritated him how quickly she'd agreed.

"Well, fine, then," Levi muttered, then made for the stairwell.

Following the striptease act was a duo juggling knives. They weren't ordinary daggers—they were hooked in a way that faintly resembled scythes. Levi studied the two girls tossing them, searching for the trick. They spun between throws, danced with blades between each of their fingers, played with the steel as though it were ribbon. It must've been a hoax.

But then he noticed the white hair of one of the performers. She was a Dove, a member of the most feared gang in the city. The assassins. It was no trick, then. He was surprised the Sauterelle let her perform, lest she frighten the audience. Or was the hair part of the show, too?

Levi slid into an empty seat at his selected table and put down a few volts. He was directly beside the handsome card dealer, who was very much the sort Levi liked in men. Delicate lips, rosy skin, all soft and boyish.

"I haven't played here in ages," Levi said casually.

"You don't look familiar," the dealer replied.

Levi gave him a moment, wondering if he'd recognize him after all. Half the other dealers here were Irons, and besides, Levi was famous to anyone who enjoyed Tropps. But when the handsome boy remained silent, Levi regretfully continued, his ego wounded. "I only come here on occasion. I like the arts scene. Pretty different from the university."

The dealer nodded, showing he'd heard, though he had to pause to finish out the hand. Levi folded the first round, as he always did. It gave the impression he wasn't an aggressive player. Gave the others a false sense of ease.

"South Side, eh? I wouldn't have guessed."

"It doesn't suit me." Levi shrugged. "But I'm good with business."

The hand ended, and to his luck, Levi was dealt an excellent new one—not that he needed one to win. But he preferred not to resort to cheating, unless he thought he might leave the den with his pockets lighter than when he'd entered.

Fifteen minutes later, Levi had won the pot. He slid the small pile of chips toward himself with satisfaction.

"You play a lot?" the dealer asked.

"On occasion." Levi glanced over his shoulder. "It's the crowds I like. No other place like this. All sorts come here."

"I don't really pay much attention," he said blandly.

Levi realized he wasn't likely to find either much information or fun with the dealer, so he decided to try for a different form of entertainment. He ordered himself his favorite drink, a Gambler's Ruin, and planned to bet his entire pile on the next hand, even if his cards were mediocre. He liked playing it cocky, especially when the stakes got high. He needed to dig himself out of the rut from last night and lift his spirits.

By the time he had his drink in hand and a new music act had taken the stage, Levi was in an excellent mood. He plucked the cherry out of the bourbon and twisted the stem between his teeth as he played, trying to tie it in a knot. It was easier to focus on this than maintaining his poker face, especially when he felt so certain he would win.

Besides the handsome but disappointing dealer and himself, there were two other players at the table: a woman who was as large as two Jacs put together, and a boy who was making a point to match Levi's every bet.

Levi held two two-of-a-kinds. Certainly the boy could've held something better, but it wouldn't matter—not if he broke first.

The dealer passed out a new card. It did nothing to help Levi's hand.

But still he bet.

The woman folded; the boy kept going. Levi sat up straighter, took another sip, added another chip. Tropps was a waiting game, one of the few where the bluff was worth more than the cards themselves. The players began with three cards but, if they played out the whole hand, ended with twelve. That rarely happened, though—players folded, players broke. Especially after the first play, seven cards in, when the players were required to turn over at least three cards.

Levi turned over his cards first, revealing the lower of his two pairs. The boy's cards were random, mismatched of suit and number. Worthless. Yet still he bet.

Levi spit the knotted cherry stem into his glass. The night was getting interesting.

But in the end, the boy broke, as Levi knew he would. Levi pressed him up until the eleventh card, then, finally, he folded. They each showed their cards. The boy had four sixes, all hiding in his hand, while Levi had finished with a full house. Levi would've lost, had they reached the last trick.

It was his favorite way to win, knowing he'd been within an inch of losing.

The boy, to his credit, didn't look irritated. He nodded at Levi with approval.

They played ten more hands. It took Levi only a few to pick out the boy's tell. Whenever he was bluffing, his eyes drifted more often to the stage, searching for a distraction to hide his expression. He wasn't as handsome as the dealer, but he had an interesting face. His skin was several shades darker than Levi's, his hair black, straight and tied at the nape of his neck. He had a small tattoo of a pair of dice beneath his jaw, and he wore a smoking jacket with a gold tie.

Levi's buzz was growing, his mood lightening, his pocket four hundred volts heavier—he was quickly forgetting why they'd come to the Sauterelle. Then he spotted Enne speaking with someone in the corner by the stage, her fur coat swallowing her small frame. He couldn't see who was talking to her—their back was facing Levi—but it definitely wasn't Reymond.

As he craned his neck to get a better look, Dice slid into the seat beside him.

"She's pretty," he commented matter-of-factly. It took Levi a moment to realize he was referring to the woman singing on the stage, not to Enne.

Levi shrugged.

Dice picked up Levi's glass and shook it. The ice cubes rattled. "You need another drink." He didn't wait for Levi's response before walking over to the bar.

Levi waited for his internal logic to remind him that mysterious boys met in cabarets were a terrible idea, and that he was here for an entirely different purpose tonight. But his logic remained quiet, subdued by the whiskey. He pocketed his chips and followed the young man to the bar.

"Do you often gamble where the other Irons work?" Dice asked Levi as he sat in the barstool beside him.

"Not usually, no," Levi replied. He unrolled the cuffs of his shirtsleeves to conceal his tattoos, though he was secretly pleased he'd finally been recognized—even if it was in the den of one of his own clients.

"It's your hair," Dice said. "Orb-maker hair. Gives you away." Levi smiled and shrugged ruefully. He'd often considered dyeing it—it wasn't as if he *used* his orb-maker talent—but he couldn't picture himself without it.

The bartender handed Levi his new drink. Levi immediately went for the cherry.

"I didn't expect to win," Dice said. He'd ordered a Snake Eyes for himself. It was a drink you ordered if you were stuck in a losing streak, a drink meant to bring luck. "I'd heard you were good. But I don't usually believe what they say about people like you."

"People like me?"

"The players. They say the city is a game, one only the reckless play."

Levi preferred to think of himself as ambitious rather than reckless. "Hmm, who are these 'they'?" Levi asked, thinking of Enne's ridiculous guidebook.

"The spectators." Dice scooted closer to Levi—awfully close—and kept his voice low. "So why are you really here, then, if not to gamble or to watch?"

The alcohol warmed him from inside out. It made everything louder and quieter at the same time. The music, the taste of the bourbon and coffee liqueur, the smell of cigarettes, the touch of Dice's hand against his—louder. The lights, the burn of the liquor, Sedric's voice in his mind as he delivered the Shadow Card, Levi's own caution—quieter.

"I'm looking for someone," he said. Up close, Dice smelled like honey and designer cologne.

"A woman?" Dice asked.

"Sometimes, but not always," he answered. "She goes by 'she.' Here, they'd probably call her Séance."

Dice nodded, tracing his thumb against Levi's wrist in a way that made everything else fade into the background.

"Another player," Dice mused. "Why are you looking for her?"

Nine days, whispered Sedric's voice.

"Do you know her?" Levi asked, his voice high and hopeful. He twisted the cherry stem between his teeth.

Dice moved his hand away so he could take a sip of his drink. "What do you think about, when you're trying to bluff?" he murmured, deftly changing the subject.

"What do you mean?" Levi asked, playing along.

"When you have the winning hand, and you know it. How

do you keep your face so still?" He tapped Levi's forehead, just above his brow bone. His finger lingered a moment too long. "And don't say 'nothing.'"

Levi hadn't been going to. "I think about the beach."

"Not many nice beaches in New Reynes, but I hear that boardwalk they're building will be something else."

Levi took another sip as his memories washed over him. They were too loud, enhanced by the whiskey. "There was a beach near where I grew up. I think of the sound of the gulls, the feeling of the wind on my neck, the smell of the salt." It was a trick he'd learned, living in that house. How to be somewhere else. How to be anywhere else.

"I just kept thinking, looking at you, that you had a winning hand. You play like you've already won."

"That's the only real way to play."

"Until you need to show your cards."

The ragtime grew louder behind them. Dice's honey smell: louder. Levi's heartbeat: louder. "Do you know the person I was talking about?"

Dice inched closer, though there wasn't much space left between them. "Don't fold so soon." Levi could feel the words against his skin as easily as he heard them.

"You know, spectators wouldn't get tattoos of dice," Levi murmured. He brushed his fingers against it on Dice's jawline, tracing the ink. Dice leaned his head back and exposed his neck to Levi's touch. After several moments, Levi pulled away so he could reach for a napkin and a pen. "Write it down for me."

"You're not *that* drunk. You'll remember."

"It's important."

Dice conceded and took the napkin. While he wrote, Levi tugged the boy closer by his tie and pressed his lips against the tattoo. Dice let out a low groan that made Levi smile. He was winning a lot tonight. He trailed higher, brushing Dice's hair aside, and kissed below his ear. Dice's skin grew hotter, and he took his time finishing the note.

Levi spared a glance at the napkin before slipping it into his pocket. It was an address.

"I can't make any promises," Dice breathed against Levi's neck. "It's just what I've heard."

"You hear a lot of things."

He smiled. "It's how I play the game."

And then he kissed Levi, and everything felt very loud, all at once. It was the kind of kiss Levi had come to expect at places like these, with charming girls or mysterious boys in the hours after midnight. The kind of kiss that was meant for that place, that time, and never again. The kind of kiss you wanted the other person to remember, even if you would forget.

He'd remember this one, he decided, as Dice slid the cherry stem out from Levi's lips and knotted it between his teeth.

Several acts in the variety show later, Levi staggered back to the table where Jac waited, his face flushed, the gold tie wrapped around his neck. They always let him keep something.

ENNE

Although she'd never admit it to the boys, Enne was rather enjoying the cabaret.

Everything about New Reynes felt unfamiliar, and the Sauterelle did, too. The burlesque fashions bore little resemblance to the chiffon and white lace in Bellamy. The dancing wasn't the sort she'd learned in school. The liquors weren't even allowed in her town.

But it was also intriguing. Exciting. For the first time since she'd left home, she was content to be out of her comfort zone, eager to explore the unknown.

"What will you have?" the Scar Lord asked over the music as he led her to the bar.

"I'm not sure I need a drink," she said, remembering how little she'd cared for the wine last night.

"You'll look more approachable with something in your hand," Reymond assured her. She still couldn't understand why Reymond had so quickly volunteered to guide her, but she found herself grateful for his presence and the power he wielded. She saw the way the people here looked at him. Like seeing him was a story they would tell their friends later that night. Like they would do whatever he asked.

If they were going to find information on Lourdes, that power was something she needed.

"Water will work," she countered.

"Has no one told you not to drink the water in New Reynes?"

Enne thought back to the water she'd guzzled at rehearsal. It hadn't tasted bad. "Is it contaminated?"

"Not polluted, just corrupted." He winked at her and laughed. Enne suspected he was the sort who always laughed at his own jokes. "Better be careful, missy. Souls can go black in this city."

The bartender, who also didn't seem to be amused by Reymond's humor, looked toward Enne impatiently.

"She'll have a Snake Eyes," Reymond said for her. "It's a signature cocktail around here. Can't say you've been here 'til you've tried it." Enne doubted she'd enjoy anything popular in New Reynes. "What's the drink of choice in Bellamy?"

"Lemonade," she said drily.

Reymond shook his head. "I'll have a Gambler's Ruin," he said. When the bartender left to prepare their drinks, Reymond lowered himself so he spoke directly in her ear. "We'll ask the staff questions first. Then the performers."

"Are you sure they'd remember her?" Enne asked, surveying the crowd. Lourdes's simple style and quiet manner wouldn't have stood out here among the outrageous clothes and layers of harsh makeup.

"It's not remembering her that we have to worry about," he said darkly. "It's them lying."

Enne didn't have time to ponder that, as their drinks had arrived. Hers was fizzy and pale gold.

Before the bartender could turn to the next customer, she asked, "Have you ever met someone here named Lourdes Alfero? She also goes by Séance." When the bartender shook his head, Enne persisted. "She's tall. Blonde. Thirties. She usually wears trousers and—"

"I don't know who you're talking about," he grunted, then walked away.

"Well, that was rude," Enne muttered. She angrily took a sip of her cocktail. It wasn't sweet enough, but it was certainly more palatable than the wine.

"He was telling the truth," Reymond said matter-of-factly.

"You seem awfully sure."

"I can see when someone is lying," he explained. "Not from a tell or whatever Levi calls it. It's my blood talent." He inspected his walking stick, as though avoiding her gaze, but Enne strangely felt as though she could still feel his eyes on her. "Not that anyone is thick enough to try to hide anything from me." His tone sounded accusatory, but she couldn't imagine why.

She took another generous sip of her drink and cleared her throat. He couldn't know anything about the volts she'd promised Levi. "You're the local, as you said. Who should we talk to next?"

The two of them gradually made their way around the cabaret, speaking to members of the waitstaff and to the bouncers. Enne did most of the talking. Each time, Reymond presented Enne as "Miss Salta," but provided no introduction for himself—he simply stood beside her and looked threatening.

They didn't find many answers—the closest they came was someone who remembered Lourdes, but had never spoken to her, nor seen her with anyone else. It was terribly disheartening. Each time someone nodded with recognition, Enne felt a thread of hope tighten in her chest, but each time, that thread snapped with disappointment. She was likely closer to finding her mother than she'd ever been, but there were no real leads. The trail could, very easily, end here.

Soon her drink was finished, and a replacement quickly found its way into her hand. The liquor eased the pain of her disappointment, as well as the aches of her horrendously sore muscles from rehearsal.

"I'm not giving up," Enne announced, her face oddly feverish.

"We'll have to find a way to talk to the performers—" Reymond started to say, but stopped, as Enne was already marching toward the backstage area. She entered a room full of costumes, makeup and smoke, the Scar Lord following close behind.

"It smells like…" Enne sniffed the air. "Like raspberry cordial." She carelessly ran her hands along the beaded and sequin dresses in the costume rack, watching them shimmer.

"It's called Mistress," Reymond explained, crinkling his nose and swatting away the smoke. "It's popular right now. An aphrodisiac. Torren-owned, I think." He pointed to the blunt stubs in the ash tray. The ash left behind a golden residue.

"Are you supposed to be back here?" a feminine voice asked. Enne whirled around, nearly losing her balance. The speaker was a woman with a wary expression, wearing a feathered hat, a scarlet slip and very little else.

"I'm a dancer," Enne offered brightly, as a means of explanation. Reymond shook his head, and the woman's eyes narrowed uneasily as she took him in.

"You look familiar," she said.

Reymond smiled. "I have one of those faces."

"Mmm-hmm," she murmured uncertainly.

Behind her, two other performers carrying a collection of knives emerged from the dressing room. Reymond patted Enne on the shoulder, making her wince again, and said, "I'll go talk to them. Don't leave this room."

"I can take care of myself."

"Sure, missy. Just don't leave." Then he skulked off to the other performers, leaving Enne alone with the woman.

The performer sat on the chair by the vanity. "What are you drinking?"

Enne looked down at her glass and was surprised to find it empty once more. "It was gold."

She raised her eyebrows. "Don't start too young, sweetie. That's how they trap you. And you're tiny as a teaspoon." She motioned for Enne to sit beside her, and Enne collapsed in a very unladylike fashion. When she leaned back, the room spun around her like a carousel, so Enne shook her head and kept herself upright.

The woman plucked the empty glass out of her hand. "I'm the vedette here—the lead performer. My name's Demi Salta."

Enne giggled. She couldn't imagine herself wearing an outfit like Demi's when she danced. "Enne Salta."

"Ah, well, a cousin wouldn't tell on me for a little preshow ritual." Demi winked, pulled a joint out of her pocket and lit it. The smoke was the color of marigolds. Demi coughed for a moment, then relaxed into her chair. "I like your jacket," she said.

"Thank you," Enne answered. She liked it, too, though she felt guilty imagining some girl in the city who was without her fur coat. But it was also very pretty.

"I'm looking for my mother," Enne said—or rather, blurted. She liked Demi, and she'd always enjoyed the atmosphere of backstage, but she was here with a purpose.

"Well, she's not back here." Demi smirked.

"I don't know where she is," Enne admitted. "She's been missing. Her name is Lourdes. And Séance. And she—"

"Maybe you're not looking in the right places," Demi said, letting out a drag. "Where else do you think she could be?"

Dead, a voice whispered in Enne's head, and she whimpered. The voice wasn't usually so loud. She could use a glass of water, or better yet, a bed.

"Don't do that, don't do that," Demi ordered wildly. "It's bad luck to cry backstage."

Enne shook her head. "I'm not going to cry." It was as much a command to herself as it was a reassurance for Demi. Just as she'd felt so often since yesterday morning, she was right on the edge of tears, a touch away from shattering. But she was growing accustomed to the feeling. Even after two drinks, she wouldn't cry.

Outside, in the cabaret, the music changed to something faster. Demi swore. "I only have a few more minutes. I have a routine, you know. It's not easy going out there if I have all my wits about me."

"I'm sorry," Enne murmured with a small sniffle.

"Oh, you're so depressing. People come here to have *fun*, sweetie." Enne frowned—she could be fun if she wanted to. Demi stood up, set down her joint and coiffed herself in the mirror. She handed Enne a tube of red lipstick. "This will look good on you. Anyone ever told you that you look like a doll?"

Enne grimaced. "A few times." With a tremendous amount of pleasure, she pictured Sedric Torren overturning his breakfast, lunch and dinner across the city. Enne applied a layer of the lipstick and eyed herself in the mirror, wondering, once again, if the City of Sin was turning her into a bad person.

She dismissed the thought and helped herself to the other makeup Demi had on the vanity. Makeup was always soothing, and besides, she knew Sedric deserved everything he was getting.

"What do you usually do to prep for a show?" Demi asked, patting down her false eyelashes.

"I repeat my mother's rules to myself, over and over." She had never admitted that to anyone. Not that it was shameful. It just made her sound...vulnerable. She wasn't quite sure why she'd done it. Demi was a stranger, but maybe that was precisely why.

"Her rules?"

"She has these rules about how to behave, about things like getting lost, or showing emotion, or—"

"You mean street rules," Demi said. She handed Enne her powder compact, apparently happy to share her products. "Like what the gangs say."

Enne stared at Demi for a moment, almost uncertain she'd heard correctly. Lourdes's rules were precious to her, and she didn't like to imagine they belonged to anyone else—let alone that they had *begun* somewhere else. And the more she remembered Lourdes repeating those phrases to her, claiming they were about etiquette, the more cheated she began to feel.

Instead of getting upset, Enne pressed some powder on her forehead and mentally filed that thought away as a question she would ask Levi later.

She should find Levi now. She was wasting time, playing with Demi's makeup. But Reymond had told her to stay here, and somehow she knew, deep down, that there were no answers waiting for her out there in the Sauterelle. Only more strangers and more disappointment.

"Every time I perform, I smoke a little of this," Demi explained. "But that's a terrible idea. Don't start it. It's already stained my teeth yellow." She tapped its excess ash into the tray, and Enne tried not to crinkle her nose. It didn't smell as good up close. "Before they got me into this, I was a little more self-sufficient. I could get that natural flush all on my own." She held up two fingers and winked at Enne, who blushed. "Pleasure isn't just for the boys, you know. You don't even need lovers at all if you get good enough at it."

Enne, in fact, had *not* known, and turned over Demi's words curiously.

Outside, the audience clapped, and Demi straightened, took a last hit of Mistress and headed toward the stage. Enne stared around the empty dressing room. She supposed she would need to find Reymond, rather than wait for him to find her. But she was tired of searching, and the room wouldn't stop tilting.

"Well, *come on*," Demi urged. "You won't find your mother while moping drunk in here."

"I'm not moping," Enne grumbled, following Demi without thinking.

They walked onto the darkened stage. The audience whispered and whistled, waiting for the next act to begin. Demi placed one hand on Enne's shoulder and peered through the crowd.

"There," she said, pointing at a young man near the front. "Go talk to him. He'll know your 'rules.'"

As the lights turned on and the music began to play, Enne scampered off the stage. She considered ignoring Demi's suggestion—Enne was exhausted and doubted it would lead anywhere—but she hadn't traveled all this way to quit just because she was tired and admittedly a little drunk.

The young man sat by himself, twirling his finger over a glass of red wine. His hair was corkscrew curly, peeking out from underneath his top hat. He put on a salesperson's smile as Enne approached.

"What can I do for you?" he asked.

"I'm looking for someone," she answered, her words slightly slurred. "Her name is Séance."

"The writer?"

Enne perked up and slid into the chair next to him. Maybe he would turn out to be a promising source after all. "Have you seen her?"

"I don't go looking for trouble, missy," he said. "*You* don't look like you do, either."

"I was told writers like her come here."

"They *did*, when they were alive." He looked at her pointedly, and Enne, again, felt herself standing at the edge of that cliff. She was tired of feeling this way. Angry for feeling this way. She could no longer tell if she needed to sob or to scream. "Maybe there's something else I can do for you," he offered. "You need a job?"

"I've got a job. What I need is information."

"Ah, but the Orphan Guild can always get you a *better* job."

"The Orphan Guild?" The name sounded familiar—maybe

something she'd read in her guidebook. Likely something to avoid. She looked around the room for an excuse, for an exit.

"Not from the city? Most people would know the Orphan Guild. It's the name of opportunity."

"I'm not an orphan," she said defiantly. Not an orphan. Not a doll. Not a lost cause.

"What are your talents?" he asked. Something about his voice reminded Enne of Mistress—sweet as syrup. The way he leaned forward, the glimmer in his eyes, it was all very alluring. He *did* have something to offer, she felt instinctively. He was trustworthy. Speaking with him was a good decision.

She leaned closer, an invisible force drawing her to his voice. She wasn't sure if it was the alcohol or something else.

"I'm a dancer," she offered to him. "And a split counter."

"The Scarhands could always use counters. We have a lot of them, in the Guild," he said thoughtfully. "A shame to scar those pretty hands, though."

He reached out and touched Enne's cheek, then turned her head side to side, inspecting her. At first, Enne let him. He was trustworthy. He was no threat.

"I'm a bad counter," she admitted, because she felt like she needed to be honest with him. "And..." She searched for the words, and it was growing more difficult to find them, more difficult to remember why she'd denied the young man earlier. "I don't want a job." She tried to peel her eyes off him and his sleazy smile to find the others. Levi. Jac. Reymond. She squinted around the cabaret, but it was hard to picture their faces. Whenever she tried, she saw the young man's.

He clicked his tongue and turned her head back toward him. Her shoulders relaxed. "Split counters aren't bad counters, missy. Maybe that's not really your talent." He leaned forward and lowered his voice. "We have blood gazers. They're complimentary."

"Blood gazers?" Enne repeated, confused.

"They can see your talents. Lots of people are mistaken about them, you know."

His words struck a nerve, and Enne shook her head, the hold of the trance fading. She squeezed the edge of the table, her thoughts veering in several directions. Talents. His voice. Mistaken. A secret.

Maybe mommy didn't really know the daddy after all, she heard Alice's sneer. But her comment had been just a competitor being cruel. It shouldn't have shaken Enne like it had.

Were you that terrible? Levi had asked about her rehearsal.

The truth was quite the opposite—she'd been a natural. She still remembered the look on Alice's face when she'd perfected the simple routine in a matter of hours. How the entire troupe had noticed her, applauded her, and the rush that had sped through her chest.

She should've told Levi instead of making it a secret. But it *felt* like a secret. Like something wrong.

Something wrong with *her*.

The more the thoughts shook her, the more she listened to the other voices, the less she remained under the young man's spell. She pushed her seat away from him.

"Stop it," she told him.

"Stop what?"

She willed herself to get up, but her body felt heavier than usual—and not from the alcohol. "Let me go."

"I'm just doing you a favor," the young man said, licking his lips. "I could give you a name of a gazer. It never hurts to know."

"I don't want to know," she snapped. She dug her fingernails into her thighs.

"Don't be thick, missy. It's free of charge."

Enne tried to gather up the strength to move, but she couldn't lift herself from her seat. His voice felt like an anchor dragging her below the surface. *It's a favor*, she heard. *He's trustworthy. Kind. Helpful.*

The young man started writing down a name and an address on the back of a business card. "She's dependable," he said, "and she owes me a favor."

Enne knew she shouldn't reach for it. She tried not to. But her arm lifted—not like a puppet, but more as if drawn to a magnet. Her fingers trembled.

Someone shouted behind her and, in a blur, ran and snatched the card out of the young man's hand. Reymond grabbed Enne by the arm and hoisted her up, seething.

"Are you even allowed in here?" he spat at the young man. His voice sounded like the strings of a violin snapping. Enne jolted from her chair, alert, awake, and backed away from both of them.

The man frowned. "Eight Fingers. You know her?"

"He's a Chainer, missy," Reymond snarled, and Enne's blood chilled as she remembered the man she'd seen on Chain Street. A debtor. A street slave. Another few minutes under his spell, and she could've been just like him. "Favors," Reymond growled, brandishing the business card, "don't count if you steal them." His breath reeked of liquor.

"I'm not like them," the boy said.

"Can't change what you are. You're a poacher."

"I'm a salesman."

"Does Levi know you're here?"

"I'm not afraid of Pup," he challenged. "Besides, Sundays are my nights off." He grinned wickedly. "I figured you might remember."

Reymond went scarlet. "Muck off, Harvey."

He yanked Enne away from the table, back toward the bar. "I leave you alone for fifteen minutes, missy, and you manage to find the seediest person here." He shook his head. "Don't tell Levi about this. He'll blame me, and he *hates* the Guild. He and Mardlin are real holier-than-thou about it." Reymond took the card out of his pocket. "What did Harvey give you?"

"It's nothing," she muttered.

"I can hear lies, missy," he hissed.

"It *is* nothing. I...didn't want to take it."

Reymond squeezed her arm tighter, so tight it hurt. "Why is it that half the time you speak, I can hear the lies on your lips?"

Enne's ears heated in a sort of shame. She hadn't realized she'd been lying to him—and to herself. She *did* want to know after all. She'd broken plenty of Lourdes's rules since leaving home, but doubting her mother felt like the worst sort of betrayal.

Reymond leaned down lower. "I don't care if you hide something from me, but I *know* you're hiding something from Levi. Why is he helping you?"

"Because I'm paying him to," she said, her voice rising. She snatched the card out of his hand and thrust it in her pocket.

"You're lying again."

She froze. She *intended* to pay Levi, once they found Lourdes. Enne didn't have access to the bank account or the volts on her own. But if Reymond told Levi, then Enne would be without help. Levi had promised they were in this together, and she thought she believed him, but it was hard to be sure. Volts were more of a guarantee than good intentions.

"Levi's in trouble," Reymond said. "He won't tell me exactly what it is, but I have my suspicions. And if I find out you're leading him into more, or if anything happens to him, then I will find you." He didn't need to add on another threat. Enne understood him perfectly well. "Levi isn't like us. He's better than us."

Us, he said. But he and Levi were both criminals—Enne was better than both of them.

"I'm not like you," she snapped.

"Lourdes was. I recognize a familiar face when I see one."

He let her go, and Enne rubbed her arm where he'd squeezed, where her muscles ached.

"They're over there." He nodded at a table in the corner, where Jac and Levi were laughing over several empty glasses.

Reymond left her to join them, and Enne wandered over slowly, slightly shell-shocked, still slightly drunk.

Levi locked eyes with her, and he smiled. It made her stomach knot. She needed to sober up.

"I like the lipstick," he said.

"Did you find anything?" she asked, ignoring Reymond's suspicious stare as she slid into the seat beside Levi.

Levi held up a napkin. "I won this."

"Impressive."

"No, there's an address on it. We'll go tomorrow."

Enne relaxed. They wouldn't leave empty-handed.

She wasn't empty-handed, though. She still had the business card in her pocket. It was a terrible idea, but she *did* want to know the truth about herself.

Of course, she'd rather hear it from her mother. And the address Levi had could lead them straight to Lourdes, which meant Enne didn't need a blood gazer. Not yet.

"I didn't find anything," Jac said sheepishly.

"I met another Salta," Enne told them. "She's dancing now." Demi was still onstage, somehow wearing even less than she had before. The raunchy music and raunchier moves made Enne flush. Still, she had to admire Demi's technique. She was very graceful.

"Maybe Levi could've gotten you a job here." Jac slapped Levi on the back.

Levi looked away hurriedly and took a sip from his already empty glass.

Jac turned to her. "Too much for your sensibilities, missy?"

"I'm not a prude," she countered, even if the suggestion made her cheeks flush furiously.

Jac snorted. "Could've fooled me."

She pointed at Levi's tie. "You weren't wearing that earlier."

"I like it," he said.

Reymond rolled his eyes. "I shouldn't leave *any* of you alone in cabarets."

"Go easy on us," Levi said, slipping his arm around Enne's shoulders, forgetting that she was sore. She cringed, but this time, didn't feel like pushing him away—drunk Enne didn't so much mind that smirk of a smile. She resisted the urge to lean into him and scolded herself—maybe Levi was the only person she knew in New Reynes, but that didn't mean they were familiar.

"Besides," he said, unaware of Enne shifting with sudden embarrassment under his arm, "we got what we came for."

Demi's act ended with her brandishing sparklers in both her hands, her leg propped against a barstool, her slip scandalously riding up. The audience—their table included—cheered, and the four of them decided that was their cue to leave.

But Enne hadn't gotten what she'd come for. As they made their way up the stairs, she scanned the faces in the crowd one last time. Lourdes was nowhere to be found.

DAY THREE

"All stories about the city are true."

—*The City of Sin, a Guidebook:*
Where To Go and Where Not To

LEVI

Levi was still nursing a slight headache the evening after their night in the Sauterelle. The vomiting had stopped sometime that morning—right before making himself a Walk of Shame, the city's supposed hangover cure. A dull ache above his brow bone lingered throughout the day—while he leaned against his shower wall, letting the hot water trail down his shoulders and back, trying to remember exactly how he'd made it back to his room last night. While he collected his paycheck—two hundred volts—from Vianca's secretary. While he sat on his couch, painting, wondering when Vianca would return from her hopeless campaigning so she could pay him out of his desperate situation.

Eight more days.

He now had two thousand, three hundred volts toward his ten thousand. The only others he could count on were the five hundred volts from the Irons' collections this week. Everything else, he'd have to earn at the gambling table. Or beg out of Vianca.

Or help Enne find Lourdes and claim his payout.

He was pondering the address Dice had given him the night

before when he heard a knock on the door. Levi shoved the napkin in his pocket and rose to answer it.

Enne waited in the hallway. She was dressed in her regular clothes, but her face was flushed—likely from rehearsal, Levi realized. He narrowed his eyes. She'd been nearly as drunk as him last night, but looking at her now, you'd never know it.

"Where's your hangover?" he asked as she marched past him. "That's unnatural."

"I drank water when I got home, like my guidebook suggested." She inspected him, her lips pursed. "You look terrible."

"Exactly what kind of guidebook is that, anyway?"

She pulled it out from her purse and examined the back cover. "I don't know. I bought it in Bellamy."

"Why do you have it with you now?"

"It has a map."

"I know where we're going."

She tapped him on the forehead with the book. He winced from his headache and swatted her away. "You couldn't tell which way was up or down last night."

He grabbed his jacket and hat, feeling sour. "We'll get mugged walking around with a map. That tourist nonsense is an affront to everything I stand for."

"What do you stand for? Bravado?"

"Obviously."

They stepped into the hallway, and while Levi paused to lock the door behind them, an older man walked past. He wasn't a hotel guest—they didn't stay in this wing. The only people who lived up here were Vianca's associates, and Levi recognized this man. He belonged to one of Vianca's Apothecary families, the ones who brewed the drugs she distributed in the city. They were treated like royalty, both in St. Morse and throughout New Reynes. The man even walked like a king, his head high, his Gershton designer suit freshly pressed, his presence impressively regal. Apothecaries disgusted Levi, who couldn't help but remember Jac during his bad days.

Enne started walking behind the man toward the elevator, but Levi held her back.

"We don't ride with him," he said in a low voice. "St. Morse policy."

"Is he Vianca's husband?"

Levi snorted. "Vianca's husband has been dead for over a decade. That's just one of her friends."

"How can the Augustines be a crime Family if there's just Vianca?"

"There used to be more. Now there's just Vianca and her son, Harrison. I heard he despises her and lives somewhere across the world." Levi shrugged. "I figure he's the only sane one in the tree."

After the Apothecary disappeared into the elevator, Levi and Enne made their way down the hallway. They waited several extra moments before ringing the bell.

Levi took a deep breath and stared at the emerald green wallpaper; the color always reminded him unpleasantly of Vianca's aura. Wherever he went within St. Morse, within the place he lived, he felt locked within her cage. She was everywhere he looked.

Every night, he wore her suit, played her games, did her dirty work. He slept in a grand suite on the top floor reserved for her closest friends and associates, on silk sheets in a royal-sized bed. But he was not her prince, not her friend; he was her dog.

And every night he spent trapped in her empire, he dreamed of building empires of his own.

He took a deep breath and tried to turn his thoughts around. Tried to convince himself that Lourdes Alfero would be waiting for them, alive and well, wherever this address was. He wanted that so badly he could feel it like an ache inside his chest. He *needed* it to be true.

Eight more days.

His desperation unsettled him. He wasn't the sort of person to seek out addresses drunkenly written on napkins, to abandon all of his logic when faced with a difficult situation. To watch helplessly as his gang crumbled. To be caught within the clutches of a delusional old woman.

The ache he felt wasn't just from the desperation to survive, but for his second chance—to be the man he was supposed to be.

The elevator opened for them, and they stepped inside. Enne wore a worried expression that matched his own, fiddling with her Mizer coin.

"What are you thinking about?" he asked, as if he didn't already know.

"I'm bracing myself for disappointment," she said matter-of-factly. In just a matter of days, Levi had come to understand that this was how she spoke when her only other option was breaking down. Her expert poker face showed nothing, but to Levi, it showed everything.

He considered reaching out for her hand—there was little else he could provide as comfort—but then the elevator doors opened. Enne pocketed her coin and strode out in front of him.

Outside, the sun was setting, and Tropps Street was only just beginning to stir. The lights glowed but did not flash. The air smelled of beckoning restaurants and that ever-present eau de piss. Levi looked to Enne, as he usually enjoyed the disgust or discomfort often apparent on her face, but instead, she appeared pensive.

"Where did you get this address?" she asked.

"A friend." Levi hadn't actually caught Dice's real name.

"That sounds very legitimate."

"You have quite the attitude today." *And everyday*, he added to himself.

He prepared himself for one of her classic, ladies-don't-have-attitudes retorts, but instead she murmured, "I was promoted today." She looked down at her shoes. There was no pride in her voice, as he would've expected. Only uncertainty.

"What do you mean?"

"The Glaisyers are considered a top-tier orb-maker family, aren't they?" Enne asked quietly.

He furrowed his eyebrows. "Yes. Why does that matter?"

"The Saltas aren't. We're common. We're for the background of a performance or for cheap cabarets." Levi could nearly hear the chip on her shoulder as she spoke. "Every day at school, every *single* day, I've stayed late after rehearsal. I've worked until my feet ached. I've fought just to be noticed, just to be included. And—"

"Where are you going with this?"

She handed him a business card. It was black with gold cursive typeface. "I'd like to go here, if your address on a whiskey-stained napkin turns out to be nothing." Her tone was unsure. It sounded more like a request than a demand.

Harvey Gabbiano.

Salesman.

Levi's blood chilled. "I know who this is. He works for the Orphan Guild. No way are we going to see him. He's bad news."

"I know that. But we're not going to see Harvey—we'd be visiting the address written on the back." She cleared her throat. "To see a blood gazer."

Levi puzzled this. Blood gazers were typically hired to determine paternity, by wealthy families embarrassed by illegitimate offspring or by sex workers seeking to determine the talents of their children. He always associated them with the opening of a joke—"A father walks into a blood gazer's office…"—but Levi had never actually met one. They weren't common.

"There are professional blood gazers, you know," he said. "No need to sneak off to some Orphan Guildworker who lives in—" he studied the address on the card "—Dove Land." All the more reason not to visit.

"If Lourdes lied to me about my talents, I'm sure she did so for a reason," Enne retorted. "There must be something to hide."

Levi handed her back the card. "Let me get this straight. You learn how to do a cartwheel, and now you think you might have an acrobatics talent."

Acrobatics talents weren't common. In fact, Levi knew of only one family—the Dondelairs. Everyone on the North Side knew their story. The daughter who'd found friends in criminals, who'd set fire to the capitol building and laughed as she bled to death. The son who'd left rubble and ruin in his wake. The family who'd obsessed over the inexplicable and the unnatural, right until the moment of their deaths. One by one, they'd hanged.

Legends of the North Side typically ended in blood.

"I've managed more than a cartwheel," she murmured.

"You don't sound convinced yourself."

She lifted up her chin defiantly. Levi tried to decide if it was cute or snobbish. "I want to go."

"Then convince me. You sound like you're asking for permission."

"I don't need your permission."

"But you want it. And I think it's a terrible idea."

"Don't I *look* like I could have an acrobatics talent?"

"I'm not arguing that you're not short enough."

Her nostrils flared. "You're intolerable."

"I'd rather *not* see the headlines tomorrow. 'Murdered girl's body found washed up in the Brint.' Intolerable, I know."

They didn't speak until they reached the border between Iron and Scar Lands. Levi turned them right, in the direction of the river and the Factory District. Within a few blocks, the bustling and lights of Tropps Street faded away, and they roamed through residential roads and warehouse lots.

"What's that smell?" Enne asked.

"The Brint." The river water was roughly the color of ham stew. "We're close."

She covered her nose. "How close?"

Levi looked at the street signs around them. He'd heard of

the road before. Probably passed it once or twice. It was some-where around here.

"A few blocks," he said, though he was no longer sure.

Levi had only just begun to enjoy the peace and quiet when Enne spoke up again. "I want to go, whether you go with me or not," she said. Levi grimaced. He was more than done with this conversation. "If nothing turns up at this place, then I'll find the blood gazer myself."

It'd barely been three whole days, and she seemed to have al-ready forgotten how she'd first arrived in New Reynes. Chased by whiteboots. Belongings gone. Frightened. Naïve.

"Don't be thick. You'd be walking straight into Dove Land alone. Maybe listen to your guidebook for once on this one and *don't go*."

"The guidebook practically says the entire city is off-limits," Enne snapped. "But I'll go anywhere to find Lourdes."

He frowned as he read the nearby street sign.

"Are you even *listening*—?"

"What's the name of that street again?" he asked. He'd thought it would be here. Instead, they'd reached the edge of a residential complex, and they stared in confusion at the empty warehouse lot in front of them and the river and South Side beyond it.

"Are we lost?" she asked.

"We're close."

She grumbled something under her breath, then pulled her guidebook from her purse.

"You're ruining my reputation," he grunted, trudging off ahead of her to retrace their steps.

"The map says to turn here," she argued.

"It's definitely not there. I remember that."

"The book says—"

"Muck the book."

Enne rolled her eyes and marched to the left, in the direc-tion that Levi was certain led to nothing more than factories and mills. He shoved his hands in his pocket and waited. No way was Enne going to go off on her own now that it was getting dark. She acted brave, but soon she'd be running back, if he waited long enough.

He tapped his foot as she disappeared around the corner.

After another minute passed, his irritation turned to worry. He pictured a trigger-antsy Scarhand crouching behind a train car as she passed, and Enne's face when she turned to find a pistol pressed against her temple. Levi felt for his knife in his one pocket and his gun in the other as he ran after her.

She was in no distress. No pistol to her head. She was leaning against a doorframe, her face hidden behind her guidebook, humming a waltz. Levi scowled as he climbed the steps beside her.

"The Wayward Inn," Levi read on the sign on the door. "Bit secluded for an inn."

The building was made of New Reynes's signature white stone and wedged in between a series of row homes. A wreath with daisies and a blue seersucker bow hung on the door.

"This is where you apologize for your pigheadedness," Enne said.

Levi ignored her and opened the door.

Inside, it was clean and empty. Levi walked up and rang the bell sitting atop the counter on a white doily.

An old woman appeared from another room. Like the inn, she was also tiny, well-dressed and unassuming. She wore a strand of pearls and a floral shawl. Levi wondered how Lourdes had managed to find the quietest, most Bellamy-like inn on the North Side. The whole place smelled like chamomile soap.

"Can I help you?" she asked, narrowing her eyes. "If you're looking for a place to say, the Wayward Inn has a strict policy that unmarried men and women are to sleep *separately*. Women are on this floor, men on the top floor and *I* sleep in the middle." This struck Levi has quite the oversight, and he wondered exactly what sort of nighttime activities occurred on their isolated floors while the old lady slept unaware.

"We're not looking for a room," Enne said hurriedly, her face red and clearly offended. Levi smiled wryly, then drummed his fingers against the counter in annoyance. He knew from experience he wasn't *that* unappealing. "We're searching for a woman named Lourdes Alfero, and we have reason to believe she could be staying here."

"The inn is empty," the woman answered, and Levi could nearly feel Enne's disappointment, as if a palpable heaviness had descended on the room. Or maybe it was his own.

Eight days. And a dead end.

"Then maybe you've seen her," Enne said, her voice and expression too collected, too poised. Levi squeezed her shoulder. "She's in her early thirties. Fair-skinned. Blonde. Brown eyes."

"There was a woman staying here like that last week," the woman mused. "She checked out abruptly, even left something behind. Who are you to her?"

"Her daughter."

"She was pretty young to have a daughter your—"

"Please." Enne's voice cracked. "We'd love to see what she left. And if you have any information…"

The woman hesitated, then leaned down and opened a drawer below the counter. She pulled out a single card, and the sight of the metallic silver back sent Levi's heart plummeting into his stomach.

It was a Shadow Card.

He had the urge to loosen his collar, or to bolt out the door. The memories of the black-and-white hallway, of Sedric Torren's menacing smile, sent goose bumps prickling across his skin.

"What is that?" Enne asked. She took it from the woman's hands and turned it over. The face was the Hermit, a representation of isolation and knowledge. It wasn't an invitation to the Shadow Game—that was reserved for the Fool—but it was a warning, just like the Tower card Levi had received two nights ago.

Had Lourdes run into trouble with the Phoenix Club?

Or worse…was the Phoenix Club following him?

It seemed unlikely that they'd guessed he would visit the Wayward Inn. His promise to help Enne had little to do with his investment scheme, except that finding Lourdes was supposed to be his way out. No one but him knew they were connected.

"It was the only thing in the room after she left," the woman said.

Maybe Lourdes had received the warning and fled the city. Clearly, she hadn't returned to Bellamy, to Enne, which meant she might have escaped somewhere else. They probably had little chance of finding her unless she intended to be found.

Or, of course, she could be dead.

"When did she leave?" Enne asked.

"About five days ago," the woman answered.

"Did she seem agitated? Nervous?" Levi questioned, his mouth dry. Five days ago wasn't long at all.

"I couldn't tell. She was quiet. Didn't say much."

Enne squeezed the card until it bent and crumpled in her hand. "Five days ago," she muttered, wiping her eyes.

Levi put a comforting hand on her shoulder and asked, "And there's nothing else you know?"

The woman shook her head. "Was she in trouble or something? I don't want whiteboots showing up and making the inn look suspicious." She eyed them shrewdly, as if she'd already made up her mind about them. "Get out. I don't want guests to get the wrong impression."

What guests? Levi wanted to ask, but then Enne ripped Levi's hand off her shoulder and stormed outside. He followed, unsure if he should tell her the truth about the Shadow Card. He would tell her later, tonight. It was dangerous to speak about things like that out in the open, especially so close to Luckluster Casino.

She leaned against a chain-link fence, and Levi waited for her to cry, as he expected she might. Instead, she stuffed the Shadow Card in her pocket, the look on her face icy. It made him uneasy, but Levi knew better than to offer her comfort now. It wasn't his responsibility to console her, even if he felt like he should.

It was a strange notion, but Levi was beginning to consider Enne as a friend—maybe even more than that. After all, they were both trapped in the same, unspeakable cage. Such a bond might not have meant much to Enne, but it meant something to him.

"Let's go back," she murmured.

Levi hesitated. Where was all that earlier talk about the blood gazer and adventuring anywhere for her mother? It was difficult to tell from her expression if she was feeling defeated or faking it—her poker face was better than most.

"Are you sure?" he asked.

"I'm tired, and, like you said, it's almost sundown." She smiled stiffly. "Maybe we'll try the blood gazer tomorrow."

Their walk back to St. Morse was silent. Levi mentally prepared a speech for what he'd tell Enne about the Shadow Card, but his rehearsed words kept falling short. Any Shadow Card, not just the Fool's invitation, signaled a probable death on the horizon. He couldn't imagine saying those words out loud, considering the Shadow Card he carried in his own pocket.

Your mother is probably dead, he'd say. *And without her, I probably will be, too.*

Halfway there, it started to drizzle. The rain tasted like smoke.

"Do you want my jacket?" he offered.

"How gentlemanly."

He slipped it off and draped it over Enne's shoulders. It swallowed her, made her look like a lost waif as she wandered through the rain. Something in Levi's chest constricted seeing her in his jacket, something an awful lot like satisfaction. It felt like a dangerous thing.

"Thanks." She slipped her hands into the pockets and tugged it closer around herself.

"We should have a talk, you and I, when we get back," he said hoarsely.

She looked up at the dark sky, her expression unreadable. "Can it wait until tomorrow?"

Levi's shoulders sagged with relief. "Yes. Of course." More than anything right now, he really needed a decent night's sleep. If Lourdes was dead, Levi would need to spend the next seven nights earning the volts the only way he knew how: from card table to card table, all across the North Side. If things were different, he'd bring a team of his best dealers with him from the Irons—but that meant telling the Irons the truth, and Levi would rather die in the Shadow Game than have his friends learn how he'd betrayed them.

He'd already dug his own grave, and he wouldn't bring the Irons down with him.

When they returned to St. Morse, they rode the elevator quietly to their floors. As Enne stepped out to walk to her own apartment, his breath hitched. He didn't want to spend the night alone. Maybe he could invite her upstairs, pour them each a drink and confide everything to her. He had a feeling she might understand his problems better than anyone.

"Here's your jacket," Enne offered, her gaze on the floor. "Thanks."

Levi took it numbly and slipped it back on. "You don't need to... I mean, you can come..."

"I'd really like to be alone," she said.

"Oh. Oh, yeah...of course." He wasn't the only one with problems, but apparently Enne didn't want to share hers tonight.

The elevator's gate closed, and Levi felt acutely alone.

Levi found Jac passed out on his couch with a five-inch cut along his right eyebrow, bruised purple and green and stitched up with black thread. The whole room smelled like his aura: light and clean, like he'd opened the window even though it was bolted shut.

Levi shook him awake. Jac sat up with a start and rubbed his eyes.

"Took a nap," he mumbled.

"Who did those stitches? A blind man?" Levi asked.

"Oh, these?" He pointed to his forehead—as if Levi could've been referencing a different wound—and gently touched the scar, flinching. "I did. Last night."

"That's not from work, is it?" he asked. Guests at Jac's tavern, the Hound's Tooth, could grow rowdy in the early hours of the morning. But sometimes Levi suspected Jac was the one starting those fights. The guests could blame it on liquor. He didn't know how Jac rationalized it.

"No. Not—"

"I thought you were done boxing." Levi fought to keep his voice steady instead of stormy. He tried to be patient with his friend, but on nights like this one, it wore at him. Sometimes he felt like no matter how much he helped Jac, it wouldn't matter until Jac started helping himself. "They always rig those games. Remember the time they slipped you something? You were out over twenty-four hours."

"Cool it. I didn't eat or drink anything. And I won. Ten volts. Not bad, eh?"

Levi didn't bother with a response. He was a breath away from shouting, but he couldn't tell if it was from anger or simply exhaustion.

Levi sighed and hung his hat on the coatrack. "What are you doing here?" He unbuttoned his jacket.

"I thought I'd check in on you," Jac replied. "Only a week left. I have one of our runners watching Luckluster—seeing if the Torrens are up to anything unusual—"

"My gun," Levi blurted, feeling around his empty pockets in alarm. He'd definitely brought it with him earlier that day. He knew better than to traverse the North Side without it. "*Muck.* My gun's gone." Then he remembered the image of a certain missy wearing his jacket, and he panicked.

"Grab what you got," Levi announced. "We're going to Dove Land."

ENNE

The Deadman District was just as picturesque as the name implied. The web of sewers reeked of grime and waste. The foul stench clung to the pavement, crusted against pipes and dug itself into her clothes so that it would no doubt follow her even after she left. The alley walls glinted from the silver metal mortar between the stones, giving each of the buildings the look of shattered glass. Red and yellow graffiti stained the rooftops—mostly symbols of some kind, but also a few names.

"'Leftover remnants of the Great Street War,'" Enne read from her guidebook. "'Seven years after the Revolution, when the city of New Reynes attempted to eradicate street crime from the North Side.'" Obviously, the wigheads hadn't succeeded.

Few of the streetlights worked, casting the streets into an ominous darkness. The city felt still here, like the whole neighborhood was holding its breath. It was a place where any heartbeat could've been your last.

She was getting close. After memorizing the remaining steps from the map, Enne slipped the book back into her pocket—

right beside Levi's gun. Maybe Enne should've brought him along, but he'd been so against the idea of coming here, and this was a secret Enne needed to uncover on her own. She needed to know the extent of her mother's lies. She needed to know why she'd worked herself tirelessly her entire life just to achieve mediocrity, when she was a natural at something else. Why her mother had watched her torture herself in silence.

No one had ever called Enne a natural at anything. Instead of making her proud, the word only left her aching. She felt the pain in the toes she'd broken in ballet. In the memories when Lourdes had scolded her for cartwheels and tumbles. In the times she'd stared at her shoulders wondering if she was too broad, too strong, too undelicate.

She reached a dead end on the street and peered at the number over the final home.

"This is it," she muttered nervously. The shutters tilted off their hinges like hangnails, and the wooden fence was rotted and termite-grazed. The sign out front directed visitors to enter through the cellar. "Charming."

Enne opened the wooden doors and crept down a damp stairwell. At the end was another door, this one with two bullet holes above her eye level. Her heart skipped a beat, remembering Levi's warnings, but it was too late to turn back now.

With one hand protectively on the gun in her pocket, she knocked.

A light shone from the bullet holes. "Who is it?" asked a female voice, and Enne relaxed slightly. She hadn't been expecting a woman.

"I'm looking for the blood gazer," Enne said, her voice high and polished, as it reverted to whenever she was nervous. "I have a recommendation from Harvey Gabbiano."

The door swung open. The first thing Enne noticed was the girl's white hair, the indicator that she was a Dove. She wore it bluntly cut near her shoulders, as if done with a razor, with a strip above her right ear shaved to a buzz.

Her skin was fair and dusted—nearly every inch of it—with freckles. She looked to be around Enne's age. Though thin, her shoulders were broad, her arms large, all bones and no muscle— as though she were built like a blunt weapon.

She looked Enne up and down. "How exactly do *you* know Harvey? Never seen him step foot on the South Side." Enne furrowed her eyebrows—she was dressed in a plain skirt and blouse that Jac had stolen for her near Tropps Street. "It's the way you speak, missy," the girl explained.

"We met at the Sauterelle. He mentioned you owed him a favor."

She scowled and opened the door wider. "Let's get this over with. I don't like being in debt to Gabbianos—even good ones." She reached into her pocket and pulled out a silver harmonica, of all things. She lifted it to her lips and played a low note, like a sigh. "My name's Lola Sanguick. Who are you?"

"Enne."

"Well, Enne—" she held out her hand "—no guns in the office. I'll keep it in my desk until we're done with our little chat."

Enne grimaced. How did Lola know she was carrying a gun? "I'd rather keep it."

"Relax, missy. What've you got to be afraid of?" Lola grinned widely. "You can keep your knives. *Those* I like."

Enne sourly handed the pistol to Lola. The worst danger was past, now that she no longer walked the streets, but she still would've felt more comfortable with the gun at her side. She'd never used one before, of course, but assumed she could figure it out if she needed to.

Lola walked away, playing her harmonica, and Enne closed the door behind her. The "office" was really a cellar with a single desk and a wine rack. Lola collapsed into her seat, deposited the gun into a drawer and pulled out a foot-long scalpel.

The color drained from Enne's face. "What is that for?"

"Do you know anything about blood gazers?"

Don't let them see your fear.

Enne could almost hear Lourdes's voice in her head as she took a step closer to Lola, a girl who looked as if she could chew Enne up and spit her out like a sunflower seed. If Enne was a white picket fence, then this girl was chain links.

"I'm afraid not," Enne responded.

Lola eyed her suspiciously. "Give me your hand."

Enne leaned across the table and held it out, trembling.

"I'm just gonna prick your finger," Lola said.

"That's a big knife just for that."

She smiled. "It is, isn't it?" She dug the tip into Enne's skin, and a droplet of blood seeped out. Lola squeezed more out of Enne's finger. The pain was unpleasant, but bearable. It was Lola herself that made Enne nervous. Doves were assassins, so just what else did Lola use that knife for?

"Almost done," Lola said gently as she pinched Enne's skin to coax out more blood. "Tell me about yourself."

"Oh, um...I'm visiting New Reynes."

She snorted. "What? No blood gazers where you're from?"

"Something like that."

Then Lola did the unthinkable. She dabbed both her pointer fingers in Enne's blood and smeared it on her eyes.

Enne grimaced in disgust. She had no qualms about the sight of blood—it was the look on Lola's face, not the blood itself, that unnerved her. Lola licked her lips and grinned, as if savoring the feeling on her murky pink eyes.

"It's not like I drank it," the blood gazer joked.

Enne's resolve wavered during the several moments of silence that passed. Maybe Levi had been right, and this was a terrible idea. Maybe she wasn't ready to hear the truth about herself. If she found out Lourdes had been lying, she'd resent her mother.

But if she found out there'd been no lie at all, and she'd doubted Lourdes unfairly, she'd resent herself.

Then Lola startled. Her gaze shot toward Enne, and she wiped the blood out of her eyes and eyelashes, smearing it onto her knuckles.

"Is this some kind of a joke?" Lola growled. She stood up and walked toward Enne before she could back away. Lola grabbed a fistful of Enne's blouse.

"No," Enne yelped.

"Then you must be pretty damn thick."

Enne's eyes flickered toward the door. Whatever Lola had seen, she didn't like it. But Enne couldn't leave without knowing the truth.

And she was getting awfully tired of people in this city calling her thick.

"What do you mean?" Enne asked coolly.

"You should be dead." As Lola reached for her knife on the desk, Enne managed to squirm out of her grip. Enne backed several feet away, close to the door. She shakily reached into her pocket for Levi's gun, then remembered with a surge of dread that Lola had locked it in her desk.

"Whatever you saw," Enne said, fighting to keep her voice under control, "there's nothing I can say until you tell me what it is."

Lola lunged so that she blocked Enne's path to the door. She held the knife out, pointed toward her. "There *isn't* anything to say. You're a Mizer, and it would be better for this whole city if you were dead."

Confusion swamped her, followed by panic. The words echoed around the cold cement walls, and Enne shivered down to her bones, trying and failing to make sense of Lola's words. The Mizers were dead. Obviously, Lola had make a mistake.

But that didn't matter. Enne could tell the blood gazer was certain by the way Lola glared at her and locked her jaw.

Whether or not Lola told the truth, if she turned Enne into the wigheads, her accusation alone would warrant a death sentence. Enne would watch tomorrow's sunrise from the gallows.

Which left Enne with three options.

She could try to talk Lola down and plead for her life.

She could escape, but with Lola forever believing this mistake and possibly revealing it to the entire world.

Or...Enne could kill her.

The last thought wasn't a whisper or a shadow. It didn't lurk. It didn't send quakes of guilt or uneasiness through Enne's heart. As her first night in New Reynes had proved, Enne could do what it took to survive. She wouldn't have lasted this long otherwise.

Enne backed deeper into the cellar, toward the wine rack. Behind her, her hand found its way onto the neck of a bottle.

"There must be a mistake," she said smoothly. "Surely you can hear yourself. How could anyone believe such an outrageous claim?"

Do I believe her? Enne didn't have time to figure that out.

"I don't make mistakes," Lola snarled.

"Everyone makes mistakes."

Lola advanced, her knife raised high. "It's nothing personal, but the person I love lives in this city, and we can't afford another street war. You'll be a weapon to whoever owns you."

"I'm just a girl," Enne countered. "And no one owns me."

Enne had always been a good liar, but her fear made her voice shake. Her words sounded obviously false, even to herself.

"It'll be quick," Lola assured her. "It'll barely hurt at all."

Don't reveal your emotions.

Trust no one.

Never find yourself lost.

"I could pay you," Enne lied.

"I'm not for sale."

"You're not even making sense. My eyes are brown."

Lola smirked and beckoned with her scalpel. "Come closer so

I can get a good look at them." As Lola took another step in her direction, Enne squeezed the bottle's neck. She was sore from rehearsal, and the blood gazer had almost nine inches on her. Enne's chances of overpowering her were low. But even if she escaped, then Lola would reveal her secret, true or not. Either option meant death. "Mizer talents don't work like the rest of them. They need to be triggered. Your eyes aren't purple *yet*."

"Then what harm could I cause?" Enne's heart pounded so hard she thought her bones might shatter. There was no negotiating with this girl. This was headed nowhere but violence.

"As long as you're alive, you're a threat."

Then Lola lurched forward to strike.

Enne jumped out of the way and smashed the bottle against the cinder-block wall. It shattered, and the pinot grigio splashed over her skirt and puddled on the floor. The two held their weapons out, as if challenging one another, although it was clear which of them had the upper hand. To Enne's despair, her bottle had broken at the end of the handle rather than the wide part, yielding a blade no longer than a few inches.

Enne lunged for the other door, but Lola jumped, aiming for her back. Instead, she cut Enne's upper arm, slicing through the sleeve of her blouse. Enne screamed and slipped, knocking against the wood of the door with a *thud* and crumpling to the ground.

Lola dived for Enne's leg, but Enne managed to kick her in the chest. Lola sprawled backward, landing hard on her tailbone with a gasp. While the blood gazer collected herself, Enne scrambled to the door and twisted the handle, and she tumbled forward into a stairwell.

Enne raced up the steps, two at a time, grabbing the railing to launch herself forward.

Upstairs was wreathed in darkness. She entered a new room and squinted at the only piece of furniture: a grand piano with a sheet draped over it, visible only as a shadow beneath the dim moonlight in the window. She frantically sprinted around, her hands held out in front of her, feeling for the wall or another door.

Before she could find an exit, Lola stumbled out of the stairwell. In the dark, Enne could hear the blood gazer more than see her as she pounced forward.

Enne narrowly missed the trail of Lola's knife. The blood gazer was slower and more uncoordinated than Enne had dared to hope. Even with Lola's height, Enne was simply more athletic. As Lola stomped and lurched, like a bear swatting at a bird, Enne danced around her and kicked her behind the knees. Lola crumbled, her boot clunking the leg of the piano, sending a cacophony of reverberations through the room.

Mere moments after Lola hit the floor, startled and knocked out of breath, Enne snatched the knife out of her grip and stepped on Lola's arm to pin her down.

"There," Enne said shrilly. She pointed the knife at Lola, her heartbeat wild, angry scarlet bursting in the corners of her vision. Enne let out a guttural groan of victory from a place inside herself she didn't recognize.

Lola stilled. Enne could make out only hints of her expression in the darkness. Defiance. Surprise. Fear. Enne wasn't used to inspiring such emotions. But she didn't falter, nor did her hand tremble as she squeezed the knife's handle. If anything, she felt triumphant. She'd been belittled. She'd been threatened. She'd been assaulted.

"Remind me what you were planning on doing with me," Enne said, her voice low, quiet and—even to her own ears—threatening.

Lola lifted her chin up haughtily. She said nothing.

Enne was now in the position to make demands, but she had little idea which decision was the wisest. Certainly, it would be safest to kill someone who wanted her dead.

She pressed the knife against Lola's throat, and the blood gazer whimpered, all bravado disappearing in a moment.

It was the whimper—not her own murderous thoughts—that startled Enne. Was she prepared to kill a girl no older than herself? Was she prepared to kill anyone at all?

Enne had left her world behind to come to New Reynes, and each new day had revealed a new sacrifice. Her freedom. Her innocence. Her identity. The more the city took from her, the more her resolve grew to protect the remnants of her old life she had left. Her hope. Her self. Her survival.

"I didn't come to New Reynes for trouble, if that matters to you," Enne hissed. "There are people I care about in this city, too."

Lola's eyes softened. Barely.

"Tell me about my talents," Enne demanded.

"Your full name is Enne Dondelair Scordata," Lola whispered, and Enne froze. "Do you see now why I'd call you a threat?"

Enne barked out a laugh. A *Dondelair*? Even in Bellamy, they knew of that family. Every word Lola uttered was growing more and more absurd.

But against all rationale, a part of her wanted to believe it. Despite their infamous treachery, the Dondelairs had once been considered one of the most renowned families of acrobatics, and Enne, who had spent her entire life considered common, hungered to be called exceptional. Just once.

But Lola was right to call Enne a threat. A Mizer and a Dondelair. Either was worthy of execution. If Lola was to be believed, Enne had been a criminal since the day she was born.

"Who were the Scordatas?" Enne asked.

"I don't know," Lola answered. "Not one of the royal bloodlines of Reynes. It came from your father's side."

Her father. The father Lourdes had claimed was a dancer, from a common family of one of the most common talents. Enne had always assumed Lourdes hadn't known her father, and Enne had rarely dwelled on him. She'd liked to imagine that he was alive somewhere, that he'd found a happy ending, even if her mother's had been tragic.

But Lola's claims meant that both of her parents, beyond a reasonable doubt, were dead.

"I don't want to kill you," Enne said. She reached for Lourdes's rules, for familiar words to recite until she once again felt at ease. But her mouth was dry. Lourdes had lied. Not just about her politics, about her double life, but about Enne's very identity, and Enne, miles away from her home, a knife clutched in her trembling hand, dried blood crusting her arm, didn't know how she would ever forgive her. "But I came to New Reynes to save someone, and I'd rather shed tears over her. Not a stranger who wishes me dead."

Lola bit her lip and lifted her head higher, away from the knife. "Please don't," she whispered.

Enne's choices, as it turned out, were one mistake after another. Tracking down Lola was a mistake—now she had secrets she didn't want and a blood gazer who could only become a liability. Finding Levi was a mistake—he knew no more about Lourdes's whereabouts than Enne did. Journeying to New Reynes was a mistake—if Lourdes could never be found, then the only other things Enne had left were in Bellamy, at home. But now, thanks to Vianca's omerta, she couldn't even go back.

Not everything she had was in Bellamy, she reminded herself. Lourdes was, hopefully, here. Levi was here. Her answers were here. Her desire to return home was only a desire to forget this place, and Enne was beyond forgetting. She had already passed the point of no return.

"Then give me a way out," Enne pleaded.

"I won't tell anyone who you are. I promise."

"Your promise means nothing. You wanted to kill me just for being who I am."

Lola glared at her. "Fine. I'll swear to you." She made a crossing motion over her chest, the same as the Irons did for Levi.

Enne nearly laughed. Swearing was for cheats like Levi and snakes like Reymond. Enne was simply a girl from a finishing school.

"What good will that do? I'm not a street lord."

"There's power in an oath. I wouldn't be able to tell someone even if I wanted to."

That didn't make sense: only talents held power. The concepts of magic or anything more than that came from the Faith, from the stories the Mizer kings told to shape themselves into gods. Like Lourdes, Enne was a pragmatist; there had been no fairy tales and ancient lore in their household growing up. What Lola claimed was impossible.

"That can't be true," Enne said.

"Like your talents can't be true?" Lola countered.

Enne clenched her teeth. Even if the oath's power was real, that made her no better than Vianca. But it was also the only option they both had left.

"Aren't you a Dove?" Enne asked.

Lola laughed bitterly. "No. I don't wear the white for…" Her mouth snapped shut, and she averted her gaze. "I'm not."

Several moments passed in silence because Enne didn't know what else to say. She lowered the knife away from Lola's neck. Lola sighed, rubbed her throat where the knife had been, and sat up. She glared at Enne with contempt, and Enne hated seeing it.

I had no other choice, Enne told herself.

"I, Lola Baird Sanguick, swear to Enne Dondelair Scordata."

That's not my name, Enne thought, too numb to interrupt Lola's speech.

"Blood by blood. Oath by oath. Life by life. I swear to live by the code of those before me—" she crossed her heart a second time "—and if I break this code, let me burn until I am only a shade."

The words left an unsettling clamor in the air, as if they existed longer than simply when spoken.

"Is that it?" Enne breathed. She held out her hand to help Lola up.

The blood gazer ignored it. "That's it," she said, climbing to her feet.

Rain drummed on the roof, and Enne could hear the rushing of water in the gutter outside.

"There's a good chance you'll never see me again," Enne started. "But if I needed to find you, would I come here?"

"Yes." When Enne opened her mouth to tell her she was staying at St. Morse, Lola said, "Don't tell me. It's better I don't know where you are."

Enne considered apologizing, but she wasn't sorry that she was alive.

She needed to go home and think about what she'd learned, and about what these secrets meant for her relationship with Lourdes—or if she even believed them.

"I'd like my gun back before I go," she said.

Before they could return to the basement, another door burst open, and Enne screamed in surprise. Levi and Jac charged inside, rain-soaked, pointing a new set of pistols wildly around the room. Jac flipped a light switch.

"What the *muck*?" Lola shouted, her arms raised, squinting in the light.

Levi's eyes narrowed as he looked between them in confusion. "Why did you scream?" he was asking Enne, but his gaze—and Jac's—was fixed on the white in Lola's hair.

"Because you scared me," Enne said flatly.

"Pup?" Lola said, shakily lowering her arms.

"Do I know you?" he asked.

"It's your hair. Not many orb-makers on the North Side."

Jac pocketed his gun. "What happened here?"

"The missy was just leaving. You should, too." Lola rubbed her temples. "I don't like guns or dogs in my office."

"You're both a little scruffed up," Levi said, making no indication that he'd heard the jibe at his nickname. "Had a bit of an argument?"

Both Enne and Lola were covered in sweat, dirt and dried blood. Enne bit her lip. She hadn't even had time to process Lola's information for herself—she wasn't sure she was ready to tell Levi. And she definitely wasn't ready to tell Jac, whom she barely knew. If Lourdes's connection to monarchists had been dangerous, then Enne's very association was deadly, and she could trust no one.

"Forget it," Enne said. "We're leaving as soon as I get my gun."

"*Your* gun?" Levi barked out madly. She squeezed Levi's arm in response, so he couldn't shrug her off. As Lola walked down the stairway to the cellar, the three of them lingered in the piano room.

"Are we keeping secrets now?" Levi hissed in her ear. His breath was hot against her neck.

She backed away from him. "I don't want to talk about this here."

"You know that girl is a Dove, right?" Jac asked. "The gang of assassins?"

"I know what the white hair means," Enne snapped. "But she's not a Dove. She—"

"Obviously not," Levi said darkly, "or you'd be dead." Enne shuddered. "I need to know what happened."

"Why do you *need* to know, Levi?" she seethed.

"Because I'm helping you, remember?"

"I was doing fine on my own." That was mostly true—she'd handled it, anyway.

"Were you?" He reached for her hand, but she quickly hugged her arms around herself. "You'd rather I leave?"

"I'd rather you stop being difficult."

He opened his mouth like he wanted to argue something else, then snapped it shut and shook his head. Behind him, Jac was peering out the window, as if he thought he'd find more Doves lurking on Lola's front lawn.

Lola climbed back up the stairs and handed Enne the gun. Levi reached for it sourly, but Enne quickly shoved it in her pocket. He didn't need two. She'd give it back to him later.

"Don't follow us," Jac warned Lola, his chest puffed out.

She picked her scalpel up off the ground and licked her lips. "Why? Worried what would happen once you split up, and it isn't three against one?" Jac paled and kept one hand on his holster.

Despite her threat, Enne strongly doubted Lola would try anything. If Enne could overpower her, she was sure Jac could as well with his strength talent. Maybe Levi, too. She wasn't a real Dove.

Enne walked to the door. "Let's go." To her surprise, the boys followed, and Lola slammed the door behind them.

No one spoke until they reached the safety of the crowds on Tropps Street.

"She wasn't that scary," Jac said. "For a Dove."

"Right," Levi said sarcastically. "You nearly mucked yourself when she picked up that knife."

"I'm not afraid of knives. One time, I cracked a switch-blade—"

"With your teeth, and it was very impressive. I was there, re-member?" Levi's voice sounded tired.

Jac elbowed Enne in the side. "Aren't you going to say any-thing?"

"Yes," she said, bristling. "Your stitches look horrifying."

"I told you," Levi muttered.

"They make me look tough," Jac said.

"No, they make you look ridiculous."

Levi and Jac continued to exchange words about the next day and Jac sleeping on Levi's couch. But no matter what Jac said, all of Levi's answers were terse, letting the silence hang in the air. He was clearly waiting for Enne to explain herself, but he was going to be disappointed. She was tired. She had rehearsal tomorrow. And she needed to think.

They paused outside St. Morse.

"That's it?" Jac asked her. "No thank you for coming to your rescue?"

"You didn't rescue me." She turned to walk through the revolving doors, but Levi grabbed her arm.

"Tomorrow," he said. It wasn't a command, but a request. For once, his expression betrayed his thoughts. He looked worried. And he was right to be.

"Tomorrow," she promised.

DAY FOUR

"Desire fame, and the city will
make you a tragedy."

—*The City of Sin, a Guidebook:
Where To Go and Where Not To*

LEVI

Levi was on dangerous ground with Enne Salta.

He'd known it since the beginning. Her connection to monarchists, Alfero's Shadow Card, whatever had happened at the blood gazer's... Enne's secrets followed her like a shadow, and Levi was shatz to mix himself up with her. If he had any sense left to him, he'd call it quits. Never mind that he'd given his word; he hadn't known what he was getting himself into, and he was already in enough trouble.

But maybe he didn't have any sense about him. Every time Enne surprised him, he craved a little more trouble.

He poured himself a cup of coffee and tried to decide exactly what he should do about himself. About Enne Salta. About Enne Salta and himself.

Someone pounded on the door. Levi scowled. It might've been Enne, and he hadn't come to a decision yet about their... working relationship. And he knew that if she barged into his apartment, all hands on her hips and flushed cheeks, he'd be incapable of anything but "yes."

It was Jac. He crossed his heart and brushed past Levi, his blond hair dripping with sweat.

Levi's brows furrowed. "Didn't you just leave?"

"I did. And I ran all the way back here," he said, panting.

"What happened?"

Jac leaned against the doorframe, gathering his breath, and snatched Levi's coffee from his hands. "There's a huge fight—" he took a swig "—in Scrap Market. Scarhands and Torren's men."

"*Torren's* men?" Levi echoed. Why would they care about the Scarhands? They might've shared some territory, but the Families and the gangs had agreed long ago not to interfere with each other, in an effort to maintain order in the North Side. The only other connection the Torren Family had to the Scarhands was the investment scheme, but they couldn't have uncovered his partnership with Reymond. Both of them had covered their tracks too well.

Still, dread knotted in Levi's throat. This couldn't be his fault.

"I didn't see it happen," Jac explained. "I ran into Chez—he was *really* running, you know? Trying to warn the other Irons away from Scrap Market."

"Where is the Market today?" Levi asked.

"Chez said near the clock tower on the border of Dove and Scar Lands."

Levi grabbed his jacket and hat off the coatrack. "Let's go."

Jac leaned over, his hands on his knees, and gave Levi a thumbs-up. He set the empty mug on the counter. "Yep. Yep, all good. Ready to go."

Ten minutes later, they were racing down Tropps Street toward Scrap Market. The morning was cool and damp from dew, and a wind blew east, carrying the smell of the sea.

"We could've taken the Mole," Jac huffed.

"No one takes the Mole." The subway system that sprawled across the city was infamously unreliable.

"No, *gangsters* don't take the Mole," Jac retorted. "You'd just rather skulk around everywhere so you look with it."

"I *am* with it." Levi charged ahead of him. "You're just getting soft."

They passed the Luckluster Mole stop. Jac groaned longingly in between pants.

"Do you know what this fight is about?" Levi asked.

"No idea."

They turned the corner into Scrap Market. It was early—too early for the Market to close—but already people were in a rush to pack up their stalls. Levi and Jac ran against the crowd, knocking vendors and customers out of their way. Down the street, the bottom floor of an old tenement—the Scarhands' residence for the day—was engulfed in flames. Smoke streamed out of the cracks in its shutters, and the closer they got, the more the air reeked of it.

They shoved their way to the front of the spectators watching the fire. A man stormed out the front door, clutching a girl over his shoulder. She kicked and pounded at his back with hands covered in scars. The Scarhands outside watched the burning building in horror. Although several had guns raised, no shots were fired. Most people seemed confused about what was happening.

A Scarhand beside Levi pointed at the balcony on the second floor, where Jonas Maccabees was fighting three men at once. Blood ran down Jonas's split lip and nose. He dodged a swing toward his stomach and collided with the balcony railing.

"What's going on?" Levi yelled to the Scarhand beside him, but he couldn't hear his response over the noise of the crowd.

Someone screamed from inside the building. A moment later, the flames exploded through the third story. The building would fall within a few minutes, and whoever had screamed was still in there. But no one dared approach. Not the Scarhands. Not the whiteboots. Not Sedric's men.

"Hold my hat," Levi told Jac, who took it before realizing what Levi intended to do.

Levi lurched forward. Within three steps, a man grabbed his shoulder. He was more than a head taller than Levi. "You can't go near there!" he hollered.

"Someone's still inside!" Levi ripped out of his grasp and sprinted to the entrance. The man tried to follow, but Levi slammed the door closed behind him and locked it.

"Who's in here?" he yelled. Fire reached for him from the walls, but it couldn't hurt an orb-maker. The collapsing building, however, could. He didn't have much time.

The man pounded on the door. Levi ignored him and ran upstairs, where there were two closed doors. He tried the first one and, finding it locked, he pulled out his pistol, shot at the hinges and kicked it open. The apartment was filled with smoke, but empty of occupants. On the balcony outside, Jonas and the men were gone—climbed down, or perhaps fallen.

Someone shouted for help from the other apartment. It sounded like Reymond.

"Reymond!" Levi screamed. He coughed from the smoke, but it wasn't enough to slow him down. He charged back into the hallway, toward the other door. "Reymond!"

There was no second yell. Levi's heart raced. *No no no.* This wasn't how Reymond Kitamura was supposed to die.

Levi aimed his gun. "If you're in there, get away from the door," he called. Still, no one answered. His stomach lurched. He had to save his friend.

Three shots. His ears rang.

"I'm coming!" He kicked open the door. "Reymond?"

But before Levi could step over the threshold, strong arms grabbed him from behind. It was the man from outside. He pressed something against Levi's hand, and his vision blackened. He glimpsed a flash of silver and struggled to hold on to consciousness.

It slipped away, and he fell into darkness.

★ ★ ★

He woke in the hallway with black and white doors.

Levi got to his feet. His clothes smelled of smoke, for some reason, and dirt was caked into the skin between his fingers. He wiped them on his pants and peered down the hallway. It stretched on endlessly in both directions. Everything was quiet.

Remembering that the black doors were locked, he opened the first white one he came to.

Suddenly, Levi was eleven years old again, and he stood by his mother's bedside, rubbing her hand to generate the warmth she was quickly losing. The covers no longer moved as she breathed. She was cold. But he was still holding her hand, still rubbing, still hoping.

This was his fault, the vision told him. All his fault.

He ran downstairs to his father, who was bent over his oven, twisting a rod into the fire. The glass orb on the end sparked white with volts, and, dimly, Levi heard screaming from inside the forming sphere, heard the auras of those who had made the volts and the anguish of their murders. It made Levi's skin crawl, made him want to throw up.

His father was muttering something about "his king," the Mizer he'd mourned all these years. It was very like him. Some days, it seemed as if he couldn't remember what had happened, where his family lived now, and he obsessed over the past like it was a lock whose combination he'd forgotten. Levi had learned by now not to ask about it.

Noticing Levi behind him, his father handed him the rod. "You do it."

"No." This was their eternal argument. Levi had tried to explain to his father before that his blood and split talents simply didn't mix, that he'd gladly accept his family's disappointment over enduring the screams he heard when sealing volts within glass.

His father growled and shoved the rod toward his son. Levi

ran through the door that led to their backyard, led to his escape, but when he crossed the threshold, he was in the hallway again, panting from the aftereffects of the memory.

Voices shouted from the black door in front of him. He pressed his ear against the wood.

"You can't go in there! You know that!" Something slammed.

"I'm sorry! I'm sorry!" The voices were female. Levi didn't recognize either of them. The second one sounded young—a girl.

"I can't do my job if you don't do yours." The first voice was softer now. "We need to keep each other safe."

Levi pulled his head back. He shouldn't have listened. The black doors didn't belong to him, but he wondered who else had seen this place.

"Levi!" Jac shook his shoulders.

Levi's eyes flew open. He rolled onto his side and coughed.

Jac smacked Levi on the back. "What were you thinking?"

"Get off me." Levi rubbed his eyes and looked at the building—or what remained of it. The top floor had collapsed, so wooden beams jutted out of the structure like fiery stakes. His mouth went dry. "Reymond was in there."

"I know," Jac said quietly. "The Scarhands' oaths were broken."

Around them, the Scarhands sat in the center of the cobblestoned street, pressing their hands to their chests as if they couldn't breathe.

It hurt when your oath broke. Reymond had once described it like a blow to the chest, and you could only sit there and wait to catch your breath. Reymond had lost his when he was a Dove, fighting back after Ivory's second cut off one of his fingers. His oath snapped. Then her second cut off another.

Reymond had always acted like nothing could touch him, but in a few hours, a coroner would identify him by his teeth.

Levi felt a surge of emotions all at once. Anger, grief, fear. If he'd been faster, he might've saved him. Stronger. *Better.*

"Jonas will be the new Scar Lord," Jac said warily.

Jonas hated Levi, so any semblance of friendship they'd had with the Scarhands was gone.

Something was crumpled in Levi's fist. He opened it and stared at the gleaming silver back of a Shadow Card, smeared with black ink. The man must've left it in Levi's hand once he'd used it to knock him out.

Six more days. Don't forget.—S.T.

"This is my fault," Levi whispered, echoing his vision. Sedric had said something about reminders; Levi hadn't fully considered what that that could mean.

"'S.T.'? As in Sedric Torren?" Jac asked, his voice cracking. "Why would he go after Reymond?"

"He's playing with me," Levi choked. It was fitting, for Sedric's reputation. Sedric was proving he knew how to hurt him in more ways than one, and he'd succeeded.

Levi turned the card over and studied the picture of a man dangling from the gallows. The Hanged Man. It meant sacrifice, a new point of view and waiting.

"I don't like this," Jac said. "This is some serious muck."

Once again, Levi was eleven years old, and he was at his mother's bedside. Just another person he couldn't save. "He was like my brother," he murmured. "And he's dead because of me."

"Sedric killed Reymond, not you."

"But it's still my fault."

Reymond's murder was a reminder. A *reminder.* They weren't kidding around with the Shadow Cards. If Levi didn't make the deadline, he was dead. He'd get the invitation card, and no one survived the Shadow Game. No one.

Worse, this might not have been Sedric's only reminder— anyone could be next. Any of the Irons, including Jac.

"I think I'm gonna be sick," Levi said. He lay on his side,

his cheek in the dirt, and took deep, slow breaths. The wooden beams cracked in between the roars of the fire. In the distance, sirens wailed, far too late.

"I thought you said the cards didn't give you visions," Jac said. "But an orb-maker wouldn't pass out from the smoke."

"I lied."

"What did you see?" He spoke so quietly that Levi barely heard him over the snaps of breaking wood. The hallway was a whole other level of shatz that Levi couldn't handle right now. In the vision, he'd thought that the black doors belonged to someone else—but the visions were just dreams. If Levi thought about them too much, he'd lose it, and he was running out of things to lose.

"What did you see?" Jac repeated.

Several yards away, Levi caught an Iron watching the scene. He didn't know her name—she was probably a low-ranking runner—nor did he think she recognized him. She smiled. An enemy lord was dead.

What she didn't know was that Reymond had saved Levi from starvation when he was twelve years old. That Reymond had taught Levi everything about being a lord. That, without Reymond, the Irons would've fallen apart years ago.

The second floor of the building collapsed, tearing the rest of the structure down with it. A wave of dirt and pebbles crashed over the street, and Levi covered his eyes. Dust coated his lips. He spit, then he grabbed his hat off the ground, shook it clean and whispered a goodbye.

Vianca's secretary looked up from her files. "Mr. Glaisyer! Madame Augustine—"

Levi threw open the door before she could finish.

He'd been working for Vianca for four years, and still her office made him nervous. Decorated in velvet and swathed in darkness, a luxurious cave with a dragon lurking within. Her menacing eyes peered at him in the dim lamplight.

"Levi," she purred. "It is *always* a pleasure."

Her aura smelled like emerald green, pines and vinegar. It wafted about the room, curling into corners, kissing the skin on Levi's neck. He shook off his revulsion and leaned against the bookcases, his arms crossed.

"Reymond Kitamura is dead," he spat. He was too furious for the words to register, even though it was he who spoke them. It felt as though he'd been shot, but was in too much shock to feel the pain.

Although Vianca didn't smile, she had a way of making her frowns look like pleasure. "Is that why you're covered in dirt?" She preferred Levi to wear suits, especially the crisp ones she bought him. Every time he stepped outside of St. Morse, she wanted the city to know he was hers. He never obliged, and the omerta never forced him. Still, he knew her wishes. He knew how she liked him.

Like a puppet, dangling on her strings.

"I was there," he fumed. "He was murdered. And it was *your* fault."

She pursed her lips and poured herself a cup of tea from the black pot with the jagged handle. Levi could tell it was her favorite blend—the tea smelled bitter, even from across the room.

"How exactly am *I* responsible for the death of *your* business partner?" she asked. Her gaze roamed up his body and his clothes, searching for tears and bruises and weak spots like a miner searching for gold.

"Sedric's thugs locked him in a building and burned the place down." Levi shuddered—he could still see the flames when he closed his eyes.

"You think killing Reymond—who was a perfectly successful criminal in his own right—was a message for you? How..." She sipped her tea. "Narcissistic."

His nostrils flared. "I *know* it was a message for me." He took the two Shadow Cards out of his pocket and tossed them on her desk.

She paled. The silver backs of the cards glinted like blades in the lamplight. Shakily, she reached for them. "How did you get these?" she rasped. She traced a long manicured nail over one of the edges, as though searching for a trick.

"They were gifts from Sedric Torren. One three nights ago. One today."

"The House of Shadows has been empty since the Great Street War." The House of Shadows was the mysterious mansion where the Phoenix Club had once played the Shadow Game. Legend claimed it was haunted.

"Not anymore," Levi said. He didn't add what he knew about Lourdes Alfero, that he might not have been the Phoenix Club's first victim since their grand reopening.

"Six more days," she read. "Until what?"

"Until my deadline. Until I'm dead." He slammed his hands on her desk. "Ten *thousand* volts. Are you happy now? Your scam is going to get me killed." He took the clock off her desk and chucked it against the wall. It shattered. Vianca didn't even wince, which only enraged him further. Nothing touched her, yet every attack pierced him. "And where were you? Away! Away campaigning for a hopeless election that's already rigged against you."

She said nothing, which was fine with Levi. He wasn't finished yet.

"And Enne! I bring her here because she needed help. Thick of me to trust that you, just once, would actually help someone. Help *me*." He panted, out of breath from shouting. The secretary outside had probably heard everything he said, but he didn't care. He was furious enough to kill Vianca...if only he could.

Slowly, Vianca stood up, and Levi instantly felt smaller. Younger. Weaker.

"I don't know how you managed to find out about Miss Salta, but we can talk about that in a moment. Let's talk about *you* first." She flicked her hand, and Levi's body crumpled automatically into a chair. As if by invisible restraints, his wrists tethered themselves to the armrests, and his head leaned back, exposing his neck. Even as he writhed, he was powerless to get up. "Let's talk about *us*." She dragged her jagged fingernail across his throat. Levi swallowed, hating the fear flooding into his chest.

"You walk around here like you're some kind of prince, but even you're disposable."

"Am I?" he challenged. He didn't know much about Vianca's other associates—she kept him decidedly separate from most aspects of her business—but he knew he was her favorite. She'd been attached to him from the moment she met him. Otherwise, why waste one of her precious three omertas on just a boy? She'd spotted a stray puppy and had wanted to keep him. Even if he was her most successful card dealer, the city was full of card dealers. That wasn't why he mattered. He was indispensable because he was the only person Vianca Augustine cared about—and that was why she tormented him.

"Of course you are," she seethed. Her nails dug into his shoulder, and he winced. "Really, Levi, I never would've expected this sort of fear from you. It's unbecoming."

"Only a fool wouldn't fear the Phoenix Club," he said. Vianca wouldn't challenge that. She feared them, too, just like everyone else who'd heard the legends of New Reynes and knew them to be true.

"I know you, dear," Vianca murmured. "You love power. You love to hold all the cards in your hand and make a good show. But your poker face needs work. I can read you like the tea leaves in the bottom of this cup." She poured the steaming tea on his shirt, staining it. The heat didn't bother him due to his blood talent, but that wasn't the point. The point was that Vianca could do whatever she liked, and Levi was helpless to stop her. "You're supposed to be great, Levi. You're the Iron Lord. Yet you let the city decide your fate for you."

"None of this was my choice," he growled.

"Really? You take none of the responsibility?" She turned away and released him from his restraints. He snapped forward and rubbed his neck where she had grazed him, as though her touch alone had left behind a scar. "Maybe you could be better. All this time, I've been trying to make you *better*."

"For what?"

She smiled and sat back down behind her desk. "Use your imagination."

He held back a roll of his eyes. She was always so mucking dramatic. Maybe she had time for her games, but his was running out.

"Why did you choose Enne?" he asked.

"You might wear a suit, but you're not exactly someone I can send to the South Side. She'll have her uses." Vianca didn't know the half of it. If she discovered Enne was the daughter of Lourdes Alfero, she'd utterly exploit her to the monarchists. And it would be Enne who was killed, in the end—not Vianca. Never Vianca.

"Like with Sedric Torren?" he asked, his voice quiet and steady and laced with hate.

"That was a fortunate coincidence. She looks very his type."

Levi clenched his fists. All of the North Side was aware of Sedric's reputation. "That's repulsive."

"Oh, I agree. Who better to strike such a man where it hurts?"

"Don't pretend that anything motivated you besides your own sick mind."

She *tsk*ed. "Watch what you say. I thought you were here asking for my help, Levi."

"It's not just help. You owe me."

"I *owe* you?"

"Sedric is going to kill me over your investment scheme, and you made Enne one of your twisted playthings. Yeah. I'd say you owe me."

She leaned forward and clicked her fingernails together. "Because I bestowed my omerta on Miss Salta, *you* are the one who deserves the recompense?"

He stumbled over his words. She made him sound like a brat. "You're dangling me as bait in front of your enemies."

"I've provided you with a place to live and steady income."

"You do that for all your employees."

"Ah, yes. You're *special*."

She was trying to make him feel like an egotistical child, and he wanted to strangle her. He wanted to summon a fire that left burn marks around her neck.

"Yes, I'm special," he growled. "I helped bankrupt all your competitors. I've made you plenty of volts dealing, not to mention *thousands* through the investment scheme. Thousands you managed to lose overnight. Your empire is falling."

Her lips played at a smile. She poured herself a new cup of tea. "And your empire? How are the Irons faring lately? How is their lord treating them?"

Oh, she was keeping tabs on his gang now? "Stop comparing us. We're not the same."

"You're the spitting image of me." Somehow her voice was proud and ruthless all at once.

"Then it's no wonder the Irons are crumbling," he snapped. "Must've gotten that from you."

He inhaled sharply as what felt like a knife twisted into his gut. He couldn't exhale. The pressure in his chest tightened, and he was sure it would crush him. He grabbed the edge of the desk in front of him. He couldn't scream. He couldn't gasp. He couldn't coax a shred of air out of his lungs.

Vianca didn't release him until he was on the floor, his back digging into the leg of his chair. Then the air burst out, and he coughed and rested his head against the ground as the ceiling slowed its spinning. He'd experienced her torture dozens of times, but he'd never get used to the feeling of suffocating.

"Enough," she commanded, her lips pursed. "What puppet is allowed to say such things to its master?"

She bent over him as he weakly got to his knees. "I've given you everything, and I *will* give you half the volts you need to pay Torren. But don't assume I care so much about you that you're invincible. I could kill you at any moment I wish."

Five thousand volts.

Five *thousand*.

He could survive this. A burst of hope filled his chest, sweeter and more relieving than the air.

"Does this cover the recompense for Miss Salta and Mr. Kitamura?" she asked.

He wasn't thick enough to answer. Everything in this city had a price, and telling Vianca off wouldn't have done him any good. What he was feeling right now, it wasn't even close to gratitude, but he knew better than to act anything less than beholden.

"I can give you the volts next week," she said.

"I only have six days left," he croaked.

"Then a few days from now. I won't forget."

ENNE

If Enne could conquer her fear of heights, then she could knock on a gentleman's door the hour after her bedtime.

She reminded herself that Levi Glaisyer was no gentleman.

When Levi answered the door, his hair was wet, and he smelled like soap and freshly applied cologne. He wore a casual pair of trousers, dark socks and a white undershirt. Something stirred in her stomach as he leaned lazily against his doorway.

"'Lo, missy," he said. "Have you come to share secrets?"

"Something like that," she said, and hurriedly brushed past him before he could see her face redden.

Last time she'd come here, his apartment had been impeccable. Now dishes lay in the sink and he'd closed his blinds, so the only light came from a dim lamp beside his couch. A half-finished art piece, mostly emerald green swirls and spikes, rested on the coffee table, surrounded by papers and oil paints. Water splotches—possibly intentional—dotted the canvas. Thin lines like puppet strings stretched from the top of the painting to the green smudges.

Interesting. She'd never imagined Levi as an artist. She couldn't tell if he was a particularly good one, though—she didn't understand what the painting represented.

"I thought we should talk about last night," Enne said. Since they'd left the blood gazer's, the black seed of doubt about Lourdes had grown into a forest, and Enne was lost in its center. She hadn't believed Lola's accusation at first—hadn't *wanted* to believe it—but the more she reflected on it, the more the pieces she knew of her past began to make sense.

He gave her a dark, expectant look and sat down on the couch, motioning for her to join him. "The part about you getting into a fight with a Dove, or the part about what the Dove told you?"

"Both." She hesitated, searching for how to begin. It would be easiest just to blurt out the truth, heave it off her shoulders and let Levi take away her burden. But she wasn't sure how long his loyalty to her would last once he learned she was a Mizer.

"You can trust me," Levi said. "Whatever it is." And criminal or not, she believed the sincerity in his voice. Whether or not she'd still been in danger, Levi had rushed into the Deadman District last night to save her. Guilt pinched inside of her. She wasn't sure she would have done the same for him.

"Once I tell you, you can't unknow it," she warned, because deceit wasn't fair to him. "And I'm grateful for all the help you've given me—I really am, but we've reached a point where my secrets are becoming…dangerous. This one isn't about Lourdes." She looked at her lap. "It's about me."

His pause terrified her. For a moment, she thought he would agree and ask her to leave.

He was all she had.

"Now you have me curious." Levi scooted closer, and her shoulders relaxed. She wouldn't be alone in this. "Are you the long-lost daughter of some wighead—"

"I'm a Mizer," she whispered.

He froze. "That's not possible."

She let out the breath she'd been holding since last night. "Scordata is my blood name. I don't know which kingdom or family it comes from. Probably a minor—"

"She must've been joking," he said abruptly. "It was a prank."

"Knowing Lourdes's history, and seeing how Lola tried to kill me after she told me the truth…I wish it *were* a joke." Enne grabbed one of the throw pillows and hugged it to herself. "That's not even all of it. She said my split name was Dondelair."

Levi choked out a laugh. "Now I think *you're* trying to fool me." Somehow, he still managed one of his smirking smiles at a time like this.

She threw the pillow at him. "I wouldn't joke about this. I'm not…shatz, or whatever you say. I know how dangerous these secrets are."

"That's some very unladylike New Reynes slang, you know." He met her eyes, and she could tell he was searching for any Mizer purple hidden among the brown. She tried not to shiver under his gaze. "Before you tell me this story, I need to know— is the blood gazer taken care of? If she knows, then—"

"She's taken care of," Enne said quietly, remembering the hatred in Lola's eyes after she made the oath.

"Good." He shook his head and stood up. "I'm going to make a drink. Do you want one?"

No, her reflexes said. But she was no longer home. No longer Enne Salta.

"Oh, um. Okay. And cookies, too, if you have them."

He lifted an eyebrow. "You made a dozen the other night. How can you even look at another one?"

"Easily. While salivating."

"Well, you're in luck. I have a box of stale tea cookies just for you."

Several minutes later, he returned with two glasses and a box of gingersnaps. The drink was amber-colored.

"It's called a Gambler's Ruin," he said. "Mix of bourbon and coffee liqueur and orange bitters. Reymond introduced me to it. Sorry—I'm out of garnish."

Enne took a sip and grimaced. She and the boys had very different tastes.

"You're supposed to drink it when you're feeling confident." He laughed hollowly. "'It's flirting with losing just for the thrill of it,' Reymond used to say."

Then Levi downed his drink all at once. He coughed afterward and wiped his lips with the back of his hand.

"Reymond's dead," he murmured.

"What?" Enne asked, certain she'd misheard.

"Sedric Torren had him killed today."

The hair on her arms rose at the mention of Sedric's name. After poisoning him, it had been easy to forget how powerful he truly was. Reymond Kitamura ran the largest street gang in the city, but Sedric Torren could still order his execution and never face justice. If Sedric ever realized the part she'd played in tricking him, she'd share the same fate as Reymond...or worse.

"Levi...I'm so sorry." She'd come here for comfort, but she hadn't even considered that Levi might need some, as well. And now that she knew, she saw the unmistakable shock in his eyes, in the rigid way he was carrying himself. She wanted to hug him, but she was awkwardly curled up on the other side of the couch. And crawling toward him, touching him—that all felt like dangerous ground. She was already on dangerous ground with Levi Glaisyer.

Instead, she reached out and took his hand. He jolted at her touch, but didn't pull away.

"Yeah," he murmured, setting his empty glass down. "I'm sorry, too."

Enne waited another five seconds—counted them precisely in her head—and pulled her hand away. She felt warm all over.

He's not like us, Reymond had said. *He's better than us.*

Feeling even guiltier than before, she took several more sips of her drink. Reymond had warned Enne against leading Levi into trouble, and telling Levi her secret definitely counted as that. She still didn't consider herself ruthless and cunning like the Scar Lord, but she was starting to see what he'd meant when he'd compared them. She'd held a knife to someone's throat. She was the girl who'd poisoned the wolf. She'd lied to Levi from the moment they'd met.

Maybe New Reynes had already corrupted her.

But another, quieter part of her suspected otherwise. Enne should've felt ill walking into rehearsal today, knowing her talent descended from such a notorious bloodline. Instead, she felt exhilarated. In Bellamy, her aspirations had been confined to keeping up and fitting in with her classmates. Never had she been given the chance to excel. Never had she tasted ambition...desire.

For the first time in her life, Enne felt confident. All those years spent agonizing over her shortcomings, all those years attempting to be something she wasn't. At what point in Enne's life had she decided that others controlled what she wanted, that she couldn't just reach out and take it?

Maybe the city hadn't corrupted her at all. Maybe she'd always been this vicious, and the Scar Lord had simply been the first to see it.

"So," Levi said, startling Enne out of her thoughts. "This is where you tell me exactly how you overpowered a fake Dove." Even though Enne had come here expecting to tell him about last night, the strain in his voice told her he was trying to shift the subject away from his friend. She decided to let him...for now. "They teach you hand-to-hand combat at that finishing school of yours?"

"Yes, of course." She grinned. "That's a requirement nowadays to become a lady. I could fight you while balancing books on my head."

"Look at that." He pointed at his arm, and Enne—foolishly—leaned forward to look. He flicked her on the forehead. "I just trembled."

She kicked him in the leg. "Rude."

Then she left her leg there, stretched out, her foot touching him. She felt like every move she made around him was a dare to herself to see how far she would go. And she wasn't sure if she was doing it simply for the thrill, from the drink...or because of something more.

But she wasn't in this city to find romance with street lords; she was here to find her mother. New Reynes was so intertwined with Levi's character that flirting with him would be like flirting with the City of Sin itself, and after all of this was over, Enne still very much intended to return home. Anything between them could only be a distraction. Besides, considering all those articles of clothing left behind in his wardrobe, Levi hardly had reason to find interest in her.

She slid her leg back.

"After Lola told me what she knew," Enne continued, "she decided she'd kill me. She said that my existence was too dangerous for the city." She paused, expecting Levi to deny this, but he only nodded for her to continue. "After that, she attacked me. She's tall, but she's not very fast. It wasn't hard to take her knife."

"Being the expert fighter that you are," he joked.

"I'm stronger than I look. *You* try keeping up with dancing and acrobatics rehearsals all day." She grabbed the box of cookies from the coffee table and tore it open. "If it wasn't for my supposed Dondelair split talent, I'd essentially be pudding right now."

"Yes. Pudding. I'm sure."

She narrowed her eyes and shoved a cookie in her mouth. "Anyway, after that, I didn't know what to do. I couldn't just... *leave.* Lola was set on killing me, and if she told anyone about my talents, the whiteboots would kill me for her." She pulled her gaze away from Levi, in case he noticed the darkness in her eyes from the things she'd done. "So she swore to me. Now she can't tell anyone the truth."

Levi leaned forward and took the box. He slid out several gingersnaps. "When you say swore…?"

"Blood by blood. Life by life. Something like that."

He straightened, then slid closer to her. She really wished he would stop doing that. The smell of his aftershave was annoyingly tempting.

"A street oath?"

"Yes."

"You're a lord?"

"I guess so."

"You've been in New Reynes *four days*, and you're already building yourself a gang? Just what have you been reading in that guidebook of yours?"

She ripped the box out of his hands. "It was the only option. It's not as if I ever need to see her again."

"You might want to. Oaths aren't unbreakable," Levi warned. "There are all sorts of rules about challenging lords and loyalty. Telling your secret to a third party? That would be hard. Killing you?" He made a slicing motion across his throat. "Give the girl a gun, call it a duel and you'll be dead."

None of that seemed very logical to her.

"Well, what else should I do?" Enne had already made up her mind not to kill Lola. In the moment, she could've called it self-defense. But now, it felt cold-blooded. Enne wasn't a villain.

"You should keep an eye on her. Keep your enemies close, and all that. And oaths get weaker when you don't see each other."

"And we'd do…what? Knit? Have tea?"

"I don't know. She probably knows a lot about families and talents, being a blood gazer. Maybe she could help us learn more about these Dondelair and Scordata parents of yours. That could lead us back to Lourdes."

Enne pursed her lips. Lourdes *was* a monarchist and a Mizer sympathizer, so maybe if they found a link between Enne's birth parents and her mother, it would help them in their search. Enne loathed the thought of returning to the Deadman District and confronting the hate in Lola's eyes, but this could be their only lead.

"You're right," she said, reaching for her drink. "We probably *should* ask Lola." The whiskey and coffee liqueur burned their way down her throat.

"There's something else," Levi said, sliding closer again. Now Enne had her arms wrapped around her knees, and Levi was seated facing her, only inches from her feet. She curled in her toes and looked everywhere but at his face. "That card left in Lourdes's hotel room wasn't just a normal playing card."

"What do you mean?"

"It's called a Shadow Card." He bit his lip. "During the Revolution and through the Great Street War, the Phoenix Club was famous for playing something called the Shadow Game. It's a card game where the invited players are…killed."

Her stomach clenched. This was it…this was when she learned that her mother was dead.

"The cards all symbolize different things. Only one card is used for the actual invitation: the Fool," he explained. "That wasn't the card in Lourdes's hotel room, which meant the one we found was only a warning."

"So either Lourdes is hiding from the Phoenix Club," Enne said darkly, "or she's already dead."

"Yes. I suppose it's been that way all along." He placed a hand on her knee. "It isn't as bad as it—"

"Why didn't you tell me about this yesterday?" She shoved his hand off.

"It was dangerous to talk about it in the open. I was going to tell you when we got back to St. Morse, but then you wanted to be alone. And by alone, I mean, steal my best pistol and stroll over to Dove Land behind my back."

Enne curled herself tighter into a ball. "This wasn't how it was supposed to be. I was supposed to come to New Reynes and discover there'd been some terrible storm—maybe that no ships had been sailing for months. And Lourdes would just be here, waiting for her chance to come home." She could picture Lourdes seated outside a café on the South Side, smoking a cigarette and reading the newspaper. In Enne's fantasy, Enne ordered herself a pastry and sat down beside her, and Lourdes told her all about the adventures she had in the City of Sin.

And then they went home.

"I wasn't supposed to be a Mizer." Enne took another sip of her drink. "How am I supposed to go back?"

After the things I've done, she added silently.

"Sometimes we're not who we want to be because we're supposed to be something else," he said. She wondered if he even believed that himself.

Enne leaned against Levi's shoulder, and he wrapped his arm around her. It was a dangerously easy move to make. She felt both comfortable and restless at the same time. Daring herself further, she pressed her cheek into his chest.

"I'm *supposed* to be dead," she whispered.

"That's not what I meant."

Enne stared at Levi's hand, palm facing up on his knee. It would be so easy to take it. But, certainly, she'd had enough thrill for one night. Any more touching and he would know what she was feeling, and she wouldn't be able to take it back. If he knew, if he slid his arm further down her waist, or brushed his forehead against hers, then all she would be able to say was yes.

"I can't even make volts. My talent isn't 'triggered' yet, or whatever Lola said." She was rambling. She crossed her arms, keeping her hand a good distance away from his. "That strikes me as very unfair. Think of how rich we'd be."

Enne bit her lip. She definitely shouldn't have said "we."

"That would…solve a lot of problems," he said slowly. "But then your eyes would turn purple, and it'd be very hard to protect you, then."

"And you would, wouldn't you?" she breathed. These words, too, were a dare. "Protect me?"

Silence. When she looked up at him, her cheek still pressed against his shoulder, he was watching her carefully. He swallowed. "Yes."

Enne had never truly had a friend. Lourdes was the only one who'd listened and advised and cared. And so she was surprised by this truth—that she had become unlikely friends with a street lord. Maybe even more than friends. When she looked at him, she saw someone invested in her search to find her mother, someone who understood the helplessness of Vianca's stare. She suddenly realized that, if he was the one in distress, then she would rush to save him, too.

"You're going to laugh when you hear this," Enne started.

"I usually do—"

"When I left rehearsal today, every single person knew my name." She fiddled with her shirt. Even after telling him the truth of her talents, this confession somehow felt more personal. Maybe because she knew it sounded absurd, even before she explained it. But still, she wanted to share it, and she knew that he would listen. "I've gone to school with girls my entire life who forget my existence regularly. I could walk beneath a spotlight and be mistaken for a shadow."

"Your schoolmates were snobbish," he said.

She shook her head. She knew it would be difficult to put into words. "It's more than that. I stand at the back of the stage for every show. I'm marked absent when I'm the first to arrive. I introduce myself again and again, only to be forgotten." Her breath hitched for a moment, and she quickly swallowed down her flood of emotions. She felt like she was carving herself open and laying it bare. The worst hurt in the world was the kind you grew to accept. "That's the reason I began to doubt. Not because of Lourdes's lies or how easily I've picked up acrobatics. But because I have never impressed anyone—not ever. But since I arrived in New Reynes, people have *seen* me."

"You impress me every time I'm with you." Levi said it so simply, as if he'd repeat those words forever without doubting them, as if those words were cheap. To Enne, they were worth everything.

Enne finished the rest of her Gambler's Ruin. As she set down the glass, her fingers trembled. All of her conflicted emotions had left her heart as sore as her body. She could lie back down on Levi's chest and sleep until morning.

"It's getting late," Levi said softly.

Enne tensed and sat up. "Oh, yes." She hurriedly straightened out her hair. "I should go."

"You don't... Yes. You should." He stood up awkwardly and picked up the glasses and the now-empty box of cookies. "You ate all of these." He tossed the box back on the table.

"You had some."

"Yeah. Maybe two."

"You said they were just for me." She stuck out her tongue.

He laughed. "I'll have to steal more for you tomorrow from the breakfast room."

She liked the idea of him keeping cookies here for her. It gave her more of a reason to come back.

Her guidebook had been wrong about one thing: the most dangerous part of the City of Sin wasn't the beckoning of the card tables or the threat of the gangs. It was the allure of Levi Glaisyer's roguish smile.

She stood up. He was in her way to the door. Standing so close, smelling like he did, looking at her like that...he was quite the obstacle.

Levi reached into the pocket of a jacket on the rack beside

him. He pulled out a key, grinned sheepishly and handed it to her. "It's a spare, to my apartment. Feel free to steal my guns anytime you want, but I'd prefer if you ask me first."

She took the key. Like the weapons he'd offered her, it felt like a dangerous thing.

"Will you be all right?" she asked. She swallowed. She definitely shouldn't invite herself to stay longer, not when he'd already suggested she leave. It was tactless. It was…dangerous. He was her only companion in New Reynes, and she was mistaking his help for something else. "I know you and Reymond were close." It wasn't fair he'd given her comfort when she hadn't returned it. "If you need to talk more—"

"I don't want to," he said quickly. "I mean, not tonight. But you don't have to—"

"Stay, I know. We can meet up again tomorrow. Six o'clock? Right after my rehearsal?"

They locked eyes, making Enne's breath hitch. His free hand reached for hers, then dropped. "I was going to say…never mind. Yes, six o'clock is fine."

Enne hesitated. The intensity in Levi's gaze made her shiver. When he looked at her, he *saw* her. She wanted to disappear into the sanctuary of a shadow. She wanted to remain here forever just to feel his stare. But if she lingered any longer, he would guess at her thoughts. She'd already surrendered so much of herself to the City of Sin, and a kiss from Levi Glaisyer would seal the deal. Her thoughts betrayed her too easily.

She took a step back. "Good night," she said breathlessly.

He licked his lips and pulled away. His poker face, as always, revealed nothing. "Good night."

DAY FIVE

"The South Side may seem safer, reader,
but remember—some monsters wait until your
guard is down to bare their teeth."

—The City of Sin, a Guidebook:
Where To Go and Where Not To

ENNE

Now in possession of a key, Enne let herself into Levi's apartment. It was ten minutes early than their planned meeting time, but Enne had come anyway, anxious from sitting around her apartment after rehearsal with nothing to do but fiddle with her token.

She heard a shower running. She leaned against the bathroom door, feeling both embarrassed and bold. "I was thinking about what you said about oaths," she said, hoping she was loud enough for him to hear. "And I have questions. I read the rest of my guidebook, and I can't find anything about them or *why* they work."

The water turned off, but Levi didn't answer.

"How often do I need to see Lola to make the oath last? Can she tell someone that she's sworn an oath to me, even if she doesn't say anything about what I am? Should I be worried—"

The door swung open, and Enne nearly fell backward.

"What oath?" a male voice asked.

She turned around and gaped. Jac was standing in the bathroom, wearing nothing but a silver Creed necklace and a towel wrapped around his hips. His blond hair dripped down his neck and chest, and Enne saw that his sleeves of black tattoos continued up his shoulders, laced down his stomach, and even grazed his hip bones. On the underside of his elbows, there were several sets of scars—bumpy, but long faded.

Enne flushed multiple shades of scarlet and quickly averted her eyes, backing away from the door.

"I heard everything," he said flatly. He held his hands up, as if Enne was a small animal he might scare off. "I don't really know you, but whatever is going on, I want to help. Levi could use it right now."

Enne hesitated. Not because she didn't trust Jac—he was sworn to Levi after all—but because she suspected Levi would be upset with her if she involved him. Secrets were the deadliest sort of weapons, and Levi had already lost a friend yesterday.

"Tell me what's really going on here," Jac urged.

"I can't," she said.

"I already know your mother is Lourdes Alfero, and I haven't told anyone," he said with a sigh. "You might as well tell me everything—about Lola's oath, what you are. And if you do, I'll tell you all you want to know about oaths and street rules."

He had a point. He already knew half the story.

"Fine," Enne agreed, bracing herself for Levi's fury later. "Just please put some clothes on."

"Are you sulking about Jac, or are you sulking about riding the Mole?" Enne asked Levi. This far down the line, the Mole's train car was empty except for Enne, Levi, Jac and a homeless man sleeping on a row of seats in the back.

Levi kept his hat low, covering his identifiable hair—he'd grumbled the entire ride about someone spotting him and ruining his reputation. The two of them stood, gripping a metal pole. "Both."

"He was very insistent," Enne said.

"I know how he can be," he muttered. "You still shouldn't have told him."

Jac sat behind them, fingering his Creed necklace. A half hour ago, in Levi's apartment, he'd been all jokes and eagerness, but since then, Enne had caught him stealing uneasy glances at her, like she was something dangerous and he shouldn't get too close.

Happy to help, he'd said. Happy until he wasn't.

She tried to convince herself that she was imagining it, but even now, she felt his gaze searing into her. She pushed her anxieties away.

Enne gestured around the train car, trying to change the subject. "The Mole isn't so bad. It's far cleaner than I expected."

"No one rides the Mole."

"It was crowded earlier, so apparently people do."

Levi grumbled something unintelligible and kicked a copy of *The Kiss and Tell* under a seat. Enne didn't know why he was pouting. This was far more preferable than walking all the way to the Deadman District like she had before, and Jac wasn't whining childishly about reputation like Levi was.

"I hope you're thinking of something to say," she said quietly, "because I'd just as rather never see her again."

"Oh, I'm not doing the talking." Levi shook his head. "You're the lord. You think of a reason other than 'I need to make the oath stronger so I know you won't kill me.'"

She rolled her eyes. "I'm not a lord."

"Maybe you weren't two days ago, but that's how oaths work. You're Lola's lord now." He flicked her lightly on the forehead. Enne grimaced. Jac's explanations earlier about her newfound title had confused her more than anything else.

Oaths are the opposite of omertas, he'd said. *Omertas force you to do something, and oaths prevent it*. Before Enne could counter that omertas also prevented her from openly discussing them, Jac was already launching on to new stories. The laws of the streets blended magical oaths, criminal legends and—as far as Enne could tell—utter nonsense. She'd left that conversation with nothing but confusion.

"Maybe you can win Lola over with your charm," Levi said.

Enne very much doubted that. Lola was as easily charmed as barbed wire.

"Don't let her see your fear," Jac reminded her, apparently eavesdropping. "That's the first rule."

It was surreal to hear Lourdes's rules from someone else's mouth. Earlier, Jac had listed all ten of them, in the exact order Enne so often repeated to herself. It was perhaps the most unexpected and unnerving of Lourdes's betrayals, and exactly the sort of thing Enne wished she could ask her mother about, if she was here. Why share these rules with Enne? Why teach her they were something else?

She sighed. It was during moments like these, of anger or sadness or hopelessness, that she missed Lourdes the most. She needed her mother to sort out her confusion, to take her hand and remind her of who she was and what was important.

"Where did the rules even come from?" Enne asked.

"From the Great Street War," Levi answered. "Veil probably wrote them."

"I heard it was Havoc," Jac said. "They were opposing street lords, Veil and Havoc. It's been eighteen years and people *still* take sides."

"It was definitely Veil," Levi repeated.

"You just say that because you worship Veil."

He stiffened. "That's not true."

"When I first met you, you were dressed like him. In costume. You thought you were pretty neat."

Levi kicked Jac in the shin, but Jac kept grinning. Enne relaxed a little at Jac's dimples. Maybe she *was* imagining the tension.

The train car stopped, and they got off. It was early evening, the height of rush hour, yet the Deadman District was mostly quiet. The rain over the past few days had ushered a cool front over the city, and Enne shivered under her jacket. She kept both hands in her pockets. Her right finger traced along the barrel of Levi's gun.

They found their way back to Lola's cellar office and knocked on the door.

Lola's green eyes appeared through the two bullet holes.

Swallowing the guilt and nervousness in her chest, Enne said, "'Lo."

Lola cursed and opened the door. Her white hair was tied into a high bun at the top of her head. "I didn't expect to see you again," she said flatly, tucking her hands into her trousers. She glanced at Levi and Jac. "And you've brought the Iron boys back. What exactly is this?"

Enne met Levi's eyes hesitantly, and he nodded, urging her to speak. It didn't matter what Enne came up with—her self-preservation was entirely transparent.

"I came to New Reynes to find someone," she started. "And after what you told me the other night...we think you might be able to help us."

"I'm no private eye."

"The names you gave me—they're our only leads. If we could find more information about my families, maybe even guess who my birth parents are, it would give us a clue."

"Who are you looking for?" Lola asked.

"My adopted mother."

Lola stared at her disinterestedly.

"Please," Enne added.

Lola made a face like she had a bad taste in her mouth. "Fine. Let me get my knives." She turned and grabbed a belt off her desk; it was covered—every inch of it—in blades. As the group returned to the Mole stop, Lola removed several knives and hid them in strategic places around her body. In her left boot.

Secured in a holster on her right thigh. Several up her sleeves. Three around her waist. One she even slid into a pocket in her top hat, which she wore to cover her white hair.

"Where are we going?" Levi asked uneasily.

"The South Side," Lola replied. "The National Library. It doesn't close until eight o'clock. They have all the census records there."

"And will we need so many knives?" Jac asked, poking at her belt. "I'm not much of a reader, so maybe I'm wrong, but I don't think the books will attack us."

Lola rolled her eyes. "It's not the books I'm worried about." She shot Enne a dark look.

Enne flushed and cleared her throat. "Are you sure we'll find the records there, even for my family?" The wigheads had certainly destroyed all the Mizer records after the Revolution. The Dondelair records might exist, but the chances were still slim. The wigheads believed the only way to defeat a villain was to erase them.

"The records will be hard for *you* to find, yes," Lola answered. "But not for me."

They hopped the gate at the Mole station and waited several minutes for the next train. Advertisements lined the tunnel walls for cabarets, the Regallière seasonal sale and Tiggy's Saltwater Taffy.

"So," Enne began, attempting to make polite conversation with the girl who had tried to murder her only two nights earlier, "are you from New Reynes?"

"Yep."

"Have any family?"

"I had two brothers, once." She kept her sentences purposefully curt and never eased her glare on Enne. "We don't need to be friends, missy."

"I'm just being polite."

"I don't want to get to know you."

"Then don't," she snapped, and turned to Levi. He looked at her red face and flared nostrils in amusement.

"We should've brought your guidebook," he said. "Check off some sightseeing."

Before Enne had arrived at New Reynes, she'd read all the guidebook's chapters on the South Side. There were a few places she would even have liked to visit: the famous university, the glamorous department stores and boutiques of Guillory Street, the national art museums. Before the Revolution, the city of Reynes had been primarily confined to the North Side, so the wealthy had fled the chaos of the uprisings and built anew across the Brint. But while they were busy constructing skyscrapers in the South, the North was left rotting from within.

The train arrived, and it was, once again, empty. Lola took a seat by the window, with Jac sitting opposite her, watching her in case she made a break for it. Enne and Levi hung near the door. Every few moments, Lola turned to glare at them or at Jac, but mostly, she kept her gaze trained out the window, playing a jazz tune on her harmonica.

Levi slapped the metal railing above their heads. "If St. Morse falls through," he said, as if Enne could simply abandon Vianca whenever she pleased, "you could do tricks on the Mole. Put out a volt meter."

Oh, how the lady would've fallen, Enne thought. "Everything in New Reynes is a show. You can't even ride to work without witnessing a performance."

"I like a little entertainment." He grabbed the same bar Enne was holding and swung himself around. Their faces were only inches apart, and the corner of Levi's mouth was turned up into one of his classic smirks. To Lola, they probably looked conspiratorial, even if they were only talking nonsense. Jac probably knew better.

Enne blushed and turned her head away, trying not to think about how hopelessly obvious she was around Levi. Considering the events and many convoluted feelings between them during the past few days, adding attraction into the mix seemed a hopeless and unnecessary complication. She might've cared about Levi, might've liked the way he looked and the way he looked at her, but her focus needed to remain on finding her mother.

"My life has enough entertainment at the moment," she breathed.

"I don't know," he teased, speaking softly into her ear. "You could always use a little more."

"Are you suggesting something in particular?" she asked warily. He had a bad habit of making her nervous, and he knew it. His smirk only got wider.

"If you want something, you should let yourself have it."

She could feel his breath on her neck. It was enough to make her break out in goose bumps, to make her stomach crisscross into frustrated knots. It reminded her of the time they'd walked down Sweetie Street, and Levi had colorfully described the workers' talents for seduction. He'd been mocking her then, and maybe he was now. But she didn't think he'd hint at something like that unless he wanted it, too.

At what point in her life had she decided that others controlled what she wanted, that she couldn't just reach out and take it? Hadn't she just thought those words to herself the night before?

She might've wanted Levi Glaisyer, but she also wanted to return home. If it came down to a choice between them, she would chose Bellamy—perhaps because she desired what she couldn't have more than what was right in front of her. But with an omerta and a thousand miles of ocean between her and home, why shouldn't she have this small consolation?

You wouldn't have wanted him five days ago, she thought. *When you were someone different. The city has already corrupted you.*

New Reynes's constant performers, flashing lights—the whole city was a show and everything had a price. Here, it was easy to forget who you were. Her desire for Levi wasn't really her own—it belonged to someone else. Someone who carried pistols in their pockets and darkness on their conscience.

At least, that was what she kept trying to tell herself.

Enne cleared her throat. "How much longer until we reach the library?" She was in desperate need of a cold breeze.

His eyes drifted away from her lips to the Mole map. "Seven more stops."

"Well then." She grabbed the empty seat beside Jac, putting several feet of distance between her and the source of her distraction. Levi didn't bother to follow. As the train car passed the next several stops and other passengers boarded, Enne did her best to keep her gaze out the window. Even so, she could still feel the heat of Levi's stare.

Lola was the first to move when they reached their stop: Revolution Bridge. It was a major station, busy with people changing lines, full of kiosks selling newspapers and food. Enne's stomach groaned as they passed a doughnut stand.

They climbed several flights of stairs before reaching the street. The change in scenery between this and the North Side was astounding. Here, the white stone buildings were actually still white, many with huge columns and gilded domes. Motorcars honked at jaywalkers sprinting across traffic circles. The men wore checkered suits, their patent leather boots clicking as they walked. Women shuffled by daintily in their hobble skirts, too fitted for them to take long strides.

"It's beautiful," Enne said.

"It's a bit glitzy," Levi answered flatly. Something had clearly soured his mood. "Not really my taste."

"And what is your taste? Cheap cabarets and malt liquor?"

"At least it's honest."

"Says the con man."

"Says the street lord," he countered. "At least I know what I want."

She bristled and took a step closer. "And I don't?" Who cared if she thought the South Side was beautiful? She couldn't even make simple conversation without it becoming a statement on her character.

"No," he dared. "I don't think you do."

Lola cleared her throat, her expression disgusted. "We don't have long before the library closes."

Enne nodded, then rolled her shoulders to try to release her tension. Now she was in a sour mood, too. Distraction, indeed. She didn't even know what they'd been arguing about. They needed to focus on what they'd come here to do.

The library was grand, both on the outside and within. The sunset shining through the stained glass windows cast the bookshelves in a sacred sort of glow. Students crowded each of the tables, pouring over textbooks and old manuscripts. The air smelled of burning candles and the dust of old books. The quiet reverence here didn't seem like it should exist in New Reynes.

"We'll start in the family records," Lola said. She led them to the third floor, to hallways of displeasing metal shelves lined with black, leather-bound books.

"It's all so…sterile," Enne said.

"The Mizers certainly treated family matters as such," Lola said. "For them, talents were commodities. Things to be bred." The accusation in her voice was clear, as though Enne was just as guilty as her ancestors, despite not knowing her family history until two days ago. She opposed their tyrannical reigns as much as Lola did. "When's your birthday?"

"February 2. Year 9." The wigheads had reset the calendar after the Revolution, as it had previously referenced the old Faith.

"Can you find her records from just her birthday?" Jac asked dubiously.

"Of course. This is what I do." Lola followed the shelves down to the ones labeled with the correct year. She grabbed several books and handed one to each of them. "These are all February. They should be in alphabetical order by blood name."

After several moments of riffling through the pages, none of them found a mention of Enne. She wasn't listed under Salta, nor even Scordata, Dondelair or Alfero. They checked every day for the entire year, but there was no evidence of her birth to be found.

"I was expecting that," Lola said nonchalantly, as if it were obvious. Maybe it was—of course Enne didn't have a birth record, being what she was. But this was only another reminder that everything she'd once known about herself was a lie. She was so accustomed to being ordinary and ignored, yet now, even with her notorious heritage revealed, she felt twice as invisible. "We'll try the family trees next." Although Lola's tone wasn't exactly enthused, it was still somewhat optimistic, and Enne clung to the hope that there would be something for them to find. Something to lead them back to Lourdes.

The family lineages were in a hallway much like the previous one. All crates and metal and fluorescent lighting. They sat on the cold white-tiled floor as Lola plucked out a laminated file labeled "Dondelair." She handed it to Enne.

"We won't find any Scordata records here—those have all been destroyed. We're lucky the Dondelairs' haven't been, too," Lola said. "What was your adopted mother's full name?"

Enne took the Dondelair file with unease. It felt criminal even to read it. "Oh, um, Lourdes Reids Alfero."

While Lola hunted for Lourdes's family tree, Enne, Levi and Jac flipped through the Dondelair file. Levi sat beside her, their shoulders almost touching, so he could examine the documents with her. Enne tried to ignore his nearness and focus.

The trees included the names of each family member, their birth dates, their death dates and their causes of death. They looked so clinical, as though they'd been written by coroners rather than historians.

The tree ended abruptly on the last page. "'Claude Dondelair,'" she read, mainly for Jac's benefit. "'Born July 10, 1884 of the old calendar. Died April 18, Year 9. Gunshot wound.'" And beside him: "'Gabrielle Dondelair. Born November 24, 1887 of the old calendar. Died February 3, Year 9. Gunshot wound.'"

Enne shivered. She recognized their names from her history classes. Brother and sister. Arsonists. Circus performers. Traitors.

"This is giving me the creeps," Jac said.

The blood didn't end with Claude and Gabrielle, however. Their mother, Geraldine Dondelair, was hanged later that year. Their split brother, Dorian Dondelair Osire, saw the guillotine. How dramatic.

"'Lo, missy," Levi said. Were they not using first names now? Enne rolled her eyes. "The day Gabrielle Dondelair died…that's the day after your birthday, isn't it?"

They exchanged a glance. That was an unhappy coincidence.

"Well," Enne said, her voice catching, "I'm sure there are other Dondelair women who could be…" She hurriedly flipped through the pages. Every last Dondelair, dead before Year 10. Not even the most distant cousins of Claude and Gabrielle had been spared. Enne pointed out the names of several women who could have theoretically birthed her before their untimely ends.

Lola returned, two more books in hand. "There's no record of this Lourdes Reids Alfero. You sure that's her real name?"

The last salvageable remnants of Enne's happy life in Bellamy were shattering. "No," she murmured. "I guess I'm not."

"You sure she's a Protector?"

"Yes," Enne said. *That* she was certain of. "Just being around Lourdes…you felt safe. She has an air about her like she's trustworthy."

"For everyone? Or just for you?" Lola asked flatly.

Enne thought for a moment. Most of Bellamy society didn't associate with Lourdes. It didn't really have to do with her frequent vacations to New Reynes, or her often distastefully honest way of speaking…it was something about her as a person, something indefinable. Other people weren't comfortable around her. They hadn't had any friends in Bellamy. It was always just Enne and Lourdes in their large, empty house, their weekends perpetually unoccupied, their telephone never ringing.

"You'd feel safe like that," Levi said carefully, interrupting Enne's thoughts, "if she'd sworn her protection to you."

It was frightfully obvious, now that Enne knew the truth about her talents. She should've realized it before. Lourdes must have sworn her protection to Enne, a seal of magic that kept Enne's secrets safer. But that also meant, by doing so, Lourdes had surrendered her ability to protect herself. She could never act in her own interest—only Enne's. Enne had always considered the practice barbaric, the sort of treachery that Mizer kings had used for their own benefit.

Why would Lourdes go to such lengths? Was it because she loved Enne? Had it been a promise to her parents? A belief that Enne's talents were something important, a piece of Lourdes's greater cause to be protected?

"Did you find anything in the Dondelair book?" Lola asked.

"Gabrielle Dondelair died the day after Enne's birthday," Jac blurted.

Lola blanched. "You must be mucking with me. Gabrielle was…infamous."

Enne waved the other pages. "*And* we have a list of names of *other* women in that family. Besides, we don't even know if February 2 is my real birthday. For all we know, Lourdes lied about that, too." She mustn't have sounded very convincing, however, because Lola stomped away.

Jac jumped to his feet. "Where are you going?" he demanded.

"To find the newspapers," she snapped. "I'm not storming off. I'm not about to—" she raised her voice "—let all the world know about this shatz. And that *she*—" She pointed at Enne, and Jac grabbed Lola's arm and shoved it down. "That she…

shouldn't be allowed to live." Her voice was quiet and strained. She could barely say the words, and Enne realized that was the power of the street oath binding her. She tried not to feel hurt at the intensity in Lola's conviction, but the words still stung. Lola thought of her more as a weapon than a human being.

Jac pushed Lola against the bookshelves. Enne frantically shoved the books back into their places. Levi was already on his feet, ready to back Jac up.

"What is your problem, Dove?" Levi asked.

"I'd think *you'd* know my problem more than anyone," Lola hissed. "Everyone knows about you and Vianca. What would Vianca do with someone like her?"

"Vianca won't know about her." Both kept their voices low. Thankfully, there was no one on this floor to hear, anyway.

"And if she demands you tell her?" Lola challenged Levi. "I know how omertas work."

Enne's annoyance piqued, as it did whenever people started talking about her like she wasn't there. She stood up and pulled the boys away from Lola. "I'm right here," she seethed. "And you might have already made up your mind about me, but I'm not from New Reynes. I go to finishing school. I spend my days dancing and curtsying and baking. I dot my *i*'s with hearts because I think it looks pretty. Whatever you think I am, you're wrong."

"Two nights ago, you almost killed me," Lola growled. "Maybe I know exactly what you are, and you're the one who's wrong."

The words hit Enne like a slap. "Th-that's *not* true."

But there was more truth in Lola's words than Enne cared to admit.

"I've lost everything to the gangs—my parents, my brothers. Every time the city finds their favorite villains, people end up dead." Lola scowled as she looked between them. "So you might be here flirting and bickering as if nothing else matters, but you're all in a *library* with loaded pistols in your pockets. Trying to find Lourdes Alfero as if the monarchists are anything other than lowlifes—yeah, I know who Alfero is." She shook her head. "This story will end badly."

Enne blinked back tears. "I didn't ask for this." Beside her, Levi put a comforting hand on her shoulder. Her anger at him from earlier disappeared, and obviously, his had, too. Arguing or not, she still had his support, and that assurance helped steady her.

Lola rolled her eyes. "Muck, missy. Crying now? You're something else."

"Can you just calm down?" Jac told her, moving between the two girls. His voice was weaker than earlier, though—unsteady. Maybe part of him believed what Lola was saying.

"Come on," Levi said, giving Enne's shoulder a last squeeze. "Let's dig up some newspapers on Gabrielle Dondelair, get what we need before this place closes and go home."

Lola cursed under her breath and walked off, Jac following close behind, grumbling about Lola's hypocritical collection of knives.

Enne and Levi trailed after them.

"She's right," Enne whispered. She yanked the gun out of her pocket and placed it in Levi's hand. "I don't want this." It felt like she was talking about more than just the weapon.

He bit his lip, but didn't take the gun. "We can leave, if you don't think this is a good idea."

"No, no," she said. "We need something. Right now all we've learned for certain is that we don't even know Lourdes's real name." She refused to leave less certain than she'd come.

They found Lola and Jac on the second floor—a much more crowded area—among the periodicals. Lola slapped a stack on the closest table, and the four of them took seats. "This is everything from that period. There's a lot. Kids at schools here write essays about this girl."

Enne slid the newspaper toward her and Levi. The headline

read "Capitol Ablaze." But of course, she already knew this story. The capitol building had to be entirely reconstructed after the fire—Gabrielle hadn't left anything behind in the ruin.

"I think I already found our answer," Levi said. "Look at this one. 'Criminal's Execution Postponed.' They had Gabrielle in custody and didn't execute her due to health reasons. And she wasn't killed until…"

Lola pointed at the paper she held. "Until February 3."

Uneased washed over her. "You can't execute a pregnant woman, can you?" Enne asked softly.

"There's even a picture." Lola turned to Gabrielle's faded head shot. Her hair was lighter than Enne's, her face softer and her skin warmer. Enne searched for some kind of resemblance, but it was hard to be certain. They had similar lips, she supposed, and maybe there was something about her eyes, but there was a grief in Gabrielle's expression that Enne couldn't see beyond.

"She's got that whole doll thing going on." Jac gestured to Enne's face, as if that served as genetic evidence.

"She looks so young," Enne said.

"She was only twenty when she died," Lola said solemnly.

Enne turned away from Gabrielle's picture, unable to look at the girl who'd been so ruthlessly executed. No matter what she'd done, it was still tragic to imagine.

"The story's right here, between the lines," Lola explained. "They discovered that Gabrielle was pregnant. Some blood gazer at the birth saw what you are." She pointed to another paper. "They issued a public apology here, saying the execution was going to be private. Back during the Great Street War, that used to mean the Phoenix Club wanted in on it. They wanted to kill Gabrielle themselves."

"You mean the Shadow Game, don't you?" Enne asked. Beside her, Levi stiffened.

"That's what I would guess. A Mizer baby would've caught their attention."

"But she died of a gunshot wound," Levi added. "Not in the Game."

"I heard there was a big chase for her, before she died," Lola said. "My brother told me stories about it. But the whiteboots got her, in the end."

"Maybe she escaped before playing the Game," Enne suggested.

"Or maybe," Levi said quietly, as Jac shot him a warning look, "she won."

Enne reached into her pocket and pulled out her token. It was warm and familiar in her hand, something she desperately needed when every new secret she uncovered was soaked in tragedy. Had the Phoenix Club known about some connection between Lourdes and Gabrielle, and that was why they'd invited Lourdes to play the Shadow Game? The card they'd found wasn't the Fool, but that didn't mean an invitation hadn't found her eventually.

What if the Phoenix Club knew Enne existed? If she were a member of the Phoenix Club, and *she* were looking for the daughter of Gabrielle Dondelair, then a seventeen-year-old girl in an acrobatics show would certainly draw suspicion. Enne was climbing her way up to becoming a real star in the St. Morse troupe, but she could no longer afford to draw that much attention to herself. If she wanted to survive, then she needed to live as she and Lourdes had lived: in the darkness, as far from the spotlight as she could.

Acrobatics was the one thing she was enjoying about New Reynes. She'd been mediocre all of her life, and the moment she'd begun to excel, she'd have to throw her ambitions away. It was the only way to protect herself, but it felt unfair.

"No one wins the Shadow Game," Lola said.

"It's not like they'd want you to know, if someone did," Levi retorted. His voice was hoarse, almost giddy. "No game is impossible to win."

Enne fiddled with her token. "So what do we have? A connection between the Shadow Game, Gabrielle and Lourdes? That's it?"

"We're digging up history," Lola said. "Did you expect better?"

"No. But I'd hoped."

She swatted at Enne's hands. "Put that key away."

"Key?" Enne asked, confused.

"Yes. That coin in your hand. Isn't that a Royal Bank key?"

Levi took the coin from Enne and turned it over, examining it. "That sounds familiar..."

"It should," Lola said. "It's in Olde Town. It's the oldest bank in the city."

Enne's spirits lifted. "You mean it's still there? We can find it?" Even if their research had been fruitful, learning the identity of her birth mother had brought her no closer to finding Lourdes. But this...

"Don't involve me," Lola said. "Olde Town is Iron Land, anyway."

Levi shook his head. "I've never heard of this bank. Have you, Jac?"

"I think there's some place like that near First Square," Jac pondered, and Enne's spirits lifted even higher. This was a real lead.

Levi rubbed his thumb on the edge of the token. "These numbers might reference a vault."

"Then we'll go tomorrow," Enne declared. "Tomorrow afternoon." She packed up their papers, eager to leave this place and the tragedy they'd uncovered behind.

"Lourdes won't be hiding in some bank," Lola said.

Enne shook her head. This was about more than just finding Lourdes now. If this was *the bank* that held the account Enne had accidentally discovered, the one Lourdes had kept secret all this time, then this meant answers. And it also meant volts. A *lot* of volts.

"You'll be there with us," Levi told Lola. "You're in this now, too. We all are."

"Involved enough to be hanged for it, you mean."

"That's a rather depressing notion, but sure. How did you put it earlier?" He grinned. "Oh, right. 'You're one of the villains, now.'"

DAY SIX

"Avarice, pride and lust—these are all modest desires. What the City of Sin truly craves is destruction."

—*The City of Sin, a Guidebook: Where To Go and Where Not To*

LEVI

Walking into Olde Town usually felt like walking home, but today, Levi had a sinking, anxious feeling in his chest. He shouldn't be worried. With Vianca's gift, his own salary, Enne's payment and two days' worth of gambling spoils, he had seven thousand of the ten thousand volts he needed to pay Sedric Torren. A few more casinos, a few more lucky streaks, and he was going to make it.

Even so, the alleys felt narrower and darker than usual, the way Olde Town probably looked to those who didn't belong. But Levi more than belonged—he owned this place. Its filth and rust and ruin were the Iron Lord's claim.

"How are you doing?" Jac asked beside him.

Was his unease that obvious? He molded his face into a neutral expression. "I'm fine," he answered.

"I know what Reymond was to you."

"I'd rather not talk about it." He didn't think his current state of mind was related to Reymond. He knew the ache of grief from his mother's death. It hadn't come yet—Reymond's death still felt unbelievable, more than anything else—but it would. This feeling just wasn't that.

"Jonas already has patrols stationed around the borders." Jac shook his head. "I know we talked about getting some dealers into Double or Nothing, but that den is right on the border. Might be too risky now. There's plenty of other opportunities in our own territory."

Already, things were changing. Levi typically met with Reymond once a week to talk about the investment scheme or the happenings of New Reynes. Reymond always paid attention to things Levi didn't care about: politics, the Families, current events. But if it couldn't earn him a profit, Levi generally tuned it out.

"You could be my second," Reymond had suggested to him several years ago. It'd been October, around Levi's fourteenth birthday. Reymond had bought Levi a beer, which Levi had pretended was his "first" drink, otherwise Reymond would've been mad.

"I don't want to be your second," Levi had answered.

"Then what do you want?"

"I want to be a lord."

Reymond shook his head. "You're better than us."

"No, I'm not," Levi had said. "Not yet."

When Levi first had the idea for the Irons' consulting business, he'd pitched it to Reymond. When he'd made a few enemies on the streets, Reymond had taken care of them. When he'd needed something—anything at all—Reymond's door was open.

Reymond hadn't been his best friend. He wouldn't sit up all night, several glasses drunk, talking about the things that haunted him. Levi turned to Jac when he was looking for a typical night's worth of trouble. But it was Reymond he'd turned to when he'd needed help.

But the one time Reymond had needed him, he'd been too late.

"Let's not talk about Double or Nothing right now," Levi said quickly, anxious to focus on something else. Maybe grief wasn't waiting around to be found. Maybe it was called.

"Chez will be expecting volts," Jac said. Today was Thursday, and although it wasn't an official Irons meeting, it was collection day. Chez delivered the volts collected from their clients to Levi, and Levi recorded them and distributed all the Irons' individual earnings to Chez. Chez was the middleman between him, his clients and the other Irons. Levi used to spend more face time with his gang, had always made a point to check in with all the Irons individually...until Vianca's scheme started dragging him down.

"Then I'll give him the volts," Levi answered seriously.

"You need those," Jac said. "I know you don't have the ten thousand for Sedric yet."

"I have seven. I can part with five hundred and earn it back tonight."

"You're good with cards, Levi, but your life isn't something to gamble."

He wasn't being reckless. He just couldn't hold out on the Irons anymore. Every time he looked at Mansi, she was a bit thinner.

All this time, Levi hadn't thought he had a choice. He was backed into a desperate situation. Stealing from the Irons had felt like his only option. But the more he interacted with Enne, the more he remembered what he was like before he came to New Reynes. Every time he lied to her, he had to ask himself: Why? Why not tell her about his own Shadow Cards? About how he ran the Irons? About the kind of man he was?

But he knew why. He couldn't bear to see the disappointment in her eyes if she knew the truth. The one thing he hadn't given to this city was his shame.

"I need to make things right," he said quietly.

Jac nodded. It was exactly the sort of language his second

understood. Three years ago, after Jac had lost months and friends and dignity to Lullaby, the first thing he did was make amends. After Levi paid Sedric and put this mess behind him, he intended to build the legacy and empire he'd always dreamed of.

Sometimes we're not who we want to be because we're supposed to be something else. That was what he'd told Enne the other night. And it made him realize, every time he felt guilt and disgust in his chest over what he was doing, that it was his own fault. Not Vianca's. Not Sedric's. His.

He was meant for more than this.

"Have you talked to Enne since yesterday?" Jac asked.

"No," Levi said. The events of the past two days flooded over him like a strong drink. The way her body had felt tucked against his. How her breath had caught on the Mole when he'd whispered in her ear. The gleam in her eyes when she'd claimed she knew what she wanted, even as she looked at him like *that*. Like she knew exactly what she did to him. The other night, when she told him she was a Mizer, he'd thought he sensed her mutual desire. But as yesterday had proved, the flirting was definitely one-sided. He couldn't let the hopeless attraction get to his head—he had more important things to focus on.

"You need to be careful around her," Jac warned.

"What do you mean?"

"I'm not sure she's good for you."

Levi stopped and stared at him. "You weren't wrong—you *did* know too much. You were already involved. But this is why I didn't want her to tell you everything else."

"Because I might get nervous about my friend's safety?"

"Because you're superstitious, and you worry too much." To those who still followed the Faith, the the Mizers were a subject of lore. Some claimed that Mizers were the first to have talents, and all other talents resulted from reactions to volts held in people's skin.

To Levi, it was all nonsense. Mizers were just people like everyone else.

But that wasn't even what really bothered him. What bothered him was that he didn't need Jac to tell him that falling for Enne was a dangerous idea.

"How well do you really know her?" Jac asked.

"Well enough. Can we not—"

"I never met Lourdes Alfero, like you did, but I know her reputation. She's cold, cunning and…dangerous. I'm not saying Enne is lying about who she is—I think she was just as clueless about New Reynes as she acted. But the way she knows all our street rules? How Lola said she almost killed her? All the muck about her talents and her family…"

"I'm not sure what you're getting at," Levi said, and he really wasn't.

"What did Lourdes have in mind for her? What is Enne supposed to *become*?"

"I don't think her goal is to become anything. She wants to find her mother, and she wants to…" *Leave.* The last part disappointed him more than it should.

"Maybe so, but…" Jac shook his head, sighing. "It doesn't matter. You're already wrecked, man."

Another detail Levi didn't need Jac to tell him. "Let's just get this meeting with Chez over with."

They walked to the edge of the square by the old fountain, which was bone dry and covered in dust. At its center, where water had once spurted, a sculpture of a Mizer queen stood, the details of her gown's fabric worn down by the elements. Someone, many years ago, had decapitated her. The head still lay in the fountain, its features no longer distinguishable.

Chez was nowhere to be seen.

"Think he forgot?" Levi asked, even though he doubted Chez would forget a potential payment.

"I can stop by the house to look for him," Jac said. "You good waiting here?"

"Yeah. Go ahead."

Jac disappeared down an alley. Levi tapped his foot and stared at the black-stained clouds, only slivers of which were visible through Olde Town's towers and spires.

Almost as soon as Jac was gone, Chez appeared from one of the off-shooting alleys. He flipped his knife around his knuckles and walked kind of stagger-like, strange for someone usually so swift on his feet. His massive shirt was damp enough that Levi could see his skin and all his ribs sticking out like piano keys. He'd probably swiped it from a drying clothesline on the way here.

It reminded him of how Chez had looked three years ago when Levi had dragged him out of the Brint and pumped life into him—a stranger, a kid. Chez wasn't so self-righteous then.

Mansi followed him, a dark expression on her face. The anxious feeling in Levi's chest tightened.

"'Lo, Pup," Chez said.

"Don't call me that," Levi said automatically, all his senses suddenly on alert. Something was wrong.

Chez and Mansi stopped in front of him. It was so quiet Levi could hear the horns from the harbor, almost a mile away.

"There's been a decision," Chez said, still twirling his knife.

"What kind of decision?" Levi asked. He looked questioningly at Mansi, but she wouldn't meet his eyes.

"The Irons want me to challenge you," he answered.

Levi stiffened. *Challenge* was a loaded term on the streets. It meant a fight to topple the lord from his seat. A duel to the death.

"You can't be serious," Levi said. He stared at his third's ribs and hesitated to reach for his own knife. No way Chez would really go through with this.

"I am. The Scarhands are under new management. It's time we were, too."

Levi winced. Chez wouldn't lose sleep over Reymond's death, but he knew Reymond and Levi had been friends. His words were meant to slice.

"I have the volts, Chez," Levi growled. "Isn't that what you came for?"

"They'd be a temporary solution to a permanent problem." Chez raised his knife to chest level. "I don't feel sorry for you. Not a bit. All that work for Vianca, and none goes to us. The Irons will be safer with you gone."

"I saved your life," Levi said, still in disbelief. "I've been your friend."

"That was a long time ago."

Levi looked at Mansi. Chez, he could believe. The other Irons, maybe. But Mansi? Mansi had looked up to him since the beginning. When had that changed?

She crossed her arms and turned away. It felt like a nail had been driven into his chest, into his coffin.

Maybe he deserved this. Maybe the Irons deserved better.

But he would still fight for what was his.

He removed the pistol he'd been carrying and handed it to Mansi. Duels were knives only. And, despite everything, if he did lose, he wanted Mansi to have it.

If he was being honest with himself, he didn't think that he could beat a Phillips in a fight—Chez had to be three times faster than him. But it was damn hard to break a street oath. He'd be hurting. Maybe that was all the advantage Levi would need to win.

To win. A challenge was a duel to the death. So it was Chez or Levi. Only one of them would be walking out of Olde Town with their throat intact.

Levi pulled out his knife and moved into a fighting stance, but his legs trembled and his arms felt weak. He wasn't supposed to die here, just another kid playing lord whom no one would remember.

Chez lunged forward. Levi dodged his knife but missed the punch he'd aimed at Chez's shoulder. His third was all skin and no bones, quicker with a blade and, of course, fast as lightning.

Chez ran forward and sank his knife into Levi's leg. Levi let out a scream and frantically jabbed his own blade as he fell, but he never made contact. Hot blood boiled out of his thigh. Chez kicked him in the side one, two, three times.

Besides the pain, all Levi could think of was how fast he'd gone down.

Four, five. His stomach flipped over, and he swallowed down a tide of vomit. If he was going to die, he wouldn't die covered in his own sick. He should've probably been thinking about something more profound, but he didn't have a family who would miss him or lovers who would weep. All he had was his dignity.

"Chez!" someone shouted. Levi's heart was pounding too loudly to hear who it was. The nerves around the knife wound in his leg screamed, and his stomach ached all over. "Stop it!"

Chez kicked Levi again, this time in the head.

Everything darkened. His thoughts whirled around his brain like a funnel, and he wondered if maybe it was the ground spinning and spinning and spinning, sucking him inside the earth.

A few more screams. Then some grunts. A clatter. Footsteps. Levi couldn't tell if it happened in a millisecond or in minutes, but then something pressed against his leg, and Levi stifled a scream.

The person bending over him was a shadow, but everything was a shadow in Olde Town. "Muck. Muck, this is really happening." The person wrenched his hand away, and the pain in Levi's leg lessened slightly. He could sense his aura, weightless and translucent. Jac. "Stay with me. You c-can't die on me."

Jac's words spun, too.

Panicked hands found their way down Levi's shirt, against his chest. A welcome warmth filled him, easing the pain, coaxing him back into lucidity.

His eyes widened. "No," he moaned, swatting Jac away.

As the hands let go, so, too, did the warmth. Levi began to shiver. Only the cold and the pain remained, sharp enough to numb everything else. All his adrenaline, gone, and with it, his sense of feeling.

All his life, gone.

The ground caved in, and he hit bottom.

ENNE

Enne stood in the hallway of black and white doors, searching for the right one. She spun in a circle, looking for something familiar. The previous door she'd opened had been her memory of the last time she spoke to Lourdes, but she couldn't remember which door it was. The hallway stretched endlessly in both directions, every inch of it the same.

She walked to a black door. Those belonged to her.

Inside, she heard thunder.

She opened it hesitantly and peeked into its darkness. Unlike her first visit to the hallway, when she had relived a memory, this time, she was a spectator.

She was in the basement of a home she didn't recognize, and a storm raged outside. A young person clutched what looked like a three-year-old Enne in her arms. As a toddler, Enne's hair had been curlier, her eyes less wide set. She was red in the face from crying, scared by the storm.

The person shushed her softly. "Loddie has you. Loddie has

you." That was the name Enne had called Lourdes when she was little.

But this person was surely too young to be Lourdes, Enne thought, even though it was clearly her. That evening, her long blond hair was tied at the nape of her neck and braided down to her waist. She wore fluid clothes, but they didn't fit her properly— it was a time before Lourdes had tailored all her outfits. Otherwise, her women's clothes were always too short, her men's always hanging or tight in the wrong areas. If Enne had to guess, Lourdes was about eighteen in this memory.

Neither the child nor Lourdes took any notice of Enne standing there, so she sat down next to her mother, curled her legs to her chest and listened with them to the storm.

Eventually, the toddler stopped whimpering and fell asleep. Lourdes leaned her head back against the wall, her face weary. She winced with every new crack of thunder and, eventually, also began to cry.

It was strange to see Lourdes like this. There was something rawer about her. In all Enne's memories, Lourdes had never cried. Apparently, she hadn't always been so reserved.

Tell me what happened, Enne wanted to say. *Tell me your story.*

But, of course, her mother couldn't hear her.

Enne didn't leave until Lourdes fell asleep. Then she slipped out and through the next black door in the hallway, eager for more forgotten time spent with her mother.

Except in this scene, Enne was alone. She was sixteen years old, and she wasn't where she was supposed to be. She crept across the upstairs hallway in her nightgown, an unused lantern at her side. Last time she'd attempted this, Lourdes had discovered her in the act, and it had devolved into a shouting match—one of the first they'd ever had. But Lourdes was on another one of her trips to New Reynes, and Enne was alone in the house, except for the staff.

She knelt in front of Lourdes's office door and pulled a pin from her hair.

It took nearly thirty minutes for her to pick the lock. She had no idea what she was doing, but the longer she sat there, fiddling, the more understanding she developed of the mechanisms. Finally, she heard the lock click, and she turned the knob and crawled into the room.

The office was stark, almost empty. She went for the desk first, yanking out drawers full of pencils and rubbish—Lourdes had always been impressively messy—searching for...something, anything to explain her mother's business in the City of Sin. Enne turned on the lantern, heart pounding, and examined the bank slips in the cabinet.

The address on the papers was in New Reynes, but neither sixteen-year-old Enne nor the Enne peering over her shoulder recognized the address.

1089 Virtue Street, New Reynes.

The statement was dated from a few months ago—from Lourdes's last trip to the city. And—both their eyes widened as they examined the document—it was for a bank account with a balance of over two hundred million volts.

Both of them gasped.

Memory Enne threw the papers back in the cabinet and slammed it closed, and the Enne who watched her remembered what she'd been thinking. It was wealth unlike that of anyone she knew, anything she'd ever heard of. Enne knew Lourdes had inherited money from her own mysterious family, but she'd never imagined anything like that.

The memory used to hold shame for Enne. This was the one time she had betrayed Lourdes's trust and uncovered a secret she shouldn't have known. But as her present self left the room and returned to the hallway, her guilt was gone. She wished she'd explored more of the office that night. Maybe she would have stumbled across another clue, something to help in the present search for her mother. Had Enne known any of the secrets she knew now, everything would be different. Enne would've journeyed to New Reynes sooner, or asked to go with Lourdes.

She found a new black door. It was the first one that wasn't a memory.

The room smelled sweet. Enne stood facing a mirror. Below her, a joint of Mistress burned in an ashtray, its soot golden, matching her costume and the shimmery eyeshadow she wore. Enne's boots were black, heeled and rose to midthigh. A garter belt snaked up her legs and disappeared underneath a corseted dress, which was sequined from navel to cleavage and crisscrossed in violet ribbon. The bust was strapless, meant to be removed more than admired. The feathers protruding from its bottom would do little to cover her if she bent over.

Still, it was hard to feel exposed when there was no one here but her. She shuffled through the cosmetic products on the counter, then reached for a sweet-smelling perfume and a lipstick black as licorice.

She examined herself in the mirror. No one would call her a doll in this outfit.

Or much of a lady.

She smiled to herself. There was no one but her to know. After all—this was only a dream.

Jazzy music played outside, and she followed it to the stage. The lights were too bright to see into the audience, if there was anyone there at all. She remembered Demi's routine with a mixture of embarrassment and thrill. Without the leering eyes of anyone watching her, she felt powerful in these clothes. Attractive. If the world were a different sort of place, she might trim off the feathers and wear it for fun.

She danced alone on the stage. Nothing suggestive...at first. It took a few minutes for her to decide such a style would be fun to try. She unlaced the ribbons on her corset.

Several minutes into the routine, she became aware of the fact that she was no longer dreaming. Her head was pressed against the pillow. Her nightdress was twisted around her stomach, her feet dangling off the edge of the bed. But she wasn't done exploring the dream just yet, so she didn't open her eyes.

At some point, in her sleepy, half-conscious state, she inserted someone else into her fantasy. An admiring gaze. Hands trailing down her hips. Lips brushing against her chest.

The light in her window brightened from the sunrise. She was now mostly conscious and exceptionally frustrated. She untwisted her nightdress and scratched an itch on her thigh, then her hand trailed up and lingered between her legs, making up for the fantasy that was slowly fading. If she were anywhere else but New Reynes—in her dormitory, in her own bedroom—she probably wouldn't have dared. She rubbed her lips together, as if she could still feel the smoothness of the black lipstick, could still feel the thrilling empowerment of the stage lights and the stranger's stomach pressed against hers.

When she finished, she was breathless and sweaty. She opened her eyes and stared at the ceiling of her St. Morse apartment. At first, she felt embarrassed, even if it was no different from that stage where no one could see her. She'd never been a prude, but inexperience lent itself to shyness, even around herself.

She climbed out of bed and sat at her vanity. Her face was slightly flushed, and the indentations of the pillow lined her cheek.

She examined her lipsticks and selected the shade closest to black.

Enne waited in the St. Morse lobby, tapping her foot. It was past the meeting time, and no one else had arrived yet. When she'd knocked on Levi's door, there'd been no answer, and she honestly wasn't certain if Lola would even show.

It was ludicrous to put any faith in dreams, but nothing about the hallway felt like one. The scenes were still fresh in her mind, the memories exact in every detail, as though she'd really ex-perienced them.

She traced her finger over the guidebook's map. Virtue Street was located in Olde Town, exactly where Lola thought the bank would be. The road ran parallel to Tropps Street, virtue and vice never intersecting.

Just as she'd begun to worry about the others, Lola strode in through the revolving doors, wearing her now-familiar top hat. She took one look around St. Morse's gaudy interior and grimaced.

"You're wearing lipstick," Lola commented. She squinted at Enne's face, as if examining an optical illusion. "It suits you."

This was the first nice thing Lola had ever said to her. She beamed. "Thank you." Enne felt it suited her, too.

"Where are the Iron boys?"

"I'm not sure. They should've been here a while ago." She shouldn't worry. What trouble could they have found by mid-morning? Maybe they'd just slept in after a long night.

"Then it's just us," Lola said. Even though there was no threat in her voice, the words unnerved Enne. She was glad she'd brought Levi's revolver—several days had passed since the night she'd stolen it, but he'd never asked for it back. Maybe she'd keep it.

Still, Lola was right. There was no point in wasting more of the day.

They ventured outside and headed to the bank. Olde Town was particularly quiet that morning, few people venturing out-side due to the sudden heat. Enne, however, relished the weather; she'd felt as though she'd left summer behind her when she sailed away from Bellamy.

She pulled her guidebook out and followed the route on the map. Neither of them spoke for some time, which was just fine with Enne, as she was too lost in her own thoughts. Without even sharing Lourdes's blood name, how would she gain access to the account? Would Lourdes have opened the account in her name or under another alias? And even if Enne gained access, what would she do with all those volts?

Lola's voice interrupted Enne's thoughts. "Can I ask you something?"

"Sure," Enne said nervously. There was no bite or threat in Lola's voice, but that was precisely why she was nervous.

"If Lourdes raised you as your mother, why do you call her by her first name?"

Enne shrugged. "She never wanted me to call her Mother." She had wondered this herself when she was younger, but even though Lourdes never discussed her own family, Enne got the sense she'd had a complicated relationship with her own mother.

"Can I ask you a question now?" Enne asked.

Lola's eyebrows furrowed, and she crossed her arms. "I guess."

"If you're not a Dove, why do you dye your hair white?"

It felt like a simple question, but clearly, it was one Lola didn't want to answer.

"Don't ask me that," she growled, then brushed past Enne and walked several steps ahead of her for the rest of the trip.

The sign for Virtue Street was rusted over, and layers and layers of kiss marks covered it in all shades of lipstick.

"We're here," Lola said. "You can kiss the sign if you'd like. It's a New Reynes tradition."

Enne grimaced. "I'll pass."

They stopped another block down the street. According to a plaque outside, the building before them was indeed the bank, but Enne could just as easily have mistaken it for a penitentiary. Wrought iron gates encircled the grounds and guarded each of its windows. Larger-than-life obsidian statues lined the walkway to the front door, but dark sacks covered each of their heads, like the sort draped over a man as he approached the gallows.

"Mizer kings, probably," Lola said cheerfully.

Enne shivered. "They could have just taken them down."

"They're reminders, not decorations."

They walked inside and approached the main desk, entirely protected by bulletproof glass except for a sliver of space to exchange documents—a harsh contrast to the marble grandeur of its decor. The woman behind the desk was elderly, with one keen blue eye and a second wooden one.

Enne slid her token under the glass. The woman snatched it up and held it close to her good eye.

"These aren't the standard engravings," she remarked suspiciously. She rubbed her thumb over the cameo of the Mizer queen. "This is very outdated."

"We'd like access to the vault that coin opens," Enne said firmly.

"You can only enter the vault if your name is on the account." The woman turned to a file cabinet and perused it for the correct number. "Hmm. There are several listed. Are you a Ms. Lourdes Orefla?"

Enne stilled and whispered to Lola, "Do you think that's her real name?"

"That's just Alfero backward, thickhead," Lola hissed.

Enne reddened. "No," she told the woman. "I'm not."

The woman adjusted her bifocals. "A Ms. Erienne Salta?"

Excitement surged in Enne's chest. Lourdes *did* put her name on the account. Maybe Enne had been meant to find this place after all.

She shoved her identification documents through the window. "Yes. That's me."

Several minutes later, a security guard led them to a rather haunting steel elevator and, from there, to the bottom-most level. The hallway had concrete walls, flickering fluorescent lighting and grated metal doors lining either side. They walked until reaching the hallway's end, where the guard gestured to a vault on their right.

Enne took a deep breath and slid the token into the coin slot.

There was a metal clanking from inside, followed by several *clicks* of unlatching locks. The handle spun counterclockwise three times before the door creaked open.

Enne cautiously stepped inside. At first she was confused—she'd expected dozens of shelves of orbs, enough to contain the fortune she'd uncovered in those bank slips.

The vault was completely empty.

She placed a hand on the wall, steadying herself. Another dead end.

"Look," Lola said, picking up a small object Enne hadn't noticed in the corner. It was a single, miniature orb made of black glass, with golden sparks glowing faintly inside. Volts were white, not gold. Which meant it wasn't a real orb.

"Is it a trick?" Enne asked, walking closer to Lola. She tried not to let her disappointment show, but her voice was catching. Had Lourdes emptied the vault since Enne had found the statement? Why leave behind this...toy?

Lola held it up to the light and examined it. "Do you have a volt reader?"

Enne did, in her purse. She held the sensor to the orb's metal cap, but nothing registered. She sighed and shoved both the reader and the black orb into her bag.

"Has the account been emptied recently?" she asked the guard.

"Why would I know that?" he snapped.

Enne put her hands on her hips and stared around the empty room. The metal walls reminded her of a prison cell, and she shivered, feeling claustrophobic. No leads, no answers. She was trapped in this city.

As Enne turned around to leave, she caught a glint at the corner of her eye—there was a faint line in the wall to her left, almost imperceptible. As she walked toward it, she made out the thin outline of a square. She ran her fingers across its edges. Her nails found a latch in the metal, and she flipped it open, revealing a keyhole.

Enne fished around her purse.

"Do you have a key?" Lola asked.

"This should do," Enne said, brandishing a bobby pin.

"You're joking. You some expert lock-picker?"

"I've done it before." *Once.*

Enne fiddled the bobby pin around the lock, searching for its mechanisms. The lock was no more complicated than the one on Lourdes's office. Perhaps Lourdes had felt the box's conceal-ment was protection enough.

After about a minute, the lock clicked open. Enne smiled tri-umphantly and yanked out the bent bobby pin.

The drawer slid open, and Enne pulled out a bronze coin. It was a token matching her own, only with a king on its face rather than a queen. It was hot to the touch—almost burning, though with no discernable reason as to why. Unlike the queen's token, this one lacked the signature ridges that made it a key. It was simply a coin.

"Feel this," Enne said, handing the coin to Lola. "It's warm."

Lola touched it, then shook her head. "Most people keep *volts* in a bank."

"Do you know what it is?"

"Seems like a regular coin to me. It's old, though. Much older than the key."

"Well, it must be important, if Lourdes took the trouble to hide it like that." That was what she tried to convince herself, any-way. She'd come here for answers but was leaving with trinkets.

The more she uncovered about her mother, the less she seemed to understand her.

Enne slid the new token into her purse, as well. She gazed around the room for any other mysterious hiding places, but found none. She swallowed her disappointment.

"So we found nothing," Enne murmured.

Lola gave her a weak, awkward smile. "It's not *nothing*—"

"Yes, it is," Enne said stiffly. She wished Levi were here to comfort her, rather than the blood gazer. Enne would probably cry if Lola's harsh words from yesterday weren't so fresh in her mind. *Crying now? You're something else.* She shouldn't care what Lola thought of her—she'd certainly made her contempt perfectly clear—but Enne still didn't want to face further judgment. She was too easily wounded right now.

Thankfully, Lola kept quiet on their return upstairs. However, as soon as they exited the elevator, Lola marched across the lobby, her boots thumping loudly on the marble floor.

"Do you have any other information on the account?" she asked the woman. Enne hovered, shocked, behind her. "Statements? Other names? Anything?"

The woman retrieved the paperwork a second time. "There's a final name listed on the account, this one with an address." She leaned closer to it, her real eye squinting. "A Ms. Zula Slyk. Number nineteen, the Street of the Holy Tombs. That's everything I have." The weight of Enne's disappointment lifted. Lola turned around, shooting Enne a triumphant smile.

"That's also in Olde Town," Lola said. "We could go now."

Enne debated for a moment. She wanted to, but her acrobatics show was that night. Even if her role in the troupe was a farce, a diversion from the real reason Vianca had hired her, she was actually looking forward to the performance. For once, she had achieved a somewhat notable role.

But her ambitions didn't matter, not in comparison to finding her mother.

"Maybe we can—"

"But we should wait for the boys," Lola said. "The Street of the Holy Tombs is deeper into Olde Town. We might not be safe if we ran into any Irons."

Enne had faced Dove Land unscathed—certainly she could manage the same in Olde Town. But truthfully, even if Lola *had* proved helpful today, Levi's presence would be a comfort. His absence today already had her worried.

"Tomorrow morning, then," Enne suggested.

"But I have Guild meetings tomorrow." Lola sounded almost let down about it. "Do you think Lourdes will be there?"

Enne stilled. She didn't want to consider that she might actually find her mother tomorrow—her chest was already weary from carrying all this repeated hope and disappointment.

"I don't know," Enne answered quietly.

She and Lola walked back outside. They leaned against the pedestal of one of the statues. The plaque with the Mizer's name on it had been shattered beyond legibility, and Enne ran her fingers over the cracks, thinking about the cracks within herself.

"If nothing turns up," Lola said, "I was thinking we could go to Scrap Market. They have old newspapers there. Ones Lourdes probably wrote for."

Enne nodded, trying not to focus on the words *if nothing turns up*. Something would. At some point, the trail needed to lead somewhere.

"That sounds good," she answered.

Lola pulled her harmonica out of her pocket. "I've always liked puzzles."

Enne almost snapped that her life wasn't a puzzle, wasn't some game, but there was no point in angering the blood gazer. Enne preferred this Lola to the one who'd wanted her dead.

Lola blew out an eerie, low note: appropriate for a garden full of hooded statues. While she played, Enne mentally recited Lourdes's rules to herself to release all the pressure in her heart. Those feelings of power and confidence she'd gained from New Reynes felt like a dream, in this moment, caught between another dead end and another lead.

She rubbed her lipstick off on the back of her hand. Maybe it didn't suit her after all.

LEVI

It was the end of Levi's Saturday night shift. He was dressed in an emerald St. Morse suit, complete with silver cuff links and sapphire velvet tie. The moment he left the Tropps Room to begin his break, he slipped the jacket off and draped it over his shoulder. He hated to wear Vianca's clothes any longer than he had to, and it felt especially wrong to be in his uniform, pretending everything else was fine.

He rolled the sleeves of his shirt up his forearms, exposing the matching ace and spade tattoos.

Vianca's woman had brought makeup to cover the impressive shiner on his left eye, but the tone was too pale, and it left him looking even more sickly than he felt. He should consider himself lucky to be walking—limping, really—only several hours after waking up. One broken rib, the doctor had said. A concussion. A minor stab wound that would leave him with a permanent scar.

And a lethal blow to his pride. He still had his tattoos, but without the Irons, he didn't know who he was anymore. He was

Levi Glaisyer, but that was the name his father had given him. The Iron Lord was the one he'd fashioned for himself.

He was surprised Chez hadn't come back to finish the job. Typically, an oath broke when someone died during the duel or if the lord relinquished their claim on their vassal. If Jac hadn't fought off Chez, Levi would be at the bottom of the Brint right now. But he wasn't dead, so the oath was still—at least partially—intact.

Regardless, Chez was probably marching around Olde Town calling himself the new Iron Lord. The thought of it made Levi feel worse than all the injuries combined. He'd been humiliated, betrayed and beaten; dying might've been a more merciful fate.

To make matters worse, Chez had stolen the five hundred volts he'd already been planning to give to the Irons. Ungrateful bastard.

Levi hadn't seen Enne since last night, and he had no idea if she knew what had happened, or if she had ever hunted down that bank. The thought of her seeing him like this was more than a little embarrassing, but she would soon find out one way or another—and besides, he wanted to catch the last half of her show.

Not needing to pay for tickets while wearing his St. Morse uniform, Levi strolled into the theater. It was dark—intermission must've just ended. He stood in the back rather than squeeze into an empty seat in the middle of a row. A dozen burlesque dancers onstage performed some kind of interpretive theater, pointing and running as a group of acrobatic birds swooped down and clawed at their heads. He spotted Enne immediately. She was dressed in black, with droopy wings that spread apart as she swung. It was obvious from only a few minutes of performing that she was one of the more talented acrobats on the stage, despite her minor role in the show. The Dondelairs were from the highest tier of acrobatics families, just as the Glaisyers were the most respected of orb-makers.

The orchestra hit a crescendo.

Crack! The "sky" broke open, and glitter rained over the performers. Lights flashed. One of the male dancers brandished a golden sword and pointed it toward the birds, but as soon as he gained his balance, one of the birds on the lowest trapeze kicked the sword from his hands. It clattered across the stage and stopped beside one of the smaller dancers. The young man grabbed it, and the moment he did, the glitter stopped falling and light poured in from above.

There was a final dance number, but the acrobats were gone. Seemed like a pretty useless story to Levi, but he didn't know much about art.

The bows began, and the acrobats took the stage as a group. Enne smiled and curtsied with the rest of them, and Levi couldn't take his eyes off her. Very briefly, Enne's gaze found his, even from all the way on the stage. She smiled wider. Levi decided the whole show had been worth it just for that.

He left soon after, and a crowd of women in flowing satin gowns and men drowned in cologne exited behind him. Levi eyed a vase of orchids on the concierge's counter. People gave performers flowers, right? But he decided against it—he already had a stolen box of cookies wedged awkwardly in his pocket— and turned down one of the small hallways that led backstage.

It was empty. When he reached a door labeled Dressing Room, Levi stopped and leaned against the wall. Enne was probably changing. He didn't mind waiting a few minutes.

A little while later, another performer popped out and startled at seeing Levi there, looking as ill as he did. Her eyes ran over his St. Morse uniform with suspicion. Levi might've been well-known in the casino, but he wasn't so recognizable outside of the Tropps Room, especially by those who didn't pay attention to the city's most notable dealers.

He self-consciously adjusted his tie and wiped at the concealer on his eye. Maybe coming to see Enne was a bad idea, but it seemed silly to turn back now.

Levi cleared his throat. "I'm looking for Enne."

The girl nodded and disappeared. Enne stepped out a moment later, still in her costume, but without her wings or feathered skirt. Heavy black stage lashes covered her eyes, and her cheeks were extra pink. Despite the fact that she looked a bit ridiculous, Levi couldn't help but stare at the way the lacy leotard hugged her waist and the makeup accentuated the pout of her Cupid's bow.

"You look nice," he managed.

She looked at him closely and gasped. "What happened to you? Are you all right?" She lifted a hand toward his face, rubbed the skin under his eye and inspected the purple bruise with concern.

Under different circumstances, Levi would've been happy to submit to her touch. But he could already see the unease in her eyes. He swatted her hand away and smiled, a bit too widely. "I'm fine."

"You look terrible."

"Really? I feel great."

She crossed her arms. "Are you really not going to tell me what happened?"

"I… I had a bit of an argument with Chez."

"Looks like he won."

He winced. "Take it easy on me."

"But Chez is your third…" She bit her lip. "I thought oaths prevented things like this."

Levi took a deep, shameful breath. "It's called a challenge, when someone tries to overthrow the lord. It's normally a duel to the death. And it would've been, if Jac hadn't shown up."

She made a face like *she* was the one who was ill, exactly the sort of pity Levi didn't need.

"Never mind that," he said quickly. "Did you visit the bank today?"

She gave him a pointed look, like she knew he was stalling. "Yes. There was barely anything in the vault. We found a strange

269

black orb and an even stranger Mizer token. I don't know what to think of either of them."

Levi had never heard of a black orb before. "Can I take a look at the orb?"

"Yes, I'll bring it tomorrow," she answered. "There was an address listed on the account. Some place called the Street of the Holy Tombs. Lola said it was in Olde Town."

Levi crinkled his nose. "I know that place. Mysterious black orbs and old coins? That's exactly the neighborhood you're looking for. It's full of the Faithful. Gives me the creeps just to walk through it."

"Well, I'm going tomorrow to call on a woman named Zula Slyk." The name sounded vaguely familiar to Levi, but he couldn't remember why. Enne hesitated for a moment before continuing. "It would be great if you could come with me, but do you think you'll feel up for it?"

"Of course I will." He cracked his neck. "Takes more than a broken rib and a cut to slow me down."

Truthfully, entering Iron Land was a dangerous notion right now, but Olde Town was *his* territory, *his* claim. He refused to let himself fear it. Besides, he'd brave worse than that for Enne— all she had to do was ask.

"Lola also suggested trying Scrap Market, if this doesn't pan out." Her face was doing that expressionless thing—she was upset.

What he *should've* done was console her. Of course something would turn up. Problem was, that something would probably be Lourdes's corpse. Levi was already struggling to pick up the pieces of his own shattered life—he couldn't bear to watch Enne go through that, too.

Instead, he said, "Scrap Market is a bad idea. It's dangerous, now that Scavenger is Scar Lord. I wouldn't risk it myself even if I didn't get the muck kicked out of me today. And you shouldn't go, either."

"I wasn't asking for your permission," she snapped. His instincts were correct—she was definitely upset.

He stepped closer and placed a hand on her shoulder. "I know that. I just think it's better if you stay away from there." His voice sounded more forceful than he meant it to.

She pushed his hand off her. "I know you've had a bad day, Levi, but don't do this. I don't need to be patronized."

He sighed. "I know that. I'm just…" *Trying to protect you.* He pulled the box of cookies out of his pocket. "I brought you these. Truce?"

The corner of her lips tilted into a smile. "Thanks," she said, tearing into the box, easily appeased.

He shifted the weight off his bad leg and closed his eyes. Even so, he could still feel the pity of Enne's stare.

"Stop looking at me like that," he said.

"Like what?"

"Like you're sorry for me." He shook his head. "I deserved what I got." He meant it, too. It was a hollow feeling—less like guilt and more like dejection. He was a pawn playing at being king. If he'd ever been anything more, if he was ever *meant* to be anything more, he wouldn't have fallen so low. Saint or crook, it didn't matter; if New Reynes was a game, then he'd already lost.

"What do you mean?" she asked.

Under different circumstances, maybe he would've told her the truth. He wanted to. Someone stronger than himself needed to hold him accountable for what he'd done to the Irons. It would be easy—all he needed to do was pull the two Shadow Cards out of his pocket.

I never pretended to be a good man, he'd say. *But I never wanted to be this.*

But he didn't tell her. Not because of the shame, but because he knew that he was a trouble she didn't need. Enne's omerta was just another example of how Levi had failed the people who depended on him. The difference between her and him was that she'd given up everything to save someone, and Levi had given up everyone to save himself.

Enne didn't deserve her *own* problems—she certainly didn't deserve Levi's, too.

Maybe he'd tell her after all of this was over. Iron Lord or not, he would find a way to pay Sedric back. He'd lost nearly everything to the city's game, but he wouldn't lose his life.

Only five days from now, when the worst was behind him, he'd tell her about all the wrongs he'd committed and all the people he cheated.

He would tell her how sorry he was for the role he'd played with her and Vianca.

And he would tell her that, even after losing everything he'd ever wanted, he still desperately wanted her.

"I didn't mean anything," he said. But when he met her eyes, he could tell that she didn't believe him. He fought back the urge to reach out and touch her again—on her shoulder, her hand, her waist. Even if he stepped closer, it wouldn't feel close enough. Enne was becoming more to him than just an attraction. She was the girl who'd come afraid to the city that could smell your fear. She'd faced the witch. She'd poisoned the wolf. She'd strolled into the land of death with her head held high and left it a lord. She was an impossible player in a fixed game, the only person not playing to win.

Maybe Levi had spent too many nights dreaming of the legends of these streets, fantasizing about the day he'd get to finally show his hand. Even after he'd lost, Enne was a fascination, a temptation and a delirious hope that the game wasn't over, but only just beginning.

She grabbed his left hand, not to hold it, but to turn it over. She traced a finger over the spade tattoo on his arm with a thoughtful expression on her face. She looked at it as if it were a scar.

"You look more lost than I do," Enne said, her voice hinting at both laughter and sadness.

In that moment, he didn't feel lost. But he would as soon as she let go.

Suddenly, the air smelled like warm, dark blue, and tasted of bourbon with a trace of espresso. It moved in swirls, like the caress of the wind picking up before a storm. Surprised, he let out a faint moan from the back of his throat. She smelled like a Gambler's Ruin.

It'd been over four years since he'd sensed a new aura, and it came upon him so unexpectedly that he almost staggered. It was so different from the others he'd known before: the quiet whisper of Jac's gray, the avarice laced in Vianca's green, the volatile flames of his father's red. Enne's aura made him dizzy, like he'd stared too long at the spaces between the stars, or dived too deep from shallows into ocean. It felt tangible enough to lace between his fingers, though it looked like curls of smoke. In the dim lighting of the hallway, it danced eerily across the carpet, the billowing train of a sapphire gown, the twisting of beasts and passions in her shadow.

Six days was an extraordinarily short time for him to start sensing an aura. And, as she held his arm, her gaze locked on his, her lips poised between boldness and uncertainty, the more five days from now seemed an excruciatingly long time to wait.

Just as his desire was about to overwhelm his sense of logic, Enne let go of him and took several steps back. Her reaction shouldn't have surprised him. They'd reached this moment before, and time after time, she'd made it clear what she did and didn't want.

"I should go," she said suddenly. "Back to the troupe, I mean. They'll wonder where I am."

You're right outside the dressing room, he thought. But Levi knew excuses—and rejection—when he heard it. The last thing he should be focusing on right now was romance, but still, her words stung.

"The Street of the Holy Tombs," he said, dragging their conversation—and their relationship—back to business. "Ten, tomorrow morning. You won't be missing me this time."

DAY SEVEN

"In the City of Sin, secrets are their own
sort of currency, and reputation holds
more power than fortune."

—*The City of Sin, a Guidebook:*
Where To Go and Where Not To

ENNE

Olde Town reminded Enne of a graveyard or a mausoleum, with the way its atmosphere evoked the decaying and forgotten, embraced monsters and nightmares.

The Street of the Holy Tombs was in the center of Olde Town, and one of the few neighborhoods with active residents. It was the cathedral to the graveyard, the beating heart of a mostly dead corpse. Ghostly wind chimes dangled in every window. Weather-worn gargoyles perched on the buttresses overhead, their faces contorted with hunger and wrath. Creeds were painted on every door, and candles burned on broken windowsills.

"It's very charming," Enne managed. With every step, she braced herself in case a wandering specter or beast jumped out at her. The Street of the Holy Tombs had a way of undermining her sense of reality.

She fought the urge to stand closer to Levi, remembering how last night she'd so nearly accepted his advances and surrendered herself to New Reynes. Every touch, every look from

Levi was a temptation to abandon the girl she'd always been. Enne might've strayed from a few of her ladylike ideals, but she wouldn't lose her entire identity. When she did leave this city, she would leave it in one piece.

"Believe it or not," Levi said, "people come to this street looking for a scare. There are museums of medical abnormalities. Catacombs lined with skulls. Nightclubs of mirror mazes and horrors."

"It doesn't look like it's all for show," she said. Creeds and any practice of the Faith were forbidden, and Enne didn't think even the greediest citizens of New Reynes would display them just for the sake of profit.

"It's not."

They found the storefront for number nineteen, a place called *Her Forgotten Histories.* A middle-aged woman with short curly hair sat outside on a rocking chair, her face hidden behind today's copy of *The Crimes & The Times,* whose front-page headline announced the two-year anniversary of the disappearance of Chancellor Malcolm Semper's daughter. The woman wore a wooden Creed around her neck, nearly twice as large as Jac's.

"Do you think that's her?" Enne whispered. "Zula Slyk?"

"I'm not sure," he said.

A white cat purred and rubbed at the hem of Enne's skirt. White cats supposedly brought bad luck, a thought Enne might not have considered if they were anywhere but a street devoted to superstition.

"Can I help you?" the woman called to them.

"We're looking for someone named Zula Slyk," Enne said.

She folded down her newspaper. "That would be me."

Don't get your hopes up, Enne reminded herself. There was an aching wound inside her from missing Lourdes, and these words wrapped it in a protective shell. If she kept her expectations low, she wouldn't feel the throbbing. If she cut off all her emotions, she wouldn't be so weak.

Zula inspected them as they walked closer. "I've always wanted to meet Vianca's other boy," she said. At first, Enne thought she was referring to Vianca's son, which was absurd: Levi and Vianca had plainly different heritages.

"Ah," Zula said, her gaze falling on Enne. "She never told me she had a girl."

Then Enne realized what Zula mean—the omerta. But how could she know? She spoke as if Vianca's shackles dangled visibly from their wrists.

Zula's amicable expression fell as Enne drew closer. She squinted at Enne's features, as though she recognized her from somewhere, or perhaps Enne reminded her of a person she would rather not see.

"Does Vianca know who you are?" Zula asked, her voice suddenly full of bite.

Enne stopped, her heart racing. If Zula knew who she really was, then surely she wouldn't be another dead-end lead. "Do you?" Enne asked, nervously, hopefully.

Zula shakily drew her hand to her chest and stood up from her chair. "Come inside. I know why you're here."

Enne and Levi exchanged a cautious glance. "What if this is a trick?" Levi whispered.

"There were only three names on that bank account. Mine, Lourdes's and hers. Lourdes must've trusted her." She felt a pang in her chest. If Zula knew Enne's true identity, then Lourdes had trusted Zula more than she'd trusted her own daughter.

Levi nodded, and they followed Zula inside.

A black printing press took up the majority of the room. Among the remaining space, desks were wedged against bookcases, papers dried on clotheslines tied to lamps and the backs of chairs. A framed painting of a martyr hung on the back wall.

Her Forgotten Histories was a newspaper. That made sense, since Lourdes was a journalist. Perhaps that was how they'd met.

Zula drew the blinds closed over each of the windows, even

shooed the cat outside. She motioned for both of them to sit at a desk.

"I should've known you'd come," Zula said. "I always told Lourdes to give you my name—who else would keep you safe? But I didn't think she'd listen. So obstinate. Never grew out of that."

Enne drew in a shaky breath. That was definitely Lourdes. "How do you know her?"

"I'm her oldest—and only—friend." There was an unmistakable sadness in Zula's voice that Enne tried to ignore.

"Well, you weren't wrong about her not listening," Enne admitted. "Lourdes sent me to Levi, not to you."

Zula barked out a laugh. "Vianca's orb-maker? Ridiculous. As if she'd send you anywhere near a woman as powerful and terrible as Vianca Augustine."

"But you know Vianca, too, don't you?" Levi said. "That's how you know about her talent. And us."

"Vianca and I share some political connections," Zula said carefully. "But no...that's not how I know." She closed her eyes, and a set of tattoos darkened on her eyelids. They, too, looked like eyes, though lacking pupils or any color. "I can see shades. That is my talent. Curses, secrets, regrets, passions, sacrifices, desires. I see them like shadows that cling to everyone."

"That's nonsense," Levi said, and Enne shot him a look. He was being rude, and they needed this woman's help.

"You see auras, don't you? It's not so different." She turned toward Enne, her eyes still closed. Goose bumps shot up Enne's arms. "Tell me, what do you see when you look at *her*?"

Levi cleared his throat and adjusted his shirt collar. "I, um..." He looked over Enne's shoulder. Enne mimicked his movement, but there was nothing behind her. She felt strangely on display. She'd never known Levi could read auras, had never thought to ask about his split talent.

Levi's gaze fell to the floor, an embarrassed expression on his face. Enne resisted the urge to fix her hair or adjust her clothes. What exactly could he see?

"Perhaps you can't see it, then," Zula said. "It's a curse. Both of you share it."

The Street of the Holy Tombs might've been a frightening place, but *this* was pushing the limits of Enne's logic. "That isn't why we're here."

"I can see it," Zula said quietly. "The hallway."

Enne instantly thought of the hallway from her dreams, the place of memories and fantasies, with the black and white doors. Both Enne and Levi quickly met each other's eyes. They'd obviously both been struck by Zula's words.

"That's just a nightmare," Levi said hoarsely.

Enne was startled, both by Levi's admission and the distress in his voice. Had he seen the hallway, too? But how was that possible? She'd seen it only in her dreams.

"It's a shade that binds you both," Zula said.

Feeling a bit shaky, and her patience quickly wearing thin, Enne pulled the first item from the bank out of her purse: the king token.

"I came to New Reynes looking for Lourdes," Enne said, placing it on Zula's desk. "I need to know where she is."

Zula looked at the token like it was venomous. "You shouldn't have removed it. It was safe in the bank."

Enne pursed her lips—she didn't deserve Zula's anger. "It's hot to the touch. Do you know what it is?"

"It's a tragedy," Zula snapped. "Countless people died because of what it is. I won't divulge its secret." Zula's vagueness was grating on Enne's nerves. She'd traveled a thousand miles and overcome horrendous obstacles to find answers, and now this woman would withhold them from her?

"Please," she said, but her aggravation was obvious through her mask of politeness. "I need to know."

"Then you'll be disappointed. You should return it."

Enne slid it back into her purse, though she had no intention of returning it at all. She retrieved the second item and placed it in front of the woman. "What about the orb?"

Zula took a shuddering breath. "I know what it is. Where did you get it?"

"It was in the bank," Enne said.

She frowned. "That doesn't make sense. Lourdes wouldn't own anything like that."

Levi picked it up and inspected it. "These aren't volts," he said, which Enne already knew. "But…" He shivered. "I can sometimes feel traces of Mizer auras left on volts, but this isn't a *trace*. It feels…alive."

"Have you ever heard of the Shadow Game?" Zula asked them. Enne's and Levi's heads shot up, and a sickly dread caught in Enne's throat. "So you have. The Phoenix Club hasn't opened the House of Shadows since the Great Street War. At least, not until eight days ago." She opened a drawer from behind her desk and pulled out a second black orb, identical to the other, except empty inside. "The Shadow Game is a game of death, and the players bet their lives. These orbs hold life energy. They are deadly poker chips."

Levi hurriedly set the orb back on the table. "Whose life is inside this one, then?"

"That's a very good question. Only one player in history has ever survived the Shadow Game, but now that she's dead, there shouldn't be any life left inside it." Zula's eyes narrowed as she inspected Enne—her gaze fixed more over her shoulder than on Enne's face. "I don't know the details of that night, but it's possible Gabrielle didn't play with her own life. She wasn't alone in the Game."

"You mean Gabrielle Dondelair," Enne guessed. "My birth mother."

"Lourdes said she'd never tell you that," Zula said sharply.

Enne's breath hitched. There was no question now. What

they'd learned about Gabrielle was absolutely true. "I saw a blood gazer. I did my research."

"You saw a blood gazer?" Zula gaped. "You know your father's blood name?"

"Do you know who he was?" Enne asked.

Zula slammed the desk drawer closed, making both Enne and Levi jolt. "I cannot speak his names."

"But...I should know. I deserve to know."

"I'd tell you if I could. His identity is protected, and he went to great lengths to see it so." That meant his secret was sealed by a Protector, someone like Lourdes. Enne felt like she was grasping at smoke, trying to connect glimpses of the past together.

Enne cleared her throat. "But he is...dead, right?"

Zula took a shaky breath. "Yes. He's gone."

Enne *knew* this. Of course she did. But it still hurt to hear it, after hoping...over and over again.

"When you said that Gabrielle wasn't alone in the Game," Levi said, "what did you mean?"

"There was only one other person involved that night. Since these orbs are used for nothing beyond the Game, and since it cannot belong to Gabrielle, then that only leaves her daughter." Zula met Enne's eyes solemnly. "Gabrielle must have been playing for *your* life that night."

Enne swallowed and stared at the orb. That was her *own* life inside it?

"The reason I bring up the Game," Zula said gravely, "is because of why you're here. Lourdes had been running from the Game for some time, but eight days ago, they found her, and she was invited to play."

The shell Enne had carefully built around her heart shattered, and no number of words or rules would piece it back together now. Before Zula even confirmed Enne's darkest fears, tears began to well in Enne's eyes.

"Muck," Levi whispered.

"Of all the stories from the Great Street War, Lourdes's was the most heartbreaking of them all," Zula said, shaking her head grimly. "Until the end, she did everything in her power to protect you. And now, here you are, a curse in your shadow, an omerta around your neck."

The past tense struck Enne deep and low, like a bell toll that shook inside of her.

She would've known, she would've felt it if Lourdes had died.

She placed a hand over her mouth. Her chest heaved, though she hadn't started to cry yet. She hadn't even taken a breath.

"With the omerta, you can't go home," Zula continued. "You must keep your secret from Vianca at all costs. And, more than anything, *stay away from the House of Shadows*. Lourdes did not die so you would, too."

"Enough," Levi snapped. He reached for Enne's hand, but Enne's gaze was firmly rooted on the floor.

"The only fortune in any of this," Zula continued, "is that you have no power yet. That's better for you. And better for New Reynes."

"Enough!" Levi hollered. He stood abruptly, grabbing Enne by the shoulder and hoisting her up, as well. Enne leaned into the support of his arm around her, holding her breath so as not to cry. She should say something, she knew. Levi shouldn't fight this battle for her. But it felt pointless, knowing she'd already lost the war. "If you were really Lourdes's friend, you could try showing an ounce of compassion."

Zula's expression hardened. "This story will end badly."

The same words Lola had spoken the other day.

This story is already over, Enne thought. *I'm trapped here, and I'm alone.*

Levi pulled Enne toward the door, and she numbly followed. "I don't expect we'll be back," he spat. He was right. Enne had no intention of ever seeing this awful woman again, even if she *had* been Lourdes's friend.

"I'm the only one left who remembers," Zula said solemnly. "If I need to find you, I will."

"Don't." Levi slammed the door.

Outside, he shushed Enne even though she wasn't crying and pressed her against his chest. "I'm sorry," he said. The words were gentle, but uselessly so. Enne was already broken. "I'm so sorry."

Lourdes had died the day before Enne reached New Reynes. All this time she'd been searching for her face in the crowds, wandering memories of her in her dreams, and she'd been chasing a ghost. Had she left earlier... Had she asked questions earlier...

"It was always the two of us and no one else," Enne whispered. "And now I'm alone."

Without Lourdes, Enne was truly lost. Her mother was the only one who'd remember the girl Enne had been before, now that Enne was already starting to forget herself. Lourdes was her lighthouse, her guideline, and now Enne had no way of finding her way back—to Bellamy, to herself or to the life she'd once lived.

Her mother had probably died thinking that, at the very least, her daughter was safe at home. And that was the tragedy of it all.

"You're not alone," Levi murmured, squeezing her tighter. Enne looked up at him, studying her own heartbreak reflected in his eyes. Finally, she began to cry.

Compared to her mother, Levi was a pale sliver of light, a fraying thread—but he was something. And so she nodded and let him guide her home.

DAY EIGHT

"Legends of the North Side are born in
the gutters and die on the gallows."

—*The City of Sin, a Guidebook:*
Where To Go and Where Not To

ENNE

Enne curled into a fetal position and leaned against the pole on a corner of the trapeze platform. The dusty windows of the practice warehouse gleamed with moonlight and the flashing advertisements of Tropps Street. She'd been here all night, ever since the show ended hours before.

It was the second performance Lourdes had ever missed.

Her mother used to claim she had the best view in the back, and last night, after her second show, Enne had checked the back row dozens of times, both out of habit and longing, staring into the faces of strangers.

Before Enne left Bellamy, she'd already had a list of questions to ask Lourdes. Since arriving in New Reynes, she felt like the city had handed her two new mysteries for every question answered. If Enne had only one more chance to speak to Lourdes, only one question to ask, it wouldn't be about her parents, about the bank or even about the lies.

Tell me your story, she'd plead. The heartbreak that Zula had mentioned, the memory of Lourdes crying while holding baby

Enne… She needed to know. How had Lourdes known her parents? What happened during the Great Street War? How young had she been?

Had she asked for this?

White chalk coated Enne's hands, and she drew zigzags with it on her thighs. Her fingernails left scratch marks on her pale skin.

Alongside her grief, a darker thought lingered, one Enne had suspected but Zula had confirmed. Enne had spent her life on the periphery of her world, no matter how hard she worked, no matter how desperately she tried. Until she arrived in the City of Sin.

Nine days ago, Zula had said. Lourdes had died the day before Enne arrived in New Reynes.

The day before Enne arrived in New Reynes, Lourdes's protection had broken.

Enne had already known Lourdes had used her talents to keep Enne safe, but she hadn't truly understood what that meant. Her mother had kept her invisible. Now Enne's memories of Lourdes wiping away her daughter's frustrated tears, of teasing her about her social ambitions—they all seemed tainted. Enne had never suffered in her life—not truly—but that didn't mean those hurts hadn't mattered to her. She'd agonized over them. She'd accepted them.

And Lourdes had watched.

Hot, bitter tears sprang from Enne's eyes. She'd cried a lot since yesterday. She'd cried for the story of her mother's life that she'd never know, for a woman she somehow both loved and resented. She'd cried for the girl she used to be. From her first lie to Levi, her poisoning of Sedric, her battle with Lola—the city was turning her into someone she didn't recognize.

But the more she thought about her life before, about her ambitions and her character, Enne knew she'd always been this determined, this ruthless. Thanks to Lourdes's protection, she'd merely lacked the opportunity to truly know herself. She was a pistol wrapped up in silk. She was a blade disguised as a girl.

Enne practiced for another hour on the trapeze, pushing her limits with tricks and moves she wasn't ready for. Repeatedly, she lost her grip on the bar, or her strength gave out.

She'd begun to relish how it felt to fall.

While climbing the ladder to the platform, Enne suddenly noticed that she had a real audience. Lola watched from far below, her arms crossed. Enne vaguely remembered something about Scrap Market, a promise she'd made Before.

"How long have you been here?" Enne called.

"Not long," she answered. "I couldn't find you in the casino. Didn't think you wanted to cancel our trip, though."

Enne had no reason to go to Scrap Market now. Digging up Lourdes's old newspaper articles wouldn't change anything, wouldn't bring her back. But telling Lola about Lourdes would acknowledge what had happened, and that seemed more difficult than pretending everything was normal.

"Are the Iron boys coming?" Lola asked.

She hadn't seen Levi since yesterday evening. He'd been nothing but kind to her, but still, she preferred to be alone with her grief. If he came, she wouldn't be able to keep up her charade.

"No," she said. "It's just us."

It was so early that the sun had yet to rise. Dew and fog clung to the streets in front of the abandoned factory in Scar Land, the noise inside piercing through the night's quiet. Since her first encounter with Lola, Enne hadn't ventured outside of St. Morse after dark, so she'd grown accustomed to the ever-present loudness of Tropps Street, where dice rattled and drunkards sang no matter the hour. Here in the Factory District, the silence felt almost tangible: heavy and cold.

Lola pushed open the factory's doors, and the two of them slipped inside.

It was almost as large as a city block, with various stalls and carts clustered in the rows between machinery and conveyor belts. The bustle of the crowd reverberated around the interior, a chorus of haggling and bidding for everything from food to weapons. It smelled of cigarettes and roasted sausage, neither of which appealed to Enne's unsettled stomach.

A hundred feet or more above their heads, children climbed the rafters and vents as if they were a playground.

"They could fall," Enne said. She twisted the inside of her dress's pocket in her fist. The crowds made her claustrophobic, though she'd never felt that way before. Maybe she simply wasn't used to Scrap Market. Maybe what she called anxiety others called thrill. But a sense of dread imbedded itself in her stomach, and every click of her heels sounded like the loading of a gun.

She shouldn't have agreed to come.

"Nah, they won't fall," Lola answered. "They're just show-ing off. Trying to get noticed by the Guild."

Enne normally would have asked what she meant, but she was too exhausted. Part of her decided that she no longer cared, that this city would always be a mystery no matter how much she attempted to understand it.

"Let's stop over here first," Lola said, pointing to a stall cov-ered with huge pieces of fabric and moth-eaten tapestries. "Ask-ing what we're asking…we might want a bit of anonymity." She ruffled through the bins of used clothing and fished out a thin black sash. "Here. It almost matches that lipstick you have."

Enne rubbed the satin between her fingers. The quality was reasonable, and unlike the rest of the clothes, there weren't any stains or rips.

Lola cut two even holes in the satin with her scalpel knife, then tied it behind Enne's head.

"Feel good?" Lola asked.

"Sure," Enne said flatly.

After they paid for the sash, Lola slipped a mask of her own out of her pocket, tied it on and led Enne to another stall. The air around it was so humid from the steam vent nearby that Enne felt like she was breathing sludge. Inside, a man with yellow lips sat on a stool holding a pipe. He wore a glove on one hand, but pieces of hay stuck out of it. In fact, his entire left sleeve was lumpy and thicker than the right.

"He's got old newspapers he's willing to sell," Lola whispered.

"'Lo," the man greeted them. "Who are you two who look up to no good?"

"My name is—" Enne started, until Lola elbowed her side. Enne reddened, chagrined—masks were useless if they gave away their names. "…we're customers."

"Pleasure to meet ya."

"We're looking for old newspapers," Lola said. "Articles by specific journalists."

"How old we talking?" He set his pipe on the table.

"Ten to twenty years ago."

"What journalists are you looking for?"

Lola nodded for Enne to speak, and Enne took a deep breath until she found her voice.

"We're interested in a writer named Séance." That was the pen name Reymond had told her, the day she'd arrived.

He sucked on his bottom lip. Its yellow color made him look almost inhuman. "Ah, you *are* up to no good. I used to read the Pseudonyms when I was young and foolish." He leaned forward. His straw arm remained in the same spot, so with his position, it made his shoulder look detached. "There was Jester—another pen name. Ventriloquist. Nostalgia. Shade."

"Do you have any of the papers?" Enne asked. She hadn't realized until now how much she wanted to read one of Lourdes's articles. Even knowing they had reached their ultimate dead end, and there was no chance they would find her mother alive, she could still learn more about why Lourdes had led her double life, and she could hear the words from Lourdes herself.

It was the closest she would ever get to her mother's story.

"I might have one that escaped the burnings," he said.

"You might?"

"It will cost ya. Fifteen volts. Or a trade."

Fifteen volts was hardly pocket change, but it was worth it. Vianca's first paycheck had already arrived, both for Enne's acrobatics performances and her other assignment. It was very generous. Enne would not hurt for volts in this city if she continued to work at St. Morse.

"I'll pay in volts," she said.

He eyed her skeptically. "Fine." His straw arm hung limply as he walked to one of the tables and reached for a box underneath. He riffled through piles of old newspapers and pamphlets.

"How'd you lose your arm?" Lola asked.

The man smiled. His teeth were even yellower than his lips. "I sold it."

Enne's stomach did an unpleasant somersault.

He grabbed a thin newspaper and a small, cheap-looking orb—gray-tinted glass, with a murky look to it—from a soup can on the table. Enne wondered if it could even hold the fifteen volts. But she pulled one of her own orbs from her pocket anyway, unscrewed the cap and paid. His shoddy orb managed the transaction without shattering.

He handed her the paper. It was called *The Antiquist*. This issue must have featured one of Lourdes's articles. Enne folded it and slipped it in her breast pocket.

"That's the only one I got," he said.

"Thank you," Enne told him, and she meant it. She crossed her arms protectively to keep the paper close to her chest. "What's your name? We haven't met many who know about the Pseudonyms."

"Sold my name, too."

"Why—"

"Thanks for your help," Lola said suddenly. She pushed Enne

out of the stall before she could finish her question. Upon re-entering the Market, however, someone sprinting down the aisle slammed into Enne's side. She yelped and nearly toppled over Lola's boots.

The girl who'd hit her had scars covering her palms. She ran out of sight, swallowed by the crowds.

In the stall across from them, a man cleared away his food cart. A pile of cabbages dropped and rolled on the floor, and a woman tripped on one as she hurried past. Everywhere, people packed. People ran.

A gun fired on the other side of the factory, and Enne's heart jolted so fast she almost retched.

"Whiteboots. It's a raid on the Scarhands," Lola said, anxiously reaching for Enne's arm. "We need to get out of here."

Hordes of people rushed toward the exit of the factory, trampling each other and clogging the only escape route. Enne and Lola followed, but it was soon clear that the crowd wasn't moving.

Even on her tiptoes, Enne couldn't see ahead. "What's happening?"

"The door must be closed."

Behind them, whiteboots charged into the crowd, their guns and batons raised. They looked like wolves herding sheep to slaughter.

A man turned and smacked Enne's side with his bag. She staggered as the heavy bundle knocked the wind out of her, and her heart slammed into her throat. Beside her, another person cursed when Enne knocked whatever they were carrying out of their hands. They were packed in here. Trapped.

Enne fearfully reached for the revolver in her pocket, but Lola grabbed her wrist and shook her head. "Don't bother," she said, her eyes downcast. "That first night, when I took your gun... I unloaded it. I never gave the bullets back."

Enne's eyes widened. She glanced down and opened the revolver's compartment, and sure enough, it was empty.

She resisted the urge to snap at Lola. Of all the times to be out of bullets… Enne might've been able to escape any real punishment from the whiteboots—though any encounter with them was a risk of exposure—but Lola had the Doves' white in her hair. It didn't matter what she had or hadn't done—she'd be marked as guilty. If anyone was feeling the pain of their lack of ammo, it was Lola.

"We need to find a way out," Lola squeaked.

Enne searched for another exit or a place to hide, but with the crowd, she could see nowhere but up. Above their heads, the kids on the rafters climbed toward a window. A boy pulled himself through it onto the roof. To safety.

Her eyes fell on a huge piece of machinery, some sort of retired generator. Not far from that was a column with two bars that branched out like a Y.

"Come on," Enne said. Their hands still clasped, she pulled Lola through the crowd and toward the generator. Stepping on a lever, Enne climbed onto the huge mechanical cylinder and hoisted herself up.

"You're shatz," Lola breathed once she realized Enne's plan. She stared at the kids near the ceiling with wide eyes.

But then she reached up and grasped Enne's hand, and Enne pulled her up. After a few moments of hesitation, Lola jumped to the column. She landed awkwardly on one foot but managed to steady herself.

Enne leaped and landed behind her. Lola scrambled up with her arms wrapped around the pole so tightly that her shirt bunched around her neck, exposing part of her stomach.

"You need to climb faster," Enne urged. "Before they notice us."

The whiteboots had reached the crowd. One of them grabbed a girl by her hair and pulled her down to her knees. Others pointed their clubs at the wide-eyed customers, who raised their arms in surrender. In the front, a group of men pounded against the closed door and screamed.

Enne swung herself around the angled pole, her back facing down, and climbed the opposite column with her legs wrapped around the beam. Now she wouldn't need to wait for Lola to move faster. The bolts on the side of the column were large enough to grasp.

Enne made it to one of the metal rafters near the ceiling. It wasn't until she'd seized it and swung her legs over that she looked down. The climb hadn't appeared quite so high from the ground. Lola, on the other hand, seemed all too aware of this. She climbed to the steady rhythm of, "Muck, muck, muck."

At least a dozen children huddled on the rafters, some as young as seven. They watched Enne in fascination and nervousness as she stood—she probably looked rather intimidating in her black mask. Below, a few people pointed at her, *saw* her. Enne was reminded once again that she was no longer invisible. She was powerful—but she was also vulnerable.

Lola appeared several feet away, dripping sweat. She hauled herself up with all the gracefulness of a walrus. "Shatz. You're shatz."

Enne ignored her and calculated the route to the window that she'd seen the boy escape from earlier. Then she realized why the other children hadn't moved: there was a twelve-foot gap between their beam and the one near the window. A huge black cord spanned across the distance, pulled taut. Several kids on either side worked to knot it to the closest beams.

A tightrope.

Lola blanched. "There's no *mucking* way."

"How did they already get over there?" Enne asked the kids.

"They came in from there. From the roof," answered a girl with waist-length black hair. She looked to be about eleven. "We took the stairs." She nodded to the opposite end of the factory, where a stairwell climbed most of the way up a corner wall to reach an office level. Enne hadn't seen it, being so far away, with all the whiteboots between here and there. She and Lola had taken a more strenuous route. No wonder the kids had looked at them with such amazement.

"We should just wait," Lola said, her voice shaking. "The whiteboots will leave eventually."

"Or come up eventually," the girl muttered.

Enne looked down again. Several of the whiteboots already stood still, watching them, waiting them out.

"The whiteboots will be gentle with you," Enne told the girl. "You're all young, what could they—"

The girl shook her head and showed Enne her hands. They were covered in scars. Enne realized all of them bore matching marks. They were *children*.

"We just swore," the girl explained. "Eight Fingers never let us, but Scavenger did."

Which meant all of them—not just Lola—were in danger.

Enne inched over to the cord. No net to catch her here.

"You could just wrap your legs around the cord and hang upside down," Enne said as Lola crawled on her stomach closer to her, her chin pressed against the cool metal of the rafter. She looked absurd, all trembling and pale. Then Enne realized that maybe it was *she* who looked absurd, confident enough to stand and give direction.

"There are holes in the wire," Lola said, indicating several bare patches with no covering. At the cord's other end, it was plugged into a machine on the ceiling. "That might be on. Touch it, and you're fried."

"Rubber soles," Enne reminded her. She flicked the cord in a safe spot. It wasn't perfectly taut, but the give wasn't severe.

"Fall and you die," Lola countered.

"Then use your clothes."

The black-haired girl slid off her jacket. She carefully walked around Enne, then slipped her coat over the cord and wrapped both sleeves around her wrists and clenched hands.

"You're actually doing that?" hissed the boy beside her. He had swollen cheeks, like he'd recently had a tooth pulled.

She shot him a devious smirk. "Yeah. Tell them all to watch."

She fell. The jacket turned over the cord, holding her, and she wrapped her legs around the wire. The other children watched in awe as she crawled upside down to the other side.

They were moving, and that was a start. "You go next," the girl called across to the boy.

Crying unabashedly, he slipped his knitted scarf over the cord and bound it to his wrists. He slowly eased his way off the beam and wrapped his ankles around the top of the wire. It took him ages to move even an inch.

"Kelvin, you gotta move faster," the girl urged impatiently from the other side. "There are others waiting." However, only a few of the others looked willing to even attempt the cross.

"I… I'm…" Kelvin stammered. He was a third of the way across now and shaking uncontrollably.

"He looks like he's gonna piss himself," another girl behind Enne, around nine years old, said loudly enough for Kelvin to hear. Enne was torn between shock at her language and fear that Kelvin actually might.

He was halfway across now. The nine-year-old took off her jacket to go next.

Kelvin's scarf snapped.

He didn't react fast enough. His ankles unlatched, and he fell, screaming. The girl on the other side reached out desperately, as if she could catch him from so far away.

The crowd shrieked when Kelvin hit an old conveyor belt with a bone-crunching thud. His blood splattered across the metal, and his neck was bent at an unnatural angle. Enne hurriedly looked away, fighting her urge to be sick.

One of the boys behind Enne vomited into his hands. The

girl on the other side hugged the beam and stared down at Kelvin's body, moaning to herself.

The crowds grew louder at the gruesome display, and the chaos below them became more and more violent. As the protesters brawled with the whiteboots, several other officials were making their way toward the stairs. Toward them.

"Time to move," the nine-year-old squeaked. "My jacket isn't gonna break, so I'm going."

She made it across. By that time, the first girl had crawled off the beam to the window. Lola and Enne shared a look, an unspoken agreement to wait until the other children had crossed, despite the whiteboots charging up the stairs. Lola closed her eyes and pressed her face to the beam. Every few seconds, she lifted one hand to make sure that her top hat was still pinned to her hair.

There was crying and pauses and cursing, but no more accidents. Everyone reached the other side.

"I should go last," Enne said to Lola. "I'll be the quickest."

"If I die, I will haunt you. And your children. And your children's children—"

"Just go." They didn't have time to waste. The whiteboots had made it to the ceiling's rafters. Although they were admittedly far away, they wouldn't be for long. Lola wore the mark of an assassin—the whiteboots very well might shoot first and ask questions later.

"Muck," Lola murmured. She put her coat around the cord and slid upside down. During that split second of falling, she bit on her lip so hard it bled. Lola muttered to herself and moved inches at a time—quickly, in a worm-like fashion that would've made Enne laugh in any other situation—and was three-quarters of the way there when her hat slid off, exposing the white of her hair.

Gunshot.

It missed. Lola shrieked and grabbed hold of the beam on the other side. Two more gunshots. Enne crouched, her stomach in her throat. *No. Please no*, she thought. *I didn't even want to come here. I shouldn't have come at all.*

Lola pulled herself onto the beam and slid forward on her stomach toward the window. She motioned for Enne to hurry, but Enne was frozen. A bullet clattered off the beam below her feet.

Enne recited Lourdes's rules to herself.

Don't let them see your fear.

She took her first step on the cord. She was steady. *Breathe.*

Never allow yourself to be lost.

She took another. A gunshot whizzed past her outstretched arm.

She ran. Quickly, lightly.

One stride. Two strides. Three strides. Then she slipped.

She caught the rope by her underarms, and for a few seconds, no one shot. They thought that she was about to fall.

Trust no one unless you must.

She raised her arms so that the cord slid into her hands. It was a miracle she hadn't touched bare wire. One kick forward turned into a swing. Two swings and she got her legs on the beam.

Lola jumped through the window while Enne lay down and kissed the metal of the rafter. Enne stood up and followed hurriedly, her acrobatic grace failing her in her rush to escape. Her foot caught the windowpane, and she toppled over the other side onto a roof. Enne landed on her back, and it knocked the wind out of her.

Lola, lying beside her, punched her shoulder. *Good job*, Enne thought she meant. *You're shatz*, she probably also meant. She couldn't argue.

Enne sat up and leaned against the wall. She was breathing hard and fighting down the urge to either laugh or cry.

The Scarhands gawked, gathered around a different window, where they'd watched Lola and Enne brave the cord. The girl who'd known Kelvin covered her face with the coat she'd used to cross, her shoulders heaving.

"We should still be moving," Enne said. "The whiteboots saw us leave." She looked out into the distance, at the unappealing view of the Factory District.

Someone tapped her arm. It was one of the kids. "Who are you?"

"Séance," Lola answered for her. Enne shot the blood gazer a furious look. What sort of game was she playing?

"Are you one of the Scarhands?" She looked at Enne's unmarked palms with confusion.

Lola grinned. "Would Scavenger be brave enough to do that?"

"No way," the girl said. She looked at Enne with the kind of reverence she had once seen Mansi direct at Levi.

Enne had nearly forgotten why they'd come to Scrap Market in the first place. Ignoring them, she pulled the newspaper from her pocket and flipped through the pages until she found Lourdes's article.

Lola nodded urgently. "We should leave." But Enne wasn't paying attention.

The ink was too blotched to read anything but the title: "Not Forgotten." The paper looked as if someone had submerged it in water.

Enne stared at the incomprehensible words and balled the newspaper in her fist. "That. *Horrid*. Man."

This had been her last chance to hear Lourdes's voice, and it had been a trick. Tears blurred her vision. Usually she'd feel embarrassed for crying in front of others, but now she no longer cared.

Lola put her arm around Enne's shoulder. It was an intimate gesture for someone who carried such conflicted feelings about Enne's well-being.

"We need to leave," Lola said. "You're the *lord*." Her words sounded forced—an act. She leaned down closer to Enne's ear.

"They're waiting for you to move. And we *all* need to get out of here."

The others surrounding them watched Enne hesitantly, as if waiting instruction. As if Enne really was a street lord.

Lola's desperate look urged her into action. They crawled across the sloping roof of the warehouse, then jumped to the building beside it. Enne landed gracefully on her feet. Lola, however, crumbled to her knees as soon as she hit the cement.

Unsurprisingly, hopping roofs was an exhausting activity. When they reached a rooftop several blocks away from the factory, Enne and Lola huffed for breath, and the blood gazer's hands were covered in scrapes from repeatedly stumbling and bracing herself. They were a safe enough distance away that the kids had begun to scatter. Now it was just the two of them.

"There are thousands of them in the North Side, just like that," Lola said. "Pulling stunts. Haunting gang territories. Hoping to be noticed by the Guild or by their lords." She grimaced. "They'd be the most vulnerable if another war broke out on the North Side. There's no one to protect them."

Enne's heart twisted into something painful and ugly. She didn't have it in her right now to listen to one of Lola's accusatory tirades.

"Why did you call me Séance?" she asked, fighting to keep the tension out of her voice.

"All lords have a street name."

"I thought you wanted me dead. 'A weapon to whoever owns me' and all?"

"I still think you're dangerous. Maybe more dangerous than I first believed. I thought the city would claim you—break you." Lola paused, looking intensely into Enne's eyes. "Now I think the city could be yours to claim."

Enne grimaced. "That wasn't your decision to make."

Lola was too late, anyway. Enne was already broken, already claimed.

"Do you want to know the real reason I dyed my hair white?" Lola clenched her fists and turned toward the skyline. "After we lost our parents, my brothers and I swore we wouldn't go near the gangs. We were young, so we worked under the table. My oldest brother was attending a music conservatory on the South Side, and once he finished, he was going to take care of all of us.

"Then I found out he'd been lying. He'd joined a gang, thought it was an easier way to provide. And when that gang fell, I watched him get shot. I watched him die."

Enne held her breath. She hadn't asked for Lola's story—she wasn't prepared for it. It was an unwelcome reminder that her tragedy wasn't the only one in the world, that she wasn't the only one who carried scars. Now she understood why Lola hated guns.

"After that, it was only me and my younger brother left. But Justin, he didn't just mourn our brother—he obsessed over him, the gangs, the North Side. He stopped caring about me. He stopped caring about anything except his own ambitions. He joined the Doves."

Lola took off her top hat, letting down her white hair. "When you join the Doves, your name is replaced with a new one. You do not leave. You speak to no one." Lola clenched her fist. "And so I moved to Dove Land, dyed my hair white and started working for the Orphan Guild…all for a chance at a scrap of information, anything to lead me back to Justin, to know if he's even alive. Even if he doesn't care, I still do."

Lola finally turned to face her, her expression unusually soft. "So I get it. We're each looking for someone. We'd each do whatever it takes to find them. In the end, we're the same. And if…" She cleared her throat. "If you *did* call yourself a lord, if you claimed real power, then maybe you could help me find him."

Enne took a deep, strained breath. It had felt wrong to interrupt Lola during her story, but now that Lola had told her truth, Enne would need to share hers.

"Lourdes is dead, Lola," Enne said softly, and Lola tensed. "She was dead before I even came to New Reynes." Enne sat and hugged her knees to herself. "I don't even know why I came with you to Scrap Market. Looking for the article was a waste of time."

She'd been deluding herself, anyway. Lourdes wouldn't have spoken to her daughter through the words of the article. It would have been ink, not a voice. She would've written about revolutions or elections or change, and none of those things really mattered. She wouldn't have told Enne that she loved her. She wouldn't have been able to hear Enne tell her that she loved her, too.

"I'm so sorry, Enne," Lola said, crouching down beside her. "How did you find out?"

"Levi and I visited the address. The Street of the Holy Tombs." Enne untied the mask and dropped it at Lola's feet. "I'm done with this now. The searching. There isn't anything left to find, and even if there was, it's too dangerous. I'm sorry about your brothers, and I'm sorry about what you thought I was. But I need to focus on staying alive."

Lola turned away so Enne couldn't see her face, but Enne sensed that she was disappointed. The two girls weren't quite friends, but they'd come a long way from being enemies.

"You're giving up?" Lola's voice cracked. "Even if she's dead, there's still—"

"There's nothing left to find."

Enne turned her back. Before she leaped to the next roof, she said one more word to Lola—a message intended for someone else, someone who wouldn't ever be able to hear it.

"Goodbye."

LEVI

Sedric expected the volts in two days, and Levi was two and a half thousand short.

Beside him, Jac licked his hands and smoothed back his blond hair. Levi straightened his tie and rolled up his sleeves to expose the tattoos on his arms. A message, just like his million-volt smile: he was the Iron Lord, strutting into a gambling tavern. His territory. His kingdom.

They turned the corner. The lights of the gambling den were dimmed by heavy shades on the windows. It was called Dead at Dawn—opened at midnight, closed at sunrise. As Levi cut through the line outside, the bouncer eyed his black tattoos and his blacker eye.

"Pup," he said. "Back from the dead. I heard Chez killed you."

News traveled fast on the North Side. "Funny. I've never felt better," Levi replied with a tight smile.

The man behind him growled for cutting to the front. Levi bristled, though only slightly. This was a gambling den, and he was—had been—the gambling lord. He could do what he pleased.

"That so?" the bouncer asked. He looked at Jac. "If Chez were lord, he'd have *your* oath. But you're with Pup. Interesting."

Jac bared his teeth. "My oath belongs to the Iron Lord."

Levi tipped his hat, and the bouncer held open the door as they passed through.

Light bulbs flashed everywhere, dangling from the ceiling by wires, and a jazz band played in the back. The air was so thick with cigar smoke that when Levi exhaled, a patch of clear air formed around his lips. Levi wove through the tables searching for a game of Tropps. They had specifically chosen this den because it wasn't a client—none of the dealers were Irons, which meant they were unlikely to encounter trouble. As Jac split from him and headed toward the roulette wheels, Levi slipped into an empty seat at a Tropps table.

The young man beside Levi wore all black clothes and an obnoxious feather behind his ear. He grinned at Levi with rotted teeth and white lips, and he reeked of dead flesh.

"Nice feather," Levi said. "That new?"

"Needed something new, now that I'm the Scar Lord," Jonas Maccabees replied. "I see *you* still got the tattoos, though. Those reminders are forever."

Jonas and Levi had never gotten along, but for some reason, Scavenger's voice lacked its usual edge. Maybe being lord suited him. Or maybe Levi's *not* being lord suited him, as well.

"I still keep wondering why," Jonas said quietly. "We never messed with the Torrens."

Levi swallowed a lump of guilt and grief. "I've got no idea."

"If Reymond was here, he'd call you a liar."

"Are you gonna cause a scene?" The night was young. There were other dens.

Jonas ground his teeth. "Not tonight."

As the dealer passed out the cards, Levi did his best to ignore

Jonas's silent fury and horrifying smell so he could focus on the game. His hand wasn't all that terrible, but not all that good, either. He carefully fiddled with the cards concealed in his sleeve.

He didn't win the first round, and the second time he drew only low cards and folded immediately. Even when he tried, it was hard not to think about the due date in two days, circling him with fangs bared. About Enne telling him she was alone. About Chez on his old throne. It didn't help having Scavenger beside him, a physical reminder of how he'd risen while Levi had fallen.

When he found his opportunity, Levi exchanged the cards in his hand for the better ones up his sleeve. It was dexterous, fast. Not even Jonas beside him had seen it. Levi didn't need to think to switch the cards—the movements were automatic, memorized from a time when he still sat on street corners, dressed as a legend long past, asking victims if they'd like to play.

His short winning streak distracted him the way only hope could. He slid a miniature tower of chips to his pile as the dealer passed him his new card. He grabbed it.

The smoke of Dead at Dawn cleared, and Levi stood in front of a white door in the hallway. Dimly, he recalled what Zula had said about the hallway, about the shade that bound him and Enne, but really, all he could think was that he needed to find a particular door. He reached forward and turned the knob of the one in front of him. It opened.

Levi stepped into a room filled with familiar smoke and murky lights. He was in Dead at Dawn, but he hadn't woken up. The men shouted. A whistle blared. After he pushed his way through the sweaty bodies that reeked of absinthe and cigars, he reached the edge of the boxing pit. Jac lay on the ground. He wore only a white undershirt and his pants—who knew where he'd left his jacket and button-up. The man above him kicked him in the side, but Jac was already unconscious.

"Jac!" Levi shouted, panicking.

The opponent lowered himself to his knees and punched Jac in the face. Again. And again. The floor below them glinted with blood and a missing tooth.

Then the opponent paused and looked up at Levi. He winked. Levi recognized him as the man who'd followed him into the burning building in Scrap Market. Who'd delivered his second Shadow Card. Who'd stopped him from saving Reymond.

This was Sedric's second reminder. First Reymond, now Jac.

Levi's heart stilled. This wasn't real. This wasn't happening. The dealer must've slipped him a Shadow Card, so this was only a hallucination—nonsense, just like anything to do with the hallway or Zula's "talent" for reading shades.

But if this *was* real, like a voice inside him warned, then Levi needed to stop it. He needed to wake up.

Levi checked his brass pocket watch, and, judging by how long he'd played Tropps before he passed out, this scene was either happening right now as he slumped unconscious in his seat, or just a few minutes into the future.

He knew only one way to wake up from a nightmare, and that was to die. Levi tapped the shoulder of the man beside him. The second he turned, Levi punched him in the nose. It broke with a satisfying crunch and a gushing of blood.

The man stumbled back into the crowd and cursed. A heartbeat later his knuckles collided with Levi's jaw. Levi moaned, hoisting himself up with the help of the barrier encircling the boxing pit, and pulled his knife from his pocket with no intention of using it. The second the man saw it, he pulled out his own, with every intention of slicing it across Levi's throat.

Three punches, one kick and thirty seconds later, he did.

Levi gasped and woke to the feeling of cold liquid being poured on his head. He sat up, his skin clammy, and wiped the Gambler's Ruin out of his eyes.

"I thought you mighta died," Jonas said cheerily. He set his empty glass down and held out his hand to help Levi up, but Levi shook his head and stood up himself. He didn't want Jonas to feel the Shadow Card hidden inside his clenched hand.

"Feeling kind today?" Levi asked, tryng to catch his breath.

"Kind?" Jonas echoed. "No one's ever accused me of kindness."

Levi's gaze fell on the table, and he cursed when he realized all the chips he'd won were gone. Whatever. Jac was more important, and if the scene from the hallway was as prophetic as Levi feared, Jac might already be in the ring.

Levi's reputation was already down the drain, and now he'd fainted in front of another street lord. Jonas smiled, and though they were the same height, it still felt as if Jonas was looking down on him with cruel delight. He'd always liked to watch Levi squirm.

But Levi didn't care about losing his reputation anymore. Not like he cared about losing his best friend.

"Never mind," Levi muttered as he shoved the card in his pocket. He grabbed his hat off the ground and turned, trying to find his way to the boxing ring.

He raced down a flight of stairs and into the room from his vision, following the word *PIT* painted in red on the walls. His wounded leg and broken rib throbbed with each hurried step.

Jac was still conscious. He staggered as the man—Sedric's man, the same from the vision—punched him in the chest. Levi jolted for a moment, seeing his vision so clearly confirmed, and then he fingered the gun in his pocket. But shooting Jac's opponent was a big risk—Levi wouldn't be able to pay Sedric back from a jail cell, nor would prison protect him from the don's vengeance. Besides, unlike Eight Fingers or Ivory, Levi wasn't a killer.

He rushed to the referee who sat on a chair overlooking the pit.

"You have to stop the match," Levi told him.

"Why is that?" the man asked, his eyes never leaving the fight.

"That boy's only seventeen. He's not of age."

"You got a birth certificate?" The referee took a sip from his glass.

Jac tripped. His opponent kicked him in the back. On the other side of the pit, the man who'd killed Levi during his vision cheered Jac's opponent on. Chills spread down Levi's back—it certainly wasn't a sight he saw every day.

He whipped back around to the referee. *"Please."* Not something Levi said every day, either.

"Get lost."

Levi spotted a bar twenty steps ahead, and he didn't even stop to think—he ran. The bartender shouted as Levi jumped over the counter and grabbed two double handles of absinthe. He charged at Levi, but Levi was already leaping back over the bar and heading for the pit. Levi yanked open the lids and poured the alcohol all over the straw-covered ground of the ring. The referee whistled, but he ignored him. When Levi snapped his fingers, a spark flew out and ignited half the pit.

Levi jumped. He hit the ground and fell into the flames, but as he rolled out into the dirt, the fire on his clothes extinguished. Jac lay on the ground, deathly still. His opponent stared at the inferno with wide eyes, and the crowd above scattered and charged toward the stairs.

Levi grabbed the opponent and twisted him around. The man must've recognized Levi from Scrap Market, because he grunted when their eyes met.

"Tell Torren that if he lays a hand on Jac," Levi snarled, "I'll burn the flesh off his bones."

Dangerous words to say to a Torren. It was the sort of thing any of the Torren cousins would take pleasure in doing to him.

Levi pulled the gun from his pocket. Before he could aim it and make a proper threat, someone else's bullet hit the man between the eyes. The man wavered for a moment, blood trickling down his brow bone, nose and lips, and then he collapsed at Levi's feet.

Above them, Jonas pocketed his pistol and motioned for Levi to hurry. No time to be fazed by the man shot two feet in front of him, Levi picked up Jac—the fire was gaining, and even if it wouldn't hurt Levi, it would burn Jac—and carried him to the edge of the ring. Jonas grabbed Jac's arm over the barrier and hoisted him over.

"Why did you help me?" Levi asked breathlessly.

"Who doesn't want Pup to owe them a favor?"

"I…" To understate it, the idea of owing Scavenger a favor sounded less than appealing. "Thank you."

Jonas snatched the black feather from behind his ear and set it on the referee's empty chair, like a calling card. "You tried to save Reymond. I didn't forget."

Jonas headed for the stairs and left Levi in the burning building with Jac. Levi gritted his teeth. This time, he wouldn't *try* to save anyone. He *would* save Jac.

Levi slapped Jac lightly on the cheek. The hideous black stitches on his eyebrow had unlaced, and the cut oozed with blood. "Wake up. Time to leave."

Jac's eyes didn't open.

Levi threw him over his shoulder—which was no small feat, given Jac's broad frame and Levi's broken rib—and hauled him up the stairs and through the gambling room.

Outside, it was still night, though it felt like hours had passed. Jac groaned, stirring slightly in Levi's hold.

"You should've forfeited, you thickhead," Levi said. He wasn't even sure if Jac had heard him. He stood his friend upright and slapped his cheek lightly again. "Walk with me. You're killing me, here." His leg, his rib, his everything screamed out in pain. Jac muttered something unintelligible and stumbled forward, the bulk of his weight still leaning against Levi's shoulder.

When they finally made it to St. Morse, Jac was mostly lucid.

Levi laid him on the couch, then handed him a glass of whiskey for the pain. He hurriedly rummaged around his drawers for first aid supplies—Jac was covered in scrapes.

Levi bent down to open the kit and winced—muck, his rib hurt.

Jac reached forward, and his fingers twisted around the buttons in Levi's shirt. "You're hurt. Let me help."

Levi pushed his hand away. Jac's split talent for taking away pain was inviting, but he knew better than agree. When Jac took away pain, it didn't disappear—Jac carried it himself. No matter how many times his friend offered, no matter the circumstance, Levi always declined. His pain was his own, and Jac always took on more than he could manage.

"I'm stronger than you think," Jac grumbled.

"But not as strong as *you* think." Levi grabbed Jac by the jaw and opened his mouth. "That's a nice missing tooth." He stuffed a wet tea bag into the empty spot. "This will help the bleeding." The scene reminded him of the Jac from three years ago, the one who'd depended on Lullaby to lull him and his pain to sleep, no matter the acts of rage and recklessness it triggered during the day. This wasn't the first time Levi had played nurse, caught between worry and anger.

"I'm sorry," Jac said, as if he knew what Levi was thinking. Jac hardly remembered anything from that year.

Levi slapped him on the shoulder. "I know. Just try to get some sleep."

He headed to the kitchen and lit the oven. He'd had this idea a while ago—a bad idea, of course. He'd just left Dead at Dawn empty-handed, and he had one more day to win back the volts for Sedric. Even if he spent all of tomorrow gambling, there was nothing to win during the day. If he was going to pay Sedric as soon as the tenth day arrived, then he had only one more night. One more chance. And he needed to win big.

Luckluster was the only other casino in New Reynes that could shell out that sort of voltage in one night.

It was a completely shatz idea, gambling in Sedric's own casino. Levi knew that.

But not if he was guaranteed to win.

He didn't remember the last time he'd made glass. The special oven he kept in his apartment was the result of a half-hearted decision from years ago to fiddle with glass cores in false dice. The con had fallen through, and he hadn't used the oven since, but he'd never bothered to get rid of it.

After nearly an hour spent kindling the oven, Levi reached inside and removed the pot of the glass mixture, which glowed a fluorescent orange. Fluorescence—he'd gotten that idea thinking about Luckluster and its famous neon lights. If he did this correctly, he'd be able to count cards alone—and quickly. Sleights of hand were near impossible to conceal from Luckluster's dealers, so with the stakes high, Levi needed a different assurance that he would win.

He needed a miracle.

He needed a con.

After melding and slicing the mixture into the proper shape, he added a solution of blue dye and tonic water to the glass. He finished it with a clear galvanizer, then set the contacts on his counter to cool.

As Levi poured the rest of the tonic water into a flask, Jac's snores echoed through the kitchen. He'd passed out, his mouth wide-open. His empty whiskey glass sat on the coffee table, and his hand was clutched around his Creed.

Levi retreated to his bedroom and lay down on his bed, still fully clothed. He fell asleep with the flask on the nightstand, a gun under his pillow and the sunrise shining in his eyes, reminding him that only one more midnight loomed before Sedric's deadline.

DAY NINE

"The City of Sin is painted white
so that the filth can stain."

—*The City of Sin, a Guidebook:
Where To Go and Where Not To*

ENNE

"My dear," Vianca said when she noticed Enne standing at her door. "Do come in. I'd usually ask you to sit, but I'm afraid we don't have time for that. I have a task for you—though not of a pretty sort this time."

Enne crept into the room carefully, the memories from her previous experience in Vianca's office making her tremble. The carpet where Vianca had strangled her without even a touch. The chair where Enne had sat when she learned she would poison Sedric Torren. The sweet, sinister smell of Vianca's perfume that Enne could still nearly taste as she inhaled.

But that last encounter was over a week ago, she reminded herself. Enne was different now. Stronger, weaker...she wasn't sure. But what mattered was that that was then, and this was now. She closed the door behind her and approached the donna's desk.

"What sort of task?" Enne asked. After returning to St. Morse from Scrap Market, Enne had collapsed and slept through the afternoon and most of the following day, but hadn't found it restful. When Vianca's woman had pounded on her door only minutes before, Enne had suspected a scolding for skipping today's acrobatics rehearsal. She had braced herself for anger, not for another assignment, and she didn't know which scenario was worse.

Vianca clutched the armrests of her seat, her knuckles whitening, her veins bulging. "There's going to be a midnight party at the House of Shadows that mustn't occur."

More than anything, stay away from the House of Shadows.

But it wasn't Zula's warning that made Enne's breath hitch. The House of Shadows was where the Phoenix Club played the Shadow Game. It was where Lourdes had died.

"Are you familiar with the House of Shadows?" Vianca asked.

"I am, Madame," she said flatly.

"Then you should be afraid."

Enne felt a coldness wrap itself around her heart, but it wasn't fear.

It was anger.

Enne straightened her posture. Lifted her head up. Looked Vianca square in the eyes. Regardless of what Zula had told her, Enne had submitted herself to enough warnings and rules for her lifetime. If the donna was going to send Enne to the site of her mother's death, then she would be ready—and, if given the chance, she would burn the place down.

"What do I need to do?"

The corners of Vianca's lips curled into a smile. "Sedric Torren is becoming a threat. I need him gone."

By "gone," Enne knew she meant "dead." The thought weighed less on her conscience than it should have, but she had hoped to never encounter that man again.

"Why me? You have dozens of others at your disposal," Enne said. Vianca had once boasted to her about the dangerous empire under her command, yet she was assigning a mere schoolgirl to perform an assassin's work.

"Because you're still my secret," Vianca said. "I can't have this traced back to me."

Vianca grabbed her tea kettle and poured herself a cup of chamomile, her hand trembling. Enne couldn't determine if age had simply weakened her hands or if the donna was truly nervous.

"Sedric will recognize me," Enne said darkly. Certainly, the charade she'd played last time would be broken.

Vianca's eyes roamed over Enne's body in a way that made her want to shiver. "I knew he'd like you. You really *do* look his type."

Enne clenched her fists as the memories of that night flooded back to her. She could feel the ghost of Sedric's hand against her thigh. "You didn't warn me what he was."

"Sedric has an army at his disposal. There were few circumstances in which you could have caught him alone or unprotected." The heartless logic in Vianca's voice made Enne hate her. For the donna, this was all a game, and Enne was a disposable piece. "If you had known, he would have grown suspicious. I played you to your own advantage."

"No," Enne seethed. "You exploited the trauma of probably countless other girls. All so you could win. I've never been so disgusted. You're as much of a monster as he is." Dangerous words to say to the commander of the Augustine Family— Enne's grief had made her reckless. She wasn't acting like herself.

Or maybe she was.

Vianca's nails drummed against her desk. "Careful, Miss Salta. You'll forget who the real enemies are in this city."

Enne examined her coolly, ignoring Vianca's words. No, she would never forget.

"Whether or not he pays Torren back tonight," Vianca said, "the preparations for his execution have already been made. The Shadow Game *will* be played tonight, at the stroke of midnight."

The Shadow Game. The weight of all Enne's anger, all her

grief, hardened in her chest. Her conscience, a soft and fragile thing, was buried somewhere inside, some place deep and dark and unreachable.

"Whose execution?" Enne asked.

"Levi's."

Then, at last, came the fear.

You're not alone.

But she would be, if Levi had been invited to play the Shadow Game.

"Why?" Enne choked. Her confidence from earlier was breaking, searing panic seeping its way into the cracks. She would lose everyone she cared about to the Phoenix Club, one by one.

Vianca's face clouded with something that could almost be mistaken as remorse. "It's my fault. But I have other plans for Levi—that's why I need you to save him."

Vianca Augustine was an excellent liar, but Enne could still hear the desperation in her voice. Levi wasn't simply an omerta for her. Not just a favorite toy. Even so, it was hard to imagine Vianca capable of anything like love or kindness. Having those feelings made her only more of a monster. If Vianca knew compassion, then she also knew the pain she caused.

"Sedric will be at Luckluster Casino early tonight, waiting for Levi to arrive with the volts. You must find Sedric before Levi does."

That only gave Enne a few hours. It was already six o'clock.

"If you do it openly, I cannot protect you," Vianca said. "You must kill Sedric quickly, and you must do it discreetly."

Enne waited for the donna to provide her another poison, another dress. But when the silence stretched on, Enne asked nervously, "What will I use, Madame? How will I get there? Should I—"

"I cannot help you this time," Vianca rasped, and Enne's mouth gaped. She would be performing this entirely on her own? "Unlike last time, this will have repercussions, and I will be the first they question. The whiteboots know my methods. They know my men. Like I said, I cannot have this traced back to me. Can you accomplish this for me?"

Enne took a deep, shaky breath. She wasn't sure if she would succeed, but she would certainly try—under Vianca's command or not. She'd already decided that she would risk danger if it meant saving Levi, and now the city was asking her to prove it.

"I will do it for him," Enne said, "not for you."

Vianca pursed her lips. "Everything you do, Miss Salta, you do for me." Enne felt ghostly fingers scrape across her throat, the omerta teasing her. Enne lifted her chin higher, unwilling to succumb to the witch's torment. "Now *go*."

For the past nine days spent in New Reynes, Enne had thought that falling for Levi would mean losing herself: her final act of surrender to the City of Sin.

But she'd been wrong. Naïvely, utterly wrong.

When she burst into Levi's apartment, breathless and heart-pounding and nauseated, Enne searched every drawer, every hiding spot for weapons. Her only gun was out of bullets.

She found none.

Frustrated, she turned to the collection of forgotten things in his closet. She found another weapon of sort—the perfect dress. Clinging, silky and black.

Then she returned to her own bedroom and tried on the costume. She barely recognized herself. For once, that felt a very good thing. This time, she would be no one's doll.

Vianca had intended her to exploit Sedric's weakness, and as repulsive as that seemed to Enne, she would play that role if she had to. However, attraction might be dangerous, but it wasn't deadly. In order to kill him, she'd first need to visit Lola, to retrieve her stolen bullets, to take whatever advice or weapons Lola had to offer.

And so she formulated her plan.

She put on her crimson-noir lipstick.

She pocketed her revolver.

When Enne arrived at Luckluster Casino, she would hunt down the wolf of the City of Sin, and she would slay him.

That was her surrender.

Lola's green eyes peered through the bullet holes in her cellar door. "I didn't think you'd be back."

"I need your help."

The urgency in Enne's voice must've been obvious, because Lola quickly thrust open the door. She scanned Enne's outfit. Rather than complimenting her or questioning the formality of her attire, she commented, "You could hide a lot of daggers in that."

"Actually, that's exactly why I'm here." Enne pulled the revolver out of her pocket. "I need the bullets back."

Lola ushered her inside. "What's going on?"

"Sedric Torren is planning to kill Levi at midnight, and I might already be too late to save him." Enne ran to the desk drawer where Lola had kept Enne's revolver on her initial visit. Inside was a pile of knives and miniature weapons, but no bullets.

"And what exactly are *you* going to do about it?" Lola asked. "The Torren Family owns half the North Side."

"I'm going to kill Sedric Torren."

Lola stared at her incredulously. "You won't make it out alive."

Enne slammed the drawer closed and grabbed Lola by the shoulders. "Levi is going to die the same way Lourdes did. I *need* to stop the Shadow Game, and all I have is a revolver with no bullets."

"The Shadow Game?" Lola's eyes widened. "The Torrens aren't part of the Phoenix Club."

"I trust Vianca's sources."

Lola's face shadowed. "So it's like that with Vianca?"

Enne let her go and stared at the floor. She couldn't bring herself to lie to Lola anymore, even if it meant Lola abandoning her.

"Time is already running out," she pleaded. "Please, Lola."

After a few moments of consideration, Lola relaxed her shoulders. She drew a key out of her pocket and unlocked a different drawer of her desk. "These were your bullets." She handed Enne three of them, then she rummaged around for additional knives and weapons. "You really *can* fit a lot of daggers in that dress."

Killing a man with a gun? That would be easy. Impersonal. Enne might not feel the guilt over murdering someone like Sedric Torren, but her skin crawled to think of how close she'd need to get to him to use a knife. To feel his hands grabbing her as she attacked him. To hear him curse in her ear as she ended his life. She wasn't sure she could do that.

"Do you have poison?" Enne asked.

Lola hesitated. "I might." She pulled out a small leather case and closed the drawer. "This belonged to my younger brother, once. But he doesn't need it anymore." There was unmistakable sadness in Lola's voice.

Enne slid off the lid. Inside was a syringe, filled with a wine-dark fluid. She reached in to touch it, but Lola slapped her hand away. "It's almost instantaneous death. Very obvious, and very traceable."

Which meant she'd need to get Sedric somewhere private. Enne shivered.

"It's an hour walk to Luckluster from here," Lola said. "A thirty-minute Mole ride."

It was seven thirty. Levi could be there by now. Levi could already be dead. "There's nothing faster?"

"Nothing that I..." Lola's face broke into a grin. "You can pick locks."

Enne's skin prickled nervously. She didn't like that daring look on the blood gazer's face. "I can pick *some* locks."

"My neighbor sells Mistress for the Augustines. Got himself

this real nice Houssen Amberlite in his garage. It's fast. And brand-new."

Nine days ago Enne would've immediately vetoed the idea. Stealing a car? It was dangerous. It was shatz.

But it was the fastest way to save Levi.

So Enne swallowed her reservations, slid the leather case into the pocket of her dress, and asked, "Can you drive?"

LEVI

Levi picked up a card. The king of clubs. He fought back a confident smile as the man next to him turned over a pair of queens and a three of spades. To reveal such an advantageous Tropp so early, the player was trying to seem cocky, even though he looked everywhere but the card table. It was the easiest bluff to spot.

Levi took a sip from a glass of the tonic water he'd brought with him from St. Morse. Nobody noticed him dab his pointer finger in the glass as he set it down. On the back of the king of clubs card, he stealthily drew a *KC* with his finger.

Normally, Levi preferred not to resort to cheating. But tonight, he could afford nothing short of winning.

The rounds continued, and Levi easily outplayed the man's bluff. The dealer called the game for the Iron Lord.

His opponent threw his cards on the table in defeat, and Levi took the pot. He'd won two and a half thousand volts tonight, which meant he had just enough to pay back Sedric—with his own casino's volts.

Levi felt the weight of the pouch of orbs in his pocket. Examined the mountain of red and black Luckluster chips in front of him.

He was done. He was safe.

He let out a sigh that he'd been holding in for months now and leaned back into his chair. Levi had never been inside Luckluster Casino, and the Torrens couldn't have decorated it in any way more opposite to St. Morse's royal grandeur. Everything was red and black: the furnishings, the lights, the attire. But despite being one of the city's two richest casinos, inside, it looked more like a cheap nightclub. The ambience and color scheme was probably meant to appear fiendishly luxe, but even to Levi—who was certainly no prude—everything about the casino seemed vulgar. Fishnets, cherry lips, black lace, scarlet nails. Satin bedsheet curtains; glow-in-the-dark artwork of lips and curves; dancers lounging in windows above the main gambling floor, their long legs and stiletto heels dangling from the bannisters.

He could finally relax, but the combination of the hypersexualized environment and the nagging discomfort of his glass contacts kept him on edge. Maybe the lenses hurt because he'd used volt glass. Certain objects in the room glowed with an unnatural shade of blue, like some of the other players' drinks and a few of the women's faces, probably from a chemical in their makeup. Looking straight into the fluorescent lights was blinding. He was getting a headache from it all.

But *two and a half thousand volts*. Yeah, the peepers had been worth it.

The dealer asked if they'd play again. What Levi needed to do was remove the contact lenses, hand over his ten thousand volts to Sedric and leave. But with his winning streak, it would've been a shame to end now. Levi hadn't earned this much in a single night in a long time.

The dealer handed out cards to Levi and the four other players. Three tens of diamonds. What were the chances?

This was his night.

After a few rounds, it was down to Levi and the man on his left. Levi, however, wasn't paying much attention, as his mind was already drifting to what he'd do after he paid Sedric, after he reclaimed his title and his reputation. For once, the future he wanted felt within his grasp.

Round after round, his opponent bet aggressively. Levi examined the man's cards. Definitely two jacks of hearts—Levi had written *JH* on the backs in a previous round, which glowed blue through his lenses. He didn't know what the other two cards were, but Levi was certain his three-of-a-kind Tropp was better.

Levi tossed a second thousand-volt chip into the pot.

The dealer nodded at them to reveal their cards. Levi showed his first, eager to admire the fury on the man's face.

Then the man showed his cards. *Four* jacks of clubs.

Levi cursed and threw his cards into the center of the table. So he was two thousand down. No need to panic yet. He'd leave Luckluster once he made them back.

The next few rounds, he continuously received mediocre hands. The peepers couldn't help him get the right cards, and the risk wasn't worth the bluff. He lost only three hundred volts.

He waited until he'd finally been dealt a good hand, then he went all in. By the time they reached the seventh round of the game, Levi had collected a royal flush, a nearly unbeatable Tropp.

Levi confidently tossed a silver three thousand–volt chip in the pot. One of the players who'd already folded whistled.

By this point, the discomfort of the lenses had developed into a pounding headache that pulsed behind his eyebrows. As soon as he won this game, he desperately needed to take the peepers out and drink a cold glass of water.

The dealer cleared his throat, distracting Levi from the throbbing in his skull. "Your cards, sir." Levi coughed awkwardly and gathered his hand.

They each showed their cards. His opponent had three jacks of hearts and two kings of diamonds. Levi hadn't seen the kings. Between those two small Tropps, he was done.

Just like that, his pile was empty. Five and a half thousand volts. Gone. Just like that.

Muck muck muck, he thought. *Why didn't I get out when I was on top?*

With very little left to bet, Levi stood. He trembled as the reality of what had happened dawned on him. He'd *had* the volts to pay back Sedric. He'd *had* his way out of this scam Vianca started. And he'd ruined it.

He could still pay Sedric a portion of what he owed. Ask for an extension. But Sedric didn't have a reputation as a merciful man. It would be all or nothing.

The Fool laughed at him in the corner of his vision. Wherever Levi looked, the Fool stared back.

Levi spotted one of Sedric's cousins, the easily recognizable and widely feared Charles Torren, watching him hungrily from a nearby bar. Levi pushed his way out of the gambling room and away from Charles's ominous, knowing stare.

The bathroom was thankfully empty. Levi bent over the counter and stared at his bloodshot eyes, his dark brown irises tinted a shade bluer from the dye. Not his best look. He took out the contacts and stuffed them in his pocket. His heart was pounding, and he tried to steady his breathing, but it was nearly impossible—due both to the anxiety tightening in his chest and the throbbing of his headache.

He'd think of a new plan. Run back to St. Morse and wake up Jac, who was probably still sleeping on his couch. They'd hide. Maybe try the smaller casinos. Peepers…what had he been thinking? He played better when he wasn't marking cards—he didn't make reckless assumptions.

Levi left the bathroom and returned to the lobby, locking his sight on the exit.

He almost stumbled as he came face-to-face with Sedric Torren. The neon red and black lights cast3 harsh shadows over the angles of his face as he loomed over Levi. Sedric loosened his necktie, as if preparing for a meal.

"'Lo, Pup. You're in a hurry." Sedric grinned wickedly. "Do you have what you owe me?"

Levi cleared his throat and rubbed his sweaty hands on his pants. "Just about. I'll have your volts to you tomorrow, as promised. Ten days, right?"

Sedric checked his watch. "Tomorrow starts in four hours, and we've waited long enough." His tone sounded more excited than disappointed, and Levi's pulse spiked in fearful response. "You know, I thought Chez Phillips would kill you before I saw you again." Sedric paused, taking in the stony expression on Levi's face. "What? Didn't think I knew about that? All of New Reynes knows you lost your throne."

The other patrons in the lobby passed Levi without so much as a glance, unaware exactly how trapped he was under Sedric's gaze.

"You want your volts or not?" Levi asked, working up the courage to keep his voice strong. "Because I can't work on those investments while I'm here talking to you."

Sedric wrapped an arm around Levi's shoulder, giving him a chummy smile that Levi knew better than to trust. "Why don't you let me buy you a drink? You look like you need to loosen up."

In his periphery, he spotted several of Torren's men guarding each of the exits. He had nowhere to escape.

This is the man who killed Reymond, Levi thought with dread. *And I have no choice but to play along.*

So Levi let Sedric lead him to a bar past the lobby. All the while, he mapped the closest escape routes in his mind and kept a reassuring hand on the gun in his pocket.

The air in the bar was so thick with smoke that the lights

looked like they wore halos. The figures inside were silhouettes and shadow, giving Levi the eerie feeling that he and Sedric were alone, even though they weren't. They sat at the bar, and Sedric ordered two Gambler's Ruins.

"So Vianca's business isn't doing well, then?" Levi fought to keep his face blank at the question, but Sedric chuckled affably. "Of course not, or you'd have paid us back by now. My family always knew Vianca would run St. Morse into the ground."

"The volts will come in soon. They're just a little late." A coil of nausea unraveled in Levi's stomach, and he hadn't even had a real drink yet.

Sedric winked at him conspiratorially. "Of course they will."

The bartender slid them their drinks. When Levi took a sip, the bourbon squirmed its way back up his throat like burning bile.

"Did you know I'm running for Senate?" Sedric asked.

"You'll look uglier in a wig." Levi cringed inwardly after he said it, fully expecting Sedric to punch him for the thoughtless remark. Levi might've carried a gun, but if he made a move for it, one of Sedric's watchful cronies would shoot him before he even had the chance. Right now, Sedric had all the power. He could hurt him any way he wanted, and Levi would be helpless to protect himself.

Rather than punishing him, Sedric merely twisted the ruby ring around his finger. "Remind me again exactly how Vianca has been investing my family's volts?"

"Bonds. Trades. Stocks," Levi answered automatically. These were the words Vianca had taught him to say. "A portfolio that provides low-risk, high-yield returns."

"Low-risk, high-yield for St. Morse, I'm sure." Sedric twirled a finger over his drink. "Poor you. *You* get the risk and none of the reward."

That was true. Vianca liked to claim that Levi got a share

of profits, but Levi rarely saw a single volt more than he made during his shifts.

"My father and Vianca had similar philosophies for running their empires. Everything under the table. All hired hands. Keeping things as low profile as possible." Sedric leaned in, as if he was truly just sharing wisdom with Levi over a couple of drinks. This was likely to be the last piece of wisdom Levi ever heard.

"But those were the old days. Favors can buy more than volts can. And I say it's better to make friends than enemies," Sedric said, a strange glint in his eyes.

Levi figured this was a very convoluted speech for Sedric to rationalize to Levi why he'd gone South Sider. The Torrens were and always would be a crime Family. Even if Sedric lusted after the old money and respectability of the wigheads, at the end of the day, those families had their names on libraries and hospitals, and the Torrens had their name on a casino.

"My new friends…" Sedric continued. "They've suspected the truth about your little scheme for a while. I was worried at first—my father had invested in you prior to his death. But as it turns out, this has all been one big opportunity for me."

"What kind of opportunity?" Levi asked, though he didn't need to ask anything, really. Sedric had obviously wanted to sit him down and gloat—whether Levi participated in the conversation or not didn't matter. But speaking made him feel less helpless. He still had a voice.

"Apparently, my friends have been rather bored for a long time," Sedric said. "They're looking for any opportunity to play, really."

To play.

Levi's grip tightened on the edge of the bar.

"I'm paying you back, aren't I? You'll get your volts tomorrow as planned, so what's the harm?"

Sedric's lips curled predatorily. "It was never about the volts."

His mouth dry, Levi took another sip of his drink. "Then what *do* you want?"

Sedric laughed, a deep laugh that echoed in Levi's ears like the clunks and thuds of gravediggers piling earth on his coffin.

"I'm delivering something to you, and in exchange, they're doing me a favor." Sedric grinned. "Whatever I ask. *That's* power, Pup. Not volts. Not sex. Not anything this city is trying to sell."

Sedric pulled out a gleaming silver card from his jacket.

Levi remained silent as he took it. Unlike the other cards, this one had no divination prophecies. It didn't need to. Its very existence foretold death.

The Fool. His invitation to the Shadow Game. Just as in his vision, when Levi had seen the card on the tombstone, the Fool strode toward the edge of a cliff, a wicked smile on his face.

Sedric leaned forward, so close that Levi could smell the coffee liqueur on his breath, and Levi's stomach twisted into knots. "You've got two hours."

"What?" Levi rasped, even though he'd heard him perfectly.

"Here." Sedric reached into Levi's jacket pocket and pulled out his flask. Levi was so nervous, so frozen, he let him. Then Sedric dumped the tonic water out of Levi's flask on the floor and replaced it with the remaining contents of Levi's drink. "A little something to keep you going." Sedric tucked it back into his pocket with a pat. Levi fought off a strong urge to vomit. "The party doesn't start for two hours. So run along, little Pup. This is your chance. Run before we catch you."

Two hours.

Two hours.

Then he was going to die.

Sedric finished off his own drink and winked. "I'll see you at the party."

Levi nearly knocked over a table on his way to the door. Out of the bar, out of the lobby, outside to where the crisp night air bit into his skin. Sedric's laugh rang in his ears, and the farther Levi ran, the louder it grew.

He turned the corner, half expecting to see Sedric standing in front of him, latched on to his very shadow. But Levi was alone.

He slumped against a brick wall, letting the stone scrape against his bare back as his shirt rode up. Sedric had told him to run, but Levi wasn't thick. He knew how these things worked. If he ran, it would make Sedric's night only more fun. Instead, he sat there trembling for several minutes, sometimes crying, sometimes feeling nothing at all.

His first thoughts were of Jac. Jac would get by without him—eventually—but for so long, Levi had been the stable anchor in Jac's otherwise directionless life. His friend might've found the Faith after his last bout with Lullaby, but would prayer alone save him from relapse? Levi and Jac had followed each other down every dark road, but Levi hated to think how his friend could so easily follow him down this one.

Then he thought of the Irons. After Levi died, Chez would be the undisputed Iron Lord, and Levi's legacy would fade: another street lord, another rotten kid, another loser in the city's game.

He thought about Reymond. *You're better than us*, the Scar Lord had once told him, but he'd been wrong. Levi had never been much of anything, and now they both would face the same fate. Out of all his regrets, Reymond was his worst. The grief rushed over him all at once, an ache worse than any of his injuries. Reymond was the only one in the world who'd watched out for Levi, and now his brother was dead.

Fourth, he thought about Enne. Now that they'd discovered the truth about Lourdes, their story had ended. It didn't matter what it could've been—it was over, and soon Levi would be gone. If she remembered him afterward, he would be the one who'd brought her to Vianca, the boy she would've been better off without.

Last, he thought about New Reynes, and that pain hurt the

most. He'd left a depressing life behind to build something better in this city. He'd bet everything he had in the game, and he'd lost. But the city wouldn't grieve for him.

The city would find some new con man, some new boy who called himself lord, and the city would play again.

LEVI

Levi spent the first thirty minutes of his last two hours wiping tears from his eyes, rooted to the same spot in the alley he'd fled to from Luckluster. If only the other gangsters could see him now. The Iron Lord. Crying when he was about to die.

Levi pictured his gravestone from the visions. If there was ever a time to cave in and pray to the Faith, as his mother always had, this was the moment. But beneath the Casion District's skyline of smoke, crouched in an alley reeking of trash and piss, Levi couldn't believe that any higher power cared about his fate.

A familiar voice drifted out of the shadows. "It's you."

Levi instinctively reached for the pistol in his pocket, tensing as Chez Phillips stepped into the moonlight. "What are you doing here?" Levi demanded. They were a long way from Iron Land.

Chez grinned slyly. "I'm making my way back to Olde Town. Never imagined I'd run into you."

Levi couldn't believe he'd have to spend the last hours of

his life with Chez, of all people. Maybe he was already dead. Maybe this was hell.

"You should cross your heart when you see me," Chez said. His forehead and neck peeled from an old sunburn, and he had an impressive black eye and walked with a limp in his step. Chez looked terrible, and this gave Levi a surge of pleasure, despite knowing that he looked no better himself.

"There are a *lot* of things I'd like to do when I see you," Levi growled. "Crossing my heart is not one of them."

"I should've killed you when I had the chance," Chez hissed, clearly forgetting the part where Jac had beaten the muck out of him before he could. Chez took out his knife and flipped it between his fingers.

"I wouldn't bother. The Torrens are after me, and they'll be pretty upset if you kill me first."

Chez laughed, still playing with his knife. "I'm not surprised the Torrens want you dead. You're a real pain in the ass. We've been better off without you."

Levi held back a wince. Despite all Chez's bravado, those words were probably true.

I'm not helpless, he thought. *If I'm going to die, I'm going to do it fighting. I'll be no one's plaything.*

"That's a shame," Levi answered.

"Oh yeah? Why?"

"Because I'm gonna take back my crown. Right now."

"What's the point?" Chez grunted. He flipped his knife again—his tell. He was nervous. Both of them were in muck shape, but if Chez won last time and was uneasy now, he couldn't have been doing well. What trouble had he run into in Levi's absence? "I thought you were already a dead man."

That was exactly why Levi wanted to fight. So he could die with some dignity—and his title returned to him.

"I've still got a little fight left in me." Levi made a show of taking off his jacket and rolling up his sleeves, exposing his Iron

Lord tattoos. Then he emptied the gun from his pocket and laid it on the ground beside him. "So maybe we can do it properly this time—no interruptions."

Chez flipped his blade in the air and caught it. As if his tricks scared Levi. Nothing could scare him now, when he had nothing left to lose.

Or maybe he was only shatz—running from one death into the clutches of another.

"You're thick if you think you can win," Chez growled. "If it weren't for Jac, you'd be dead right now."

"If it weren't for me, you'd be dead, too. Floating in the Brint where I first found you." Chez's jaw locked. Levi found most of the Irons that way—desperate and near death. It was why he'd thought they were loyal to him. Now he knew it was also why they hated him. "Why would you chance walking around Scar Land? Seems kinda desperate. Just how well are the Irons fairing without me?"

Chez lurched forward. He was about three times as fast as Levi, but now Levi knew better than to try to outmaneuver him. He jumped out of the way and immediately went for Chez's feet, grabbing his shins and yanking him to the ground. Chez tumbled on top of him, and his head smacked the cobblestones.

Levi wrestled him on to his back, then he pinned his arms down. Chez's knife flew from his hand and landed a few feet away with a clatter.

"I don't owe you anything," Chez said, his voice slurred from hitting his head. Blood stained his brown hair. "I never asked to be saved."

"Everybody's asking to be saved," Levi answered.

As Chez gradually regained his senses, he struggled more against Levi's grip.

"Even if I don't kill you right now," Levi snarled, "I win. I outfought you. That makes me your lord again."

Chez spat in his face. "Like hell it does."

All of the week's anger and frustration getting the better of him, Levi summoned his talent and let his skin warm. Chez screamed as steam rose from his wrists where Levi's fingers were wrapped around them. His skin began to blister, pink and oozing and raw.

"I'm not gonna kill you, Chez, but maybe these shackles will remind you that I own you, no matter how far away you run." When he let go, rings of raw flesh circled Chez's wrists, raised and inflamed—more gruesome than Levi had intended. Chez howled more.

Holding Chez's arms down with his legs, Levi paused to savor the moment. He took a triumphant swig from his flask.

Levi stood, closing his eyes to savor the victory. But when he opened them again, he caught a glimpse of his reflection in a window and startled. The look on his face...

He was the spitting image of Vianca.

Click.

In barely a moment's time, Chez had pressed the barrel of the abandoned gun to Levi's head. Levi grabbed his arm and tried to shove him away, but his third held steady. "Back down from being lord, Pup," he demanded, panting. "Or I swear I'll paint the wall with your thoughts."

In a real challenge, you couldn't shoot your lord. No one inherited the oath from a bullet. Every gangster knew that.

But Chez didn't need Levi to remind him. "As far as I'm concerned, this never happened," Chez hissed. "No witnesses."

So Chez would kill him after all. Levi would die here, another lord lost to these streets.

"Any last words?" Chez asked.

Levi couldn't think of any. None that hadn't been said before or wouldn't be said again.

But Levi still had one last card up his sleeve. He'd never swallowed his mouthful of Gambler's Ruin.

He spit it out, snapped his fingers and a roar of fire erupted between him and Chez. First, there was a scream. Then a gunshot. Levi was already on the ground, his ears ringing, eyes closed, arms clutching his broken rib. Something thudded to the cobblestones a few feet away, but it took several moments for Levi to regain his composure and look.

Chez lay on his back. His fingers reached for the knife he'd lost earlier, but he was clearly in too much pain to move. The skin on his face, neck and chest had burned cleaned through, exposing a mess of blood and bone and tissue. He made a gargling noise, and tears glistened in the corners of his left eye. The right one was gone—now an empty socket filled with crimson and black, wet and bulging.

Levi gagged, both at Chez's appearance and the smell of it all—the burnt cloth and burnt flesh. He stood frozen under the terror and hatred of Chez's glare. He wondered if Chez would die. Instead, he lay there, grinding his teeth, the blistered parts of his chest still heaving up and down. He shook all over, and bits of spit dribbled down his chin.

Maybe you should kill him, a voice in Levi's head told him. *Maybe that would be better than this.*

But he wasn't sure Chez would die. If Levi killed him, would it be mercy, or would it be murder?

It already is murder, he thought. *You did this.*

He nearly killed you.

Yet you were the one who asked to fight.

He was your friend once.

In the end, Levi retrieved his gun and left Chez there for someone else to find. He didn't know if that was the right decision or the cowardly one, but the longer he watched him, the more he hated himself.

He doesn't have to die. Only you do.

After he finished throwing up against an alley wall, Levi made his way back to Luckluster. There was still no point in running. This was the last chance he had to write his legacy, and no matter how terrified he was, at least Levi would be remembered for how he didn't beg.

Luckluster's red lights sparkled all the way down the street. Levi sighed and leaned against an empty motorcar, taking in the glory of the Casino Distrct.

Someone tapped his arm. Levi jumped, brandishing his gun, and tripped over the curb.

It was Lola. She was dressed as she usually was, in her top hat and leather boots.

"What do you want?" he asked. She was awfully far away from Dove Land, and Luckluster didn't seem her type of haunt.

"We thought you were inside," she breathed.

"Who's 'we'?"

"Me. And Enne."

Levi frowned. Enne shouldn't have any idea where he was. Levi hadn't told her about the scheme—it was the one thing he'd done right. So why was she here?

"Vianca sent her to save you," Lola explained. "And to kill Sedric Torren."

Levi's heart screeched to a halt.

He'd had it all planned: his death, on his terms. He'd have no one else's blood on his hands tonight. Especially not Enne's.

"Where is she?" he rasped.

"You just missed her." Lola glanced worriedly at the red neon lights. Levi hadn't thought she gave a muck what happened to Enne, but clearly he'd been mistaken. "She's already inside. She's looking for you."

Levi didn't bother responding as he sprinted toward Luckluster, where his killers were waiting for him.

ENNE

Lola had lied about her driving skills.

They sped down the streets of the Deadman District, the motorcar swerving and skidding through every turn. Enne whiteknuckled the door handle each time Lola slammed the brakes.

"You said we needed to get there fast," Lola pointed out.

At this point, Enne would just be thankful if they got there alive.

After narrowly missing several cars, road signs and pedestrians, they screeched to a halt a block away from Luckluster.

Lola pulled something black and silky out of her pocket—Enne's mask from Scrap Market. "You might need this." She slipped it into Enne's concealed pocket, beside the leather box with the poison.

"Knock him dead," Lola said cheerfully.

Enne grimaced. "Really? That's distasteful."

The lights of Tropps Street danced around her, flashing in no particular pattern. They made her feel the way she had after drinking those Snake Eyes at the Sauterelle.

"Better him than you," Lola replied gravely.

"If I'm not out by eleven..." Enne paused before repeating her mother's oft-used phrase. "Then I'm dead."

Lola nodded solemnly. "Be careful." And Enne knew that she meant it.

Enne took a deep breath, shoved down the storm raging in her insides and walked down the block and through the revolving doors. Where Vianca had decorated St. Morse to resemble an old Mizer palace, all gaudy opulence and vintage luxuries, the Torrens had opted for New Reynes's famous burlesque sinfulness. The staff wore uniforms easily mistaken for lingerie. Red carpet lined the floor and stairwell, darkened by dirty footprints, and scarlet lights blinked against the black-and-red-striped walls. It reminded her of a fun house. Even the jazz band played a carnival tune that beckoned players to contortionist shows and roulette tables.

Enne checked the gambling rooms first, then the theater, the ballroom. Neither Sedric nor Levi were anywhere to be found.

Maybe she was already too late.

As she dashed around the corner, Enne collided with a man with his back turned, his white button-down a canvas for the dancing shadows and crimson lights.

"I apologize. I didn't see—"

The stranger spun around. He smelled faintly of citrus cologne, and he had a fading black eye and complementary ace and spade tattoos on both his arms.

Any relief she felt at finding Levi safe quickly vanished. If Sedric Torren sighted Levi, then Enne had little idea how she could save him.

"Levi?" she croaked. "You need to get out of here—"

"No, *you* need to get out of here." He grabbed both of her arms and pulled her close, nearly knocking her into his chest in his urgency. He backed the two of them into an alcove off the lobby, away from the bustle of the crowd. Enne's back pressed against a door leading to a coatroom.

"You don't understand." She tried to shake him off, but he only held her firmer. "Sedric Torren—"

"I know why you're here." She could smell the bourbon on his breath. "I can't let you do it."

"Why not?" she hissed. "I'm trying to help you."

"I'm not letting you get yourself killed. Especially not over me."

"It's not only you. It's..." She tried to say Vianca, but the omerta caught the name on her tongue. And, of course, there was something else. The cold, angry hurt inside her that wanted to end Sedric Torren and put a stop to the Shadow Game forever.

"Let me help you," she urged.

Levi swallowed, then gently tucked a strand of hair behind her ear. The touch was delicate, hesitant, as if they had time for such tender gestures. "You can't help me. *You're* the one who needs to leave."

Didn't he know her better than that by now? She had thrown everything away to save someone she loved before, and she would do it again for him.

"I thought we were in this together," she murmured. "You and me."

"Not in this. This has always been *my* problem."

His gaze moved down her dress, and he wore a look somewhere between longing and pain. She leaned in to him, and her hand found its way into his. Her head felt dizzy from the flashing lights and nearness of him, but even as her heart urged her to move closer, her mind compelled her to resist. The expression on Levi's face scared her. Not because of the desire in his eyes—the desire she shared, as well—but the desperation. As his free hand moved around her waist, his other pinning hers to the wall, Enne realized he really believed that this was his last night, his last chance. This wasn't simply attraction. This was him attempting to leave this world without regret.

He bent low until his forehead pressed against hers, and the space between them felt negative and infinite all at once. Her heart stirred, begging her to surrender.

"Promise me," he whispered. "Promise me you'll be safe."

She couldn't promise that. Vianca had given her orders, and Enne intended to see them through. There would be more nights spent with Levi Glaisyer. This wasn't their last chance.

We won't die tonight, she swore silently instead.

"Promise me," he repeated, and she felt his breath against her lips.

She squeezed his hand. "You asked me to trust you once. Now I'm asking you to trust me."

His expression faltered. "I won't let you—"

"Please."

Breathless, she slid out of his grasp and disappeared into the crowd before he could catch her, praying she hadn't made a heartbreaking mistake.

Enne followed the pull of the omerta toward the bar, where it whispered to her that she would find her mark. Her hands were clammy with sweat, her chest tight with fear. She would have to face Sedric Torren again. Him and the terrible, nauseating way he looked at her.

After a few moments, she stopped to glance back at Levi for a last push of courage.

He was gone.

"No," she whispered. She shoved her way back to the alcove, but Levi was nowhere to be found. Maybe he'd left, just as she'd pleaded. Enne should've felt relieved, but bullets of worry buried themselves in her chest. This was not the night to make assumptions.

Had they found him already? Had they killed him?

She had no time to search. The omerta was steering her toward the bar, and the clock was ticking. Whether or not Levi was safe, she would find out from Sedric Torren, and she would finish what she'd come here to do.

The room was dark and hazy with smoke. A single figure sat at the bar, one with broad shoulders and slicked-back hair.

Sedric Torren caught her eye and gave her an inviting smile.

All at once, she was back in the St. Morse theater. Sedric's hand had found its way to her thigh, and her mind had found its way somewhere else as she waited for the poison to work, waited for the night to end. Sedric's mind, too, had seemed somewhere else. Fabricating reasons to lure her away, imagining the things he would do in the dark, the way he'd tell her she'd wanted this, the secrets and shame he'd convince her to keep.

She'd seen it all in his eyes then, and the same look was there now.

Enne reminded herself how far she'd come since that night. She was not Vianca's doll. She'd walked into the Deadman District and emerged a lord. She carried poison in one pocket and a gun in the other.

She was a blade disguised as a girl.

Taking a deep breath to calm herself, she slid onto the stool beside him.

"'Lo, Sedric," she said.

He inspected her dark lipstick and slip of a dress. His eyes traced over her face, her chest, the rest of her body. She could see the calculations in his head, trying to guess how old she truly was and whether he would still have her, anyway.

"Emma Salta," he said, all smiles and snares. "I didn't think I'd see you again. You spend an awful lot of time in casinos for such a young lady."

It was so easy to slip back into that role. It felt like retreating to a different part of herself, a place where she didn't need to think, didn't need to feel.

"You don't look happy to see me," she said, feigning offense.

"You look awfully different."

"I'm trying to impress," she said. "You were right. Vianca wouldn't hire me. I thought I would dress the part this time."

"You're asking me for a job?"

She couldn't tell if she was fooling him. Everyone in this city had a perfect poker face. Lying was more of a necessity than a skill in New Reynes.

"We danced last time," she reminded him. "It seemed a sort of audition."

"You're awfully ambitious." He placed his hand under her chin and lifted it up. Her stomach twisted into a knot, and she fought the urge to slap his fingers away. If the bartender wasn't hovering so close by, she'd pull out the syringe now. Anything to prevent him touching her.

"I'm sure we can discuss some type of…arrangement," he said. "There's a private room here no one's using."

A trap, she knew. But she needed to get him alone. There was no other way.

"That would be great," she said.

He waved away his men, then whispered something to the bartender that she couldn't hear. The bartender gave her a pitying look before walking away, and Enne clenched a fist behind her back in response. She wasn't the first girl. Everyone in this casino was complicit.

"Come on," Sedric said, putting his hand on the small of her back. It felt nothing like Levi's had—*his* touch had felt warm and protective. Sedric's felt wrong.

They entered a small dining room. He pulled out a chair for her at one end of a glossy table. Like the rest of the casino, the decorations were red and black. Red carpet. Black iron chandelier. Red candles. Black place settings. Enne settled into her chair, wondering just how many people had watched her walk in, how well they'd seen her face. If they found Sedric dead here later, would they remember her?

She couldn't kill him yet, however. Not without knowing where Levi was.

"I sent the bartender for a few drinks," Sedric said, winking. "Don't worry. I won't tell anyone."

"Oh. Are you celebrating anything tonight?"

"You could say that. I managed to catch a criminal who was scamming a lot of people for a long time."

Levi.

While Enne's heart hammered, the bartender returned with their drinks, and she took hers—a sparkling pink liquid in a glass with a lollipop dunked inside. He handed Sedric a Gambler's Ruin. "I helped a lot of people, maybe even got myself a few votes in the next election."

To avoid responding, Enne took a sip of her drink. She couldn't help noticing how delicious it tasted. Sweet as sin.

"You like it?" he asked, indicating the drink. "It's called a Lollipop Lick." Still trying to feign politeness, she nodded shakily and set down the glass. His smile widened.

"What's going to happen to this criminal?" *Please, please let him still be alive.*

Her skin felt flushed all of a sudden—she was breaking under her nerves. Sweat rolled down her back, and she wished this dress wasn't so tight on her hips.

"He's to be executed. I arranged it myself." Sedric licked his lips. "Why so curious?"

"No reason." She raised her glass and prayed he didn't see it shaking. "Cheers to your success."

Sedric raised his glass and clinked it with hers. Then, to Enne's shock and discomfort, he took her hand in his. It was such a little, unassuming touch, but to her, any touch from him felt repulsive. Every move he made was a rehearsed act, designed to seduce, to ensnare.

"You know," he said, "you're an excellent dancer, but I had no idea you were also so talented in acrobatics."

"What?" Her heart sped up in panic. Did he know?

"Don't be coy, my dear." His eyes slithered over her once again, and Enne flinched. "I saw your show, and you were quite dazzling. One of the other acrobats told me your name is Enne Salta. You should've corrected me. I've been saying your name wrong this whole time." Enne wrenched her hand away from his and let it creep toward her pocket. Her lie had unraveled, but it wouldn't matter for much longer. She'd finish this right now.

But her hands trembled as she slid the case out, and she struggled to get a grip on it with her sweaty fingers. Thankfully, he didn't notice her fumbling beneath the table. "I searched for you that night, but I couldn't find you." He leaned forward again, took her other hand again, smiled again. She was too dazed to push him off. Her cheeks burned, yet she was cold, shivering from the coolness of her sweat. Her vision darkened and lightened like she'd stood up too fast, though she hadn't moved an inch from her seat.

This couldn't be normal. Couldn't just be stress or alcohol.

Amid her haze, she tried to focus on the black case in her hand. One puncture. That was all it would take to end him.

"I never had the chance, but I wanted to find you," Sedric continued. "To buy you another drink."

Enne's eyes flickered to the Lollipop Lick.

"Are you feeling all right?" he asked, not sounding the least concerned. "You look a little pale."

Then Enne realized what he'd done. Her chest heaved bit by bit, as if a crank needed to pry it open to inhale. This couldn't be happening.

"I guess that's just the effects kicking in," he said casually.

Her balance veered, and Sedric placed his hand on her shoulder to steady her. As if he still had her best interests at heart.

He'd drugged her. How naïve of her to take a sip of that drink. To believe, even for a moment, that she'd had him fooled.

"Don't worry, it won't kill you," he assured her. "You'll wake up soon enough. I wouldn't want you to miss the fun."

Her grip slackened. The leather case slid back into her pocket.

Her shoulder hit the edge of the table, but she barely felt any pain—only nausea. Her thoughts were thicker than grime. She knew something was wrong—she was in danger, Levi was in danger—but for the life of her, she couldn't remember why. The man in front of her smiled—she couldn't recall his name, either—a not-quite-handsome smile. He reached into his jacket and pulled out something shiny.

"Brought you a gift," he whispered. He tucked the silver rectangle into her hand. A man in a jester's hat grinned up at her from the face of the card. She looked back at the man to ask what it was—she knew it, knew it, but couldn't remember—but he and everything else were gone.

LEVI

This was Levi's last night to live, and he hadn't even gotten a kiss goodbye.

The black silky hemline of Enne's dress disappeared into the crowd, and he cursed under his breath. He wouldn't let her do this.

He started pushing through the Luckluster patrons to follow her, but was quickly blocked by two of Sedric's men. As Levi tried to slip past, he stumbled over one of their canes.

"Watch it!" one of the men said, catching Levi by the arm. His front tooth glinted gold.

Something sharp stabbed Levi in the neck. He yelped, then felt his body go slack. Another arm slid around his middle, hoisting him up. Levi fought to move, tried to lift his head to search for Enne's black dress, but he was paralyzed. Even his mind was going numb.

Someone nearby gasped.

"He's just drunk," a voice said. "Real lightweight, this one."

All at once, the red lights went dark.

★ ★ ★

Levi woke sitting against a stone pillar, his hands tied behind him, an ache in his lower stomach. A man stood over him, presumably having just kicked him awake. He was well over six feet tall and half as wide. Levi moaned and pulled at the ropes binding him to the pillar, but they only scratched his wrists.

"Rise and shine," his captor said. A hint of gold flashed as he smiled, revealing teeth that were pointed like a shark, and Levi realized it was the same man from Luckluster. "Almost thought you'd miss the party. That would've been a right shame."

One light bulb dangled above them, and from the looks of the room, they were in a basement. The cold cement walls reeked of mold, and a distant laughter echoed from a wooden staircase that led upstairs.

"Where am I?"

"The House of Shadows."

Levi's skin crawled. So this was the haunted mansion where the Phoenix Club played the Shadow Game. The haunted part, he reminded himself, was just a superstition. Levi had imagined this place as more…luxurious, decked out with black velvet and silver opulence. But his surroundings looked much like the basement of any shambled home in Olde Town.

It took him a moment to remember he was here to die. That he hadn't been able to stop Enne from disappearing into the crowd at Luckluster. He swallowed down a wave of panic. Where was she now?

"Now, don't worry," Shark said. "I got your jacket and hat over there with your invitation." He nodded to a pile of Levi's belongings a few feet away. His pistol and the Shadow Card gleamed on top.

"That's generous of you."

"Don't be smart. I'm here to prepare you for the Game, but I've been told not to touch your pretty face." Shark leaned down to examine Levi's black eye. "You're already fairly roughed up. Where've you been hurt?"

"My right leg," Levi said. "And a broken rib."

"Well, I'll be sure to find some new spots, then."

Levi braced himself as Shark grabbed beneath his arms and lifted him like a bag of straw.

"It's a lot easier if you stand up," he said, then threw a staggering punch at Levi's shoulder. It dislocated with a *pop*.

Levi shouted and fell forward, caught by the ropes tying him to the pillar. Every breath he took ached. The man raised his enormous boot and kicked Levi's hip bone—not hard enough to fracture, but definitely enough to bruise.

Shark kicked him once in each shin as Levi sputtered.

"Nothing personal, you know. I don't even know your name."

"It's...Levi," he breathed.

Shark punched his chest, forcing the air out of him and hurting his ribs enough to make Levi scream. The force of it sent his body colliding with the pole behind him.

"I didn't say I *wanted* your name."

His fist slammed into Levi's left thigh.

Levi had reached the point where he felt himself retreating. It was an old, familiar feeling, of curling into that cold place in his mind where the aches of his body and heart couldn't follow. Though the place was meant for comfort and self-preservation, it had its costs: each time he returned there, he left pieces of himself behind, pieces he sometimes never found again.

When he'd left home, he thought he'd left this place behind him, as well.

He leaned unsteadily against the pillar and concentrated on reality. On the pain all over. On the dim overhead light. On the smell of mold and the taste of blood.

The final blow got him in the side of the neck. Levi's head knocked against the pillar. He slumped over and puked—for the second time that night. Even as he vomited whatever remained in his stomach, he was both in the basement and that somewhere else. Here and not here.

When Levi finished retching, Shark cut the rope binding him. "Don't bother running. You know you won't get far."

Levi didn't think he could run at all if he tried. His hands fell limply to his side, and Shark handed him his suit jacket and hat. Levi took it with dread, knowing it meant the night's festivities were about to begin.

"Now let me get a look at you." Shark's eyes ran up and own Levi's body. "Oh—my mistake." Before Levi could brace himself, Shark put two hands on his shoulder and shoved it back into its socket. Levi screamed and staggered back.

"I'll be keeping this gun of yours." Shark pocketed the pistol. "But here's your invitation." He slipped the Shadow Card into Levi's breast pocket and patted it with a malicious grin. "Look sharp. Now we go upstairs. That's where the fun is."

Fun for him, maybe. The only thing waiting for Levi was death.

Shark pushed him up the stairs, and Levi's bones ached with each step, so painful he needed to bite his tongue to keep from crying out. A fog of cigar smoke greeted them at the landing, and they entered a dark room with all black furniture that matched Levi's original vision for the House of Shadows. Two men lay on couches in the corner, too transfixed by the women in front of them to notice Levi and his captor. The women giggled teasingly and played with their transparent slips, their legs miles long in silver shoes with heels like razors.

"You know," Levi wheezed, "this isn't as bad as I thought."

Shark grunted and shoved him up another flight of stairs.

"Is Sedric Torren here?" Levi asked, though he doubted that Shark had news about whatever had happened to Sedric and Enne.

"Never knew him to miss a party," he replied.

Each time Levi heaved one leg painfully in front of the other, he thought, *this is one of my last steps.* He knew he should feel terrified—earlier, he had. But now that he was here, the House of Shadows felt too surreal to warrant anything but numbness. Maybe the effects of the sedative hadn't fully worn off. Maybe he was still in that someplace else, trying to protect himself from reality.

They entered his execution room.

Ten people sat around a long felt-topped table, and others spectated from chaises in the room's corners. Their skin had a gray cast to it, like the skin of a peach gone shriveled and moldy, and it was impossible to guess their ages. They looked neither young nor old, neither alive nor dead. They stared at Levi with empty eyes, their expressions still. All that moved was the shadows across their faces, flickering in the light of the metal candelabra.

The black-and-silver-striped walls made Levi feel as though he were entering a cage.

"Our first guest has finally arrived," one man said. His face was long, and his chin hooked outward into a point. His mostly gray hair was parted down the center, sharpening his severe widow's peak. Levi had seen his picture before, of course, but the black-and-white newspapers failed to convey that Chancellor Malcolm Semper was equally gray-cast and haunting in person.

Shark left, and the *thump thump* of his feet on the stairs echoed around the room. Levi scanned the faces of the Phoenix Club for Sedric, but none of them were him.

"Levi Glaisyer, why don't you take a seat?" Semper gestured to the chair beside him.

"Where's Sedric?" Levi asked.

"Mr. Torren isn't a member of the Phoenix Club, so he doesn't participate in our Game."

Levi limped to his chair and settled into the rigid leather seat. Was this where Alfero had sat when she died? Or Gabrielle Dondelair when she won?

The only remaining empty chair was directly across from him.

"We will explain the rules once our final guest arrives," Semper said.

So Levi didn't even warrant a solo execution. He wondered who else the Phoenix Club had decided to play with tonight.

"We weren't expecting another player," said a woman Levi recognized as Senator Josephine Fenice. Her wild silver hair draped across her body down to her waist. She was Semper's right hand and the woman who personally oversaw the execution of the previous Mizer royal family of New Reynes—even the children.

"I received a last-minute message," Semper explained. "Mr. Torren feels he has more to offer us. He's very eager to please."

Levi's heart stuttered at the mention of Sedric. What had happened between him and Enne? Did she finish what she'd come to do?

"Who is the player?" Fenice asked.

"The message didn't say," Semper answered. "Only to expect him here at two."

Levi had little idea of the time, only a guess that it was almost midnight. He heard the ticking of a clock in the back of his mind, counting down to the tenth day, counting down to his end. He tried to push away his concern over Enne. He needed all his concentration.

Once upon a time, Gabrielle Dondelair had won this Game. He needed to forget about all the legends, all the nightmares. The Shadow Game was a game like any other; there were winners, and there were losers. He wasn't helpless. He wasn't finished. He needed to remind himself who he was.

If anyone in this city had a chance of outplaying unbeatable odds, it was the Iron Lord.

ENNE

Enne's head smacked against glass, jolting her awake. Her eyes flickered open briefly, but, glimpsing Sedric's face, she immediately squeezed them shut again. She heard a door open, and a warm summer wind kissed her skin. She was in a motorcar, but her surroundings were slanted awkwardly to the left. The noise of Tropps Street was gone. The events of the evening gradually returned to her—Levi's disappearance, the drugged drink, the Shadow Card—and she held her breath to keep from crying out.

Sedric cursed and climbed out of the car. The door closed.

She eased her eyes open. Voices murmured outside, their tones escalating. Judging from that and the tilted angle of the car, they must've been stuck in a ditch. The windows were darkened with screens, so Enne had no way of confirming this—nor any idea where in the city they were.

She quietly reached for the abandoned suit jacket on the seat in front of her. Inside, she found her revolver from earlier, which Sedric had stolen. Rather than take it and alert him that she was awake, she emptied it of bullets and slipped them in her pocket, where the leather case with the injection was still carefully concealed among folds of satin.

The Shadow Card was sitting on her lap, the face of the Fool laughing up at her. It was the invitation card, she knew, but whose? Had Sedric meant it for her, or was he only delivering her Levi's? She didn't think Sedric knew Enne and Levi had any connection.

Only two things were clear now: Enne still needed to kill Sedric Torren, and she needed to stop the Shadow Game.

Voices. Footsteps. The seat tilted forcefully. The engine roared, and the motorcar jolted forward out of the ditch.

The door opened. She closed her eyes, feigning unconsciousness.

Someone—Sedric, probably—sat opposite her, bringing the odors of sweat and cigar smoke with him.

As the car resumed its course, she didn't move for another ten minutes. Enne desperately hoped he couldn't hear her heart pounding.

When the car finally stopped, Sedric lifted something to her nose. The stench of ammonia made her lurch. "Sleep well, doll?"

"Where are we?" She forced her voice to slur, as if she was just coming to.

"A place known as the House of Shadows." A malicious grin spread across his face, sending dread seeping across Enne's skin. "You might say it's the best gambling in the city."

Sedric opened the door and stepped outside. Over his shoulder, Enne caught her first glimpse of the House of Shadows. The name couldn't be more appropriate—the dark stone of its exterior looked as rough and jagged as a cavern wall, and though lights danced in the windows, they were muted behind fishnet curtains. A faint bass rumbled in the air, and a flute whispered a mournful melody into the night. Beyond the tall evergreen trees lining the driveway, the city's skyline glittered in the distance.

Zula's warning whispered through her mind. *More than anything, stay away from the House of Shadows.*

On her first day in New Reynes, Levi had told her that the Phoenix Club orchestrated the Revolution and the deaths of all the Mizers, so Enne understood the risks of entering their lair. But the fear she'd heard in Zula's voice that day—it sounded as though there was more to the House of Shadows than simply politics and history. Whatever dangers awaited her inside, it was something more. Something Enne had never known before.

Sedric handed her an envelope. "Take this to Malcolm Semper."

She sucked in a breath. The *Chancellor?* He was the most powerful man in the Republic, and the leader of the Phoenix Club. Her heart clenched as she took the envelope. He was the man who had murdered Lourdes.

"They're expecting you," Sedric told her.

"Expecting me for what?"

"For the Game."

Enne's breath caught. At the edges of her vision, she glimpsed shadows. The ghost of Gabrielle Dondelair. The silhouette of Lourdes. They had both tried to protect her, but in the end, they would all face the same fate.

"Unfortunately," Sedric continued, "I won't be able to watch—I'm not a member of the Phoenix Club. But rest assured, I'll be exploring the other entertainments the House of Shadows has to offer."

She let out a shiver as she slipped the envelope in her pocket, unsure if Sedric was giving her an opportunity to save Levi, or her own death certificate.

"They don't know who you are," he told her, a grin playing on his features. He was relishing this. "They don't particularly care. Times are changing—repeating, so they claim. And so they're playing again."

"Playing because...of the times?" Sedric wasn't making sense.

"There's a price to keep the devil away, when the devil comes knocking." He grabbed her by the wrist and pulled her out of the motorcar. She stumbled onto the grass. "Tonight that price is you."

As far as Enne was concerned in that moment, the city was full of devils. Sedric Torren. Vianca Augustine. Malcolm Semper. She'd paid a price to all of them already.

Very suddenly, Sedric slapped her across the face. Enne gasped and backed protectively against the side of the motorcar, her cheek stinging.

"That was for St. Morse," he snapped. He stepped closer to her, and fear bubbled up in her throat. She glanced around, but there was no one nearby to witness—not even their driver. They were alone.

This was her chance. But his glare rooted her to the spot.

"Black Maiden is a rather uncommon flower," he said. "Imported. Untraceable. Neither of the Families own it. Where did you get it?"

She could still hear Vianca's words in her mind. *This cannot be traced back to me.* The omerta grasped a bony hand around her throat, cutting off her air.

He took a threatening step closer, and Enne instinctively lifted her arms to protect her face. "Who are you working for?"

She could do nothing but stay silent.

His fingers brushed a strand of hair behind her ear, sending millions of chills of warning down her back. "I won't ask nicely again," he hissed. His fingers slid through her hair and squeezed. He jerked her head back, and tears formed in Enne's eyes from the pain. She slipped her hand into her pocket and fingered the edges of the leather case.

"Is it Vianca?" He pulled her hair harder, and she whimpered. The omerta forced her to shake her head. "Tell me."

"No one," she lied, slowly sliding the case out of her pocket.

In some ways, that was the truth. Vianca might have given the order, but if she killed Sedric Torren, she would do it for Levi.

He slammed her head against the car door. She cried out, stars spinning in her vision. The case dropped silently onto the grass.

Please no, she thought.

"You're lying," he said. He relaxed his grip on her hair and instead slid his hand to her throat. His chest pressed against hers, and she tried to stretch away, to put as much distance between him and her as possible, but his hip bone was jammed painfully into her side.

He won't kill you, she told herself. *The Phoenix Club is expecting you. He already said so.*

That didn't mean he wouldn't hurt her first.

His grip on her throat tightened. She let out an involuntary sputter.

"You will die tonight," he growled. While he spoke, she managed to lift her calf up and hooked her finger around the strap of her heel. She carefully slid it off her foot, trying not to lose her grip on it. She was dizzy from lack of air. "It will be long. It will be painful. The last time there were two players, the Phoenix Club didn't get to have their fun. I told them this time they could have it with you."

Enne knew exactly which game Sedric was referring to—the night Gabrielle had played to save her daughter's life. As anger flooded through her, Enne squeezed the heel and, with all the force she could muster, jammed it into his eye.

Sedric howled, letting go of her and covering his eye with his hands. Bloody tears dripped down his cheek. "You *bitch*," he snarled.

Enne shoved him away and frantically bent down, breathing heavily and feeling around for the leather case. She found it and slid off the lid. She had only just gotten a grip on the syringe when Sedric kicked her in the side, sending her sprawling.

Then he grabbed her by the front of her dress and hoisted

her to her feet. His left eye was squeezed shut, but there was so much blood, Enne couldn't be sure there was much of an eye left. His other arm aimed, ready for a punch. Before he could take a swing at her, she kicked him in the groin and slid out of his grasp.

She landed face-down on the grass, the syringe still clutched in her first.

When she looked up, Sedric had his revolver pointed at her. He clutched his eye with one hand, and there was a feral look in his other. He laughed madly. "You really should've let me have my fun."

Then he pulled the trigger.

Click.

His cursed and opened the revolver's empty compartment. Then he looked at her, his eyes wide, as she lunged forward and stabbed the syringe into his leg.

She would *not* be his victim tonight.

He would be hers.

Within moments, his limp body fell on top of her, his stomach on her back. She grunted and pushed him off, disgusted by the feel of him against her. He rolled over in the grass, staring with one eye into nothing.

She shakily got to her feet and looked down at his body. She felt no remorse. Not for him, not even for herself. Rather than breaking her, her surrender left her cold and steady with anger, with resolve.

Enne picked up the envelope Sedric had given her before he'd slapped her. He'd said something about two players, which meant Levi was inside—alive, but preparing to play the Shadow Game. If she was going to save him, she needed to join him in the House of Shadows.

She picked the revolver up from the ground. She only had three bullets. From the way the music carried, she assumed the House of Shadows was far from empty. Could she burst into the room, gun raised, and force Semper to let Levi escape? Would that be enough? Or would she be shot down herself before she had a chance?

She loaded the revolver and tucked it into her pocket. Her fingers brushed against the cool ribbon of the black satin mask Lola had given her. She pulled it out and tied it around her eyes, same as she'd done at Scrap Market. The mask covered very little of her face, but it offered at least a small amount of protection. If she and Levi managed to make it out of this alive, then no one could know who she was—otherwise, the Phoenix Club would easily discover it was she who'd slain Sedric Torren.

With her lipstick reapplied and her blood-stained heel back on, Enne knocked on the front door of the House of Shadows.

A huge man opened the door, and the loud music from inside blasted through her ears.

He blinked at her for a few moments, and then his jaw dropped. "It's you," Shark said, his golden tooth glinting.

Enne tensed as she recognized him—one of the whiteboots from her first day in New Reynes. He knew that she had a connection to Lourdes, the woman they'd killed here only the week before. He'd seen her without her mask.

Her mind blanked except for one, desperate idea.

She took out the revolver, aimed it between his eyes and pulled the trigger.

The noise and force of it startled her so much she yelped. His body thudded to the floor, and she stood there for a few moments, her pulse a violent current, ready for someone to come running. No one did. She wondered if anyone had even heard over all the music, which pulsed loud enough to drown out everything.

She stepped over his body and the pooling blood to enter the House. The cold shell inside of her hardened with each step. Apparently she'd left her soul back at Luckluster—probably back in Bellamy.

The air smelled strongly of several kinds of smoke, and she scrunched her nose and tried to blow away the odor with the envelope. A light shone in the next room, but the hallway was otherwise cast in darkness. She shoved the revolver in her dress as she made her way through the House.

A few men lying on the carpet glanced up blankly as she entered, but their attention was quickly recaptured by a giant pipe shaped like a candlestick on the table before them. Enne eyed a stairwell in the far corner of the room. A sinister force pulled her in that direction, guiding her toward her demise. She began to climb, her hand sliding up the smooth ebony railing.

There was a single door at the top of the stairs. Behind it, she heard a rhythmic ticking, like a clock or a heartbeat. She hitched her breath and turned the knob, opening the door cautiously.

Over a dozen lifeless faces peered at her as she stepped inside, but her gaze immediately fell on Levi. All the color drained from his face as he met her eyes. He was hunched in his chair as if it hurt him to straighten up, and an ugly red mark glared at the side of his neck. Enne's heart skipped in alarm—he'd been hurt again.

Enne closed the door behind her, and the music from downstairs disappeared, as if nothing existed outside this room. The ticking, too, was gone—maybe she hadn't really heard it at all.

"The other player, at last," one man said. Enne recognized him immediately: Chancellor Malcolm Semper, the Father of the Revolution—and her mother's killer. Her heart clenched, all the anger and grief and adrenaline seizing her at once. "Please take a seat, my dear."

She tried to reach for the revolver. This was it—she'd made it to the Game in time to stop it. But her hand was frozen at her side—not from the omerta, but some other power in the room. The same sinister force that had led her upstairs. She swallowed down a scream of panic.

"I believe you have Mr. Torren's letter, don't you?" Semper asked.

Enne froze. She didn't have any choices left. She was weapon-less, powerless, and she had walked directly into their hands. She'd made a fatal error for the second time that night, and now it was too late.

After a few moments of horror, she regained her composure enough to hand him Sedric's envelope. Semper tore it open and scanned the contents, then cleared his throat. "It seems… What is your name?"

"Séance," she said, the name Lola had given her. The name her mother had once used, long ago.

Semper blinked, as if startled for a moment. Maybe he, too, glimpsed the ghost of Lourdes at the edges of his vision.

He returned to Sedric's letter. "Mr. Torren has recommended that Séance be the one to play."

"What?" Levi hissed. Enne froze. What did that mean? Weren't they both supposed to play?

"Well, with your background in cards, Mr. Glaisyer, you don't need to prove your prowess. Perhaps this newcomer should be given a chance to impress."

Levi shook his head. He looked utterly defeated.

"Take a seat," Semper urged her, and Enne carefully claimed the only empty one at table. Every few moments, she tried again to reach into her pocket for the revolver, but to no avail. If she ran—if she *could* run—that would mean leaving Levi here, and she'd already come this far. No matter how panicked she felt, she couldn't abandon him in his final moments. She wouldn't be able to live with herself afterward.

"Don't bother eyeing the door, dear," Semper said. Every monster in this city always found a pet name for her. "The Game began the moment you stepped into the House. The rules are binding. There is no escaping. No cheating."

That explained why Enne couldn't reach for her gun. There

was a magic to the Game, like there was in oaths. A magic she couldn't explain.

"During the Game, the player typically bets their own life," Semper explained, "but since there are *two* guests, it will be Mr. Glaisyer's life on the line, and Séance the player."

Enne's heart sank. It should've been the other way around. She didn't know anything about cards.

"Last time we did this—" a younger woman started.

"That was a mistake," Semper snapped. "Besides, these two don't even know each other. Isn't that right?"

They were referencing the Game of Gabrielle Dondelair, when it had been Enne's life on the line. They had no idea that same child sat in front of them now, prepared to play the Game a second time.

"I've never heard of him," she answered. Levi shot her an annoyed look, as if he could honestly be worrying about his ego at a time like this.

"Players don't just walk through our door," the woman from earlier snapped. "If you don't know him, then why are you here?"

The words came easily. "To win," Séance answered.

Semper smiled. "People do not play this Game to win, my dear. They play this game not to lose."

DAY TEN

"Some say the City of Sin is a game,
so before you arrive—ask yourself, dear reader,
how much are you prepared to lose?"

—The City of Sin, a Guidebook:
Where To Go and Where Not To

ENNE

"The rules are not that complicated," Semper started. The room was so dark that he was merely a shadow across the table. "Eleven players and twenty-two kinds of Shadow Cards. In the beginning, every player will start off with two." He dealt out the silver cards and slid them to the players at the table. "Best not to look until you understand the rules," he said, just as Enne was reaching for hers. She drew her hand back, heart pounding. The nine other players stared at her with such detachment that she wondered if they were sleeping with their eyes open. If they were even interested in this Game, where Levi's life was the prize.

Semper continued his explanation as a man behind him placed a massive stack of silver-backed cards on the table. There were ten decks of the Shadow Cards within the large one, which meant there were ten of each kind of card. Each round, the players wishing to compete for that round's card would place one orb in the center. The objective was to collect all twenty-two Shadow Cards.

The men standing around the table gave each of the players

a silk pouch. When Enne opened the bag, she ran her fingers over tiny orbs made of black glass, identical to the one she kept within her nightstand at St. Morse.

"These are unique orbs," Semper said. "They're filled with your life force, not volts."

"How is that possible?" she asked, as though she'd never seen one before.

"There are many mysteries in the House of Shadows. Why don't you hand the orbs to Levi?"

How it works doesn't matter, Enne thought. *All that matters is us making it out of here alive.*

But only one person had ever won the Game, and she'd died that night, anyway.

Enne slid Levi the bag. His face rigid, he placed an orb on the inside of his elbow and filled it with volt-like lightning that was gold instead of white, in the same way one might fill an orb if they'd carried volts in their skin. One. Ten. Thirty. Fifty orbs, all filled. He handed her back the bag, looking as gray as the members of the Phoenix Club.

She literally held his life in her hands.

"The orbs empty after they're bet, so if you bet all of the orbs, Levi will die," Semper told her. "The Game will last three hours. If you have failed to collect the twenty-two Shadow Cards by that time, the orbs will deactivate, and he will also die." Enne tried to catch Levi's eye, but his gaze was fixed on the stack of Shadow Cards.

Semper set a metal timer the size of a mousetrap on the table, its clockwork and wires visible, as if inside out. Each round, he would deal the players as many regular cards as there were bets. Eight cards for eight players betting, for example. From there, those players competed for the card up for grabs that round. Everyone played one card per trick until they ran out, and the highest card of the trick collected the others. Whoever ended with the smallest number of spades won the round and the Shadow Card. Ties were decided by dice.

Semper shuffled the normal deck. It *thump-thumped* on the table.

"There's one other catch," he said. Of course there was. "The Shadow Cards, once the Game begins, develop divination properties. When they touch your skin, you'll see a flash of your life according to the card. What has already happened, or perhaps what could have happened, had you made different choices."

Levi finally looked at her. She held his gaze, her heart lodged in her throat, and silently told him that she could handle this, that it would be okay, that he had more than three hours left. But the fear on his face remained. She wouldn't have believed herself, either.

"What's the point of the divination?" she asked Semper.

"To remind the players of the stakes."

As if they needed reminding that they were about to die. It didn't matter that Levi's life was the one at play—the Phoenix Club would certainly never let her leave the House alive when this was over.

"You may pick up your cards," Semper instructed. He slapped his hand on the timer, which jolted to life.

Tick, tick, tick.

Enne grabbed her two Shadow Cards. As soon as she touched the top one, an image filled her mind, momentarily ripping her away from the room. She was in the dining room of her Bellamy house, and she stared up the stairwell at the first door. Lourdes's office, always locked. The house felt crowded with secrets.

The vision changed. She was slightly older, wearing a deep burgundy gown and waiting in a queue. Someone announced the name of the girl in front of her. When he called Enne's name next, Enne glided down the white-carpeted steps and entered a glittering ballroom, finally Lady Erienne Abacus Salta.

The room returned. Enne gasped and, after a few moments, shakily lifted the Shadow Cards. The first was the Moon, which had given her the memory of her home. The second was the Chariot, which had shown her entrance into society after graduation. That wouldn't ever happen now. *Lady Erienne Abacus Salta.* She couldn't even truthfully claim that name anymore.

My life will literally flash before my eyes, she realized. The all-encompassing nature of the visions reminded her of the black-and-white hallway from her dreams. Maybe whatever mysterious forces that enveloped the House of Shadows were also responsible for how Levi and Enne shared that place.

She didn't think she'd learn the answer now.

Semper flipped over the first Shadow Card up for grabs. It was the Empress. Eight people put in an orb, including her. The hand Semper dealt her was almost all high cards, and from what she remembered about the rules, that wasn't a good sign. But she hadn't understood much from his explanation.

Semper played his first card, the three of spades. She used her lowest spade, the jack. Of course, that turned out to be the highest card and she took all of the cards, including five spades. That was five strikes.

At the end of the round, she had more spades than anyone, which eliminated any chance she might have of collecting the Empress. She could almost feel Levi's anguish from across the table. Three people had collected zero spades, and they rolled the dice to determine who won the round's Shadow Card.

One orb missing. Forty-nine left.

Five rounds went by. She played four and lost them all.

Tick. Tick. Tick.

Semper flipped the Lovers card. Enne placed her bet, and to her luck and surprise, received almost all low cards. She managed not to collect any spades and won the prize.

As soon as she took it, an image appeared. She was in Levi's bed lying on her back, the top buttons of her blouse scandalously undone, her hair draped over his pillow. He was on all fours over top of her, his lips pressed against her chest. She sighed and breathed in the smell of his cologne, playing with the hairs at the nape of his neck. His hand traced from her shoulder down her arm until his fingers interlaced with hers. He lifted her arm above her head. Pressed his stomach against hers. Breathed her name into her ear.

It was a very sweet surrender.

With her free hand, she tilted his face to meet hers, raised her head to meet his lips—

It was over. Her cheeks must've been furiously red, since Semper smirked as he flipped the next card. Levi gave her a faint, congratulatory smile for winning the round, but his expression also seemed to ask, *What did you see?* She was obviously flustered. She looked away, sure he could read the embarrassment and truth in her eyes. They'd been pushing the boundaries of their relationship since she'd arrived.

Her body still burned at the thought of what might have been, but she forced the lingering thoughts of the illusion from her mind. She needed to focus.

Five more rounds passed. She bet only once—during a round when not many others did, since her chances of winning would be highest—and lost.

Tick. Tick. Tick.

An hour went by. Two more remained to collect nineteen cards.

She bet on the next five hands and won two: the Wheel of Fortune and Death. First she saw herself, stabbing the syringe into Sedric's leg, every moment of the scene as real and bloody as it had been earlier than night. When the image changed, she was collapsed in Vianca's office, the donna watching apathetically as the omerta drew out her last breath.

Tick. Tick. Tick.

By the end of the second hour, she'd won four more Shadow Cards, which meant she had one hour left to win thirteen.

Before, Levi wouldn't look her in the eyes. Now he looked nowhere else. He crossed and uncrossed his arms, tapped the table, shifted in his seat, cracked his neck, all while keeping his gaze locked on hers. She knew she was losing. He knew she was losing. She couldn't say anything because she'd told Semper that she didn't know him, but she wanted to scream *I'm sorry, I'm sorry, I'm sorry.* His eyes told her he wanted to say the same.

She bet on the next card. Semper seemed to take an eternity to deal their hands, and she wondered if he was moving slowly on purpose. With over two dozen of her orbs already played, Levi looked much less himself. His dark skin was growing increasingly transparent, and a whiteness was seeping the color out of his brown eyes.

Enne was going to have to sit here for fifty-five minutes and watch him die. The thought made her shake with panic.

She tied with another woman for the next Shadow Card. The woman rolled first. An eleven.

Enne watched Levi as she tossed the dice, refusing to look at the number. He smiled slightly, and she knew she'd won.

Then she looked at the dice. A nine. She'd lost. His smile had been for comfort.

Soon she'd lose the entire Game, and it would be her fault both of them would die. Had she not been here, Levi could've played himself, and then he would have stood a fighting chance. All that bravado about trying to save him the way she should've saved Lourdes…she'd only made everything worse.

Tick. Tick. Tick.

Fifty minutes left.

She refused to let them die because the timer ran out. If this was their end, it would be only after she took a chance and bet everything she had and never stopped trying.

Semper turned over the next card.

The World.

She was the first to place in her orb. Semper was second. She looked around and realized that there were three people already out of orbs, and the rest were observing indifferently. Their lives weren't on the line. They already knew that she'd lose.

Only two players remained in the round. Semper played a four of hearts, and she played her three. All she had was the ace of spades, which meant if he played any spade, she'd lose because she'd have the highest card and would be forced to take them both.

He played the six of diamonds. Then he took her ace of spades, and she took the World.

Upon touching the card, the sensation came suddenly, inexplicably, and all at once. A pain radiated across her chest, starting at her heart and seeping through her veins. She felt feverish, hyperaware of ever pulse of her blood, every churn of her insides. When she closed her eyes and tried to determine the pain's source, she had the eerie feeling that there was another presence inside her. A silhouette lurking inside the edges of her mind. Something that hadn't been there before.

As the pain gradually faded, she became aware of a change in the room. Nearly everyone present was still and lifeless, yet she felt a cold energy in the air. There were threads everywhere. They weren't something she could feel or see in a literal sense, but something she still understood was there. They hummed against the Shadow Cards, against the black orbs, against the timer. They circled around each of the players' wrists, binding them—all of them but her. Even though the threads weren't connected, they all felt as though they were part of the same fabric: different strings of the same piano. And the Game, she realized, was the song.

She nervously placed the World with the other Shadow Cards she'd won. Whatever had happened, whatever she'd thought she could sense—she must have been imagining it. She was at a breaking point of fear and nerves. For a moment, she'd cracked.

In forty-eight minutes, when the timer rang, Levi would die, and so would she. She needed to hold herself together. She ignored the strange sensation and returned her focus to the Game.

Levi blinked a few times, and by the way he did it, Enne thought he was trying to tell her something. A signal. He rubbed his eyes repeatedly, but she'd stopped paying attention. Semper had flipped over the next card, and she was determined to win it. Much of her panic from earlier was gone, replaced solely with resolution.

She won the next six Shadow Cards.

Tick. Tick. Tick.

Twenty-eight minutes left.

More people joined in, but only a few. Most were out of orbs. They must have all started out with different amounts.

Enne had sixteen orbs left, and even in the near darkness of the room, she could tell Levi looked within inches of death. His skin reminded her of wax paper, and all his veins showed through, particularly around his eyes.

The next round went by, and she was the only player to bet—Semper already owned that Shadow Card. It automatically went to her.

Then three people bet. Enne won again.

Tick. Tick. Tick.

She lost the next.

Tick. Tick. Tick.

And won the one after.

Tick. Tick. Tick.

Twenty minutes. She still needed four cards.

Tick. Tick. Tick.

But she was almost there. She was almost there.

There were five players left, including Semper and her. The other three played *every single* hand. They must have believed that there was a chance that Enne would win.

She won the next card. Fifteen minutes left.

And the next. Twelve minutes left.

Then she lost. Eight minutes left.

She won. Three minutes left.

Only Enne and Semper still had orbs to bet. He flipped the Hanged Man, but they both already owned that, so he flipped another. They both owned that one, too. And another. And another. It seemed that they were after the same card.

Tick. Tick. Tick.

The Devil. When he reached it, there was only one minute left.

She couldn't lose. The presence in her mind—the one she'd imagined—felt larger and more imposing. All the threads in the room hummed. The song was reaching its final movement.

Semper dealt them each two cards, moving slowly, *so slowly*, and she wanted to strangle him, she was so anxious and frustrated. He was trying to stall.

He played his first card. A four of spades. She had to follow suit, and the only spade she had was the jack.

Which meant she'd lost. She'd lost, and now they would both die.

Because not only would Semper have all the cards and win the Game, but the timer would inevitably run out. Only twenty-eight seconds left.

If she played her card, she'd watch Levi die. If she did nothing and waited, she'd still watch Levi die.

Twenty-four seconds left.

She could… She could…

Seventeen seconds left.

She needed time to think. Just for a second. Just to get her bearings straight and stop the Game and tell Levi that she was sorry and—

Stop the song, whispered the presence in her head. *Stop the song. Stop the song.*

It was her own voice. Her own sense of self-preservation speaking. The threads hummed around her, binding everything but her. If she listened closely to the song, she could almost hear the notes skipping. Something was wrong with its tune. The Game wasn't as it was before. The rules…the rules were broken in a way they weren't before.

Ten.

Nine.

Eight.

She reached into her pocket.

Seven.

Six.

She pulled out the revolver.

Five.

She stood and pointed the gun at Malcolm Semper. Her chair screeched like the cries of someone waking in their coffin.

Four.

The women gasped. The man beside Enne leaped up to knock her over. But her finger was already on the trigger, and she fought to keep her balance.

Three.

STOP THE SONG, it screamed.

Two.

Enne obliged.

One.

The gun fired. The bullet smashed the timer into a hundred pieces of clockwork and, all at once, the threads silenced, the song cut off.

The man forced her down, and her chest slammed on the table. She gasped as his weight crushed the air out of her lungs. Someone ripped the gun from her hand.

It was Levi.

Semper reached to flip over his last card and win the Game.

"*No!*" Enne shouted.

Levi pointed the gun at Semper's head and shot.

Screams. The sound of chairs scraping the wooden floor. Enne's ears were ringing from the sound of the gunfire. She craned her neck, searching for Levi.

The table jolted as Semper's body hit it.

"That was for Lourdes," Levi whispered, and she loved him for it.

With her cheek pressed against the black felt of the table, Enne stared at two things: the lifeless eyes of the man who'd killed her family, and the Devil card soaking in the devil's blood.

LEVI

"Don't. Mucking. Move," Levi shouted, pointing the gun around the room. The Phoenix Club watched him with wide, dead eyes and remained motionless. You couldn't kill them with time, but you could kill anything with a bullet.

"Put the gun down," Josephine Fenice said calmly. Too calmly. He'd just shot the *Chancellor of the whole Republic* right in front of her, and he would happily shoot her next. He certainly wasn't calm.

"Let her go," Levi ordered the man pinning Enne against the table. The man raised his arms, and Enne hurriedly straightened. Her eyes, once brown, were now blazingly violet. Her aura, too, had shifted from swirls of dark blue to a violent storm of purple and silver, deepening the original smells of coffee and bourbon with hints of gunpowder.

Auras weren't supposed to change.

It was dark enough in the room that he doubted anyone else had noticed her eyes during the Game, but now...now the two of them held their full attention. He needed to get Enne out of here before anyone figured out who—and what—she was.

"Séance," Levi said, even if the name sounded shatz, "go stand by the door." Enne did as instructed, and Levi's shoulder relaxed once she was safely tucked into the corner, far enough away that the Phoenix Club wouldn't see her Mizer eyes.

Levi reached for the remaining black orbs and returned their energy to his body. He didn't feel any different afterward than he had before: exhausted, the blood pumping so slowly inside him that his gears felt stuck together. Most of his life energy—whatever that was—was gone. He wondered how long it would take to regenerate.

If it ever *did*.

Levi backed toward the door. Every part of him ached, but muck—it felt good to move. He didn't think he'd walk again.

"We'll only find you again," Josephine said matter-of-factly. "You can't run from us."

From the moment Levi left this room, he would be a real criminal. He'd always been a cheat, but he'd never caused enough trouble that he'd needed to hide. Starting tonight, he would be a wanted man. Wherever he ran, the Phoenix Club would follow.

Gabrielle Dondelair had lasted only a few hours.

Enne grabbed his arm reassuringly. "We're leaving."

She opened the door, pulled Levi into the stairwell and slammed it closed. They raced downstairs—a feat nearly impossible for Levi in his current state. Besides his multiple injuries, his body was three-quarters of the way to death. Enne had to prop his arm around her shoulder just to keep him upright.

"Enne," he hissed frantically in her ear as she helped him down the steps. "If we see anyone at all, you need to close your eyes."

"What do you mean?"

"They're purple."

She tensed, but didn't look as shocked as she should have. What had happened to her during the Game? "Did they see?"

"I don't think so. We'll talk about it when we're alone." Once they made it out of here.

This had been the room with the dancing girls, but now it was empty. Behind them, laughter and music echoed, coming from somewhere deeper in the house.

Enne pulled him through an archway. The next room smelled strongly of Mistress's signature sweet smoke, and a few men slept on the floor. They didn't stir as Levi and Enne dashed toward the exit.

This was too easy. They had simply let them escape. Did the Phoenix Club believe the House of Shadows to be that well protected? Or that they'd meet their fates by the end of tonight?

Enne swung open the front door, and Levi took a deep breath of fresh air and tried to push his anxieties away.

Then he tripped over the body.

He crashed down, knocking his head on the man's shoulder with an agonizing *whack*. Enne landed face-first on Levi's back. Her knee jammed painfully into his wounded leg, and he let out a long, stifled curse.

"Sorry. Sorry," she said, scrambling up.

Levi stretched himself onto his knees, then nearly let out a scream. He was face-to-face with Shark, the man who had beaten him in the basement. Blood had pooled over the concrete step, trickling down from the bullet hole in his forehead.

"Muck." He reached for Enne's hand and nearly jumped to his feet. He'd accidentally laid his palm in the blood, and he hurriedly wiped away the red on his pants, feeling ill.

"I forgot he was here," Enne murmured.

"How long has he been here?"

"Since I arrived."

"Since you...*you* shot him?"

She nodded, her face grim. "Let's go."

Levi bent down and carefully removed his pistol from Shark's pocket and shoved it into his own. If they were going to survive the rest of the night, they both needed protection. "Let's go," he breathed, reaching shakily for Enne's arm to steady him.

Together, they raced across the front lawn and the woods adjacent to the estate's long driveway, toward the glittering skyline of New Reynes. They could still faintly hear the ghostly music from the House of Shadows in the air.

Levi shivered. Tonight, they'd been the entertainment.

They made it to the main road and waited several moments, hoping for a carriage or motorcar to pass by so they could beg a ride. None did.

"It's a long walk back to the city," Enne said, her voice hitched. "They've probably already called the whiteboots. They'll know we can't have gone far." He felt her trembling beneath him.

"We could take the Mole. No one takes the Mole," Levi said, never so eager to ride the subway in his life. If they kept running, they'd find a station within a few minutes.

"The whiteoboots will look there," she answered. She placed a hand on her forehead, breathing deeply, trying to steady herself.

The cool nighttime wind, the agony of every step, the adrenaline of nearly dying—their reality crashed over him all at once, and Levi let out a manic laugh. "Maybe we should consult your guidebook. What does it say to do in this situation?"

Unamused, Enne grabbed his arm and yanked him down the street. He tried to keep up, but it was almost impossible to run. Standing up alone was a struggle, and the pain from his broken ribs and dislocated shoulder were enough to make him faint.

"It says we change our clothes and call Vianca," she hissed.

"Good plan."

They ran for a few more minutes before they reached the eastern edge of the Factory District, even beyond the realms of Scar Land. Levi couldn't remember the last time he'd been so far from downtown. They crept down an alley between two apartment buildings. Enne pointed to a clothesline several floors above them and started toward a metal escape stairwell.

"Wait here," she whispered, unwrapping his arm from around her shoulder.

Levi nodded, doubting he could make such a climb in his condition. He slumped onto the ground and leaned his head against the wall. The alley reeked of garbage and the odors of the Brint. Very faintly in the distance, he heard the calls of sirens. They were probably meant for them.

He was exhausted. He was beaten. He was light-headed. Even though he should've been focusing on their escape, his thoughts jumbled together, and he fixated on only one question.

Gabrielle Dondelair had only lasted hours. How much longer until the Phoenix Club found them?

Enne returned with several articles of clothing. She tossed him a shirt that was clearly several sizes too large. "Get dressed," she commanded. "And turn around."

He raised an eyebrow—they were in far too much of a rush for modesty. But still, he stood up painfully and faced the wall, hyperaware of the approaching sirens, hyperaware of Enne in some state of undress behind him. Both of these thoughts made his heart pound.

"Those look terrible," Enne said from behind him. He realized she was looking at the swollen bruises on his back.

He shot her an annoyed look over his shoulder. Hurt as he was, he couldn't change as fast as her. He was wearing very little. "I don't remember giving *you* permission to peek."

She flushed indignantly. "I thought you'd be done. Now hurry up. We need to find a pay phone."

He grumbled and pulled up the too-big pants. Enne was dressed in trousers, a checkered men's button-up and a pair of socks. Her dress and heels were discarded on the ground.

"I know that dress," he said, managing a smirk. She'd obviously pulled it from his closet. "You wear New Reynes well."

Her blush deepened, but after he finished dressing she propped his arm over her shoulder again. "Come on."

They hurried out of the alley, away from the direction of the sirens. Enne pointed ahead, where a yellow phone booth stood below a streetlamp. They raced toward it.

"Do you have volts?" he asked.

"Yeah." She rooted around her pocket, pulling out a tube of lipstick, the gun and the silk mask. All the girlie necessities, apparently.

Finally, she pulled out a small orb, bright with volts.

They slid into the phone booth. Enne held the orb up to the meter, and Levi stood behind her. There wasn't much space, so his chest was pressed against her back. He coughed awkwardly and drummed his fingers against the metal counter, waiting for her to suggest he wait outside. She never did.

Outside, the distant sirens approached. They didn't have much time.

"Is it safe to call the phone operator?" she asked hurriedly.

He reached over her to the number pad. "Vianca has a private line."

After he dialed the numbers, Enne held the phone up to both their ears. He held his breath, listening to the ringing. Enne's face was only inches from his. He stared at all the strands of hair that had fallen from her bun and now draped across the slopes of her neck and shoulders. She had goose bumps, he noticed.

"This is St. Morse Casino, Vianca Augustine's office," the secretary answered.

"We need a motorcar," Enne said frantically. "At the…" She squinted at the Mole station outside. "At the Paidalle station."

"Who is this?"

"It's us," Levi growled. "We need a car."

"Oh. *Oh.* Yes. I'll tell her—"

"And send another car to Luckluster Casino," Enne told her.

"There'll be a girl there. Tall. Fair skin. Top hat. Black laced boots. She'll be looking for us."

"Yes. I'll let her know."

Enne hung up. "I hope Lola's still there, but it's been hours."

"I'm sure she's fine, even if she's gone." Levi held his breath. Bent over like he was, his mouth was awfully close to her neck. He cleared his throat. "We need to find somewhere to wait." A place where there wasn't negative space between them, and where they wouldn't be so exposed.

Levi opened the glass door and stumbled out. They stood on a strip of sidewalk that cut down the middle of a street, forking it on either side. The shops around them were closed, metal security doors down and locked. With nowhere else to wait, they climbed down the steps of the adjacent Mole station and collapsed in a corner—close enough to the exit to still hear the sirens and faint noise of the city, but deep enough inside to remain out of sight.

Both of them panted.

"How long will we wait, do you think?" she asked.

"Maybe thirty minutes. We're a long way from St. Morse."

She cringed, and their eyes met. Anything could happen in thirty minutes. They could be dead in thirty minutes.

Swallowing down his panic, Levi stretched out his legs and winced at the burning in his muscles. They sat shoulder-to-shoulder, legs out. Enne, he realized, was barefoot except for the socks. Her hand was outstretched beside him.

We will survive this together, he thought, sliding his hand toward hers. But taking it would be as much for comfort as it was for desire. They were on a run for their lives—temptation never came at the proper time.

A rumbling filled the halls as a train sped through the tunnels below.

"My eyes," she whispered. "How am I supposed to hide them?"

She locked her gaze with his, and, again, he was taken aback by how changed her face looked. How her aura had once smelled of a Gambler's Ruin, but now also smelled of smoke.

How very difficult it was not to kiss her.

"You're in luck," he said, shifting nervously, knowing he should put more distance between them. He didn't. "Because it so happens that I have the world's most uncomfortable pair of blue contacts in my pocket this very moment. Perfect for concealing royal lineages and cheating during card games."

"You're mucking with me," she said, eyes narrowed. "You're doing that face."

"What face?"

"That smirk of yours."

He reached into his pocket and pulled out the case of contacts. "I can make you better ones, at some point. These will do for now."

"Why do you have these?"

"A series of very poor decisions. Just put them on."

She walked to the nearest advertisement on the wall and studied her reflection in the tarnished glass. "I don't even look like me." Her voice was a mix of both wonder and bitterness.

As Enne struggled to put on the contacts, Levi once again contemplated whether this was his last chance. The sirens outside echoed into the night, and when Levi closed his eyes, he still heard the sound of the gunfire that had ended the Shadow Game.

It would be easy. He would beckon her closer, grab her hands and close the distance between them. If not for her, he would've died tonight, and he would've died alone. If death was still their fate, then why shouldn't he kiss her just like he wanted? Just like he knew she wanted, too? In Luckluster, he'd seen his desire reflected in her eyes. They might have survived the Game, but who was to say they would survive the night?

They had always been in this together.

But as she turned to him, her purple eyes now concealed with blue, a fear settled in Levi's heart. She'd poisoned the most powerful don of the North Side. She recited street rules to herself. She was the daughter of a notorious arsonist, raised by a woman who'd lived a life within the shadows.

She was a Mizer. She was impossible.

They very well might die tonight, but the real danger stood only an arm's length away. He could kiss Enne, in hopes of surviving the night—or he could let go of his desire, in hopes of surviving tomorrow.

"How do I look?" she asked.

He swallowed. "You look different. But the purple is gone."

She took an unsteady breath and sat down beside him.

"Do you feel different?" he asked quietly.

"I feel…" She shook her head. "It sounds sort of shatz, honestly."

"Try me."

"I had the gun with me the whole Game, of course," she explained. "But I couldn't reach for it. Semper said something about the Game binding the players the moment we entered the House, so no cheating was allowed. But as soon as I touched the World card…everything changed." Levi nodded. That was the moment he'd first noticed the new colors of Enne's aura. "It was like I could *see* the magical threads of the Game, holding it all together, playing a song, and there were no more threads around *me*. And I could feel—can still feel—this presence in my head. Something that wasn't there before."

Levi's skin prickled. Every word she said reminded him how much danger they were in, how dangerous she was. "You're absolutely right," he said, trying to sound teasing when really, he was terrified. "You sound shatz."

She shoved him in the shoulder. "You should be nice to me. I can make volts now, or however Mizer powers work."

"And you should stop hitting me. I'm more wounds than person."

She reached out and brushed the bruise on his neck, gently enough that it didn't hurt.

"These aren't from Chez," she said softly. "These are new."

The memory of his last encounter with Chez returned to him, leaving a foul taste in his mouth. "I saw Chez tonight, too."

Her eyes widened. "Did he try to challenge you again?"

"Not exactly. I started it. And...I also ended it." Levi clenched his fist. He wished he could guess whether or not Chez was still alive, but he truly had no idea. He'd never meant to go that far.

"You don't have to tell me," she murmured.

But there was nothing else to tell. She understood, and he could already see the unease on her face.

It was the same unease he felt when looking at her.

"Tell me about what happened tonight. Everything before the Game. Like..." He reached into her pocket and pulled out the mask. "Where did you find this? Not really something ladies just carry around with them."

Enne snatched the mask from his hands. "There was an incident, of sorts, at Scrap Market." She told him the story. How Lola had changed her mind about Enne and about the oath. How she'd come up with the name Séance, taken from one of Lourdes's older pseudonyms.

Then the story continued. How Vianca had called her into her office. How Enne had found Lola and stolen a car. How the blood gazer gave her the poison Enne brought with her to Luckluster.

At some point during her tale, she rested her head on Levi's shoulder. He struggled to pay attention to anything other than the way her body felt pressed against his, and his attempt to forget his desire became a muddled afterthought. He wondered if she knew what she was doing to him.

"I woke up in Sedric's motorcar outside of the House of Shadows," she said.

The words gradually sank in. "He *drugged* you? Did he hurt you?"

"Only a little. I killed him before he had the chance to do more."

Sedric Torren was dead.

"What?" he asked, even though he'd understood her perfectly. His mind spun. This changed…*everything*. The Torren family was without a don. The upcoming election was without a candidate. The North Side had one less monster on its streets.

"You already know I had to kill the guard, too. The one who opened the door," Enne continued. "I keep waiting for everything to hit me, but I don't feel bad. I don't even feel like I *should*."

"I killed the Chancellor," Levi whispered, only just remembering now, as they confessed their sins in the dark. That would change everything, too.

Enne gave Levi's shoulder a gentle but comforting squeeze. "He was a terrible man."

Even so, Levi had never killed someone before. He'd never thought of himself as a killer. That was Ivory. That'd been Eight Fingers. But not him. He felt like he'd been stained in some uncleansable way, that the person he was before was somehow purer than the person he was now. He didn't mourn the Chancellor, but he mourned himself.

The chorus of sirens outside grew louder. Several cars were speeding through the streets above, searching for them. The two held their breath as the sirens passed by the station. They had been lucky in their hiding spot for now…but soon their luck might run out.

"Vianca's motorcar should be here soon," he whispered, hoping to reassure himself as much as her.

Even in the dark, she looked pale. "What if the whiteboots come and we need to run? We told Vianca this is where we'd be."

"I told you—no one takes the Mole. They'll never find us here."

She pressed her hand over her heart. "Don't joke. I'm actually terrified."

"So am I. That's why I'm joking."

There were footsteps on the stairs of the station.

Levi and Enne immediately stood up and backed into the corner. Enne pressed against him as they each pointed their guns at the mouth of the stairwell. Levi bit his lip to silence his breathing. He could feel Enne shaking. She reached for his hand, and he squeezed it.

"Together," he whispered.

The woman who appeared, however, wasn't a whiteboot. She also brandished a gun, but she relaxed once she saw them. "You're here." She was dressed like one of Vianca's typical gangsters—a fedora hat and a tight, pin-striped dress. "We need to hurry. The whiteboots are already at St. Morse."

Relief washed over him—they wouldn't die, not here, not yet. Levi slid away from Enne and lowered his gun. He took a shaky step toward their savior.

"Then where do we go?" he asked.

"Oh, we're going to the casino. We're just not walking through the front doors."

ENNE

Enne had never been so grateful to step out of a motorcar. She and Levi had spent the entire thirty-minute ride crouched in the back seat beneath blankets, jostling painfully each time they'd skidded around a turn, holding their breaths each time a siren passed.

They were parked in front of a den called The Palace, but the majesty of the den began and ended with its name. It was a tall, narrow building wedged between a casino and an apartment complex off Tropps Street. The *P* and the *c* of its neon sign flickered cheaply. The exterior reminded Enne of a pastry shop: all swirls and pastels and glitter.

"Is this Sweetie Street?" Enne asked.

"No," their driver answered. "We're only a block from St. Morse."

Their driver quickly led them inside the den, a firm hand on both their shoulders. Despite the late hour, The Palace was empty, but the air still reeked of smoke and the overwhelming smell of orchids. They walked around cushions and through sheer curtains to the staff room in the back. Enne tried to figure out exactly what type of New Reynes entertainment was offered here. Potentially all of them.

Their trek was long and winding—appropriate for two criminals running from the law. Down the steps. Across the basement. Through a trapdoor. Into a tunnel that stank of sewage. Enne shivered. They were in the bowels of the city.

"This leads directly to St. Morse," the woman explained. "We'll take the private elevator to Vianca's suite."

The hair on Enne's neck rose at the thought of visiting Vianca's personal residence. Enne whispered to Levi, "Have you been there?"

"No," he said grimly. "I've not yet had that misfortune."

"What do you think she'll do with you? It's not as though you can deal cards anymore." Unlike Enne, the Phoenix Club knew exactly who Levi was—and where to find him.

"I'm not leaving New Reynes," he said firmly. "Vianca would miss me too much." He elbowed her in the side. "You would, too, right? After all, we're partners in crime now."

She smirked to conceal her embarrassment. She had a thousand reasons for not wanting Levi to leave the city, the chief one being the way he was looking at her right now. Like it was just her and him and no one else.

They reached the elevator at the end of the tunnel. The woman ushered them inside but didn't follow. The lights flickered, and the elevator rose with a jerk.

Enne's stomach clenched. They were about to enter the donna's true lair.

She reached for Levi's hand, seeking courage and comfort. At first, he tensed, then he laced his fingers with hers, sending a nervous spark across her fingertips.

"What do we tell her about the Game?" he asked hoarsely. "I'm sure her little spies have told her all about what happened in the House of Shadows. She'll know you were there."

"We tell her that *you* played." It was safer for Vianca to assume that Levi had won the Game. Vianca knew Levi's card abilities—she'd believe that story. If she knew Enne had played and cheated the Game, she'd grow suspicious as to why.

"And if she knows otherwise?" Levi asked, squeezing her hand in warning.

"How could she? She had spies in that room?"

"I'm not sure what the Phoenix Club has told others."

Enne pressed her free hand to her heart and felt its pounding. "I don't have any other ideas." Her voice hitched in panic. Vianca couldn't know the truth. They needed more time. They needed a better lie.

Levi wrapped his arms around her and hugged her reassuringly. She let herself lean into him. She let herself sigh. It'd been a long night.

"We've faced scarier things than her," he said.

"I know."

Just as in the phone booth, she was hyperaware of him behind her, how his chest felt pressed against her back, warm and steadying. It would be easy to turn around. To slide a hand behind his neck. To pull his lips to hers. She held her breath, certain Levi could feel the racing of her pulse, could hear the desire in her thoughts.

Then the elevator doors opened, and Levi and Enne sprang apart.

Vianca was perched on an armchair in a sitting room, her snake eyes leering at them curiously. "Well, wasn't that a picture." She set down her teacup on the end table. "I found *this* one in your apartment, Levi. Lucky I found him before the whiteboots did." She nodded at Jac across the room, who was several shades of green from being so close to Vianca. He looked like he'd just found the monster beneath his bed. "I also fetched that girl you requested." Lola sat beside Jac. She fiddled anxiously with her harmonica in her lap.

"It's been quite a night, hasn't it?" Vianca frowned, scanning Levi. "You've looked better, dear."

"I've felt better," he croaked.

Vianca stood and wiggled a bony, ring-covered finger at Enne. "You first, Miss Salta. You and I need to have a little chat."

Even something called a "little chat" with Vianca sounded dangerous. Enne gave the other three a parting, desperate glance before following Vianca into the next room. Levi nodded at her reassuringly, reminding her once again that they had faced worse this night.

Don't let them see your fear.

Never allow yourself to be lost.

Trust no one unless you must.

Two days ago, Enne had been certain that she was broken beyond repair, yet still her mother's words held their familiar power, winding Enne back together.

Just not all the way back, she thought as Vianca closed the door behind them. The ache of missing Lourdes and her old life would never leave her. All she could do was keep surviving, keep playing. In ways that were both better and worse, Enne wasn't the same girl who'd arrived, lost and alone, in the City of Sin.

"Séance," Vianca said with a hiss. "A rather interesting choice of name."

They were in what appeared to be Vianca's parlor. Like the rest of St. Morse, it was furnished in her typical dark, antique fashion—cheap luxury that bordered on gaudy. Each upholstery had a different sort of print. Dozens of glass gemstones dangled from the chandelier above the couch, a piece of costume jewelry set out as decoration. On the largest wall of the room, there was a portrait of what Enne imagined must've been Vianca's family: Vianca, years younger, though clearly recognizable; a man who didn't smile; and a boy with a princely grin.

"I would never have guessed it. I mean, *look* at you," Vianca said, gesturing at Enne's body. "I imagined you easily discarded."

Enne was still frozen by the door. She shouldn't be this para-lyzed by Vianca, not when she'd already slain one monster to-night. But fear didn't need to be logical to be felt.

"Don't just stand there like a wallflower," Vianca snapped. "Take a seat." She patted the spot beside her.

"Yes, Madame." Enne sat as far away from Vianca as she could without looking rude.

"So polite. I wish Levi spoke to me that way." Vianca's eyes narrowed as she inspected Enne's face. "You look different."

It took everything in her to conceal her panic. "I... I haven't slept, of course. It's nearly morning."

Vianca waved her hand dismissively, and Enne's shoulders re-laxed. Levi's contacts had worked, even under the donna's cal-culating inspection. "You'll have time for rest after we're done. I need to hear if the rumors are true." Vianca leaned forward gleefully. Happiness was an emotion that didn't suit Vianca's face. "Is Sedric Torren dead?"

Enne nodded, swallowing. If she closed her eyes, she could still feel his hand around her throat and the repulsive lust in his stare.

"And the Chancellor?"

"Yes, he's dead."

Vianca laughed with such mirth that—to Enne's horror—she reached forward, grabbed Enne's hand and shook it in excitement. "The whole city is talking about you—about Sé-ance. How you killed them both."

Enne startled. "But Levi was the one who killed Semper."

"*My* Levi?" Vianca echoed, dumbfounded. "How *interesting*. But the truth hardly matters. What's important is what people say, what the papers are printing. Your Séance character is about to become the most notorious criminal we've seen in almost twenty years." She laughed and gave Enne's hand a last little shake. "You must tell me *all* about it."

"About...the murders?" Enne asked. She fought the urge to

look away from the donna's face. Her many frown lines coiled unnervingly when she smiled.

"Yes. And about the House of Shadows."

Despite not having properly rehearsed her words, the lies flowed easily. Vianca was so enraptured, she listened to the entire story without asking questions.

"When Levi won, and the Game finished, its rules were over. So he stood, pointed his gun—" she swallowed again "—and shot the Chancellor in the head."

Vianca clapped. "Delightful. Delightful."

Then the donna leaned back and studied Enne a second time. The presence Enne had felt during the Game—her Mizer abilities—hummed inside her, and she nearly tremored, imagining Vianca's stare peering straight through Enne's lie.

"This whole act you put on is quite convincing," Vianca purred, "but I'm starting to believe you were corrupted before you ever set foot in this city." Vianca grabbed Enne by the chin and peered at her closely, turning her face from side to side. Enne shuddered and kept her gaze fixed on her lap, in case Vianca noticed the faint outline of the contacts. "Are you a pearl, or are you a bullet?"

There was an unpleasant truth to Vianca's question. Enne wished she knew the answer herself. She'd like to consider herself a pearl, but pearls were breakable, and she had proved herself not to be.

Maybe she could be both.

"I have *excellent* plans for you, my dear," Vianca cooed, relinquishing her grasp on Enne's face. "But for that, we must talk in the morning. I want to speak with Levi now. Send him in."

"Yes, Madame," Enne responded, more than eager to leave.

Enne slipped out the doors into the other room, and the others snapped to attention. Levi immediately stood and came to her side. "She didn't notice the contacts," Enne whispered.

"Good. Anything else?" His hands found her wrists, and he turned her arms over, as if examining her for injuries.

"She wants to see you."

He eyed the closed door warily, then he took a deep breath and cracked his neck. "The night's almost over." Enne didn't know if he was reassuring her or himself.

Then he molded his face into something expressionless and entered Vianca's parlor. The door closed behind him.

Enne tried not to worry about whatever meeting was unfolding in the other room. Levi had braved Vianca for years before she'd met him, but the way he'd braced himself before walking in, the little bit of fear in his eyes—it almost broke her heart. Because he felt just as trapped as she did, and it was a terrible way to feel.

It was too easy to let her feelings slip out of control. It had nearly happened in the pay phone booth. In the Mole station. In the elevator.

The Phoenix Club knew Levi's face now. They'd be hunting for him. Enne's purple eyes were deadly enough—it wasn't safe to fall for someone with a bounty on his head.

Even if she already had.

She collapsed on the seat beside Lola. From across the room, Jac tossed her a box of spice cookies. Enne hadn't even realized how hungry she was. She thanked him and tore into them.

"Levi told us," Lola said. Her eyes found Enne's. "What have you done?"

Enne was too exhausted for words. She wasn't prepared for another round of Lola's paranoid accusations. "I thought we were past this." It wasn't a question—it was a challenge.

Lola shifted awkwardly. "We are. I mean, I waited at Luckluster for hours."

"And I told Vianca to find you. I wanted to make sure you were all right." Enne handed her a cookie. "Because we're friends."

Lola nodded numbly.

"So, Enne," Jac said. "Does your new power thing mean we're all about to be rich? I'm your friend, too."

She might've laughed if she weren't so tired. Since the Game, she'd worried about her eyes all night, but somehow Jac had managed to find humor in her dangerous situation. He, too, had seemed wary of her talents before, and maybe he still was, but she also trusted him. Yes, she would also call him a friend.

Levi, Jac and Lola—only they knew her secret. It was now the four of them against the entire city.

"Priority number one, in the morning," he said. "I've always wanted a car. Something really sleek. Like an Amoretti. In white."

"As if you'll be driving in the near future," Lola said. "You're the second of the street lord who helped kill the Chancellor. Maybe you should talk to Vianca after Levi and beg for her protection, too."

Jac blanched. "I hadn't thought of that." Enne tried to come up with something comforting, but found she had nothing to say. Lola was right. Through no fault of his own, Jac had lost his freedom, too. "So I'm a wanted man now, eh? That means I need a street name. The other seconds have street names."

This time, Enne did laugh. Jac managed to find reasons to smile when there should have been tears.

"The other seconds are scarier than you," Lola told him.

He raised his eyebrows incredulously. "You're *her* second. You're not scarier than me."

"Yes, she is," Enne said, popping a cookie in her mouth.

"I am," Lola agreed. "And Enne's scarier than Pup, too."

Jac pondered this. "True." Then he shot Enne a teasing smirk.

"I am *not* scary," Enne grumbled. "I'm elegant. And charming."

"You can be all three," he ceded, and Enne decided that was satisfactory.

Her guidebook had been right about the City of Sin. It was morally decrepit. It was disgusting and rotten. It was stained black to its very core.

But her guidebook had been wrong about one thing—it had been wrong about *her*. She had entered New Reynes as delicate as glass. She had even shattered. But as it turned out, beneath the dust and shards, something stronger lay within her, a substance less easily broken.

She would never forget the ache of her mother's death, but she would also never regret uncovering the truth—about Lourdes and about herself.

Even deep within St. Morse, Enne could still make out the wail of sirens outside. She could still hear the echoes of engines roaring, timers ticking and guns firing.

Her guidebook claimed the City of Sin was a game.

She'd made her first move.

LEVI

"Levi, my dear," Vianca cooed as Levi entered the donna's unholy, unfashionable lair. "Look at you." She *tsk*ed with feigned concern as she examined the bruises on his eye and neck. "I'm surprised you can walk."

He sat on a chair across from her, and it made him as stiff and uncomfortable as she did.

"Miss Salta has proved to be quite an impressive young woman," Vianca mused.

He didn't like that smile on her face. "Yes, she is," he answered carefully.

"Tell me—how does it feel to be a celebrity? You've always wanted that, haven't you?"

Levi had always wanted to be a legend. Maybe he was, after tonight. But he was also a target.

He leaned back into the seat and winced from the pain in his ribs. "It could feel better."

"The whiteboots have searched your apartment—and this casino—from top to bottom. They'll be leaving soon. You and the rest of your...associates can sleep here tonight, in Miss Salta's apartment. I have my men watching every entrance and floor. Starting tomorrow, I've made arrangements for you to stay with a friend of mine named Zula Slyk. She lives on the Street of the Holy Tombs."

"We've met before," he said drily. The idea of bunking with Zula and her unsettling ramblings about shades and curses sounded less than appealing. Though, admittedly, he'd live just about anywhere if it meant escaping St. Morse.

"You know each other?" Vianca asked, surprised.

"I know everyone in Olde Town."

"Yes, I thought you'd like to stay within your little territory." She said it as though she'd kept his wishes at heart. "I've never understood what you see in that place. It's a stain on New Reynes."

"Can we trust Zula?" he asked.

"Oh, yes. You're not the first runaway she's stowed, and I've known her a long time. We run in similar circles." She smiled in a way that was nearly giddy. In all the years Levi had known Vianca, he'd never seen her smile like that. Her yellowed teeth, her flaky lips—he actually preferred her scowl. "With Sedric removed, the monarchist party actually has a chance. Only four months left until the election—I can't imagine they'll find someone else suitable in time."

"You know I hate politics."

"I'm sorry—am I boring you? With the Chancellor dead, this is set to be the most important political moment since the Great Street War, and you're at its center. You should be paying attention."

Levi was treading dangerous waters. When Vianca launched into one of her political tirades, there was no interrupting her for hours. It wasn't that she bored him—he just had no desire to review the night's events with her. She was the reason he'd nearly died.

"It's been a long night," he said, hoping that would satisfy.

"Yes, well…" She lifted her chin higher, and Levi braced himself for whatever insults she would throw at him, as she usually did in each of their conversations. "All of this business with the investment scheme—I didn't know what I was getting us into. More specifically, what I was getting *you* into. And I am genuinely sorry about that."

Levi was too stunned to do anything but nod. He'd never heard Vianca apologize. He'd always thought remorse was beyond her.

"I'm set on making it up to you," she said. "I thought you should know."

Oh, no, he thought, sure that whatever gift she was planning would prove to be another death sentence in disguise.

"Go rest," she told him. "By tomorrow, the whole city will know. By tomorrow, everything will be different."

Levi mumbled some parting words and rejoined his friends in the other room. Lola and Jac were bickering about something, and Enne was finishing off the remaining crumbs in a box of cookies. The scene was so normal he wanted to laugh, if doing so wouldn't make his whole body ache.

"Vianca has arranged accommodations for me at Zula Slyk's," he said.

Enne set down the box, her lips pursed. "You have to go *there?*"

"I'm leaving tomorrow. Vianca offered up your apartment for all of us tonight."

She raised her eyebrows. "How generous of her."

Several minutes later, the four of them were sneaking silently down the stairs toward Enne's apartment on the eighteenth floor. Her hallway was mainly for staff, and no one was awake at this hour—it wasn't quite sunrise. Enne fumbled with her keys in her pocket, then unlocked the door.

"I'm getting the couch," Jac declared. "Dove, you can have the floor."

Eager as he was for rest, Levi hadn't dwelled on the potential awkwardness of their sleeping arrangements. Enne's apartment was very much designed for one person. One bed. One couch. He swallowed down the heat building in his stomach, creeping its way to his face.

"The girls get the bed," Lola said drily.

"You changed your mind about wanting to kill her, what, yesterday? Are you sure you deserve slumber party status?" Jac then shot Levi the dirtiest, most suggestive look he could manage. As if he were being helpful. Levi's face went hot in embarrassment.

Enne cleared her throat, looking everywhere but at Levi. "Yes. The girls get the bed."

"If you think I'm sleeping on the floor," Levi growled at his second, "you're mucking mistaken." Then, when Enne and Lola had disappeared into the bedroom, Levi smacked Jac on the back of the head. "Don't do that."

"I was trying to help you."

"Yes. Don't do that."

"You don't normally need my help."

"Enough." Levi kicked him off the couch and stretched out on the cushions. It wasn't the most comfortable, but he wasn't anticipating getting much sleep. Not with the sirens calling from the streets below. Not while thinking about Enne asleep in the next room. He closed his eyes anyway and tried to quiet his mind.

The water in the bathroom was running. He peeked one eye open.

"I should say good-night," he mused out loud.

"Yes, you should."

Levi gave him a rude gesture as he stood up and walked to the bathroom. Enne was in a nightdress, leaning over the sink and removing the contacts from her eyes.

"You were right," she said, blinking painfully. "They do hurt." She snapped the contact case closed and turned to him, shaking her head. Her eyes were slightly bloodshot—and very purple.

"Stop looking at me that," she snapped.

"I can't help it."

"I already feel like I'm wearing a costume, like this isn't actually my face." She pressed her hands against her cheeks, as if making sure her other features were still the same.

Jac shouted from the next room, "Oh, are your contacts gone? Do we get to see?"

"I'm not a sideshow," she muttered.

Jac appeared in the doorway. He gaped at her, then gave an exaggerated bow. "You look like Queen Marcelline."

"Before or after she was beheaded?" Enne shoved him away, grimacing. "And look at this," she told Levi, leading him into the bedroom. Lola was perched on the edge of the bed, looking very absurd in one of Enne's nightdresses. She glared at him suspiciously and wrapped a blanket around herself.

"Oh, is she showing you the 'magic coin'?" Lola asked.

Levi scratched his arm nervously. "Is that a euphemism for something?"

"Lola's just saying it like that because she can't see what I'm talking about." Enne grabbed a large bronze coin off her dresser, one slightly larger than her token. It was the same one she had shown to Zula. She pointed to the cameo of the king on its face. "Look at his eye. It's purple."

Levi examined both the coin and Enne with mild concern. "You've been wearing those contacts too long." Behind him, he sensed Lola creeping out of the room.

Enne groaned. "I swear it's purple. And feel it. It's warm." She thrust it into his hand.

"You've been holding it," he said.

"It was on my nightstand! And you remember how Zula talked about it."

He rubbed his temples and set it back down. They all needed some rest. "Yes. It's very spooky."

"You're giving me that smirk again."

"This is just my face," he said, stepping closer and smirking wider.

She had to tilt her head to look up at him. "Yes. It's very vexing."

"I'm sorry my face vexes you."

They grew silent. Levi was all too aware of the tumbling violet waves and smoky smells of her aura, of the heat of her skin, of how close they were to each other. What was actually vexing was that *she* was giving him that look again, that biting-her-lip, holding-her-breath look that tempted him so damn much.

"I'm not positive when we'll next see each other," he said.

"Vianca said she wanted to talk to me again in the morning," she said, grimacing. "She said she has 'plans.' I'll want to—I mean, we should talk afterward." She flushed and looked away from him.

"I'll find us a place in Olde Town to meet."

That was how all their meetings would have to be from now on—secret. This was the life he had ahead of him, and he already knew the most dangerous thing he could do was fall for someone like Enne. Levi had flirted with disaster for over a year now, and everything in his life had crumbled for it. It was time he focused on the empire he was always meant to build. It was time he played his cards safe.

Even if he didn't want to.

"It's late," they both said at the same time.

"Get some rest," she said, smiling weakly.

"You, too."

Levi walked back to the sitting room with his stomach in knots. He'd made his decision. But—so help him—if Enne had called his name. If she'd turned him around. Asked him to come back.

He would've surrendered to his desire without a second thought.

Lola and Jac were whispering conspiratorially on the couch.

"You can stop gossiping," Levi said flatly. "Let's all go to sleep." He shooed them away, lay down and closed his eyes, making it clear he didn't want to talk.

"We had bets," Jac said.

"Good night, Jac."

"I owe Lola three volts now."

Sirens blared from outside the window, which didn't make for the best lullaby. Levi listened to his pulse beat against the throw pillow. It reminded him of the timer ticking down during the Shadow Game and those ten seconds when he'd thought for sure he was a dead man.

But he wasn't dead yet.

The City of Sin was a game, but not everyone was a player. Before tonight, Levi hadn't just wanted to play—he'd wanted to win. He'd thought all that separated the players from the observers was desire.

That had been his first mistake. He hadn't understood the rules. The game wasn't about empires and legends and legacies. It was about power, and it was about death.

It was too late to fold—the city had brutally marked him a player tonight. But if he wanted to survive, he needed to change his strategy. Desire would undoubtedly be his downfall. As Semper had remarked before the Shadow Game…

People don't play this Game to win, my dear. They play this game not to lose.

Nevertheless, when the sirens finally lulled Levi to sleep, he didn't dream of caution or escape.

He dreamed of being king.

EPILOGUE

In a city several hours south of New Reynes, one less merciless and despicable, a telephone rang in the hour before sunrise.

A man slid out of bed, careful not to wake the woman beside him. He reached for three things: an eyepatch, a robe and a gun. The eyepatch because his left eye was gone, cleaved out many years ago on the night New Reynes caught fire. The robe because he was naked. The gun because he knew better than to be without it.

He slipped silently into the hall, where the phone was ringing. He picked up the receiver, but didn't speak.

"You told me never to call," a woman said, "unless I had an opportunity." It'd been many years, but her monotone, lifeless voice was still recognizable, still made the man shiver. They weren't friends, but they shared a common enemy.

He considered hanging up. It'd been eighteen years since he stepped foot in the City of Sin, and, at some point during his travels, he'd promised himself to never return. Unlike the city where he lived now, the man was both merciless and despicable—

but not entirely so. And New Reynes had a way of corrupting whatever remained of a pure soul.

As he moved to end the call, the woman spoke louder, "You'll be delighted to hear who has died."

He quickly pulled the phone back to his ear. "Was it my mother?"

"No."

Wishful thinking, he thought. His mother was too stubborn to die.

"It was Semper…and Sedric Torren," the woman said.

The man's eye widened. Eighteen years of peace, and New Reynes might just catch fire again. "Tell me what happened. And what you're offering."

The woman recounted the story of what had occurred only hours before, of two street lords named Séance and Levi Glaisyer.

"I accept," he said.

"There's a train leaving at six. A man will be waiting for you there, and he'll escort you to the House of Shadows." She hung up.

The man lowered the receiver to its cradle and returned to his room.

It'd been a useless promise, he knew. One born out of frustration, waiting for that phone call, waiting for his chance. No matter how many cities he visited or how many people he met— it didn't matter. His destiny had always been in the City of Sin.

To burn his mother's empire down.

Within minutes, Harrison Augustine had dressed, packed his belongings, and walked to the station. Even hours away, he sensed the rising smoke of New Reynes.

It tasted sweet.

★ ★ ★ ★ ★

ACKNOWLEDGMENTS

This story has seen me through three graduations, through first romances and first griefs, through world-traveling adventures and questionable basement dormitories and cramped apartments. I have thrown all of my dreams into this book, and, in return, this book taught me how to write. But this has been far from a solo endeavor. Over the course of the many years spent on this story, I have whisked some thrill-seeking readers away to the City of Sin, and I have countless to thank.

First, to my own gang. To my editor, Lauren Smulski: this story found its happily-ever-after thanks to you, and I could not ask for a more passionate advocate for this book. To my agent, Brianne Johnson, who found this series the perfect home at Harlequin TEEN, and whose editorial insight changed the entire way I looked at these characters. To my publicist, Siena Koncsol, who gives the best pep talks and has worked tirelessly to put my words into the hands of readers. To Bryn Collier and the rest of my marketing team, thank you for your enthusiasm in championing this book and all my books.

To Christine Lynn Herman, my partner in crime, thank you for reading every snippet as soon as I write it, for crying over all my milestones with me, for editing this book with such patience and fervor. You know this story better than anyone and still haven't grown tired of it. That's good—I have a lot more books I need you to read for me, for I trust no one more. Thank you for being my first reader, my last reader, my idea springboard, my fellow trash lord, my first mate of many ships, my gossip buddy and my best friend.

To Meg Kohlman, Melody Simpson, Joan He, Akshaya Raman, Kat Cho, Katy Pool, Claribel Ortega, Janella Angeles, Amanda Haas, Mara Fitzgerald, Axie Oh, Maddy Colis, Ashley Burdin and Ella Dyson…I could not ask for a savvier critique group or writer cult. Your support means the world to me.

To Molly Jaffa, whose editorial feedback remains all over this story: thank you for your energy and your patience with me as I hunted for my true vision for these characters.

This story has seen an army of readers and supporters over its journey. In no particular order, many, many thanks to Jena DeBois, Deeba Zargarpur, Kristy Shen, Audrey Dion, Emmy Neal, Kelly Ferraro, Kate Maffey, Marieke Nijkamp, Lindsay Smith, Brenda Drake, Jadzia Brandli, Tamara Felsinger, Stephanie Diaz, Hafsah Fazial, Michael Waters, Courtney Washburn, Nikhita Prabhakar, Jessica Harvey, Steph Stessa, Raven Ashley, Kay Cox and Kelia Ingraham. You are all honorary Sinners.

To my parents, who have been with me every step of the way in producing this book. To Ben, who has listened patiently to my ramblings about these characters since the day I met him.

To my Pikachu pillow—you saw a lot of tears over the course of this journey.

To the many characters who were once part of this series, but were tragically cut—I cringe when I think of you and any early drafts of this manuscript, but I won't forget you. I'm sure I'll recycle your names somewhere.

And to you, dear reader—I hope you heeded my advice and avoided the City of Sin altogether, for no one truly leaves it uncorrupted.